USA TODAY BESTSELLING AUTHOR

MAGGIE ALABASTER

USA TODAY BESTSELLING AUTHOR

JO BRADLEY

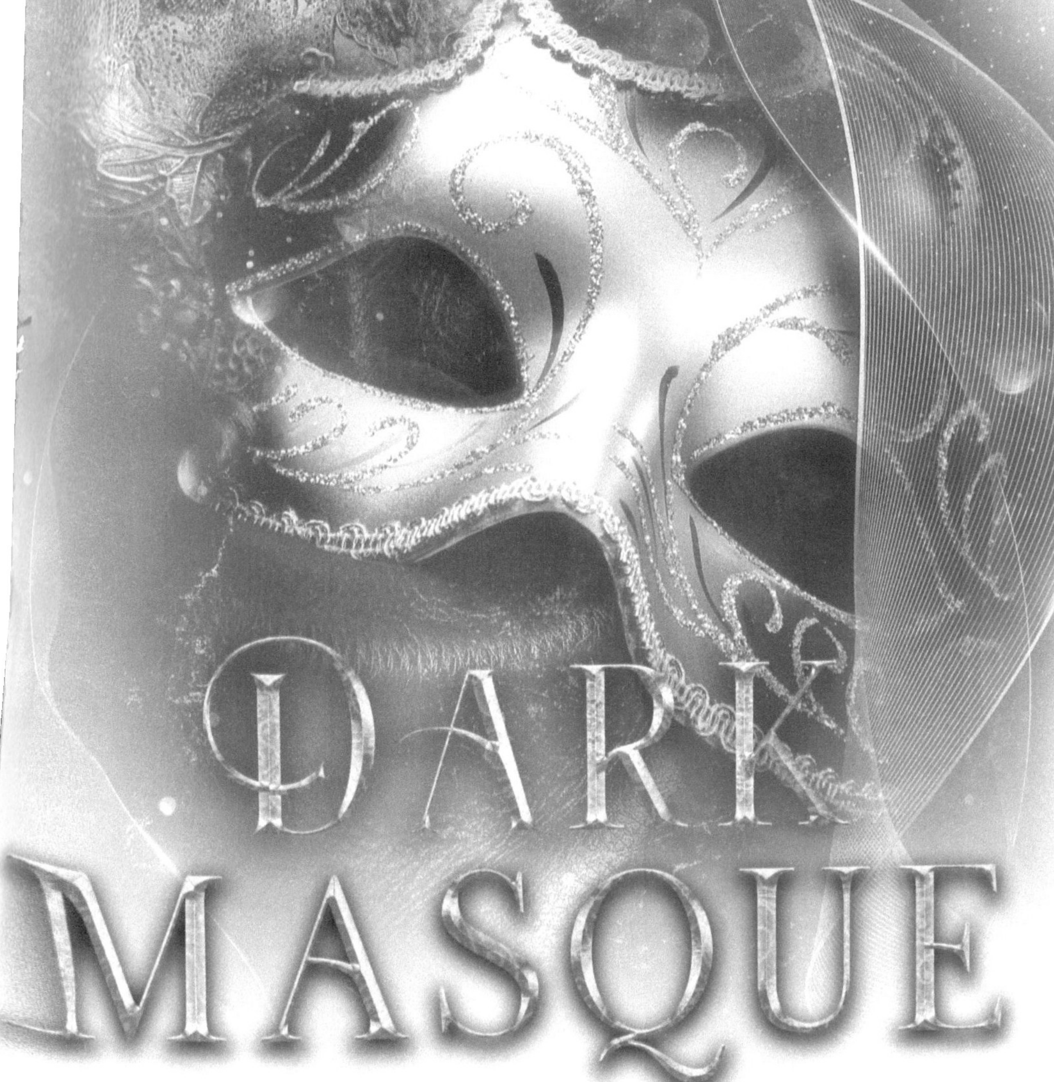

DARK MASQUE

BOOKS 1-3

Cover by Atra Luna Designs

Edited by Lily Luchesi

Proofread by Nora Hogan

BAIT

DARK MASQUE BOOK 1

CHAPTER 1

KENNEDY

Whoever she was, she came so loudly she wouldn't have heard me sidestep them in the dark.

Apparently, I wasn't the only one sneaking away from the masquerade ball to get some air. Although, judging from the noise, she was getting a fuck load more than air.

"Oh yeah, baby, just like that," a male voice groaned.

I wrinkled my nose and hurried on through the trees. They probably didn't hear the twig snap under my foot, or the music that poured out of the ballroom and into the night. They wouldn't have heard anything but the roar of blood through their veins, and their moans.

I slanted away from them and headed toward the lake.

I pushed my mask off my face and up onto the top of my head. Strands of hair fell around my face, knocked loose by the elastic on either side of the mask. I pulled the clip out and let the rest of my red hair fall down my back, wild and wavy.

I picked up my skirt and stepped carefully over a fallen log. My black chiffon gown was long enough no one noticed I wore flat shoes instead of the heels my mother wanted. In sequin stilettos, I would have fallen flat on my face.

No thank you.

She also wanted me to wear pink, like I was still a kid or something. Pink would have clashed with my hair like bubblegum on a tomato. Thank fuck she listened to reason in the end. Although, only because she was busy with plans for her wedding. Fighting with me took a back seat for a change.

"I was on my way."

I froze at the sound of voices up ahead. How many couples had crept away for air?

I cocked my head and listened. The sound which carried on the breeze wasn't fucking. It was talking. Several voices. Tense, tight.

My breath held, I stepped toward them on silent feet.

"I tried to leave, but the boss, he needed..." The tremble of fear in the speaker's voice sent a shiver up my spine.

I stopped. I shouldn't be here, listening. Whatever was going on, they were out here in the night for a reason. Obviously. People didn't sneak around in the dark just for the hell of it.

"That's crap and you know it," another voice said. Also male. "We've given you enough chances. How many is it now?"

A third voice spoke but I couldn't make out the words.

"Please..." That was the first man. His words were accompanied by the sudden tang of urine. "I was an accident, I swear."

"Bullshit," the second guy growled.

Another shiver passed down my spine. I should leave, right now. Run. Or better yet, sneak away before they knew I was there.

Instead, I took a few more steps forward. A skewer of light from the ballroom faintly illuminated four figures. Two stood facing a third. He was restrained by the fourth, his arms held behind his back. They all wore dark suits. Masks, like the one I wore on top of my head, covered three of their faces. Only the restrained man had a bare face. No one I recognised, although I only arrived in Dusk Bay a week ago.

One of the masked men nodded to another. He drew something out of his pocket. A faint click and the light reflected off a slim blade in his hand.

Shit.

"Can we have some fun first?" the guy beside him asked. He cocked his head and smiled. "I bet he screams really pretty."

The restrained man sobbed. "Please… I swear I won't—"

Whatever he was going to say was cut off by the slice of the knife across his throat. He let out a gurgle. Light reflected off a gush of blood which poured from his open neck. His eyes bugged out of his face and he sagged.

I clapped a hand over my mouth. They just… Murdered the guy.

I hoped to hell they couldn't hear my heart racing. In my ears, it sounded louder than a passenger plane engine. Multiple rapid cracks of thunder.

My stomach turned. I wished I hadn't eaten my last several meals. They all threatened to make a violent reappearance on the ground at my feet.

I swallowed hard and forced several breaths in and out, silent and shallow.

I had a sneaking suspicion these guys wouldn't leave any witnesses alive. I had to calm down, not panic and do something stupid.

I crouched, shrunk as low as I could and held my breath.

"That was anticlimactic," the guy without the knife said. He snatched the blade and shoved it into the victim's eye. He pushed it in deeper, twisting it.

A short cry was cut off as the knife entered the man's brain.

Fucking hell. My knees trembled violently, threatening to dump me onto the ground. I gripped the trunk of the tree beside me for support. Hoped like hell they didn't hear the leaves rustle.

"That's much better." The bloodthirsty guy pulled the knife out before the man fell to the ground. "Do I need to give you guys lessons in interesting ways to kill people?"

"Nope, we'll leave it to you." The guy who had been restraining the other man clapped him on the back. "Maybe you should write a book."

"I should, shouldn't I?" Mr Bloodthirsty grinned. "I could call it *One Hundred and One Ways to Eliminate Your Friends and Eviscerate Your Enemies*."

"Maybe you could shut up. We have to get out of here," the first guy said. "We need to dispose of this." He slipped off his suit jacket and rolled up his sleeves.

I caught a glimpse of the mask he wore on his face. Black with splashes of red here and there. A black feather slanted from the top of either side of the mask, across his forehead.

Simple, but menacing, even without a murder involved. In this context it was fucking terrifying.

“Come on, grab the asshole.” He nodded toward the others. They picked up the dead man between them. Grunting under his weight, they hefted him up to waist height.

I pressed myself down lower, until my thighs almost touched the layer of dry leaves on the forest floor. I adjusted my left foot slightly to keep from toppling. My shoe found a twig.

It snapped louder than a stockwhip.

All four of us froze. The four of us that were still alive.

"Is someone there?" the guy with the red and black mask growled, deep and low. A sound that would have been hot as fuck if I wasn't absolutely certain he would cut my throat if he knew I was there. Or maybe I’d end up with a blade in my eye.

Hard pass either way.

"Go and look. We'll take care of this." He barked orders like he expected to be obeyed immediately.

I didn't wait and see who came after me. I rose, picked up my skirt, turned and ran. I headed away from the light of the ballroom, into the deepening shadows. My heart raced harder than ever.

Every passing second, I expected someone to explode out of the trees behind me and catch me.

Years of gymnastics and aerial silks meant I was graceful, but I was also terrified. And more or less running blind. Any moment now, I'd trip over a stick or a log and smash my face into the ground. Or my dress would snag on something and tear loudly. Or—

"I know you're there," a sing-song voice called out behind me. "I know what you saw. Why don't you stop and let us talk about it?"

Oh, fuck nope.

I trotted behind a tree and ducked down low. My palms were slick with sweat and I was about ready to piss myself too. I forced deep, measured breaths in and out, to keep myself from holding it. Nothing would give me away like passing out and crashing onto the ground.

Footsteps approached. The snap of a twig, the swish of a branch, the soft murmur of leaves under his shoes.

Crunch.

Crunch.

Crunch.

"I could turn on my phone and find you," he said easily. "But where's the fun in that? The thrill of the chase is much more entertaining. Then when I catch you, I'll know I've earned my trophy." He rubbed his palms on each other.

Oh good, I was going to end up one of those stuffed heads people have on their walls. He might have a collection of them. One hundred and one for every way he knew to kill.

I pressed myself down smaller and closed my eyes. I was even more grateful now that I wore a dark dress and not pale pink. That would have stood out like the proverbial dog's balls, even in the middle of the night.

"I know I'm supposed to find you, and catch you, but you know what, I don't think I will right now." He sounded like he was turning around in a slow circle. "I think, sooner or later, I will find you. You'll come to me and then we'll deal with you. I'm going to enjoy knowing you'll spend every day wondering if this will be the day when I catch my prey. If this will be the day when you end up in my trap. If this is the day I make you mine. I'm going to enjoy making you squeal, little mouse."

My mouth went dry. What kind of twisted, sick fuck was this? Oh yeah, one who liked to stab people in the eye. I had a feeling that, given the chance, he'd take his time, make the man suffer before he died. One thing I knew for certain was, I didn't want to end up that way.

"They're going to be pissed off I let you go, but don't worry. I'll deal with them. I know just the way to handle them, like I know how to handle you. You're probably thinking I don't have a clue, but I know more than you might imagine. Such a sweet perfume, little mouse. I don't mean the stuff you dabbed on behind your ears and on your wrists. I mean the scent of you. Your pussy. Your arousal. Your *fear.*"

He took a long, slow sniff of the air. "Intoxicating."

Oh God, this guy was out of his mind. There was no way he could really smell me, was there? Okay, maybe my perfume, but not *me*. Not how scared I was.

No, he was guessing. It wasn't much of a stretch. I was hiding in the dark from someone who murdered another person. Whose friends were out there, disposing of the body.

How would they do it? They probably had one hundred and one ways of getting rid of a corpse. Would I be one hundred and two? Would they dig me a shallow grave in the forest and leave me there, dusting dirt off their hands? They wouldn't give me a second thought after that. While I decomposed down to my bones, they'd get on with their lives, doing whatever shit they did.

I had to stop thinking this way, it was making my fear worse. If he couldn't smell me before, he would if I kept going like this. I tried to calm my racing mind. He didn't know where I was or who I was. Once he walked away, he wouldn't find me. I might change my perfume, just in case, but otherwise his game would go unplayed. There would be no hunt, no prey, no trophy. All I had to do was stay calm and not freak out. Freaking out would definitely give me away, like waving a huge red flag while standing in the middle of the road.

"I'll see you soon, little mouse," he said. "Or maybe it will be later. Now I think about it, later would be better. Your fear will taste sweeter then. Like honey and wine. Like the smoothest chocolate melted down until it's liquid. Like cum. Perfect for drinking." He smacked his lips and turned to disappear into the trees.

I stayed crouched there for a long time, listening to the distant music, the lap of waves against the side of the lake, the whisper of the breeze and the pounding of my heart.

CHAPTER 2
KENNEDY

"Isn't it just wonderful here?" My mother spread her hands and gestured at the view out the window.

Helen Knight had expensive taste. She always had. Nothing but the best homes in the best neighbourhoods, with the best schools, reached by driving the best cars. Apparently, my father made sure we were well taken care of, even though he was absent from my life.

My mother made sure to spend as much of what he gave her as she could. All of the luxury I grew up with was nothing compared to this.

The house was huge, set in ten of the best acres in Dusk Bay. On one side were elaborate gardens and an enormous swimming pool. On the other was a cliff with a sheer drop and stunning view of the ocean.

"It's fine," I said vaguely, only half hearing the question. It was probably something wedding related. I didn't know why she asked me. Whatever answer I gave, she already made up her mind anyway. In the end, smiling, nodding and agreeing was the only way to go.

Not to mention I couldn't stop thinking about the other night. Over and over in my mind like a constant, instant replay. Blood spurted out of the man's neck. The twist of the knife in his eye. The guy who stood so close to me in the dark and claimed he'd find me. It was all I could think about when I was awake. All I dreamt about when I was asleep. The knife, the mask tattoo, the blood. Everything blurred together in my mind except the fear. That lingered like it happened moments ago.

Mum looked at me sharply. "What's wrong with you lately, Kennedy? Every time I try to talk to you, it feels like you're on another planet."

She was right, I was and unless I wanted to answer a pile of questions I had no answers for, I was going to have to pretend nothing was wrong. What in the world would I say anyway? The three masked guys killed a man. They didn't know who I was. I didn't know who they were either. If I went to the police, I suspected they wouldn't find a body. Or any sign of a struggle. No proof anything happened, except my word. I risked leaving the killers a trail that would lead straight to me.

I had no choice but to keep quiet.

I forced a smile. "I'm sorry, I was just thinking about what UNI classes I need to take."

That was a flat out lie and we both knew it. I was in the final year of my computer science degree. I knew exactly what I needed to take to finish.

At Mum's insistence, I'd agreed to complete my final year here at Dusk Bay instead of on campus. A decision I was starting to regret. As far as I knew, no one on campus was a murderer. None I was witness to anyway.

A flicker of movement out the window caught my eye. The massive iron gates that led into the property opened slowly. Before it was open wide enough, a sleek black SUV rolled inside.

I winced, but it slid through effortlessly and came to a stop outside. The driver must have missed hitting the iron by a hair or two on either side.

The guy that climbed out of the passenger seat had a scowl etched on his face, like somehow it might be his permanent expression. His hair was blond and short, slightly longer on the top than on the sides. His square jaw was covered with a light smattering of stubble. Both his face and body looked like they were carved out of stone, cold and hard. A dark blue T-shirt clung to broad shoulders and chest, and flat stomach. I bet myself he had abs for days, but his face was all, 'don't fucking touch me.'

So, of course, that was exactly what I wanted to do.

The driver looked just as cut, but where the first guy was blond and blue-eyed, this guy had dark hair and dark eyes. The kind that could see right through you, because he can't be bothered to look *at* you. His white T-shirt contrasted with tanned skin. I couldn't help wondering what he'd look like if that T-shirt was wet and clinging to every dip and groove of his body. Droplets of water cascading from his hair and face when he shook his head. His...

That thought made my mouth dry and sent a rush of warmth through my body.

I swallowed hard.

A third guy got out of the back of the car. The sides of his mouth turned up in a smile. He said something to the blond, and got a glance in return, but no other response. For some reason, that made him grin. He pushed dark hair out of his eyes and moved around to the back of the car to open it and pull out a suitcase. To go with his dark hair, he was dressed completely in black. A t-shirt like the other two, over ripped jeans. His hair was pulled back in a bun.

Unlike the other two guys, he looked completely at home.

"Please say he's my stepbrother-to-be," I muttered. According to Mum, he'd just finished his degree at Brutham Academy and was returning to Dusk Bay to work for his father.

The guy with the white T-shirt stepped around and yanked the handle of the suitcase out of the other guy's hand before rolling it towards the house.

Crap. Of course it couldn't be the guy who actually looked friendly.

My mother hurried over to the door to greet them, but I hung back.

"Mannix!" She greeted him with open arms.

He gave her the shortest hug in human history, before stepping aside to let the other guys enter.

"Helen." He nodded towards the blond. "Ares." Then to man bun. "Isaac."

Isaac grinned and held out his hand to Mum. "Everyone calls me Ice. It's nice to meet you."

"It's nice to meet you too, Isaac," Mum said. Apparently, 'everybody,' didn't apply to her. She turned to look at me and waved me forward.

"This is my daughter, Kennedy Knight."

I didn't miss the way all of the guys raked up and down my body with their eyes. Or the way Ares curled his lip at me. Ice regarded me with interest. Mannix's expression was unreadable, but he carried an air of annoyance at my existence.

Ice surprised me by stepping forward and grabbing me up in a bear hug. "Don't mind those two. They'll be nice when they get their heads out of their asses."

I hugged him back. He smelled nice, like a combination of musk and cinnamon.

"When will that be?" I asked sweetly.

Ice chuckled. "Hopefully some time this decade, before they suffocate on their own shit."

"Fuck off," Ares growled. "Not everyone likes annoyingly cheerful." His sneer seemed to be the default expression every time he looked at me. Although, he looked at Ice the same way. Maybe he was just a dick.

"My theory is that he got out on the wrong side of the bed about twenty years ago," Ice whispered loudly to me.

Ares flipped him off.

"Is my father around?" Apparently Mannix was done with the pleasantries. If you could call them that.

"He's upstairs in his office," Mum said. She didn't seem concerned at any of their attitudes. Then again, she was so deliriously happy with Leo, she probably wouldn't notice if the world ended right in front of her face.

"I need to talk to him, then I'll drive you clowns home," Mannix said.

"I could drive Ares home," Ice offered.

Mannix and Ares both said, "No!" At the same time.

"The last time you drove, we ended up in a ditch," Ares growled.

Ice shrugged. "Practice makes perfect. How am I supposed to get perfect if you don't let me practice?"

"Practice in your own car," Mannix said.

Ice reached into his back pocket and pulled out his wallet. He opened it and grabbed hold of a credit card between his thumb and forefinger. He held out to Mannix.

Mannix looked at him funny. "What the fuck are you doing?"

"Buying your car," Ice said easily. "Then I can drive my own car. And you can buy yourself a new one tomorrow. Win-win."

Rich boy problems. I knew Mum loved Leo, but I suspected she also loved the fact he had more money than God. So did Mannix, and apparently his friends. I couldn't even imagine buying a car on a whim. Even if I could afford it, I liked to think things through.

Mannix shook his head and turned to hurry up the stairs. His feet thumped heavily all the way to the top, like he was announcing his presence with each step. Or trying to break through to the space under the stairs.

Ares leaned against a wall and crossed his arms over his ridiculously broad chest. He'd be hot if he wasn't looking at me like something the cat dragged in.

Yeah, fuck you too, asshole.

Ice slipped his credit card back into his wallet and shoved it back in his pocket. "I guess I'll go car shopping tomorrow. Wanna come?" he asked me.

"She's probably busy," Ares snapped.

Ice's eyes were still on me, when he said, "Doing what?"

Before I could answer, Ares said, "Washing her hair or getting her nails done. Some shit like that."

I glanced down at my natural, bitten nails. I'd never had acrylic on them in my life. As for washing my hair...

"What is your problem?" I asked him. "I met you approximately three minutes ago and you've already decided you don't like me?" Apart from wondering how his tongue would feel on my clit, the feeling was mutual. I'd bet half my trust fund that his cock would fill me up and then some. Ugh, I needed to stop that line of thought right now. If I didn't, I was going to drip on the hardwood floor.

"Kennedy," Mum hissed, as though I was the antagonist in all of this. "Let's not have any unpleasantness. Perhaps we can all get some coffee. I'm sure we would all get along if we got to know each other."

Ares gave me a sarcastic smirk.

I badly wanted to flip him off, or better yet, kick him in the balls, but I didn't want to upset Mum. Thank fuck he didn't live here. With any luck, I wouldn't have to see much of him or Mannix.

Ice seemed okay, if a bit strange, but if hanging out with him meant hanging out with them, I'd have to pass. Just because they were all hot didn't mean I had to give them the time of day. I needed to find my own friends, which meant going to the gymnastics studio to see if I could spend some time in the gym. With any luck, I'd meet a hot coach and forget all about these three guys.

"I could go for a coffee," Ice said cheerfully. "Knowing Mannix, talking to Leo will take ages. And may or may not involve one or both of them bleeding."

I snorted a soft laugh. At least, I thought he was joking. My stepfather-to-be was nice enough, but he was intense. Like Mannix, he had an undercurrent of something dark. Like if you lifted the lid, you'd find a rolling boil of violence. He'd never hurt my mother, but other people? If anyone lay a hand on her without her permission, he'd want to rip their arms off and shove them down their throat.

It was… Sweet. Would he act on that though?

That brought me back to that night and the tang of blood and death. It wasn't just that night, I realised. Dusk Bay had a feeling about it. Like it was teetering on the edge. On the edge of what, I had no idea, but I had a very strong feeling I should be scared of it.

CHAPTER 3

KENNEDY

"So much for not seeing them," I muttered under my breath.

For people who didn't live here, Ice and Ares were here all the time. As far as I could tell, they both lived a handful of minutes away, but whenever I saw Mannix, they were with him. Ice was friendly enough, but the other two hadn't thawed a drop. Ironic that they were colder than he was.

They must have heard me mutter, because Ares turned to give me his customary sneer.

Mannix matched it with his usual annoyance at my presence.

Okay, I got it. This was his house and I wasn't even legally a stepsibling. I was just the daughter of his father's fiancée. Still, did he have to look at me like I was trespassing?

"Hey, what are you doing?" Ice slipped into the chair next to me. He didn't even pretend he wasn't looking at my laptop screen. "Oh, essay writing. Yeah, I don't miss that."

"I'm sure you don't." I closed my laptop and tried not to look at Mannix when he gripped the hem of his T-shirt and pulled it off over his head with one hand. Why the hell was it so hot when guys did that?

On the other hand, did he have to strip off right in front of me? I was supposed to be concentrating on university work, not counting his abs—eight—or admiring the V of his hips. I really shouldn't be memorising his tattoos, or how fucking thick his biceps were. Or the way his thighs looked like he could crush a watermelon without raising a sweat.

Crap, I was wetter than the pool right in front of me.

I could study in my room, but it was a nice day to sit under a wide umbrella beside the sparkling water. Right, I was only here for the pool, not the view of the guys when they came out at the same time every morning for a swim. I totally didn't work here so I could watch them do laps and splash each other, all shirtless and hot.

"Ice," Ares growled. He looked at me like somehow I'd be a bad influence on his friend.

I met his gaze glare for glare until his eyes slid away like I wasn't worthy of another second of his time. If he thought I'd be intimidated, he'd have to think again.

He pulled off his T-shirt and threw it across the back of a chair. He dove into the pool right in front of me, clearly knowing he'd leave a splash behind.

"Asshole." I grabbed my laptop and turned so it didn't get wet. If it did, the fucker could buy me a new one. Yeah, hell would freeze over before he did that.

Mannix grinned. Apparently the sight of me pissed off amused him somehow.

I resisted the urge to flip him off.

Don't take their bait, I told myself. For some reason, they seemed to have made it their life's goal to make me as unwelcome as possible. I wasn't going to let them get to me. Right now, this was as much my home as it was Mannix's.

"How are you friends with these assholes?" I asked as Mannix leapt into the water, his arms around his knees. The splash from his bomb sent droplets of water flying, covering the top of the table. If I hadn't moved my laptop, it would have gotten drenched.

Ice shrugged. "They're okay when you get to know them."

"How will I do that when they don't want to know me?" Did I really want to anyway? I should at least try to get to know Mannix, if only for my mother's sake. I owed Ares no such consideration. If anything, I owed him a big, fat fuck you.

"If they don't, then I get more time with you," he reasoned.

I brushed a tangle of red hair off my face and looked at him in surprise. "At least one of you is nice." He wanted to spend time with me? His friends would love that. Not.

He smiled, which was just as panty melting as any set of abs, but said, "Don't be fooled. I'm nowhere near as nice as I seem. If anything, I'm less nice and more dangerous than those two clowns." He jerked a thumb in the direction of Ares and Mannix, who were freestyling neck and neck up and down the pool.

I'd seen their routine often enough to have it memorised. They started with a few laps of freestyle before switching to butterfly, then backstroke and finally to breaststroke to cool down.

"I don't know, you seem a lot nicer than them. Did you meet on the swim team or something?" They all seemed to know how to do the strokes correctly. At least, as far as I could tell. I was no expert on swimming techniques.

"Something like that," Ice said. "We all like getting wet." He gave me a smile that left me in no doubt about what he was referring to.

Hint: nothing to do with pool water. Or any other kind of water for that matter.

My face heated, which made him smile wider. He also liked to get to me, but in a different way from the other two. It was hard enough to focus with them around, without one of them flirting with me.

"I'm sure you do," I said awkwardly. "Shouldn't you be swimming too?"

"Yes, I should." He hopped up, but before he walked away, he leaned over to whisper in my ear, "Are you wet already, Beautiful?" His warm breath brushed the side of my neck. My skin pebbled. So did my nipples.

Before I could answer, he straightened up, winked and walked away to the other side of the pool before stripping off his shirt and diving in.

He might be right about being dangerous, especially to my heart rate. More than that though. He also had a simmering undercurrent of violence, but kept it behind a friendlier mask.

The thought of masks took me back to that night and my pulse quickened.

Dusk Bay was a combination of violence and sex that shouldn't be heady, but it was.

Not the murder, that was terrifying, but the sense that three guys doing laps across the pool in front of me knew how to use their bodies to hurt other people. Fists, feet, thighs. My money would be on them in a fight. What if they fought each other? I didn't know who'd win, but imagining them wrestling made me hotter than hell.

I scooped up my laptop from my lap and glanced down at the table. I sighed. The surface was too wet to put my computer back down. As tempting as it was—and it really was—to pick up Ares' t-shirt from the back of the chair and wipe the table with it, I decided I didn't need him hating me more than he already did.

I couldn't stop him from being an asshole, but I didn't need to be one as well.

Reluctantly, I stood and carried my laptop inside. I set it down on the kitchen island and opened it. Before I slipped into a stool, I glanced back at the door. Through the clear glass, Mannix watched me. A hint of a frown was etched on his brow. When he saw me looking, he turned away and disappeared under the water.

What the fuck was that frown for? Had he and Ares deliberately wet the table to drive me away? Was Mannix pissed off it hadn't driven me far enough? Maybe he wouldn't be happy until I moved out, or left Dusk Bay.

If that was the petty game he and his friends were playing then too bad. I wasn't going anywhere. For one thing, Leo's house had the best Wi-Fi I'd ever had access to. It was crazy fast and strong everywhere in the house.

Yeah, for good Wi-Fi, I'll put up with the occasional hostile glance. Priorities.

Besides, the guys were assholes, but they were good to look at. Ice was right, I got wet around them. Especially when they took their shirts off. There was definitely danger in that. Being attracted to guys who hated my guts would get me nowhere.

I sighed and flipped open my laptop. I opened a search window and typed in gymnastic studios nearby. There was one in town. According to their website, they had aerial silks for me to practice on. Hell yeah. A lot didn't, since it wasn't a recognised gymnastics apparatus.

I grabbed my phone out of my pocket and shot off a text message about renting the gym or doing a class. Whatever it took, as long as I got to practice. It was that or ask Leo to bolt some silks to the top of the staircase. If Mum asked, he'd probably do just that, but I wasn't going to meet any hot coaches if I stayed here. Just hot assholes who weren't worth my time.

I closed the web browser and opened my essay file. Information security analytics might be as boring as hell to a lot of people, but it fascinated me. Every day it seemed like another big corporation was hacked. When I finished my degree, I wanted to prevent those hackings. Companies owed it to their customers to keep their information safe, not let it be sold on the dark web. Maybe I was an idealist, thinking I could actually prevent cyber attacks, but at least I could help to minimise them, and clean up afterwards.

All of that was shorthand for, Kennedy Knight is a massive nerd. A nerd who would get a lucrative job after I graduated. There was nothing to be ashamed of here.

I read over my work, making corrections here and there before I started on the conclusion. I was so absorbed in my work I didn't notice the guys got out of the pool until the door slid open behind me and they strutted inside like all three of them owned the place.

I kept my gaze on the screen, but watched them move around in the corner of my eye.

Mannix went to the fridge and pulled out drinks for the other two and himself. They all twisted off the caps and tossed them down on the island next to my laptop.

They were obviously trying to piss me off, so I ignored them.

"Are we going to that party tonight?" Ares asked.

That was obvious too. He wanted me to know they were invited and I wasn't. Whatever.

I had more important things to worry about than their petty games. Although, a party would be fun and a good way to meet people.

I tapped my keyboard as though I hadn't heard.

Mannix leaned his elbows on the island and looked right at me. "I think we should."

"We should take Kennedy with us," Ice said.

Ares and Mannix both stiffened.

"You want to come, don't you, Kennedy?" Ice slid a hand under my hair and rested it lightly on the back of my neck.

Luckily I was sitting, because his touch set me on fire and made my knees weak. My breath hitched. I know they all heard it.

Which kind of come did he mean? To the party, or orgasm? Of course, he probably meant both, and that would have been my answer if I could speak coherently.

"She's not invited," Ares snapped.

"She's invited if we bring her," Ice said easily. "You want to come, Kennedy?" He squeezed the back of my neck and I had the strangest sensation that he wanted to wrap his fingers around my throat and squeeze. And squeeze until the light left my eyes.

I was terrified and turned on at the same time.

"I'd love to," I said finally.

I ignored Ares' growl of irritation. And the deepening frown on Mannix's gorgeous face.

I hope like hell I didn't live to regret agreeing to go.

CHAPTER 4

MANNIX

"Why the fuck did you invite her?" I growled. "What part of *she's not fucking invited* did you not get?"

It was typical of Ice to invite first and give a shit about the consequences later. Or not at all. Right now, he didn't seem to give a crap about the bomb he threw in the middle of the three of us. Girls like Kennedy Knight and her mother were nothing but trouble. Women in general.

Kennedy, in particular, was too fucking cute for her own good. The moment I first laid eyes on her, I wanted to tear her clothes off and slam my cock into her wet heat. I bet anything she was tight. Girls like her always were. The ones who went about pretending they had no idea how fucking hot they were. But they knew. They always did. Why else would she walk around my home in a singlet and tight little shorts? She might as well be waving a flag with the words, 'bend me over and fuck me,' written on it.

And I wanted to. That was a problem. Especially in light of the fact Ares and Ice also wanted to bounce her on their cock. The guys were my brothers, but I didn't want to fucking share.

No, the best thing I could do was stay as far away as I could from Kennedy fucking Knight and her perfect tits. At least until the other guys lost interest, because my pretty little stepsister-to-be was *mine*. I couldn't wait to teach her the way I like my cock sucked. The thought of her mouth, her throat, made me hard.

"I invited her because I wanted her to come," Ice said unapologetically. "All study and no play..." He waved a hand in the air. "Blah blah blah. You wouldn't want the Cassani family to get a reputation for being boring, do you?"

I grunted in response. "Like that will happen. No one would dare say shit like that about us." They wouldn't because either I'd kill them or I'd have one of my father's people do it.

Everyone in Dusk Bay knew that. We didn't have quite the power of the DiMarco family, who ran the city, or the Brantley family, who ran the state, but my father was a loyal minion of them both. Ric DiMarco and Caleb Brantley trusted him as much as they trusted anyone. And by extension, they trusted me.

I knew more about my father's business than anyone except him and my older brother Gunnar. Whatever was asked of him, of us, we'd do it. Anything from running guns and drugs to trafficking diamonds and even people.

"The bitch is trouble," Ares said. Like Ice, his family were local to Dusk Bay. More loyal minions of Ric and Caleb. The three of us went to school together, then went away to Brutham Academy. Brutal Academy, they call it. If you make it through your first year there alive, you have at least a fifty-fifty chance of surviving until graduation.

First year exams include hunting down other students by any means necessary. It was a perfect opportunity to get rid of any threats who would pose a problem at some point in the future. I was hunted by a member of the Bell family, who took it upon herself to rid the world of any threats to them. I can still feel my hands around her throat, squeezing until her body went still and the last breath slipped from between her lips. Shame, she had one of the tightest pussies I'd ever fucked. She made her choice when she chose the wrong side. She deserved a slower death than what I gave her, but I couldn't take the chance she was working with someone else. It was her or me and it wasn't going to be me.

"She's almost harmless," Ice said.

Ares grunted. "She's either harmless or she's not. And she's not. She's a ticking time bomb in the middle of a field of sheep."

I cut him a look. "A field of sheep, bro? Do I look furry to you?"

"Isn't it fleece?" Ice asked.

"Whatever," I grunted. "Either way, I'm no lamb." Kennedy might be though. A sweet little lamb, ready to be led right to her own slaughter. After I fucked her until her body was boneless. Until she begged me to stop. No, I'd still keep going. I wanted to make her cry. I wanted her so sore she couldn't walk for a week. For a month. When she couldn't take any more of me, I'd still give her more. When I was done, she would know exactly who she belonged to. Who owned her.

"She's a pain in the ass and the sooner she gets the hell out of Dusk Bay, the better," Ares growled. "The better for us and the better for her." His blue eyes were dark with anger or lust, or a combination of the two. Ever since I've known him, he was a dark and complicated guy. I could count on one hand the amount of times I saw him smile. According to him, he was born fucked up. That sounded accurate to me.

"The better for us and the better for her," he said again.

Usually, I agreed with him, but not on this. Kennedy wasn't leaving. I wouldn't allow it. If she tried, I'd hunt her down and bring her back, whether she wanted to return or not.

Thing is, I knew he didn't want her to leave either. I saw the way he looked at her. He was already mentally pinning her down under the weight of his body and slamming his cock into her.

I curled my hands into fists under the table and kept them there to stop myself from punching Ares in the face. It wasn't his fault he was hot for her, but I needed to find him someone else to obsess over. Ice too. Him being nice to her, touching her, that was also a problem. I wanted to push him into the pool and hold him under until he stopped kicking.

I wouldn't though, because he was my brother. Both of them had short attention spans when it came to women. In a week or two, they'd be drooling over someone else and leaving me to make my move.

I glanced over to where she sat, talking to Daisy Lasalle, of all people. Known by most people in Dusk Bay as Daze, she was my older brother's girlfriend. At the same time, she's screwing Ric DiMarco and Caleb Brantley's right-hand man, Hilton Blake. She was as powerful as any of them, as deadly. Anyone who crossed any of her boyfriends, or her, would wish for death, instead of the slow torture they'd inflict on them.

Anyone with half a brain was scared of her. Including me. Right now, she was smiling and laughing at something Kennedy said. I couldn't tell if the two women becoming friends would be a good thing or the worst idea ever. I had no trouble telling Kennedy who she could and couldn't be friends with, except for Daisy Lasalle. If I wanted to keep my cock intact, I'd stay out of that. As it happens, I'm very attached to my cock.

"See, she's making friends already." Ice nodded toward the pair. He smiled like an indulgent father who was happy his toddler was playing nicely in the sandpit with another kid. Or sharing the red finger paint.

"Perfect." Ares scowled but he said, "If Daze doesn't scare her into running out of town, nothing will. Any minute now she'll start telling Kennedy how she likes to ask her boyfriends to break thumbs for her. Or about the time she and Ric locked a guy in his own cool room to die slowly."

I smiled. That was pretty epic. From what I've heard, the cool room walls and door were too thick for anyone to hear him shouting. Who knows whether he froze or suffocated. Either way, it wasn't a quick and cheerful death. I doubted Daze or Ric lost any sleep over it. Knowing those two, they probably talked and laughed about it while they fucked. Judging by the fact he always had half-healed knife wounds on his neck, things got wild at their place.

I won't lie, I'd stick my cock into her if I got the chance. Most of the guys in Dusk Bay would. They'd probably lose their cock five seconds later, but it might just be worth it.

"Do you think she knows what this place is like?" Ice propped his elbow on the table and rested his chin on his hand. His hazel eyes lingered on Kennedy. "I mean, she seems innocent to me. Like she thinks we all have pet bunnies, and spend our weekends mowing lawns and growing chrysanthemums."

"You did have a pet bunny and grew chrysanthemums," I pointed out. His parents paid someone to mow the lawn.

He looked over at me, a dreamy expression on his face. "Yeah, Mr Flopsy. I was so sad when he died. But then I got to cut him up and see how he worked." The memory of that brightened him up a little. Typical Ice. I'd seen him slice animals and people and marvel at the blood, bones and muscles and the way everything fit together, and came apart. No wonder he studied forensic pathology at university. He loved nothing better than a good autopsy.

Sick fuck.

I wasn't entirely convinced Mr Flopsy hadn't met with a nasty Ice-related accident, but he seemed genuinely upset when the thing died. Maybe he'd killed it by accident. If he had, it was the only time he ever killed anything or anyone by accident. It might have given him a taste of blood and death. A thirst he enjoyed slaking whenever he could. I've never met anyone who enjoyed killing as much as he did. It was almost like he needed to murder someone to start his day, like normal people drank coffee.

"Did you dissect the chrysanthemums too?" Ares asked, his tone scathing.

Ice cocked his head at him. "No, those were for my mother. She liked to have fresh flowers everywhere." A mischievous glint in his eye added, "Your mother liked them too, right before I—"

Ares growled deep in the back of his throat. "Don't try to imply you fucked my mother. I'll rip off your dick and shove it down your throat."

"I wasn't trying to imply anything," Ice said as though he was saying it outright. He probably had fucked Ares' mother. Almost everyone else in Dusk Bay had, except me. I wasn't into older women who liked to be in control. I preferred to be the one in control.

"You're an asshole," Ares said.

"Maybe, but I..."

I tuned out their bullshit and looked around the party as though I wasn't keeping a close eye on Kennedy. I made a note of everyone she spoke to, especially anyone she was friendly with. Particularly if they had a cock. If they thought they were going to touch her, they could think again.

I'd cut their fucking hand off and smack them with it, then stab them in the stomach and let them die slowly. I'd make Kennedy watch so she knew what would happen to anyone if she let them touch her. Then I'd tie her to my bed and punish her by making her ass black and blue with my hand before I fucked the hell out of her.

Everyone would learn not to touch her. Including her. By the time I was done with her, she'd know not to touch herself. I'd be the only one to touch her, to get her off.

Me.

And when she came, she'd scream my name and be grateful to belong to me.

CHAPTER 5

KENNEDY

"So... I'm supposed to go in this morning to check out the gymnastics place," I said slowly.

Mum and Leo both looked at me over their coffee cups. Their expressions matched except for Leo's slightly raised eyebrow.

"I don't have a car." I thought back to Ice offering to buy Mannix's car like it was nothing. It was probably nothing for Leo too, but I wanted to buy my own car when I had my own money. I hadn't needed one back in Sydney, I took the train everywhere, or rode my bike. Public transport didn't come to this part of Dusk Bay. And it was too far from anywhere to ride.

"If I could borrow one..." I started tentatively. Leo had a collection of them, but most of them were crazy expensive, like his white Shelby Cobra, and a classic Rolls-Royce. All I needed was an old rust bucket. Or a little hatchback.

"I'll drive you," Mannix said, his voice tight. He was standing in the kitchen, his back to the bench. His long fingers were curled around a black mug full of black coffee. The same shade as his soul.

He gave me a look like I'd insisted, instead of him offering.

"What a lovely idea," Mum said. "It's so nice to see you two getting along."

I gave her a watery smile. He let me tag along to the party, but didn't say a word to me all night, or since. It seemed like every time I turned around, he was watching me, trying to figure out a way to get rid of me. Every time I caught him looking, he immediately looked away and stalked off into another room.

Mannix looked at Mum like maybe she was crazy, but didn't say anything. It was obvious to everyone we weren't exactly friends.

That begged the question of why he offered to drive me in the first place. Was this his attempt to make an effort to get to know me, or was I going to end up disposed of, like the man at the ball?

Yeah, okay, I was being a little bit paranoid, but I *had* seen a man murdered. Part of me wanted to ask if Mannix knew anything about it, but he and his friends weren't in town at the time. Did Leo know? Did I want to know if he did?

No, that was something better not discussed, not thought about. Forgetting was easier said than done though. My nightmares were still full of blood and masks.

"I have to go into town anyway." Mannix shrugged. There was that look again, like somehow he thought I was making him drive.

"I don't want to be a hassle—" I started.

Mannix put his coffee cup down on the bench hard enough to make me jump. He smirked. Apparently making me startle was hilarious and intentional.

Asshole.

"Like I said, I'm going anyway. If you want a ride, you have five minutes." He scooped up his cup and put it in the dishwasher.

"Five minutes sounds accurate," I told him as I put my bowl and mug in the dishwasher beside his cup. I gave him a sweet smile when he scowled at me.

"It would still be the best five minutes of your life." He gave me a dark look and strode away toward the garage.

"Dream on," I said under my breath. He might be hot, and sexy, and the thought of him touching me set my blood on fire, but he was still a jerk and my stepbrother-to-be.

I hurried off to change into leggings and a loose T-shirt. I shoved my feet into running shoes and trotted down the stairs as Mannix backed the SUV out of the garage. I thought he might drive off without me, but he stopped long enough for me to slip into the passenger seat. I barely got the door closed before he gunned the engine and flew down the gravel driveway. I managed to drag my seatbelt over me and click it into place before he braked heavily and waited for the gate to open.

"Thanks for offering to drive me." Maybe if I was nice to him, he'd be less of a dick back to me.

A girl could hope, right?

"If I hadn't, Dad would have spent my inheritance buying you a car," he said.

"I never would have expected him to do that."

"He'd still do it, whether you expect it or not." He accelerated hard and the SUV jumped past the gate and onto the road.

I sighed because he was probably right, but I couldn't help that.

"I don't want his money or yours," I said firmly. "I can make my own money. I don't need to live off a parent or stepparent." Wasn't he doing exactly that? Daddy gave him a job. Leo probably brought him this SUV. He got to live in a mansion and be a jerk all day with his asshole friends.

Mannix snorted with disbelief. "So if we get home and one of those cute little bright pink cars with a pretty little pink ribbon around it was there, you're gonna say no to it?"

Pink wasn't my favourite colour, but it would be difficult to refuse a gift like that. "I don't—"

"Of course you're not going to fucking say no," he snarled. "Girls like you don't get anywhere if they say no."

I glared over at him. "What's that supposed to mean? If you're trying to suggest I haven't worked hard at university, or at—"

He cut off a white van and flipped the driver off out the window. "Learn to drive, dickhead."

He glanced over at me. "I'm saying girls like you want to say yes. You get off on making people happy. Don't tell me I'm wrong, because we both know I'm not."

He wasn't wrong. But was it bad to be a people pleaser?

"What does that make you?" I asked. "The kind of guy who gets off on telling people no for no reason? Who won't give an inch, even if it's in your best interest to do it?"

He shrugged one shoulder. "Maybe. It's better than being a pushover."

"Is it?" I challenged him. "Seems like being a nice person makes life easier for everyone, especially myself."

"An easy life is an illusion. The world is a shit hole. No amount of nice is going to change that, it just gets you screwed over." He seemed to be speaking from experience.

"Who hurt you?" I asked. "Aren't you a bit young to be that cynical?"

He stopped the SUV at a traffic light and cut me a look and a bitter smile. "I'm not cynical, I'm a realist. The universe isn't sitting there waiting to give you what you want. The only way to really get what you want and what you need is to fucking take it. That's why if Dad gives you a car, you'll accept. Even if the car comes with a blowjob."

I grimaced. "I definitely wouldn't take it if it did. And Leo wouldn't cheat on my mother."

"Who said he'd be the one to receive the blowjob?" Mannix gave me a look like he'd happily drag my face down to his lap and make me suck him off while he drove.

"Does your family often give gifts with conditions attached?" I asked.

"Frequently." The light turned green and he turned his attention back to the road. "No one in the world gives gifts without strings attached. There's no such thing as a free blowjob."

"You should get that on a T-shirt," I said dryly. "Maybe sell them at the local market. You might make a few dollars. I'm sure Ares and Ice would come and help you out." Ares and Mannix would scare all the customers away, but Ice might sell a few. If nothing else, it was an interesting mental image.

"I'll save one for you," Mannix said. "A white one that's tight around your tits. No bra. You could make a few dollars giving paid blowjobs. I'd be first in line."

I believed him. He hated my guts, but he'd enjoy seeing me on my knees, my lips around his cock. His eyes on mine as I sucked his thick length. His hips moving slowly back and forth, grunts of pleasure slipping from his mouth.

I shook my head to get the thought out of it. I should one hundred percent not be thinking about him like this. He might not appreciate it if I left a puddle on his seat, even if it was because I was thinking inappropriate thoughts about my stepbrother-to-be.

"I know I need money for a car, but I'm not that desperate." I adjusted my position on the seat.

"Yet," he said.

"I have no plans to be that desperate ever," I retorted. I wouldn't knock anyone who was employed in the sex industry, but it wasn't a career I aspired to have.

"Shame, I hear it pays well."

"If you're so worried about Leo giving away your inheritance, maybe you should look into it for yourself. I'm sure you'd be popular." Lonely, rich housewives would probably pay a ton to fuck him. Men too.

"No one would be able to afford me." He looked smug.

I snorted. At least we were getting along with each other now, more or less. This was the first halfway decent conversation we had since we met. This might be as good as we got with each other.

He pulled up in front of the gymnastic studio and killed the engine.

"I'll be back in an hour. That should be long enough for you to do your shit." He was telling, not asking. If I wasn't ready to go when he got back, I'd have to find my own way back home. He wouldn't regret leaving me behind for a moment.

"An hour should be plenty," I said lightly. "Thank you again for—"

"Are you going to get out sometime today?" His inpatient tone matched the dark look in his eyes. Evidently he'd exhausted his quota of pleasantry, and was done with me.

Our tentative peace was at an end.

"Yeah." I pushed the door open and climbed out. I'd barely shut the door behind me when he pulled away from the curb and roared off down the street. I was lucky he didn't run over my feet. That was probably his plan.

Not today, motherfucker.

Why did he have to be so fucking hot and an asshole at the same time? Had something terrible happened to make him so cynical? Maybe he witnessed a murder too. Seeing that, living with the memory, would mess with anyone's mind. It was certainly messing with mine. I considered therapy, but dismissed the idea. I couldn't talk about it without risking giving away details. As much as I'd like to trust a therapist to keep things confidential, I'd be naïve to think the chance of details getting out was zero.

"I'll see you soon, little mouse. Or maybe it will be later. Now I think about it, later would be better. Your fear will taste sweeter then. Like honey and wine. Like the smoothest chocolate melted down until it's liquid. Like cum. Perfect for drinking."

The words were seared into my mind like a brand. I played it over and over again until the idea of melted chocolate made my stomach turn. In my dreams, he took a few steps forward, found me, and tore me open like their victim. Sometimes I dreamt they drank my blood. Sometimes I was still alive when they did it.

If he found me, if *they* found me, I was screwed. Worse than screwed, I'd be dead.

I pushed down the flutter of fear that rose in my chest and stepped through the door and into the gym.

CHAPTER 6

KENNEDY

This was my happy place. Right at the top of the thick line of bright blue silk.

Technically, stretch polyester, but whatever. I was the most alive with my back arched, hands outstretched, thighs the only part of me gripping the fabric.

I wound the silk around my wrists and let myself drop, face first. I caught myself a couple of centimetres off the mat and grinned at the rush of adrenaline through my body.

A handful of younger gymnasts taking a kid's class stopped to watch, gasped and clapped. Their coach, a guy around my age named Charlie, clapped louder than the kids.

The gruff head coach, Nicola, had palmed me off to him when I walked through the door. She muttered something about renting out the silks for a couple of hours a week and that she'd consider hiring me to teach. Then she disappeared into her office with a cup of coffee and hadn't emerged since.

I tipped over forward and landed on my feet.

I tugged my t-shirt back into place as Charlie dismissed the class. The kids went running off to their parents who waited near the door.

"It's been a while since we had anyone who could use those." He gave me an easy smile. With sandy blond hair, blue green eyes and the body of a gymnast, it was easy to like Charlie. He was a pleasant change from 'grumpy asshole'.

"I'm a bit rusty," I admitted. "It's been a couple of months since I got to practice."

"If that was rusty, I'd love to see you when you're warmed up and competition fit." He waved back at a couple of the kids as they waved vigorously and giggled. They looked at him with huge eyes that screamed crush.

I got that. If he was my coach, I might have a crush on him too. On paper, he was exactly the kind of guy I should go for, but he didn't get my pulse racing like Mannix and his friends. Figured I wouldn't be into the first nice guy I met since I got to Dusk Bay. Hopefully he wasn't the only one in town. It would be a long year if he was.

I sighed. "I wish I had time for competition training. At least I can get in some practice here and there." I eyed the clock and then the uneven bars. I had a few minutes before Mannix returned.

"Spot me?" Charlie probably had a life to get to, but he didn't seem to be in a hurry to leave.

"Absolutely." He waited until I chalked my hands and got into place under the lower bar. "Ready?"

I could get up there myself, with the help of the ladder beside the bars, but I decided to let him put his hands around my waist and lift me up to the lower bar. I didn't even mind when his hands lingered a little too long, or the way his toned body felt close to mine.

It was nothing like the rush of heat I got from looking at Mannix, Ares and Ice, but it was pleasant enough.

I started to swing back and forth to build momentum, then leapt onto the higher bar. Back and forth, round and round until everything around me was a blur. I was rusty at this too, but muscle memory took me through a routine I'd practised a billion times. I could even hear the cheesy competition music playing in the back of my mind over and over.

I dropped to my feet, stuck the landing and presented, raising my arms above my head and smiling as Charlie clapped.

"You probably guessed Nicola wanted me to watch you and give her my thoughts on whether or not she should hire you," he said lightly. "She'd be crazy not to. How did you never make the Olympic team?"

"I injured my knee right before the trials." At the time, I was devastated, but that was a few years ago now and I didn't miss the pressure of competitions and the need to succeed. I was happy to do this for fun and maybe for profit if Nicola gave me a job.

Charlie sucked in a breath with sympathy and winced. "That's a bummer. I was never quite good enough. Which is my way of saying I didn't take it seriously. I was too busy clowning around on the rings to win a competition, much less qualify for any big ones." He seemed unworried.

"One more go?" He jerked his head towards the uneven bars.

"I have time for one more." I stepped into the circle of his hands and let him lift me. I'd just gripped the lower bar and started to swing when the door opened with a crash.

I startled so hard my hands slipped and I fell to the mat on my ass. Nothing was hurt but my pride, but that had a pretty big dent in it. I knew better than to react to sudden sounds like that. If I did that during the competition, I'd lose a bunch of points.

Dusk Bay definitely had me on edge.

I looked over to see Mannix standing inside the door, his expression as dark as thunder. He wasn't looking at me. He was looking at Charlie like he wanted to rip his head off and use it as a bowling ball.

I stood up and dusted chalk off my hands. "Looks like my ride is here."

"You know this guy?" Charlie asked uneasily.

That was a good question. Honestly, I hardly knew Mannix at all.

"He's my stepbrother-to-be," I said lightly. "I'll hear from you or Nicola?"

Charlie managed to force his eyes away from Mannix's glare and smiled. "I'd say within a day or two. But you'll be back to practice, yeah?"

I returned his smile. "Definitely, if I can get someone to drive me." I narrowed my eyes at Mannix, hoping he'd get the hint to chill out. I didn't know what his problem with Charlie was and I didn't care.

Charlie was a nice guy and hopefully soon a co-worker. Nothing more.

"Hurry up," Mannix snapped. He turned and stomped out the door toward the SUV.

I shrugged at Charlie and grabbed up my stuff before I trotted out after him and slipped into the passenger seat.

Like before, he barely gave me time to close the door and fasten my seatbelt before he pulled away from the curb.

"What is your fucking problem?" I asked him.

"Why was he touching you?" Mannix snapped.

I stared at him. "What?"

"Why. Was. He. Touching. You?" he said again, slowly and deliberately.

"He wasn't…" I shook my head. "He's a coach. He was lifting me up to the bars. That was all. Why? Are you worried I was giving him a blowjob before you got there?"

Apparently that was the wrong thing to say, because Mannix's face turned red. He screeched the SUV down a side street and slammed on the brakes so hard I almost bounced my head on the dashboard.

"What the hell, Mannix?" My head spun for a moment. "Are you trying to kill us?"

Judging by the expression on his face, that was exactly what he was trying to do.

He lurched towards me. I backed up until my shoulders hit the SUV's window. The expression on his face was intense, his eyes darker than ever.

He grabbed a fistful of my hair and curled it around his fingers. He drew me toward him until my face was a couple of centimetres from his. His breath was blazing hot on my cheek.

My heart thundered through my chest. I could hardly think, barely breathe. Being so close to him was an attack on all of my senses. Heat radiated off him, churned with a dose of fury and lust. If I looked down, I knew I'd see his hard cock pressed against the zipper of his jeans. The feel and smell of him was pure sex.

Oh fuck.

"Why did he touch you?" he growled. His teeth were gritted

together, bared like a wild animal. If Charlie was here, he might bite his head off with one snap.

"I told you, he's a coach. He was doing his job. Nothing else. It was harmless." I swallowed hard. "Why do you care anyway?"

His fist tightened around my head to the point of pain. "Because no one touches you," he said slowly, his tone menacing, bordering on terrifying. "No one touches you but *me*. Do you understand me? *No one.*"

My head spun harder. What the hell was he saying? I was convinced he hated my guts, but then he said things like that? He was going to give me whiplash with his sudden change.

"I don't—"

He pulled me until his stubble scratched over my lips and the side of my cheek. My eyes watered from the pain, but I didn't want him to stop. Didn't want him to let go.

"Princess, I know you want me as much as I want you. You want me to fuck you until you scream. I see it in your eyes every time you look at me. Did you think I wouldn't notice? Did you think I wouldn't feel it too? The moment I set eyes on you, I knew you were mine. You knew it, too, didn't you? Your pussy is dripping right now. Dripping for me."

I didn't know how to answer that, so I let out a breathless whimper. I was wetter than hell. Yes, I wanted him to touch me, but I still wasn't convinced he didn't hate me. I was also not convinced I'd say no to anything he tried to do to me. Yeah, I wanted him so bad it hurt. I wanted to spread my thighs and let him bury his face between them. I wanted to feel him fill me with every centimetre he had.

"You are mine and no one touches you but me," he said again. "I don't give a fuck if he's a coach or a fucking gynaecologist. No one lays a hand on you. Do you hear me? Do you?"

"Ye— Yes I do," I said, my voice barely above a whisper.

He paused for a moment, then brushed his lips over mine. It was barely a kiss. A feather light touch. And then he released my hair and sat back.

"We should get back," he said like nothing happened. "I have things to do. If you need to go anywhere, I'll drive you. I'll watch the whole time you're there if I have to."

I combed my fingers through my hair to straighten it and sat back up in my seat. "That could make it difficult to teach if you're lurking around all the time." My heart slowed gradually, but my whole body throbbed with need. What would it be like to have him on top of me? Inside me? The thought threatened to consume me like an inferno.

"Don't give me an excuse to lurk around then," he said. As if I was somehow responsible for the actions of someone else.

Okay, I didn't need Charlie's help, but the whole thing was harmless. Apparently Mannix didn't see it that way.

"I have a feeling you'll lurk anyway," I said.

He cut me a look as he restarted the engine. "I take good care of what's mine. I might even buy you a pretty little pink car with a pink bow, myself."

I believed him.

"I prefer black," I said.

"I think I'll just drive you around myself for a while." He drove the SUV back out into the main road, but just as wild and reckless as before.

"Fine, but maybe don't kill me with your driving," I said. That would really put a dampener on this...whatever this was. I couldn't deny the attraction but could I handle his intensity? Did I want to try?

For some reason I wasn't even sure of myself, I actually did. As well as being hot, Mannix was fascinating. When he wasn't being an asshole, I felt safe from the world around him. Like...if anyone hurt me, he wouldn't hesitate to protect me from and deal with them.

The question was, who would protect me from him?

CHAPTER 7

KENNEDY

I was dreaming but I couldn't get myself to wake up. In my dream, several figures started towards me. Three wore black head coverings like they were executioners. A fourth had no face, but his neck was wide open, gaping and shining with blood.

They shuffled towards me. Their hands were by their sides, but at the same time, they seemed to be reaching for me.

"We'll find you, little mouse. There's nowhere you can run and hide from us. Nowhere we can't find you."

I couldn't tell which one of them was speaking. Maybe it was all of them. The words echoed through my mind like they were on feedback, on a continuous loop. Speaking over each other more and more, becoming louder and louder like a crescendo.

Something pinned my wrists to either side of my face. The figures got closer. I writhed and struggled, but couldn't move. They were going to catch me, and when they did, I was dead. If I let them touch me, I would wither and die or turn into dust.

I couldn't let them touch me. Whatever it took, I had to stop that from happening.

I struggled harder. Tipped back my head and screamed.

And screamed.

"Princess. Princess, come on. I've got you. Shhh." Vice-like hands gripped my wrists, holding me tighter.

My eyes snapped open and I found myself in dim light.

My bedroom.

Mannix lay beside me, his fingers hard around my wrists, his face centimetres from mine.

"There you are." His grip relaxed slightly. "Another nightmare?"

"Another…" I blinked a couple of times, still trying to orient myself.

"You've had them every night since I got here." He let go of my wrists and propped himself up on his elbow. "This one sounded worse than the others."

Slowly, I managed to register two facts. First, Mannix was in my bed. Second, he'd come in here to help me when I was having a bad dream.

Wait, there was a third fact—he was naked except for a pair of boxer shorts. It went to show how disturbed I was after the nightmare that I didn't notice that straight away.

He brushed hair off my sweaty brow. "You okay?"

"I— Yeah." I wanted to tell him everything. To get the memory of that night off my chest. I didn't know him well enough to know if I could trust him, so I just said, "Thanks."

He grabbed up the water bottle I kept beside my bed and offered it to me. I took a couple of sips and set it back down.

"Better?" He cocked his head at me. He seemed genuinely concerned. Maybe the aloof guy he'd been since he first pulled up with Ice and Ares was an act to protect himself. From what though?

"Much better. I'm sorry if I disturbed your sleep. I guess moving to a new place has me more on edge than I thought." That was lame, but that was all I could come up with right now.

"Dusk Bay has that effect on people." He slipped a hand under the hem of my singlet and across my stomach. "I'll have to give you something to keep your mind off it."

A shiver went all the way through me and left a pool of heat in my core. His fingers were calloused, rough on my skin, but enticing.

"Mannix…"

His mouth right next to my ear he whispered, "Tell me something,

Princess. How many guys have touched you? How many guys have fucked that tight little pussy?" He spoke as though he would track down every last one and trim their cocks off at their balls.

My tongue darted over my lips. I whispered, "None."

His hand stilled and he drew in a breath of surprise. "None? My sweet little Princess is a sweet little virgin?"

"Yeah. I just never… Found someone I wanted to… be with." There were opportunities, but none that excited me the way Mannix, Ares and Ice did. What would Mannix do if either of his friends touched me? It didn't matter in Ares' case, since he obviously hated my guts, but Ice was sweet. How far would Mannix really take it? It was one thing to say no one else could touch me and another to act on it. Especially when the other guy was a close friend.

"Good." He lowered his mouth to mine and kissed me softly.

Just that gentle touch set my body on fire. Strange how a guy who could be so forceful, could also be so sweet. His mouth tasted of mint and some kind of spice.

His tongue slipped between my lips and stroked over my teeth, probing deeper like he wanted to explore every bit of me.

His hand slid up my stomach, to cup my breast. He palmed my nipple until it was rock hard. Then he worked on the other one.

"Tell me how much you want me, Princess," he whispered between kisses. "Tell me you want me to fuck you."

Did I? I mean, yes I did, but this was going so fast.

"I want you to…touch me," I said tentatively.

"Just touch? I can start with that." He peeled up the front of my singlet and moved down to trace circles around my nipple with his tongue. This was already far more than I ever did with anyone else.

"This nipple is mine." He closed his lips around it and sucked, while at the same time teasing me with his tongue. "And so is this one." He switched over to my other nipple. "So tasty."

His touch felt so good. Better than good, it felt right.

He abandoned my nipples and kissed his way slowly down my body. He hooked his thumbs into my panties and ripped them in two.

"I'll buy you new ones." He unapologetically tossed both pieces aside and moved down lower. He parted my thighs with firm, but still gentle fingers.

"Has anyone else licked you down here?" His eyes were intense on mine.

"No, no one."

Was he really about to... I'd thought about this more times than I could count, but when his tongue grazed over my clit, it was so much better than I could have imagined.

He groaned. "Fucking hell, Princess, you taste like pure addictive sin." He lapped at me a couple of times before he added, "This pussy is mine too. Mine to taste." Lick. "Mine to nibble." Lick. "Mine to make come."

I could only moan in response. I was speeding towards an orgasm faster than Mannix's driving. My whole body was on fire, burning like his touch was hot oil on an open flame.

I stiffened when he slipped a finger inside me. It felt strange at first, and more than a bit mindblowing.

He raised his face and said, "Relax, Princess." He slid his finger in and out slowly. "You feel amazing and so fucking wet. This is practice for when you take my cock."

When I finally let myself relax, he slid in another finger. He stroked me inside while his tongue worked the outside.

"Come for me, Princess," he said, his voice muffled by my thighs. "Show me you're mine."

I couldn't have stopped myself if I wanted to. He shattered me into a thousand, breathless, bucking pieces. The world exploded into a prism of light, lost in the sound of thundering blood. With my fingers or a vibrator, I'd never come so hard. Or stayed up in the atmosphere so long.

I finally flopped back onto the mattress. He slipped his fingers out of me and scooted up to press one between my lips.

"See how delicious you taste? My delicious Princess." He held it there while I sucked it clean. The combination of my juices and the salt on his skin were divine.

He lay down beside me and gathered me up in his arms. "I won't fuck you tonight. I want to, but I'll give you a little bit of time to be ready for me. I'll come to you every night and make you come for me. And when you're ready, I'll fuck that tight little pussy. Just like my father is probably fucking your mother right now. When they get married, nothing has to change between us. When I'm your step-brother, you'll still be mine."

He stroked my hair, tangling his fingers in the soft waves.

He whispered in my ear, "Tell me who you belong to."

I swallowed. My voice a little shaky, I said, "You. I belong to you. Soon I'll be ready for your cock." He was right, I needed some time to think about it and process everything. I wanted to feel him inside me, but not tonight. Not yet.

"Of course you will. You're my princess. I'm going to claim you fully. Every beautiful centimetre of your gorgeous body. I'm going to fill you so much you'll overflow, but you'll still beg for more."

"You think I'm gorgeous?" I said sleepily.

He chuckled, low and deep. "You're the most gorgeous woman I've ever seen. The more of you I see, the more I think, I know, every bit of you is absolutely fucking beautiful."

My face heated. What? When I looked in the mirror was a girl with bright red hair, pale skin and a bunch of freckles. I was cute, but I'd never seen myself as beautiful before.

The way he said it almost made me believe it. If he kept saying it, someday I would.

"What will your father say?" If Leo hated the idea of us being together, he could easily kick me out of his house and his son's life, even if it meant upsetting my mother. Leo was the kind of man who got what he wanted. That must run in the family.

"Leave him to me. It won't be a problem."

Why did those words leave me slightly chilled?

"Are you worried your mother will object?" he asked.

"I'm not sure what she'll say," I admitted. She'd want me to be happy, but the situation was all kinds of complicated, especially if things turned bad. On the other hand, it wasn't as though Mannix and I were related by blood. Where was the harm in us making each other feel good? "What will Ares and Ice say?"

"They'll be jealous as fuck," he said, sounding smug. "They both want you too."

"They do? Ares—"

"Ares has his head stuck up his ass," Mannix said. "With good reason, but that's another story. Let's not talk about them anymore. Do you want to talk about the nightmare?"

I shivered. "Not really. I'd prefer to forget about it. Will you stay with me for a while?" With his arms around me, I might sleep without dreaming. If anything could keep the darkness away, it would be his muscles and the comfort of his warm body.

"You couldn't make me leave if you held a gun to my head," he said.

I got the impression he meant that literally. Maybe the reason I thought he could keep the darkness away was because he was part of it. It might curl itself around him so they could comfort each other.

If I thought he was dark, then what did that make me? A girl who lay in the arms of her stepbrother-to-be while his face smelled of me, knowing he wanted to claim every part of me, inside and out.

What would he give me in return? His body, certainly. But what about his heart?

What about mine? A guy like him could tear me apart and walk away, leaving me shattered on the floor. I should guard my heart against him, but part of me didn't want to. A reckless voice inside told me to let go, but I didn't want to jump into freefall without some kind of parachute.

Right now, I didn't even have a scrap of fabric.

CHAPTER 8

KENNEDY

"So," Ice drawled, "what are you studying?" He stood at my shoulder, his breath brushing my neck.

"Computer science," I said without looking away from the screen. I was trying to play it cool, but I hadn't read a word since he entered the kitchen. After what Mannix said about him and Ares wanting me, I was hyper-aware around all three of them. More so than before.

"I'm sure that sounds super geeky." It was a great way of scaring guys off. Too many of them couldn't deal with a smart woman. I couldn't deal with a guy who was threatened by someone with brains.

"I think it sounds super cool." He put his hands on my shoulders and lightly started to massage the knots.

"I was going to ask what you studied but I'm guessing it's massage therapy." I dropped my head forward and let him work, while keeping half an ear out for Mannix and Ares.

Mannix had said something about a problem with one of the cars. Ares went to help him, leaving Ice and I alone. I presumed they were letting the mechanic onto the property, because I doubted these rich boys knew much about engines.

But if Mannix was going to get pissed off about Ice touching me...

Ice chuckled.

My heart skipped a beat and started racing. *It was just a laugh,* I told myself. Why did it get to me so much?

"No, I studied forensic pathology. I'm fascinated about how one part of the human anatomy is attached to another. Like this—" He squeezed my shoulder lightly. "Is attached to this." He traced circles around the top of my chest with the pad of his thumb, brushed across the top of my breast.

"And this—" He slid a finger down my arm and traced circles around the crook of my elbow. "This innocent little crook is an erogenous zone."

It certainly was. I was going to go wild if he kept doing that.

I shivered.

"The whole body is full of interesting muscles and nerve endings," he continued. "A touch here can elicit a reaction there." The heel of his hand slid over my collarbone. My nipples immediately pebbled in response. He moved his hand up and down, slow and light.

"Is that making you wet, Beautiful?"

Without waiting for an answer he moved his hand over to my other collarbone.

I swallowed hard. His touch was like pure electricity on my skin.

"The funny thing is, the body can react without physical stimuli. Sometimes all it takes is words."

He braced himself on the kitchen island, one hand on either side of me, almost but not quite touching me. He whispered in my ear.

"I want to tear off all your clothes, sit you up on the bench top and bury my face between your legs. Then, when you're as wet as hell, I want to impale you on my cock, all the way to my balls. I want to feel your wet heat around me, muscles convulsing. I want to feel the friction as I fuck you slowly, then quickly. I want to feel my balls burst as I come inside you, filling you all the way up."

He breathed hard out his nose. "Did that make you even wetter? It made me hard as fuck."

He adjusted his pants as he stepped away from me. "They say the brain is the sexiest organ in the human body. I think it's incredible because I can arouse you—and myself—but I can also scare you with words."

"I'm sure you could." I knew all too well how terrifying words could be. And he was right, I was wet from both his voice and imagining him doing those things to me.

"What are you doing?"

My eyes snapped up, toward the door.

How long had Mannix been standing there? Ares was right behind him. They both looked pissed.

"Keeping Kennedy company," Ice said lightly. "I think we need to talk, the four of us. There's something very much in the air that needs to be cleared." If he noticed the glares they both gave him, he showed no sign. He wasn't intimidated by them one bit.

That made one of us.

Mannix stepped up behind me and placed his hands on my shoulders. A gesture of pure possessiveness. Could he see the blush on my cheeks? Surely he must have noticed my reaction to Ice's words and touch? The touch was innocent. Ish. The words? Definitely not.

"What the fuck are you talking about?" Ares demanded.

Ice stepped around to the other side of the island and nodded at me. "I'm talking about Kennedy."

The air was thick with testosterone. I could almost smell it.

"She's mine," Mannix growled.

"I think she should be ours," Ice said reasonably. He could have been talking about last night's soup, or the rising cost of eggs.

"You've gone fucking soft in the head or the cock," Ares snarled.

Ice looked at him like he'd asked him what his favourite colour was. "My head and cock are as hard as ever." He looked back to Mannix. "We share everything, why not her?"

"You guys are out of your fucking mind." Ares muttered something to himself about people thinking with their cock before he stalked out of the room.

I might be out of my mind too, because I was wondering what it would be like to be sandwiched between Ice and Mannix.

Ice shrugged. "Don't you think it should be up to Kennedy to decide?"

I was wondering when one of them might remember I should have a say in this.

Mannix's fingers tightened convulsively, digging into the bones of my shoulders.

"Princess…" He was obviously not used to asking for other people's opinions, or for permission. Although, he respected my choice not to fuck him last night when I wasn't ready, so maybe there was room for him to respect my other choices.

"I like you both," I said slowly and carefully. "I don't want to come between you." I didn't realise my inadvertent innuendo until Ice grinned.

I snorted softly. "Okay, I sort of do, some day. But I don't want you to fight over me. I don't want to mess up your friendship with each other or with Ares. I'll move out of it becomes a—"

"No," Mannix said quickly and with force. "No moving out." He was silent for a while and I could almost see him chewing his thoughts and trying hard not to spit them out.

"You both want this?" he asked finally. "You two and me? Ares too if he stops getting his dick in a knot?"

I looked at him over my shoulder. "What do you want?"

He regarded me intently. "I want you. If it means sharing you with guys I think of as my brothers, then so fucking be it."

"You can fuck me too if you want." Ice grinned.

I expected Mannix to deny wanting to do anything like that, but he didn't. He gave Ice a long look and then returned his gaze to me.

"It's agreed then. One of us will be the first to fuck you. When the time is right."

I glanced over to Ice, who nodded.

"Works for me. As long as I get my turn." He gave me a look that made me even wetter than any of his words had.

At this rate, I was going to leave puddles behind wherever I went. I could hardly believe we were casually discussing me dating all three of them. Screwing all three of them. I was turned on enough to let them bend me over the kitchen table and fuck me here and now.

"One condition," Mannix said. "No one touches her but us. Not that dickhead coach, no one."

"I can agree with that." Ice opened a drawer and pulled out a large knife. "I know just what to do with them if they overstep." He drew a precise line in the air, then peeled it back with his fingertips as though opening a chest cavity. He reached in and curled his fingers around an imaginary heart. He pulled his hand back and cocked his head, pretending real blood dripped from his fingers.

"I know how to make it look like an accident." Ice tossed the imaginary heart over his shoulder.

I pictured it hitting the wall and sliding down, leaving a smear of blood behind it.

"Why bother?" Mannix shrugged. "We could leave it as a warning."

Was it wrong that I found all of this incredibly hot? Fucked up, but hot. I mean, it wasn't like they'd actually act on it.

Would they?

"I guess I belong to both of you then," I said softly.

Ice, who was swishing the knife around in the air, froze and smiled. "I like the sound of that. Our girl. Our *smart* girl," he added.

He glanced at Mannix. "I bet your father can think of a hundred ways to put a computer science major to good use."

Mannix grunted. "Probably, but let's not get ahead of ourselves."

I wanted to ask him why, but he gripped my chin, turned my face toward him and kissed me.

Ice, with the knife still in his hand, skipped around the island, turned my face the other way and kissed me too, all teeth, tongue and stubble.

In the corner of my eye, I saw the knife near my shoulder, a hair or two from my ear.

Like the knife was that night in the forest. Right before it was pulled across the man's throat. The gush of blood… The gurgle…

I gasped involuntarily.

"Figures you'd be a shit kisser," Mannix told him.

"No it's just—" I leaned away from the knife. "It's just *that*."

Instead of taking it away, Ice trailed the tip of the knife down my cheek, slow and careful. It tickled slightly. My heart raced as the light glanced off it. One slip of his hand and he'd slice my cheek open.

"I would never hurt you," he said softly. "This is just a tool. Sometimes used for bad, but mostly just to cut onions." He took the blade away and made a series of tiny dicing gestures in the air. "Occasionally steak." His dicing became a cut of what looked like very well cooked beef.

"Knives don't hurt people, people hurt people?" I didn't take my eyes off the blade. I put a hand to my cheek, but I knew he hadn't broken the skin.

"Exactly. And sometimes people hurt themselves," Mannix said. "But if anyone tries to touch you, they will end up resembling an onion. I've seen the way Ice works, he could do it too."

I believed him.

"I wanted to be a doctor." Ice held the blade up in front of his face as though fascinated by the stainless steel. "A surgeon. But I decided autopsies would be more interesting than surgery."

"Fewer malpractice suits from dead people," Mannix said dryly.

Ice grinned, his smile eerily cut in two by the blade. "Yep."

"What did you study?" I asked Mannix. Partly because I wanted to know and partly to change the subject and stop looking at the knife.

He shrugged one shoulder. "Business. Someone has to step into Dad's shoes."

I had a feeling there was more to it than that, but he didn't seem to want to elaborate. I didn't ask. If there was more, he'd tell me when he was ready.

"What did Ares study?" Apart from the inside of his own asshole.

"Believe it or not, psychology," Ice said. "I'll leave it to you to ask him why."

Considering he wouldn't give me the time of day, I doubted he'd give me an answer to anything that might vaguely resemble a personal question.

It was difficult to see how I could avoid making waves between the three guys, but if they wanted to try, then I would. As long as knives were kept for cutting food and not people. Especially me. I believed them when they said they wouldn't hurt me. I also believed them when they said they'd hurt anyone who touched me when they shouldn't. At some point, maybe I could confide in them about what I saw that night. If anyone could keep me safe from three crazy masked murderers, then these guys could.

Right?

"Did someone mention skinny-dipping later tonight?" Ice said innocently.

No one had, but the idea sent a thrill of excitement through me. Naked in a pool with two, maybe three hot guys. Dusk Bay might not be so bad after all.

CHAPTER 9

MANNIX

"You're out of your fucking mind," Ares snarled. His blue eyes were dark and narrowed, razor-sharp glare directed straight at me. "You two are going to share a woman, and think I should too?"

I shrugged and sipped my beer. "Kennedy isn't just any woman."

"No, she's your step sister."

"Not yet she's not." I hooked my ankle around another pool chair and dragged it over so I could put my feet on it. "Who cares anyway? She's smoking hot, smart and her pussy tastes better than this beer." I held up the bottle for a moment before taking another long sip.

Ares groaned. "You know how her pussy tastes?" He shook his head. "I should have known you'd fucked her already. How long did it take you? An hour?"

"I didn't say I fucked her," I said. "We didn't get to that. Not yet. But we will." Soon. I didn't want to rush her into anything she wasn't ready for, but I wouldn't wait too long. My cock ached thinking about her.

"What, is she a virgin or something?" Ares laughed. He stopped when he saw my expression. "Really?" Now he looked interested. "I didn't know there were any of those left in Australia. In Victoria, anyway."

"That explains the vibe I got from her," Ice said thoughtfully. "Naïve, innocent and sweet. Three of my favourite things."

"You could be describing me," I joked. They both laughed. I was the exact opposite of innocent and naïve. We all were.

"So, you need help corrupting this girl?" Ares asked. "Moving to Dusk Bay would do that sooner or later, without my help."

"I don't want her corrupted," I said firmly. I sighed into my beer bottle. "Sooner or later she has to know who we are, what we are and what we do."

"The Devils of Dusk Bay," Ice said softly. "Wasn't that what your father wanted us to be?"

"Haven't we lived up to it yet?" I raised my eyebrows at him.

"I think we have a way to go." Ice sipped his beer. "Our reputation is growing, but there's always room for more."

"You won't be happy until people are pissing themselves at the idea of us," Ares told him.

"Isn't that what you want too?" Ice asked. "I'm just happy if I get to do a little carving once in a while."

"Once in a while being at least once a day," I told him. Ares and I liked to take care of business, whatever that meant at the time. Ice, he seemed to be in it for the bloodshed. I once saw him torture a man for three days, for the fun and fascination of it. He claimed he wanted to see how long the man would last with no tongue and in constant agony. He got off on it.

I've known him all my life, long enough that I got him, for the most part. He was harmless unless you were the wrong person. I basically made my life's work not to be the wrong person.

"And you think someone sweet, innocent and naïve isn't going to freak the fuck out when she finds out who we are?" Ares asked.

"She might be sweet, but she's not stupid," I said. "She has to know the kind of people my father and her mother are, even if it's deep down. Sooner or later, she'll face the truth and we'll help her through it. She belongs to us and *with* us. She'll be fine." She had to be, because if she wasn't, then she'd be one of the wrong people. I couldn't guess how long Ice would keep her alive to listen to her pretty screams. I suspected it would be days at least.

"You seem very sure of that," Ares said. "What happens if we tell her and she turns on us? Do you have the balls to do what needs to be done?"

"I have balls of iron," I said coldly. They were constantly hard around my Princess. Aching to release into her gorgeous body. I wished she was here with us right now for me to do just that. Last time I saw her, she was in her bedroom, studying. After a long day of teaching gymnastics to a room full of brats, I decided to leave her to it. As long as I knew exactly where she was, I could give her a bit of space.

"Is that why you're reluctant to get involved with her?" I asked Ares. "Are you worried she'll make you soft?" I was goading him on purpose. Ares wouldn't turn soft for a puppy, much less a woman. But this arrangement only worked if everyone agreed.

"Fuck off," Ares snarled. "Do you want me involved with your girlfriend so you can see my cock once in a while?"

"I've seen your cock plenty of times," I said. "It's nothing special. Not as big and thick as mine."

He flipped me off. "That's bullshit and you know it."

I shrugged. "Keep telling yourself that. The point is, we hang out together all the time. If Kennedy is going out with all of us and fucking all of us, then we don't have to worry about any bros before hos shit." The three of us were a tight unit. The last thing we needed was three other people breaking that up.

"I'll think about it," Ares said. "I'm not saying I wouldn't rail her in a heartbeat, but I don't know if I want to share with you fuckers. I've never been big on taking turns. I might just hunt down my own pussy. You dickheads aren't going to let her get in the way, are you? Posse before pussy, like we agreed."

"She won't get in the way," I assured him. He was a stubborn prick sometimes. He'd come around eventually, but if he didn't, then whatever. More holes for Ice and I.

"She can be part of our posse," Ice said. "The Devils and the Beautiful. She could be the Beautiful Devil."

I preferred my nickname for her, but I didn't bother to mention it. We didn't have to share every single thing.

"Are you listening to yourselves?" Ares asked. "What guarantee do you have that she'd want anything to do with any of us when she knows what we're really like? You say she'll be fine, but what if she's not? Can you really imagine her with blood on her hands?"

"She doesn't have to have blood on her hands," I argued. "She's learning how to prevent people from hacking systems like my father's. She could be useful for that. I bet anything she knows how to hack into those systems too. Imagine how much fun we could have, fucking with the Bell family bank accounts." She could probably make herself a billionaire with a few keystrokes. That would be all kinds of awesome.

"Is your psychology degree telling you sweet, innocent people will only ever be that?" I asked. "Because I know it's not. Even people who think they're decent are really assholes deep down."

"It's not even deep down for some people," Ares said pointedly.

I grinned unashamedly. I gave up trying to be nice a long time ago. Around at the same time I noticed Ares seemed to have more fun being his honest, nasty self. The only one of us who even tried was Ice, but I always suspected that was an act to gain people's trust. He was the only one of us people would turn their backs on. Ironically, he was the one they should never look away from, if they preferred their internal organs inside their bodies.

Ares and I killed when we needed to, but Ice did it for fun. For shits and giggles. These days, we tended to leave most of the killing to him. He'd complain if we didn't.

"I feel like you have the rest of your life planned out, with your stepsister right in the middle of it," Ares said slowly.

"What's wrong with that?" I asked. "I'm going to take over my father's business and she'll be by my side. That's where she belongs. The three of us and her. Think how powerful we'll be. We might even be powerful enough to challenge Caleb Brantley some day. Or Reuben Brantley." The thought gave me a chill up and down my spine. The idea of that much power made my cock hard. We would be above any law, anywhere. We could do whatever we wanted to whoever we wanted and no one would dare stand against us.

"Don't say that too fucking loud," Ares warned. "The walls might have ears here too." He gestured around the dark pool area. The only lights were the handful under the water, and those inside the house.

"If they do, I'll deal with them." If I had to take out my father or my older brother, Gunnar, to keep my two other brothers safe, then that's what I'd do. Ice would have fun dissecting Leonardo Cassani, in spite of the fact my father let him get away with a lot of things others wouldn't. Ice was only loyal to him up to a point. Once he was off his leash, he'd go wild. Figuratively speaking. Ice's version of wild was understated and methodical. And very bloody.

"How are you going to deal when Reuben Brantley sends an assassin after you?" Ares asked.

"He won't," I said with certainty. "As far as anyone knows, we're loyal to the people we're supposed to be loyal to. We'll keep doing that as long as it covers our asses. Whatever it takes for us to survive and thrive." At the end of the day, that was all that mattered. There was nothing I wouldn't do to ensure that. No one I wouldn't step on, step over or kill. Whatever I had to do, I'd do it.

"Has it crossed your mind that your precious stepsister and her mother might be working for someone who doesn't have our interests at heart?" Ares asked. "You're so sure she's sweet and innocent, but what if she works for the Bell family? Or is one of them? She's only a year or two older than Chloe and Lila Bell. They could be best friends for all you know."

"You think I'd let someone like Helen Knight into my home without a very thorough background check?" I asked coolly. Who did he think he was talking to? I sure as fuck wasn't born yesterday. No one crossed the threshold without me knowing exactly who they were and why they were here. I made sure of that.

"Who would have the skills to make a background check come up exactly the way they wanted?" Ares asked thoughtfully. "Oh, I know. A computer science major. Just because her file says she's a twenty-one-year-old university student who does gymnastics in her spare time, doesn't mean she's not really a thirty-one-year-old spy for another mob family."

I snorted. "She's definitely not thirty-one." He planted a seed of doubt in my mind though. He was right in saying Kennedy could have changed the information with a few clicks. On the other hand, we had people working for us who had the skills she was just learning. If anything was changed, chances are they would have found it.

If it was there to be found. I knew as well as anyone that meetings often took place face-to-face, but there would be some record of that, somewhere. On her phone perhaps? I'd take a look later. I wanted to make sure she wasn't talking to any other guys anyway, or letting them talk to her. If she was, I'd let Ice take care of them.

Speaking of Ice, where the fuck was he?

I glanced around, but he was nowhere to be seen. In a flash of realisation, I knew where he'd gone and why.

"Motherfucker."

CHAPTER 10

KENNEDY

I pinched the bridge of my nose and squeezed my eyes shut. I'd spent way too long staring at this report. The words on the screen were starting to blur together.

Just a bit longer, I told myself.

I glanced at the time in the bottom corner of the screen. It was close to midnight. Early for me, but not after a long day of coaching. Nicola offered me a job as Charlie suggested she would, but then I ended up covering for him when he got sick. Food poisoning, apparently. Hopefully that was all.

I hadn't forgotten how Mannix got all pissy about him touching me. It was completely innocent, but I knew Mannix saw it differently. If the tables were turned and he was the one lifting a woman up to the uneven bars, I might be jealous too.

Or if Ice did it.

Okay, Ares too. He was a free agent and could do what he wanted, but I couldn't help thinking of him as mine, if only a little bit.

I blinked and tried to focus on the screen.

"All work and no play..." Ice whispered as he silently pushed my door open.

"Hey." Once, I would have been annoyed at the interruption, but today I was glad for the chance to take a break. I closed my screen and put my laptop on the table beside my bed.

"Are the other guys with you?" I leaned over to look past him, but the corridor was dark and empty.

"Nope, I snuck away when they were having a deep and meaningful conversation about cock size." Ice grinned and stepped into the room. He shut the door behind him.

"Who would win that argument?" The skinny dipping hadn't happened yet so all I had to go on was my imagination. Which I admit was very fertile. When I wasn't having nightmares, I was dreaming and fantasising about all three guys. Fantasies that left me wet and panting, and tracing circles around my clit with my fingertips.

The bed dipped as Ice sat down beside me.

"Ares," he said. "Although, Mannix and I give him a run for his money. He just happens to be thicker than us. Mannix is a bit longer. Mine slants to the left a little, but has the added bonus of some jewellery."

My eyes widened. "Jewellery?" My mouth was suddenly dry.

"You want to see?" His hands hovered over the button of his jeans. His eyebrows were raised and he looked straight at me. Not pressuring, not being sleazy, just happy to share.

"Um." Great, now I looked like a complete idiot. I'd never been ashamed of being a virgin, but the only cocks I ever saw were on the Internet. Unless you counted the shared bathrooms in preschool, which I didn't.

He placed his hands on the top of the bed covers behind him and leaned back.

"I didn't mean to make you uncomfortable. I'm sorry if I did."

I licked my lips. "You didn't. I've just been thinking a lot about…" If my face was any hotter I'd catch fire.

"External and internal stimuli?" he asked.

"Right, that." I hadn't been able to think of much else, even with the gymnastics class and the report I was supposed to write. I felt like my senses were full of the smell and feel of Mannix and Ice.

"Would you like some more?" he asked softly.

I swallowed hard.

"Yes, please," I whispered.

He slowly raised one hand as though I was a wild animal, and cupped my cheek. He stroked the pad of his thumb across my jawline and leaned in to brush his lips over mine.

Gradually, his touch became firmer, kisses more demanding. He swiped his tongue across my lips and into my mouth.

Before I lost my breath completely, he drew back.

His hand still on my cheek, he said, "Close your eyes."

My heart raced, but I shut them.

"Imagine me sliding my hands up under your shirt. Across the tight, smooth skin of your stomach. Up to the bottom of your breasts."

As he spoke, I could almost feel him doing those things. He wasn't. The only place he touched me was my cheek. His voice was so hypnotic, so enticing, he gave me tingles everywhere.

"Imagine my fingers circling your nipples. You know how that feels, don't you? You've touched yourself?"

"Yes," I whispered.

"Good," he said softly. "Imagine me rolling those stiff little peaks between my thumb and forefinger. They feel so perfect."

I didn't open my eyes, but I knew he had his closed too, imagining the same thing.

"Picture my mouth around one of your nipples. Sucking like a baby trying to get milk. Then sucking the other one. At the same time, my hands slide off your panties. You take off my pants until we're lying side by side, naked. I take your hand and guide it down to my cock. You curl your fingers around my length, stroking and teasing. You position me outside your pussy. You're wet. So wet. I slide inside you. All the way in, nice and deep."

I groaned. "Please…" I wasn't exactly sure what I was asking for, but I needed to feel, not just imagine.

"Please what?" he asked, his mouth right near my ear. "Tell me what you need."

"I need…" I hesitated. "I need it to be real. I want you to…" I could barely think straight, much less put the thoughts into coherent words.

His next words were so faint, I almost didn't hear them.

"Fuck you?"

My body trembled. Was that what I wanted? Did I need to take more time to think about it? I knew he'd respect me if I did, but I didn't. I wanted this. I wanted him.

No louder than he had spoken I said, "Yes."

The word barely left my lips before his hands gripped the hem of my shirt and he was pulling it over my head. I took off my bra hours ago, so my chest was bare, nipples as hard as blush coloured rocks.

"I thought your breasts would be beautiful," he said, sounding reverent. "But they're even more incredible than I imagined." His tone was still hypnotic, but he did all the things he said he would, first with his hands and then with his mouth.

When I was panting and ready to beg for more, he pushed me back gently until I lay on top of the covers. He hooked his fingers into my panties and tugged them off.

Then, not without a flourish, he undid his jeans and pushed them down.

I stared.

The tip of his cock was decorated with two long bars which crossed over each other, a ball at all four points like a compass. Like he'd said, his cock pointed north-west, towards me but with a slant.

"What is..." I pointed tentatively.

He glanced down. "It's called a magic cross." He gripped my finger between his thumb and forefinger and brought it all the way until it touched his cock. He was hot and hard. Gently, giving me time to pull away, he guided me until my fingers were all the way around his length.

"Have you ever touched a cock before?" he asked.

My tongue darted over my lips and I shook my head. "Never. It feels— thick."

His laugh was soft and deep in the back of his throat. "Thank you. I don't mind my cock being described as thick." He pried my thighs open with his hands and let them explore the insides of my legs and up to my pussy.

He took his time with every movement. Every stroke. Every circle. When he slid his fingers inside me, he did it with care, like he didn't want to hurt me.

When I came against his fingers, he smiled. The orgasm he drew out of me was like a cascade of fireworks, stars and heated blood. I was so wet I must have coated his hand with my release. Judging by the way he sucked his fingers when he took them away from me, he didn't mind. In fact, it seemed like he was having a tasty snack.

"You make the most beautiful sounds when you come. I look forward to hearing them many, many times."

He was equally careful when he knelt between my knees and positioned his cock outside my entrance.

"Beautiful girl, Mannix said you were a virgin."

"Yes," I whispered. Was Mannix going to be pissed I let Ice be the first? He might be, but I didn't want to stop now. I was ready for this. Wanted it. Did it bother Ice that I was so inexperienced? He didn't seem concerned. If anything he seemed pleased, like he wanted to be my first. That was such a guy thing I would never understand. This was too much thinking right now. I let it all go. All that mattered right now was the moment.

"Perfect," Ice said. "I want you to look at me. Watch me while I slide into you. I want you to watch me take your virginity. I'm going to watch you give it to me. Giving it to me so generously."

I locked my eyes on his and felt him press himself into me. At first, it was just a little bit, just his pierced tip. He waited until I relaxed, then pressed in a little further. Then further. And further until he was all the way inside my body.

It felt strange, but wonderful. So full. I couldn't believe I'd waited so long for this. And yet, I waited just long enough.

"Fuck," he said softly. "You're so incredibly tight. You feel amazing around me. Like you were made to take me inside you."

He started to move, slowly at first, then gradually faster, but always meticulous and careful. Never once did he lose control.

"Would you like to try being on top?" he asked.

"I'm not sure how," I admitted.

He smiled and rolled us over until I knelt on him, his cock still deep inside me. He placed his hands on my hips and helped me rise and fall until I got the rhythm. It wasn't until a couple of bounces that I realised if I angled myself, I could rub my clit on him. I did that a few times before he worked his fingers in between us and rubbed me himself.

"Simultaneous orgasm is difficult to achieve, especially the first time, but it's worth a try." He smiled up at me.

"No pressure," I said. I read about people coming at the same time, but it always seemed so difficult. Like trying to sneeze simultaneously.

His smile widened. "None at all. I just want you to enjoy yourself. I am. It's not going to take me long before I come inside your beautiful body."

For some reason, his words got me going more than ever. That and his touch, and the way his piercings touched me inside.

External and internal stimuli. He knew what he was doing with both of those things.

"I'm close," he whispered, his eyes half closed.

"Me too," I said. "I—" I groaned as I came for the second time. This time so intense I arched my back and rubbed my clit against his fingers with something close to desperation.

We didn't come at the same time. He was at least two or three minutes behind me, thrusting up into me before he stilled and groaned loudly.

"God, Beautiful. Fuck, fuck, fuck, yeah. You're amazing. Absolutely perfect. Your body is ahhh… So good."

I slumped over him. He flopped down to the mattress just as the door flew open.

CHAPTER 11

KENNEDY

"The fuck, bro?"

Mannix stood silhouetted in the doorway, Ares a few steps behind him.

"Hey," Ice said easily. Hands still on my hips, he eased me off him with a wet plop and tucked me in down behind him. He placed his hands behind his head and crossed his legs at his knees. He looked perfectly comfortable being fully naked in front of them.

"We're just hanging out, right, Beautiful?"

"Um. Right." The blood still pounded through my body and hadn't quite returned to my brain yet. Between that, the guys' sudden appearance and trying to get my head around having had sex for the first time, I was lost for words.

We didn't do anything wrong, but would Mannix and Ares see it that way?

They were both looking at me hungrily and with twin erections.

"Was that what you wanted, Princess?" Mannix's voice was tight, his eyes on Ice before they flickered over to me.

For a moment, I thought Ice would answer for me, but he turned his face to look at me.

My face slightly hot, I sat up and raised my chin. "Yes, it was. It was what I wanted." I wasn't going to apologise for it, even if Mannix was mad at not being my first.

Mannix nodded, then said to Ice, "You're a sneaky prick. We were in the middle of a conversation and you sneak off to fuck our girl."

Ice crossed his legs the other way. "Sometimes you have to seize the moment when it arises. You two can compare cock size all day if you want. I'm going to use mine for what it's intended for. Fucking."

I remembered what he said about the other guys, and looked speculatively at their groins.

"Can you guys shut the door on your way out?" Ice asked.

"Who said we're leaving?" Mannix stepped all the way into the room. "We just got here. Right, Ares?"

Ares hesitated. "It's getting late. I should get home before my father starts wondering where the fuck I got to." He backed away.

Mannix shrugged. "Suit yourself." When Ares disappeared, followed by the sound of his footsteps heading down the stairs, Mannix closed the door and stepped over to the bed.

"So you two got to have fun. Which one of you is going to suck my cock?" His hands went to the button of his jeans.

I drew in a shaky breath. What would it be like to close my lips around his tip? To slide my tongue across his seem and taste his precum? To feel him thrust in and out of my mouth? Was I ready for that?

Before I could answer, Ice sat up and said, "I will."

Now my heart was really hammering. I wasn't the only woman in the world who got aroused by watching, or reading about two men being intimate, but to see it in person?

Yes please.

Mannix only hesitated for a moment longer before he undid his jeans and pushed them down his hips. His erection jumped free. Ice was right, he was longer. He also had a piercing, but only a single ring at the tip of his cock.

He stepped over and pressed his cock between Ice's eager lips.

My eyes wide, I watched Ice lick his way up and down Mannix's length, from his tip to his balls. Up one side and down the other, then down and back up again. He took him all the way into his mouth and started to suck. The sound and sight turned me on all over again.

"Touch yourself," Mannix said. His eyes went from the guy on his cock, to me. "I know you want to."

"I—" My tongue darted over my lips.

"Touch yourself," he said again, more firmly this time, like he expected to be obeyed.

"Okay." I lay back against the pillows and put my hands between my legs. The entrance to my pussy was sticky with Ice's cum, but I found my clit and started to rub circles around and over it with my fingertips and nails.

"Good girl," Mannix said. "Play with your nipple."

I slowly slid my other hand over my stomach and pinched my nipple. My eyes fluttered shut.

"Open your eyes," Mannix said. "I want you to watch what Ice is doing to me. Watch me fuck his mouth like someday I'm going to fuck yours."

He rolled his hips slowly, pushing himself deeper into Ice's mouth. He groaned. "Bro, your mouth is all kinds of fucking incredible."

Ice chuckled, but didn't stop sucking.

Watching them together turned me on so hard I was close to coming within a minute or two.

"You two are so fucking hot," Mannix whispered. He thrust harder and faster.

Ice took every movement and rolled with it, even when Mannix was so deep I thought he might gag. I didn't think they'd done this before, but I suspected Ice had thought about it. Both of them had.

Without thinking, I said, "Can you come in his mouth?" Where the hell did that come from? Oh, right, reading romance novels. Where else?

Mannix groaned. "That's my girl. *Our* girl. I *will* come in his mouth for you. What do you want him to do with my cum?"

I considered suggesting Ice spit it out, but I didn't think that was what any of us wanted.

"Swallow it," I said softly. I was right on the edge right now. The sound of Ice's mouth sucking was driving me wilder than wild.

"You heard her," Mannix said breathlessly. He grunted like a wild animal. His hips stilled as he came.

Ice slid his lips off Mannix's length and turned his face to look at me. The corners of his mouth tipped up in a smile before he swallowed, then licked his lips.

That threw me over the edge into a third, mind and earth-shattering orgasm. My whole body rocked against my fingers, the whole world disappearing except the faces of both guys who watched me intently while I came.

My back arched and I cried out. I bit my lip to keep from screaming.

This house was big, but I didn't need my mother to hear what I was doing. Thankfully, her and Leo's bedroom was right at the other end, so I could have shouted at the top of my lungs and probably not been heard. Still, I didn't want to be too loud.

Mannix stepped out of his jeans and walked around the bed to lie down on the other side of me.

Both guys snuggled into me and somehow managed to get the covers over the top of us.

"That was awesome," Mannix said, sounding sleepy.

"Can I ask you something?" I asked, addressing the question to both of them.

"Anything," Ice said. "I'm an open book as well as an open mouth."

He knew just the right words to say to make my heart race and my mind picture them together again. That would be an instant replay in my brain for a long time. Potentially forever.

"Have you two ever… Done that before?"

"No," Mannix said.

"I've thought about it plenty of times." Ice rolled me onto my side and rested his hand on my ass. "We've talked about it, but we've never acted on it."

"Except the time we shared a kiss," Mannix said.

"Right. But we never talked about it." Ice sounded regretful. "I thought maybe Mannix regretted it." He picked up his head and looked over me and to the other guy.

"No, I never regretted it," Mannix said. "I was worried it would change our relationship too much. But seeing you like this tonight, with our Princess, and willing to suck me off, I wasn't gonna say no."

"Neither was I," Ice said. "I was starting to think you'd never ask. I can't tell you how many times I thought about getting my lips around that cock of yours."

"Would you go further with each other?" I asked tentatively. I already changed their relationship but neither seemed to mind. That didn't mean they wanted to do more than they already had. I could picture it though, and if the sight was as hot as the mental image, then it was definitely something I wanted to see. And hear.

Mannix ran the back of his knuckles down my cheek. "Do you want us to, Princess?"

"I only want you to do what you want to do," I said carefully.

He chuckled. "That wasn't what I was asking. That goes without saying. I want to know if you want to watch us fuck?"

I cleared my throat. "If you do it, and want me to watch…" When he narrowed his eyes I changed my wording. "I'd like to watch."

"Then, if we fuck, you can watch," Mannix said. "There's nothing wrong with asking for what you want. It's the best way to get what you want. If you want either of us, or Ares, tell us. The same way I tell you what I want. It saves a lot of time and bullshit."

"I want a new black hatchback with a bright red ribbon," I said half joking. "Make that a black ribbon."

"Consider it done." Mannix nodded like it was no big deal.

"You don't have to do that," I said with a small laugh.

"How else do we fulfill your dreams?" Ice asked. "If you tell us what you want, we'll make it happen. That's what we do. We make things happen."

Why did that send chills through my body?

"Yes, we do," Mannix agreed. "We'll give you everything you ever wanted and more."

"More than you ever dreamt of," Ice agreed.

"More than any Princess ever had." Mannix dragged his knuckles over my lips and down the line of my jaw. "You'll learn that belonging to us has lots of benefits. No one will dare fuck with you, like they don't dare fuck with us. We'll make sure you're protected wherever you go and whatever you do. We look after what is ours."

"Yes, we do. We all look after each other." Ice squeezed my ass.

"Including Ares. Don't worry about him, he'll come around. He needs us, we need him and he wants you too much to walk away."

"I hope he does," I said. "I feel like there's a piece of the puzzle missing." I also didn't want him to stomp off every time he saw me. He spent so much time here, he might as well live here too. The last thing I wanted was for him, for any of them, to feel uncomfortable here.

"That's exactly how I feel too," Ice said. "I thought we had everything figured out, but we didn't. Now we've met you, I know how this is supposed to go. The four of us against the world." He slid the tip of his finger down my ass crack.

I shivered deliciously. Could I keep up with two guys, much less three? Even knowing how inexperienced I was, they all still wanted me. And each other. I could very easily fall into this warm, tight web they wove around me, and I wasn't sure I'd mind. One thing I knew for sure, once I got in, it might be difficult to get back out again. Maybe even impossible.

I wasn't sure how I felt about that, but right now I was safe, held between two smoking hot guys. Guys who seemed to care about me as much as I was coming to care about them.

If this was a trap, maybe I'd jump in feet first and never look back.

CHAPTER 12
KENNEDY

"Nice wheels." Charlie looked sideways at the shiny new Porsche Taycan. The long black ribbon was gone, but the car was still ridiculously incredible and undoubtedly expensive.

I couldn't bring myself to look at how much it was worth. At a guess, I'd say more than a small house in a rural town, and less than a luxury apartment in Sydney or Melbourne. As presents went, it was extravagant. None of the guys would let me refuse it, although Ares muttered something about me spreading my legs for it. When I left for work, Mannix and Ice were busy growling at him for saying that.

"Uh, yeah." How did I begin to explain how I came to have a car like this? "It belongs to my mother." I hated to lie, but the truth was hard for me to believe, much less explain, to someone I barely knew.

"Are you feeling better?" I asked. When he looked confused, I added, "Nicola said you had food poisoning?"

"Oh, right. Food poisoning. Yeah that was… You know, rough. Don't eat chicken that isn't cooked properly." He didn't meet my eye as he spoke. He quickly turned to unlock the gym door and stepped aside to let me enter.

"So that guy the other day, he's a friend of yours?" He followed me in but skirted around me to walk to the office. I had a feeling if he could cross to the other side of the street, he'd do that. What the hell was going on? He'd seemed friendly up until now.

"Mannix? Yeah, I guess you could say we're friends. My mother is marrying his father. We live in the same house." He told me I belonged to him, but we hadn't talked about being boyfriend and girlfriend, or anything official.

Just because he bought me an insanely expensive car didn't mean I'd assume he saw our relationship the same way I did.

"Right." Charlie placed his bag under the desk and sat in the chair to pull off his shoes. "So he's...family?"

"I suppose you could say that." I put my bag beside his and leaned against the desk to take off my own sneakers.

Charlie flinched and turned the chair away from me.

What the hell?

"Are you okay?" I asked. "You seem really... I don't know, on edge. Did I do something to upset you?" I hadn't had enough to do with him to have pissed him off too much, had I?

Some people *were* touchier than others. Mannix and Ares, to name two.

"No," Charlie said quickly. Too quickly. Like he was worried about upsetting me. His eyes flicked to the door and he looked nervous.

"If you're worried about Mannix suddenly coming in like the other day, he's working," I said.

Charlie relaxed visibly, but only slightly. His body was still wound tighter than a corkscrew.

I frowned at him as I tossed my shoes down beside my bag. "Did something—"

The gym door opened and the flood of children began. Charlie looked relieved to have been interrupted and hurried away to gather his class to one side of the gym.

My class consisted of a group of six five-year-old girls, who would all start school in a few months. Right now, their skills consisted of bouncing, running and some basic tumbling. One of them might be a future champion. Right now, they had crazy short attention spans. It took all my energy and attention to keep them from wandering off or chatting amongst themselves too much.

I kept half an eye on Charlie during the class. He had a group of four boys the same age as the girls. Since boys used different apparatuses, their gymnastic skills were different from the girls. They could often learn together, but where possible they tended to be separated. At least two of them seemed more interested in running up and down the mats than in learning anything. That was one way to work off excess energy. They must be exhausted when they got home. I knew I was.

Charlie didn't say a word to me when the class finished and the next one started.

This was a group of younger children and their parents. My job was mostly to guide the parents while the kids walked over beams a finger width off the floor. Most of the kids looked less interested than the energetic boys, but the parents seemed to have fun.

Charlie disappeared into the office during the class and closed the door. Maybe I misjudged him the first time we met. He seemed nice and friendly then. Now, he didn't seem to want to know me. I wasn't necessarily here to make friends. I was here to make money. But it wouldn't hurt if he was nice to me. Would it?

"That's it for today, thanks for coming." I stood by the door and waved each parent and child out until they were all gone, then closed it behind the last of them and stepped into the office.

"Break time until the after-school crowd gets here," I remarked.

Charlie grunted. He was bent over the desk, eyes on the computer screen.

I watched his back for a moment, then crouched to feel around in my bag for my lunch. When I stood up again, he hadn't moved. For some reason, that annoyed me.

"Did I do something wrong?" I asked.

I remembered what Mannix said about asking for what I wanted. What I wanted right now was a straight answer. Was that too much to ask?

I thought he wasn't going to respond, until he sat back from the screen and half turned his face towards me. "It's nothing, I'm busy. These invoices won't send themselves."

I perched on the side of the desk beside him. "I could help."

He glanced at my legs, bare up to the hem of my shorts. "No," he said a bit more forcefully than was necessary. "I mean, I'm fine. Nicola or I would need to sit down and explain how to do it."

"I did invoicing in my last gym, it's the same software." Even if it wasn't, it was exactly the thing I picked up in about thirty seconds flat. "I'm a computer science major too," I said lightly. Anything to relax some of the tension in the room.

He ran his fingers through his short hair. "I can't let you do anything without Nicola approving it anyway. Right now, you're only approved to coach."

"Yeah, okay." That was, or at least *sounded*, legitimate. Nicola was the boss after all. She might want to see what I could do before she gave me extra duties. After all, there was a difference between saying you could do a thing and actually being able to do it. She might have been burnt before by people not living up to their hype. It happened all the time. No doubt when she was ready, she'd take a look at what I could do and decide then.

"I guess I could tidy up out there." I nodded to some boxes and mats which were slightly out of place.

He looked relieved. "Yes, you could go and do that."

I gave him a long look but he already turned back to the screen and hunched over again. For some reason, he seemed to want me as far away from himself as he could get me.

Was Mannix really that scary standing in the door glaring at him? A little bit intimidating, sure, but not that scary. Not to me anyway. I wouldn't have thought he'd be too scary to Charlie either, but what did I know? I hardly knew the other coach.

It took me all of two or three minutes to straighten everything, before I sat on a box to eat my lunch.

I peeled open the box and frowned at the contents. I'd only packed a sandwich and a banana, but the box now contained an additional red velvet cupcake topped with black sprinkles and an edible decoration in the shape of a crown. If I had to guess, I'd think it was a collaborative effort between Ice and Mannix. I wouldn't have thought they were so romantic, but they had bought me a car. What was a little cupcake in comparison? It was sweet of them.

I was good and ate the banana first, but then couldn't resist biting into the cupcake. It was light and fluffy, and delicious. I presumed Ares hadn't contributed to it, because it didn't contain sand or gravel, or as far as I could tell, poison. Would he dare to do that, knowing the other guys might be pissed off? I liked to think, in spite of his glaring and sneering, he wasn't really an asshole. The jury was still out on that. Hopefully at some point, he would have a chance to prove me right.

I was licking crumbs off my fingers when I glanced towards the office and saw Charlie, his eyes on me. Before he realised I was looking, I saw his expression. He had the same hunger in his eyes as the guys did when they looked at me. Unlike their bold, unapologetic lust, his was laced with caution. Like he was looking at something he knew he couldn't have. But that didn't stop him from wanting it.

He realised I saw him watching and ducked down, out of sight. I was starting to think maybe he was slightly unhinged.

For the first time since we met, I felt uneasy about him. I didn't think he'd touch me or do anything to me, but working with him might be more difficult than I hoped. I wasn't going to quit. In spite of the guys' assurances they'd make all my dreams come true, I still wanted to work and make my own money. If there was anything my mother taught me, it was never to rely on other people for financial support. Especially her.

Whatever happened, I'd always want to take care of myself. I fully intended to pay the guys back for the car, even if it took me years to do it. I was going to need one hell of a good job to make enough money for that.

Soon I'd have my degree and I had a shit load of determination. I knew I had what it took to succeed. My eventual goal was to have my own company, making and maintaining security software. I had plenty of ideas brewing in the back of my mind, but I'd need a lot of money for those too. Much more than a gymnastics coach would ever make, but this was a start.

With any luck, Leo and Mum would let me keep living with them so I could save.

Who was I kidding? Mannix would insist I stay, regardless of what they said. Could he overrule his father? Probably not, but he'd try. He was at least as determined as I was. That was part of the reason I was attracted to him. In spite of his harder edge, we had some things in common. Backing down if we wanted something very much, was not an option for either of us. Not for the other two guys either, although Ice covered it by being easy-going.

Now I was thinking about the way his cock felt sliding into me, thrusting in and out. I couldn't wait to do it with him again, and with Mannix.

Okay, and with Ares. At some point, I'd need to sit down and talk to him. We needed to clear the air.

I hurried off to get a big drink of water before the next class started. There wasn't time for a cold shower, so it would have to do. I could distract myself from that line of thought by wondering again why Charlie was behaving so strangely.

That was another conversation I needed to have at some point. But not today.

CHAPTER 13

KENNEDY

"You and my son seem to have hit it off." Leo glanced into my cup. When he found it empty, he picked it up and placed it in the dishwasher. He pulled out two clean cups from the cupboard and started the coffee machine.

"I guess you could say that," I said carefully. I made a note not to play poker against either him or Mannix. I had no idea what either of them were thinking most of the time. Leo might be making casual conversation, and he might be about to ream me out.

He glanced at me over his shoulder and raised an eyebrow. "You wouldn't say that? I got the impression you two were getting close." He turned back to the coffee machine just in time to not see my face get hot.

"Is that a problem?" I asked. Was I poking a hornet's nest with a question like that?

"That depends how many cars you need. Cappuccino?" He paused with his finger on the middle button of the coffee machine.

"Yes please, and one is extravagant enough," I said awkwardly. "I only needed an old, secondhand rust bucket."

Leo pressed the button and the machine rattled away happily. He turned around and braced his hands on the top of the island. The look he gave me was so Mannix I had to hold back a smile.

"You're going to be my stepdaughter soon. A Cassani. We have a reputation in Dusk Bay that I prefer to uphold. That means no one in the family drives around in a rust bucket." He punctuated the statement by tapping a couple of fingers on the veined, white marble.

"I wouldn't want to embarrass the family, but a Porsche?" This wasn't an argument I could win, that was obvious. In the game of pick your battles, I wasn't going to fight this one. But I could make my point. "There's plenty of cheaper cars. Are you angry he spent so much?"

"It's only money." Leo straightened up and crossed his arms over his chest.

I hadn't realised until then Mannix was very much a younger version of his father. His older brother must look like their mother. Did he have the same stubborn arrogance? Probably; it seemed to run in the family.

"If you need a replacement on a weekly basis, then it will be a problem, but in the meantime, accept the gift and enjoy it. Most twenty-one-year-olds don't drive around in cars like that."

I grinned at the understatement. "That's very true. I do appreciate it, I'm just… not used to getting gifts like that." My mother liked to be extravagant, but never like this.

"If my son has set his sights on you the way he seems to, then get used to it."

The coffee machine fell silent. He turned to pick up my coffee and handed it over to me before putting his own cup under the spout and pressing a different button.

"Thank you." I could get used to having a fancy coffee machine like this. Not to mention the quality of coffee Leo preferred. I was a tea drinker until I moved in here. I still was, but a good cappuccino helped to get me through a long day of study.

"So you don't have a problem with Mannix and I?" I asked while I waited for my drink to cool.

"Should I?" Leo picked up his black coffee and sipped. Without sugar or milk, it must have been hot, but he showed no sign of discomfort.

If anyone was uncomfortable, it was me. I shifted on my stool.

"Well, you and Mum are getting married. Some people frown on stepsiblings having a relationship with each other."

"What do you think?" He seemed genuinely curious.

"I think," I said carefully, "as long as we don't secretly find out we're biologically related, then it's not a big deal. But… if things don't work out between us, it could get ugly."

"And if things don't work out between your mother and I, the same could happen." He drank another gulp of coffee. "Things could get complicated. On the other hand, I've always thought life was too short not to take what you wanted, and worry about the consequences later."

"That sounds like something Mannix would say." I smiled.

Leo smiled back. "At the risk of being immodest, he learned from the best."

"Of course he did," I said. "It seems he learned well." In spite of being a closed book, Leo was easy to like. He was smart and respectful and obviously loved my mother.

"Where do the other two boys fit in?" Leo asked over the top of his mug.

I wasn't sure what he wanted to hear, but I decided on the truth. "Ice and I are also involved. I think he and Mannix might be involved with each other too." I watched for Leo's reaction, but he was neither surprised nor upset to hear that.

"I don't know about Ares," I added after a moment. "I think he hates me."

Leo smiled at my grimace. "I think Ares hates most people, including himself. I'm sure you'll have him eating out of your hand in no time. Did you know your mother and I started that way? When we first met, we couldn't stand each other."

I cocked my head at him. "No, I didn't know that. I thought it was love at first sight. For her anyway."

"Lust at first sight, maybe, but you don't want to hear about that. We eventually realised we had more in common than different. We're both strong personalities."

"That's for sure," I said dryly. Once they set their sights on each other, there was no going back for either of them. I thought it was my mother who decided they should be together, but now I knew it was mutual. No one in the world could make Leo Cassani do something he didn't want to do.

"It's a trait you've inherited from your mother. That's clear to see. And one of the reasons I will allow you to be with my son. He doesn't need a weak willed woman he can walk all over. Or a weak willed man, for that matter. People like Mannix and I destroy people like that, even if we don't mean to." He seemed to be referring to someone in particular and I wondered if it was Mannix's mother. I could definitely see how guys like these would tear apart anyone without the strength to stand up to them. I wasn't sure if I was strong enough, but I'd have to be, or he'd eat me alive. Literally and figuratively.

I decided my cappuccino was cool enough to drink and took a sip. I half closed my eyes in appreciation of how delicious it was. I could do worse than a stepfather who made coffee that tasted like this.

"This is so good."

Leo grinned. "Of course it is. Nothing but the best for our family." He toasted me with his cup, then said, "Mannix says he thinks you'd be an asset to my business. Once you've finished your degree."

"I'm not really sure what you do," I admitted. None of the guys gave me much detail, apart from Leo being powerful in some way.

"Lots of different things. I deal in transport, real estate, human resources, things like that. You could say I have my finger in several pies. Most of those pies are connected by some kind of computer network."

He smiled wryly. "You can tell by that description that I am *not* a computer person. I'd like someone close to me, someone I can trust, to be my computer person. If you're interested?"

"I'm definitely interested," I said quickly. It was an opportunity that could make me enough money to start my business the way I wanted to. When I proved myself, I might even convince him to invest. I had a feeling proving myself was going to require me to work my ass off, but that was okay. I wasn't afraid of hard work and I knew I was more than capable of doing the job.

"Of course you are," he said as though he never expected any other response from me.

What would he have said if I said no? He probably would have kept asking until I said yes, or strongly encouraged Mannix to convince me. Fortunately, that wasn't a problem.

Except for one thing.

"Shouldn't you interview a bunch of people before you decide?" Hiring me because we were more or less related, might be a rash move on his part. I didn't want anyone to think I got the job based on anything other than my skills. Hell, people would think that anyway. I'd prove them wrong.

"I know what I want and what my business needs, and that's you," he said simply. "Your mother and Mannix agreed and I trust both of them implicitly. Also, I spoke to your university and they gave me their endorsement."

My mouth formed an O. "I didn't realise you'd dug so deep."

"I always do before I approach anyone." He gave me the impression he now knew my panty size, my favourite food and that I wanted to get a tattoo of an owl on my ankle someday. Did he also know what happened that night during the ball?

No, he couldn't. He couldn't read my mind and someone like him wouldn't be involved in murder.

Right?

"I didn't mean to imply you wouldn't check out every prospective employee. I guess I just assumed…"

He raised his eyebrows at me and waited until I finished. Of course he wouldn't make it easy on me, not when he clearly expected honesty from me. He wasn't the sort of man people lied to and got away with it

I cleared my throat. "Maybe you were doing a favour for Mum. Or Mannix."

Leo put his empty cup aside and leaned his weight on his elbows. "I love your mother and my son very much, but I don't do favours like that. Not when it comes to my business. If your mother insisted I hire you, I'd still do a thorough check of you and your skills to figure out if and where you fit. And if you didn't, I'd tell her no."

I couldn't resist asking, "And if Mannix asked?"

Leo chuckled. He ducked his head for a moment, then looked back up. "Same deal. I don't trust anyone's judgement as well as I trust my own, not even my sons'. Either of them. They would be the first to bitch at me if I hired the wrong person and lost a chunk of their inheritance down the toilet."

"I'm sure they wouldn't be—" I started.

"Oh they would. They definitely would. Both of their life goals are to end up richer than me. They might even achieve it. They both have the balls for it." He looked approving.

I couldn't speak for Gunnar, but Mannix certainly had the balls and then some. Leo was right, he was ambitious. There was nothing wrong with that, so was I. I didn't necessarily aspire to be richer than Leo, especially since he was already richer than God, but I wanted to be comfortable and secure for the rest of my life. Whatever it took to achieve that. I never wanted to have to worry about money.

"I should leave you to finish your study," he said finally. "The sooner you finish, the sooner you can start to be valuable to me."

His words gave me the slightest shiver. There was nothing sexual in what he said, but for some reason, I felt like a commodity.

CHAPTER 14

MANNIX

"Hey." I closed the door behind me and stepped over to the table.

It was covered in a variety of knives. If I hadn't met Ice, I would have assumed there were only a few different kinds of knives. You know, the ones for putting butter on bread, the kind you used to carve a chicken or some shit like that, steak knives.

There's a lot fucking more than that. Ice owns one of every single kind. Actually, that's not true. He owns a few of each. At least a dozen were spread across the table right now, each covered in a smattering of blood and other bodily stuff. I guessed it all came from the guy who hung from the ceiling in chains. He seemed to be missing most of his toes and all but his pinky fingers.

One of his kneecaps was exposed, all white and shining. The other looked to be shattered in several pieces. His face was crisscrossed with knife marks, including several across his nose.

Ice glanced over his shoulder and grinned. "Hey. You're just in time. Our friend here was just about to tell us everything he knows about Samuel Bell and his operation."

"Oh, he was? That's great." I crossed my arms over my chest and cocked my head at the man. "You might as well. He's just started with you. I've seen him keep guys alive for weeks." That was only a slight exaggeration. Ice had a knack for pushing people right to the edge, then bringing them back. He would have made one hell of a doctor, if he didn't get a bit too much enjoyment out of torturing people.

The man grunted and spat a mouthful of blood in my direction.

Ice casually walked over to the side of the room where the other end of the chain was wound around a hook in the wall. While the man whimpered, he gripped the chain and pulled, tugging the man off his feet. He dangled from the ceiling with his full weight on his damaged wrists.

I guessed it wasn't the first time he'd hoisted the man up like this.

I turned my head to the side and said, "That looks painful." Prick got no sympathy from me. He worked for the wrong side. His life choices probably didn't look so good right now. Neither did his life expectancy.

Ice grinned. "Doesn't it? It's one of my favourites. If it doesn't get them talking, it gets them thinking about talking. And if it doesn't do that, at least I can do this." He lifted up his foot and shoved it into the man's shattered knee, pushing him back before he let him go.

The man screamed as he swung back and forth, and twisted around, legs kicking and twitching.

"You get to have all the fun," I remarked.

Ice laughed. "I really do, don't I? You can join in at any time, if you like. You know what they say, the more the merrier."

He got off on this. Judging by the tent in the front of his pants, he really, really did. And that was hot as hell. I'd always had a thing for him, but seeing him here in his element made me hard too.

His gaze dipped to my groin and he took a step towards me. "It looks to me like you want to play." His hand slipped around the back of my neck and he drew me to him. He gave me a hungry kiss, stubble grazing against mine, tongue tasting my lips, before he pulled back.

"As much as I want to play some more, your father expects answers from this asshole."

I wanted to drag him over to me, push him down to his knees and make him suck my cock.

He was right though. My father expected results, and if he didn't get them soon, he'd start asking why. Worse than that, he may decide someone else would get answers quicker. We couldn't afford to fuck up so soon. Or at all. Fucking up was not an option. Not today, not ever.

Ice loosened the chain and let the man fall to the floor. He screamed as he landed on his feet, and would have crumbled to his ass if not for the chains holding him a bit too high for his comfort.

"I really don't want to keep hurting you," Ice lied. He could have kept going for days. He'd probably do it even if he didn't get paid. "Just tell us what we need to know and you can have a nice, warm shower. Maybe some coffee and pizza. Or beer. I might even patch you up and send you on your way. How about you start by telling us your name?"

"You're never going to let me live," the man growled.

"He's stubborn," Ice said. "I'm gonna call him Stuart. Stubborn Stuart. You know what they say?" He glanced at me, one eyebrow raised.

I decided to take the bait. "What do they say?"

"If you name something, then you have to keep it." Ice nodded. "I don't usually bother naming the people I work with, but I'm particularly attached to Stuart here. I could keep playing with him for days. He's been a ton of fun."

Luckily the building was soundproofed, and this room was down in the basement. The whole of Dusk Bay would have heard Stuart screaming otherwise. Not to mention all the other people Ice worked with.

Stuart groaned. He tried to lash out at us, but it was a weak attempt at best.

"I think he's trying to get us to kill him," I remarked.

"You know, I think you're right."

Ice stepped closer to Stuart, almost nose to nose. "Let's do a deal, Stuart, my friend. Tell us what we want to know and then you can die. All of the pain will go away. All of your broken bones and cuts and bruises will stop hurting." He spoke in a soft, melodic tone, like he was promising something wonderful. Considering the state Stuart was in, it probably would be.

I made a mental note a long time ago not to get on the bad side of my friend here. He knew more ways to fuck people up than anyone I ever knew. Physically at least. Ares knew all the ways to get to people mentally. Me, I knew how to hit them financially. How to make their businesses crumble down around their pathetic ears. With Kennedy on board, we could attack them remotely before moving in for the kill. We'd be the perfect team of destruction and retribution. Justice, if you wanted to put it that way.

"Okay," Stuart said weakly. "I'll talk. To him." He awkwardly jerked his head in my direction.

"Ouch." Ice pouted playfully. "I thought we were getting along so well." He stepped back and gestured for me to approach.

My eyes on Stuart, I moved over to him, not quite as close as Ice got, but close enough to hear.

"Talk," I snapped.

Stuart huffed out a breath. "You're a motherfucker. Your father is a motherfucker. Your days are numbered and so are his."

I lashed out and punched him in the stomach.

He grunted, then howled in pain. The sound only lasted for a second or two before his eyes widened and he fell still.

"Mannix!" Ice drew my name out like a whine. "Did you kill Stuart? You weren't supposed to kill Stuart." He stepped over and poked Stuart in the arm with the blade of one of his knives. The steel went right through skin and muscle and grazed against bone with a grinding sound.

"He's dead all right. That sucks. Now who am I going to play with?" He sighed, but his expression quickly returned to a smile. "Lucky for me, I can play with you and Kennedy. And Ares when he stops being a giant twat." He gave me a sideways hug and almost stabbed me in the hip with the knife.

I jumped to the side. "Watch what you're doing. I don't need you to stab me with that." The dickhead could have cut off my nuts or my cock. If he did, his would be next. I'd shove them down his throat and leave him like that for a while.

"Of course not, I have something much better to stab you with." He grabbed his groin and grinned.

My heart thudded in my chest like a hammer. I couldn't forget the way his mouth felt around my cock, and the way Kennedy watched us and got herself off. The whole thing was etched into my brain like a tattoo. Hot and hard. Both of them were beyond perfect. Them and Ares, they were the people I wanted to walk alongside on this fucked up journey, this twisted life of mine.

"As much as I'd love to, I need to report to my father." I sighed. I didn't want anyone taking him out, but at the same time I looked forward to the day I didn't have to answer to him any more. I could just get Ice down on his knees in the fresh blood on the floor and let him blow me off. Or maybe I could let him chain Kennedy up and we could—

I shook my head. For now, I needed to focus on what I had to do, and that was tell my father about Stuart, or whatever his fucking name was.

"What are you going to tell him?" Ice asked. "The only thing I got from him was a lot of sass, and a few days of fun. Also right there, on his thigh, that's dried cum. I was having so much fun, I couldn't help myself."

I patted him on the shoulder. "You keep doing you, bro. I'll tell my dad someone is coming for us, but Stuart didn't know who it was." At least half of that was true, maybe all of it. Whatever, this was a fact he couldn't check against Stuart's word. The fact, he already knew to be true, this just confirmed it.

"Sounds reasonable," Ice said. "Maybe he can bring us someone else to play with."

I could think of at least one person I'd like to hand over to Ice and his knives. I had a conversation with Charlie, the gymnastics coach, after seeing him touch Kennedy the other day. The memory of his hands on her still made me furious, murderous.

Of course, I was nothing but pleasant to him, merely outlining exactly what would happen to him if he touched her again. I would have liked to stop him from even looking at her, or being in the same room as her, but she insisted on working at that gym, and the owner was resistant to my offers to buy the place. Charlie's sudden disappearance might freak Kennedy out, so I had to make do with a warning for now.

"I'm sure he'll find someone soon enough. If someone like the Bells are coming after us, then people like Stuart here are going to come out of the woodwork. You might need a bigger workspace. Maybe a trainee to help you with your toys."

Ice's eyes widened. "Do you think Kennedy would enjoy this? I could teach her all the things. I wonder if she likes red, too. It's my favourite colour. I like all shades of it. Especially her hair and the exact colour of fresh blood."

"You're a sick fuck, bro," I said affectionately.

He grinned. "You say the sweetest things."

"Of course I do," I agreed. "I'm a nice guy." No I wasn't, not even a little bit. I prided myself on being who I was. Hard, tough, always in control of everyone and everything around me. I was exactly the guy my father moulded me to be. The son he made in his own image, but with a harder edge, because I didn't try to be nice. Except to the three people on the face of the planet I give a shit about. For them, I would give up my soul.

Everyone else, could get fucked.

CHAPTER 15

KENNEDY

"Night."

Working until after dark and locking up the gym with Charlie was disconcerting, until he hurried away down the street towards his car. He walked like he couldn't get away fast enough.

"Night," I said to his disappearing back. He quickly became a shadow amongst parked cars and dim streetlights. The smell of garlic hung in the air from a nearby restaurant.

I found myself alone, and shivered. Only the occasional passing car reminded me I wasn't really alone. I might as well have been as I walked to my car. My whole body was on alert, my mind replaying that night yet again.

"I could turn on my phone and find you, but where's the fun in that? The thrill of the chase is much more entertaining. Then when I catch you, I'll know I've earned my trophy."

"There's no one here," I said under my breath. "You're overreacting because of that night." Of course I fucking was. It wasn't every day I saw a man get killed. It wasn't every night a murderer followed me through the trees. Taunted and terrified. How long would it be until I didn't freak out walking around alone at night? The fear may never leave.

Maybe past me should have been more careful, but the dark never bothered me before.

It bothered me now. A lot.

Headlights loomed behind me.

Fumbling slightly in my haste, I pressed the button on my key to unlock the car and wrenched the door open. I all but threw myself inside and slammed the door shut behind me.

The car sped past without so much as slowing.

"Stop being paranoid." I tossed my bag on the seat beside me and started the car. She purred like a big cat. I couldn't stop myself from smiling. She was an extravagant gift, but she was beautiful.

Using the Bluetooth connection with my phone, I put on the latest album from my favourite band, Wolf Venom, and pulled away from the curb.

I glanced in the rearview mirror as headlights appeared around the corner a hundred or so metres back. I didn't give them any more thought until I drove through a couple of sets of traffic lights and they were still there.

So what? I asked myself. *They're just heading in the same direction I am.*

Every so often, I'd glance up. They were no closer, but no further away either. I couldn't make out anything past the headlights, but it didn't look like a truck, and it wasn't a motorcycle. That narrowed it down to about a million other kinds of car.

I turned the stereo up for my favourite song, "Before I Stay", and sang along while trying to keep myself from what was more than likely an unnecessary freak out.

"You want to give me all of your soul,

But your eye is on the door.

Your hand is on the handle ready to turn,

But you step toward me."

I was the first to admit I had a crap singing voice, but here by myself, no one could hear me anyway, so I sang at the top of my voice. This song was so good, I couldn't help myself.

Ironic how, according to the media, the guys in the band all shared a girlfriend, the solo singer Abbie Hart. From the sound of it, she toured the world with them and they all fell in love. How adorable was that? Not to mention inspirational. If she could handle multiple boyfriends, maybe I could too.

The song ended and I glanced up to see the car still behind me. It was a little closer now.

A shiver passed through me. I thought about calling one of the guys, or Mum, or Leo, but what would I say? *Hey, I'm driving home and a perfectly innocent car is behind me, but it's scaring me.*

Yeah, that sounded pathetic to me too.

I was only about five minutes away from home. Less if I went slightly faster. I couldn't rule out the possibility it was a police car behind me, hoping the woman in the fancy car would make a mistake and they could book me. Since that would suck, I stuck to the speed limit, but not a kilometre under.

I passed through the suburbs and into the more affluent part of Dusk Bay. Here, all the houses were enormous, and situated on several hectares of land. Most of the homes were set back from the road, so, apart from my headlights and the ones behind me, I travelled through the darkness.

I startled slightly as something darted across the road. It was just a possum, I told myself. They were everywhere around here. Them, kangaroos, and the occasional wombat. I didn't want to hit any of them, but especially the last two. They were a really good way of fucking up a perfectly good car. Not to mention I didn't want to kill any animals. All they were doing was trying to live their lives, like I was trying to live mine.

I swallowed in relief when I saw the big iron gates appear out of the darkness. I turned into the driveway and fumbled for the remote to open them.

Where the hell was it? It had to be somewhere in my bag. Please don't tell me it fell out somewhere.

I glanced out the window and saw the car was still there, but it had slowed down to almost a crawl.

Shit.

Trying as hard as I could to keep my panic at bay, I felt around in my bag until my fingers closed around the remote. Of course it was right at the bottom.

I pulled it out and aimed it at the gate before mashing the pad of my thumb against the button.

The gates never opened so slowly.

A finger.

Two fingers.

A hand.

An arm.

The car was still coming, its lights brighter now.

Just when I thought about getting out and running, the gate opened wide enough for me to gun the car and fly through.

One hand on the steering wheel, the other on the remote, I pressed the button to close the gate behind me.

In the rearview mirror and both side mirrors, I saw the car come to a stop just outside the gate. It stayed there for a minute, maybe two, then leapt forward and roared away into the darkness.

That wasn't fucking weird at all.

My heart in my throat, I drove the rest of the way up the driveway and waited again, this time for the garage door to slide open.

I slid the car in carefully and closed the door behind me. Only when I heard the clang of metal hitting concrete did I dare to kill the engine.

With my heart still racing, I reached for my bag and clutched it to my chest. I put my hand on the handle as the door opened.

I couldn't stop the shriek of fright that slipped out of my mouth.

Mannix leaned, looked into the car and grinned. His smile faded when he saw he hadn't startled me. I was genuinely scared.

"Hey," he said softly. "Didn't mean to scare you. You okay? You look like you saw a ghost."

I let him help me out of the car and close the door behind me, but it took me a moment to compose any kind of coherent words. When I finally managed to put more than one syllable together, I told him about the car.

"It was probably nothing," I said finally.

His expression was like a rock wall. Unreadable and unbreakable.

"Stopping outside the gate as you come in isn't nothing. You should have called me."

"I didn't want to make a problem if there wasn't one," I argued.

"Next time, call me," he said firmly. "It doesn't matter if it's not a problem, but what if it was? What if the other car tried to drive you off the road? Or worse."

I didn't know what would be worse than being driven off the road, but his annoyance was both genuine and partly directed at me. Should I find that sweet or irritating? It wasn't my fault some dickhead followed me home.

"I should start driving you again," he said half to himself. "It wouldn't have happened then."

"You don't know that," I pointed out. "We still might have been followed." As far as I knew, he wasn't invincible.

"You wouldn't have been alone," he growled. "If anything happened, I would have handled it." He gave me a look like he could have handled anything, including being run off the road.

"Nothing happened," I said lamely.

"This time." He pried my bag away from my chest and folded his arms around me. "I don't want anything bad to happen to you. Okay? I care about you. The idea of anyone trying to hurt you or take you away from me makes my blood boil."

He exhaled heavily out his nose. "There's a camera at the gate. I'll take a look at the footage and see if there's anything to be seen. A number plate, some distinctive features, something."

"You don't think you'll find anything, do you?" I asked softly. The headlights would have obscured most of the car, blinding the cameras to everything, including the number plate.

"Chances are, I'll see nothing but a nondescript, dark-coloured car. Whoever it was, they were probably too smart to let themselves be identified." I didn't need to see his face to know he was frustrated, his voice was full of it.

"You don't sound surprised that this happened," I said. Angry, but not surprised.

"My family… our family has our share of enemies." He leaned back to look at me. "That's one reason I worry about you being out there by yourself. Some of them wouldn't hesitate to use you to get at the rest of us."

My heart froze. "You think whoever it was, was actually after me?" Was it the three men I saw murder that man? Were they enemies of the Cassani family? Business competitors? What sort of business required murder? What the hell had I got myself into?

"It's possible," he agreed. "Or it was some kind of warning. One I can't ignore."

I looked into his eyes. "What are you going to do?" Should I tell him about that night? Maybe something I saw would be a clue to whatever happened tonight. What had I really seen though? A man killed, three men, a red and black mask. That was about it. Nothing useful. If I thought of anything, I would tell him. Until then, what was the point?

"Don't you worry about it," he said vaguely. "I'll deal with it. I'll keep you safe."

I believed him, but I was worried how far a guy like him would go to do that. He wouldn't kill anyone for me, would he? No, he probably just meant he'd go to the police and talk to them. What would they do, though?

I leaned my forehead against his chest and sighed. All I knew right now was a whole lot of nothing and that was no use to anyone. I hated feeling helpless and useless. I'd have to find a way to help keep myself safe, so I didn't have to rely on Mannix or anyone else. I was an independent woman. I could do this. I had to. Otherwise I'd never be able to sleep at night.

"I've got you." Mannix rubbed his hand up and down my back. "I won't let anyone hurt you, even if I have to keep you here at the house forever."

He meant the words to be comforting, but the fact he even thought that might be a necessity, was the most chilling thing of all.

CHAPTER 16
KENNEDY

"You couldn't make out anything from the security camera?"

Ice looked as pissed off as Mannix had. Although, pissed for him was still a lot less intense than it was for Mannix or Ares.

Ares smirked at me like I was making something out of nothing. Ice and Mannix looked ready to pull off heads.

"Nothing," Mannix said. "Not even Kennedy arriving home. At least half an hour was completely blank."

Ares frowned. He looked more annoyed that he might be wrong than at the idea something might happen to me.

Asshole.

"That doesn't sound like a coincidence to me." Ice rubbed a hand over his jaw.

"No, it doesn't." Mannix scowled. "Kennedy, I need a list of the families whose kids do gymnastics in that last class. In fact, the whole fucking gymnasium. They'd all know when you finish. And that Charlie prick. The boss too."

I gaped at him. "I can't just give personal information out. That's all kinds of illegal."

"So is intimidation." Mannix was unmoved. "When you screw with our girl, I don't give a fuck about your privacy. All fucking bets are off. Can you get into the club's systems?"

I blinked and shook my head. "Are you suggesting I hack in?"

Ice sat forward eagerly in his chair. "Can you? I'd love to see that."

"Hacking is also illegal," I pointed out.

"Yeah, but can you do it?" Ice wasn't even slightly deterred by the illegality. If anything, he looked aroused.

"It's a simple system," I said slowly. "It wouldn't take much effort to get in, but—"

"Then do it," Mannix said. "We need to know if someone there is coming after you so we can stop them."

"Is this where you say I do something illegal or I'm going to be stuck in these four walls for the rest of my life?" I asked. I didn't like either option particularly much.

Mannix smiled. "That's exactly what I'm saying. You have access to those files when you're at work, so what's the big deal? You're just accessing them from a different place. And it's for a good cause."

I sighed. "If they have some software that tracks this back to here…" I could go to prison. I could certainly kiss my career goodbye. My degree too. This was all kinds of fucked up. Was I even considering doing this?

"We'll say Ares did it." Ice grinned.

Ares flipped him off. "Fuck off. We'll tell them she was working from home. Trying to help streamline their system. If I know anything about computers, they need it."

Nicola only just let me help with invoices, but Ares was right. The filing system the gym used was out of date and clunky, to say the least. I could easily improve it for them. I thought about offering, but I wasn't sure the excuse that I tried to do it for them from home would fly. Hopefully no one would find out what I was about to do.

I stood up, grabbed my laptop from where it lay on the island and sat back down before I opened it.

"For the record, I think this is a bad idea."

"It's a good idea if it stops anything bad from happening to you." Ice scooted over beside me, until his thigh touched mine. "In fact, I think it might be a good idea if Ares and I moved in here for a while."

To Mannix he said, "Do you think Leo will mind?"

"When I tell him why, he'll be fine with that," Mannix said. Judging by the expression on his face, he didn't much care what his father thought. If he decided they should move in, then they would.

"You wouldn't mind, would you, Beautiful?" Ice asked.

"That depends if you guys are planning to take turns following me around or some shit like that." I tapped my screen and looked for the gymnasium's website.

"That's a good idea," Ice said. "I volunteer to take all night every night." He grinned. "Don't worry, I'll let you get an hour or two of sleep here or there."

My heart skipped a beat at the idea of what he'd do to keep me awake for the rest of the time. That part didn't sound so bad.

"I don't need a bodyguard," I said.

"Guarding your body would be a bonus on top of all the other things I would do to it," Ice said.

"Could you stop thinking with your cock for two seconds?" Ares growled.

Ice shrugged. "I could, but why would I want to? Have you seen how hot this woman is? You can't tell us you don't want her as much as Mannix and I do."

Ares grunted and scowled, but he didn't deny it.

Mannix came to look over my shoulder. "Are you in yet?"

Ice grinned. "If I was in, you wouldn't have to ask."

I caught Ares' eye as we simultaneously rolled our eyes. I smiled, but he only smirked in response. Fine, if that was the way he wanted it. I wasn't going to lose any sleep over his attitude.

Mannix patted Ice on the shoulder. "Me too, bro, me too. Princess, are you in the gymnasium's files yet?"

"Almost." It was difficult to work with them talking about sex so casually. And my brain picturing where on each other they might slide into. Thinking about them fucking each other made my core hot. I needed to focus before I started to drip.

A couple of minutes later, I said, "Here we are. The names, addresses and telephone numbers of all the students and staff, present and past."

"Can you print it out?" Mannix asked.

"Can I make a hard copy of evidence I committed a crime?" I winced. Whatever could go wrong from doing that?

"No one will ever know it came from you," he assured me. "Besides, my father and I have connections. You wouldn't get in trouble for doing something so minor."

"Is that how you get away with driving so fast?" I asked, only half joking.

He grinned. "Exactly. It helps to know people." He sounded like he meant half the city was in his pocket, but I didn't ask. If that was true, it was better I didn't know. I suspected at least some of it had to do with how rich they were. People with that much money tended to get away with a lot of shit regular people didn't.

Although, if it was true, who really were these guys?

I turned my attention back to the screen. "It should be printing out now in the study."

Leo had his own office in another part of the house, but the study was there for everyone to use. Mostly, I liked all the books in the floor to ceiling bookcases. Not that I got much time to read, but it was one of my favourite pastimes.

Mannix nodded and slipped through the door to the study. He came back a couple of minutes later with a few sheets of paper stapled together.

"This should be everything we need. I'll look through it and see who we can rule out straight away. Nova Lasalle and her family, for one. My father works f— with Daisy Lasalle and Ric DiMarco. If they wanted Kennedy dead, she'd be dead."

"I met Daze at the party you didn't want me to go to," I said slowly. "Nova is a nice kid." I frowned. "Wait a minute, what do you mean if they wanted me dead, I'd be dead?"

The guys exchanged glances. Something seemed to pass between them.

I looked from one to the other. "Is someone going to explain?"

Finally, Mannix said, "They're powerful people. Sometimes powerful people do things to get what they want. Sometimes those things are illegal."

"No shit." I nodded to the paper in his hand. "But killing people?"

Were Ric and Daze behind the murder of that man? From the way Mannix was talking, I should definitely keep my mouth shut about what I saw. If those two were that ruthless, not to mention Daze's other two boyfriends, I might end up dead. In spite of one of her boyfriends being Mannix's brother.

I rubbed the bridge of my nose. When did all of this get so complicated? And deadly?

"Desperate times call for desperate measures." Mannix shrugged. "Be glad they don't want you dead. From what I gather, Daze likes you. In this town, that's a good thing."

"You're scaring her." Ice spoke softly and put his arm around me to pull me closer. "We won't let anything happen to you, I promise." He kissed my forehead. "If anyone is going to do any killing, it will be us killing anyone who dares to lay a hand on you, or try to hurt you in any way."

"That might be a bit extreme," I said. Of course he didn't mean that literally. That would be crazy.

"Not even a little bit extreme," he said. "You belong to us and anyone who tries to mess with you, is going to learn not to."

"What he said," Mannix agreed.

Ares grunted.

"See, Ares agrees." Ice waved his hand in the direction of the other guy.

Ares looked at him like he didn't agree at all, but only grunted again.

"So what are you going to do to the people on the list you can't rule out?" I asked tentatively. All this joking about killing, if it was joking, put me on edge. If I gave all those names to the guys and they did something stupid, that would be on me. I should have refused to do it. Shouldn't I?

On the other hand, if whoever followed me tonight was on that list, and the guys could find them and hand them over to the police, then that would be a good thing, wouldn't it? I'd be that much safer.

Not just me, I quickly realised. They might do the same thing to other people. Dusk Bay might be safer without them driving around in it. Maybe there was some dubious logic in there, but it made me feel better. For now anyway.

"Don't worry about them, we'll deal with it," Mannix said. "Most of these people will be completely innocent. They have nothing to worry about. It's only the ones that aren't, that I'm concerned with. Including that Charlie prick."

"You think that was him?" I frowned. I'd considered it, but the way he disappeared so quickly…

He could have driven around the block and waited until I was leaving, to come up behind me. Why would he do that though? If he wanted to scare or intimidate me, he could do that at work. Although, he couldn't do it without me seeing him. Was he that much of a coward that he had to hide behind his car? If he was, what else might he do?

"Maybe you shouldn't go to work for a few days," Ice suggested.

"She shouldn't go at all," Mannix growled. "We can pay for everything she needs."

"I'm going to work," I said firmly. "If it's him, he's not going to try anything in front of all the kids. Or Nicola. And if it's not him, then it doesn't matter."

"I'll do everything I can to find out who it is before you have to work again." Mannix tapped the paper against his thigh. "That will solve a lot of problems. Even if Charlie wasn’t the one driving that car tonight, I don't trust him. I don't like him being anywhere near you."

I sighed. "You've made that clear. He hasn't touched me again. We just work together, that's all."

"That better be all." He didn't add what he might do if it wasn't. By now I got the idea. At best, he’d make threats. At worst, he'd carry them out.

The question was, how far would he really go?

CHAPTER 17

MANNIX

"I have a list of potential threats." I tapped the sheet of paper against my thigh. Ice, Ares and I went over the list last night and I made a new one, leaving off anyone we ruled out. A lot of them were people known to us, or friends of ours. I underlined anyone we already knew was dubious. Some of the people on the list had a history of resentment toward those who ran this city. At least a dozen were completely unknown. I left Charlie Lynbrook on the list. His name was underlined twice.

"I'm sure my father has made you aware he believes someone is stirring up trouble."

I looked around at the faces in front of me. Daisy Lasalle, Ric DiMarco, Hamilton Blake and my brother Gunnar. Only an idiot wouldn't be alert around them. None of them, including my brother, would hesitate to kill me if it served their purpose.

I wouldn't hesitate to do the same if I had to. For now, I didn't have to. But I did have to tell them what I knew. If I didn't, and someone came after them, my life wouldn't be worth shit. And they would find out, that was guaranteed. Nothing went on in Dusk Bay they didn't know about sooner or later.

Gunnar gave me a doubtful look and put his hand out. "Let's see what you found, baby brother."

I handed him the sheet of paper, but resisted the urge to tell him to fuck off. I wasn't that much younger than him.

"Where did this list come from?" Daze asked. She regarded me with those big, dark eyes. She could almost pass for someone as sweet and naïve as Kennedy, but there was an edge to her that was sharper than any of Ice's blades. People underestimated her at their own detriment. Which was exactly how she liked it.

She was everyone's best friend, their sister, until she cut their throats. She was hot, there was no denying that, but I preferred not to have my cock burnt. Not to mention the three men in the room would take pleasure in making me suffer. I didn't want to find out how many days I'd last under their treatment.

"An associate of mine," I said carefully. "I have reason to believe they were followed by one of the people on this list, and that their intentions were to cause harm. At the very least, to intimidate. This happened right outside my home, which leads me to believe it goes further than just my associate. My father agrees it's probably something bigger than that."

I only had a brief conversation with him, but he was concerned. Not worried, but interested in having me take care of the matter before it became a major problem.

"They're getting bold," Ric said. He had an interesting array of scars on his neck. None deep, it almost looked like several people tried to cut his throat, but failed. That fit with the man I knew. If anyone would have a throat of iron, it would be him. Not to mention that if several people wanted to kill anyone, it would be Ric DiMarco. He'd pissed off his fair share of people.

"Do you have any evidence they're going after anyone but your father?" Hilton Blake fixed me with his cold blue eyes. Of all the men in the room, he intimidated me the most. He was the right-hand man of the most powerful mobster in the state, the second most powerful in the country. That made him connected and deadly. If his bosses wanted me dead, I'd be dead last week.

I understood the reason he asked that question. If this was just about my family, his bosses might cut us loose. Why bother themselves with our troubles? Being a loyal minion only got you so far. I was determined not to let him turn on us.

"We cornered Eric Parsell a couple of weeks back. He suggested the Bell family were putting out feelers into Dusk Bay." That was all we got from him before he met with an unfortunate accident involving Ares' knife and his throat. And then Ice's knife in his eyeball.

"And we're just hearing about this now because…" Daze cocked her head at me, a dangerous glint in her eye.

"I had no proof," I said, unflinching. "It was just a rumour until someone dared to follow my associate home from work."

"Associate or step sister?" Gunnar asked. Of course he would know. Dad probably told him. Or one of the staff. Whatever, I had nothing to hide.

"Step-sister-to-be and my girlfriend." I ignored the looks of surprise. It was good to see they didn't know everything.

"You believe someone is trying to get to you through her?" Daze asked.

I nodded. "I think someone assumed she was an easy target." When I found them, I'd use them for target practice. The guys and I had a place we liked to take people once in a while. We'd release them and hunt them down. If they got away, they'd be free.

They never got away.

"I met Kennedy at that party the other day." Daze frowned. "Put the word out that she's under my protection. Anyone who touches her can deal with us." She nodded to include me in that group. It was just as well she did, because I had no intention of handing them over if I got to them first. Whoever it was, they were mine to fuck with and tear into shreds. If there was anything left when the guys and I were done, then they could have them.

"I appreciate that," I said. "She doesn't deserve to have anything bad happen to her." I was sorely tempted to insist she stay at home, focus on her degree and on me and the other guys. It would be a lot easier to keep her safe if she didn't leave.

Being the beautiful bird she was, she needed to spread her wings and fly, even if it was only short distances. The three of us guys were now taking turns keeping an eye on her at all times. I'd spent hours this morning sitting in my car outside the gym, watching who was coming and going and making sure she was all right. She had no idea I was there, and that was okay.

Right now, Ares was reluctantly watching her while reading up on shit for his masters degree. Personally, I didn't know why he bothered to continue studying, but if he enjoyed it and it didn't get in the way, then he could do whatever the fuck he wanted. Apparently he was determined to get his PhD someday.

I supposed Doctor Ares Turner had a ring to it. Ice was taking a break, but he wanted that title too. Doctor Isaac Miller sounded fancy as fuck. Me, I was okay just being Mannix Cassani. I didn't need any fancy titles.

Although, now I thought about it, I wondered if Kennedy would do a PhD too. Fuck, I'd be surrounded by doctors. Good thing none of them would be the medical kind, not really. The medical kind were a pain in the ass. Sometimes literally.

"Are you the right person for her to be hanging out with then?" Gunnar asked. "No offence, little brother, but trouble follows you around wherever you go. If she's so nice, she might be better off nowhere near you."

I didn't bother to try to hide my irritation. It was just like him to judge my life choices.

"That's up to her," I said coldly. "If she wants to walk away, she can." It wasn't that simple. I wouldn't let her go without a fight. If she decided to leave, I'd have to convince her to stay. Or force her. Whatever it took. She was mine, no matter what.

Gunnar gave me a look like he was reading my mind, but since that was impossible and I didn't care what he thought, I ignored him.

"I can keep her safe," I said firmly, "don't worry about that. But knowing she has extra protection can't hurt." Unless it made her an even bigger target than she already is. In which case, we'd get her out of town. Out of the country if we had to.

"Of course it can't," Daze said. "Most people know not to fuck with what's mine. That includes anyone under my protection."

In the corner of my eye, I caught Ric staring at her. The front of his pants tented. Clearly I wasn't the only one who appreciated a woman who had power and knew how to use it.

If it wasn't for Kennedy, my cock would have twitched too. Neither my cock nor I would cheat, especially not on someone as gorgeous as my Princess. I'd be a fucking idiot to do that to her. I couldn't wait to fuck her. I knew she was a thousand percent worth waiting for. Sure, I was a bit pissed off Ice screwed her first, but my cock would feel her wet heat around me soon enough. Maybe tonight.

"We'll take a look at this list of yours." Hilton took it from Gunnar and skimmed his eyes down the page. "If anyone on it is up to something, we'll know soon enough." He didn't look like he believed they'd find anything.

It was an effort to keep from bristling, I reminded myself who his bosses were and forced myself to keep my face expressionless while I nodded.

"I'm sure it will be useful. When it is, I hope you'll bring us in to deal with them. Ice Miller, in particular, has a useful skill set for dealing with people who step out of line."

"I've heard that." Daze twirled a section of hair around her finger. "I'm a big fan of breaking fingers myself, but it sounds like he takes it all to a whole new level. I'll have to sit in on his work someday."

I smiled. "I think you'll like what you see." She might be just the person to introduce Kennedy to our ways. The darker, bloodier aspects of it, anyway. Women bonding over torture and murder, what could be better?

"I'm sure I will," Daze assured me. "You boys didn't spend all that time at Brutham Academy without learning skills that will be useful to me. To all of us."

That was the point of Brutham Academy. All of the degrees were tailored not just to gain employment, but to help all the student's families in their criminal activities. Not every student came from a mobster family, but those who didn't tended to end up in the life anyway, persuaded there by their friends, and the lure of money and power. Those who refused tended not to last there very long. They either left, or they died. Either way, they got weeded out quickly.

Even those who came from mobster families got weeded out

quickly if they weren't up to scratch. The level of hazing at Brutham was brutal, to say the least. It sucked when you were in first year, but by the time you got to your third or fourth and got to haze the newbies, it was worth it.

I got particular pleasure out of seeing Ice trying out some new pain inflicting techniques on the Brantley twins, Hunter and Parker. Those two were a pair of smartasses if I ever saw them. They'd do well at Brutham. Their kind always did. It didn't hurt that they were Reuben Brantley's youngest brothers. Even hazing had its limits when there was the potential of dealing with someone as powerful as him. Fuck that. Fun only went so far.

"I hope to show that my skills are, as you say, useful," I said. Useful enough that they might sidestep my father in future dealings and come straight to me.

CHAPTER 18

KENNEDY

"So, psychology, hmmm?" It wasn't the most exciting conversation starter, but it was a start. I was making an effort at least.

Ares barely glanced up at me and grunted. He looked back down at his laptop.

Okay then.

I took the opportunity to study him, since he was trying so hard to avoid looking at me. Or interacting with me in any way.

He wore a tight-fitting black T-shirt that moulded to his muscles like a second skin. His biceps looked like they were going to burst out of his sleeves. A tattoo of a snake slithered down his arm, ending just before his wrist. His torn black jeans were equally tight, showing off muscular thighs. Long, pale lashes lay across the top of his cheeks. What was it with guys having lashes like that? Mine were almost nonexistent.

"Like something you see?" he said without looking up. "Didn't your mother teach you it's rude to stare?"

"Didn't yours teach you to use your words and not caveman sounds?" I retorted.

"There's no such thing as cavemen," he said. "They never really existed."

"Neanderthal sounds then," I conceded. "Either way, it's not real, modern speech."

"Neither are emojis, but I bet you use them when you text your little friends." He tapped at his keyboard.

Little friends? I couldn't deny using emojis. Didn't everyone?

"Are you saying you don't use emojis?" I asked in disbelief. "I bet you do. Your favourite ones are probably the doughnut, and the hot face."

He glanced up long enough to shake his head at me, before looking back down. "Your favourite one is probably the eggplant. You don't seem to be able to get enough of Mannix and Ice's."

I'd had sex all of once in my life and he was trying to slutshame me?

"First of all, I'm pretty sure the eggplant emoji is everyone's favourite. Second of all, are you jealous because I've been spending time with them and not you? Or are you just pissed off that you're on guard duty?"

A frown flickered across his brow. "I'm just studying. Trying to anyway. When Mannix suggested I stay here, I didn't realise I'd be subjected to constant interruption."

"You're denying you're my guard today?" I asked. I wasn't fooled. Was anyone?

"Is that why you're being annoying?" he snapped. "Because you don't like the idea of being watched over? Let me tell you something." He fixed his gorgeous blue eyes on mine. "I have better things to do than babysit a spoilt brat like you." He raised the pitch of his voice and said, "*Buy me a new car. Make it as expensive as fuck and I'll spread my legs for you.*"

Rather than showing him how offensive his words were, I just smiled.

"Is that what it takes to get you into bed?"

He snorted. "You fucking wish. You have the other two eating out of your hands and wrapped around your pussy. Not me. I see right through people like you."

Okay, now I let my irritation show. "People like me? What is that supposed to mean?"

"It means you saw how much money Mannix has and moved straight on in. How many days were you here before you fell on your back and spread your legs?" He looked disgusted.

"Fuck. You." I returned his look. "I don't care about his money. Or Ice's. Or yours, for that matter. In case you hadn't noticed, I'm studying so I can get a good job and make my own money. I don't need, or want, anyone else's. He didn't have to buy me a car. He sure as hell didn't need to buy me an expensive one. You might not have noticed, but Mannix is headstrong and makes up his own mind about the things he does. And people he does."

I hesitated for a moment, then added, "Are you that threatened by me?"

He barked a laugh. "Why would I be threatened by you? One little car driving behind you and you're ready to jump out of your skin." He raised his voice again. "Mannix! Ice! There's a car behind me! O! M! G!"

I stared at him. "You saw the tape. You saw the way the car stopped outside the gate. You don't think that was fucking weird? I bet anything if that happened to you, you'd wet your pants."

"Not a chance," he said immediately. "I would have put the car into reverse and smashed the shit out of the other one. Or made the asshole get the fuck out of there. Or I would have led him to one of the dozens of places in Dusk Bay where I could have gotten behind him, boxed him in and beat the shit out of him. I wouldn't have run away."

"Me trying to beat the shit out of someone wouldn't end well for me," I said. "For one thing, we don't know if there was one person in the car or five." A woman alone with five men would definitely be bad news for me. I'd take running and hiding over that any day.

He shrugged. "Next time, call for help and we'll beat the shit out of him. Or them. Or whatever."

"Are you saying you'd come to my rescue?" I asked. "Even though I'm a spoilt brat, according to you."

"Just because I don't like you doesn't mean I want anything bad to happen to you," he said. "Besides, the other guys would drag me along, whether I wanted to go or not. Now they've staked their claim on you, they're not going to let you go, no matter what it takes to keep you."

"What about you?" I found myself asking. "Are you going to try to stake your claim too?" Did I want him to? He was a massive asshole, but sitting this close to him made my body throb. I couldn't help imagining the way it would feel to have his hands on me, touching me, parting my thighs. His face diving between my legs. His cock sliding into my pussy.

His eyebrows quirked. "Flushed cheeks, dilated pupils, shallow breathing. All classic signs of arousal. You hate my guts, but you *want* me to claim you." He sat forward slightly. "If I took you over to that couch," he jerked his head to the side, "bent you over it and pulled up that skirt of yours, you'd be dripping for me. I wouldn't need to touch you, you'd be so wet, I could slide my cock right in. I could pound you so hard I'd ruin that precious little pussy of yours. And you know what you would do? You'd beg me for more."

He sat back and looked smug.

I cleared my throat and waited until my racing heart slowed. What was it with these guys and their ability to get me going with only words?

"That sounds like a yes to me," I said when I could finally speak. "You do want to stake a claim to me."

He did, I saw it on his face, but he rolled his eyes. "If I ever lose my self control and fuck you, that would be all it was. Just a fuck. If you ever think I'll have feelings for you, forget it right now. The only feelings I have toward you are annoyance, irritation and..." He paused for a moment. "No, that's about it."

"Good," I said. "Because that's exactly what I feel for you too."

"I'm glad we understand each other. I'd hate for you to be living under some delusion in which Mannix, Ice and I are some kind of harem for you. As long as you're with them, I'll tolerate you, but only for their sake."

"I'm glad we cleared that up." I picked up my empty coffee cup and slipped off my stool. "I'll do my best to stay off your cock."

"You do that," he said as though this was some kind of rational conversation we were having. "I'll do my best to stay out of your pussy."

"Good." I turned on the coffee machine. "I'm sure, between us, we can prevent any nasty accidents."

"That might be the most sensible thing I've heard you say," he said.

That was bullshit; I'd said plenty of sensible things in his presence, but I didn't dignify it with an answer. I didn't know why he decided to hate me, but he had and apparently there was nothing I could do to change his mind. I asked myself why it mattered so much, but the only answer I had was that he was Mannix and Ice's friend and it was easier if we all got along. It had absolutely nothing to do with the way my pulse raced whenever he was around. Or the way he'd come to my rescue with or without the other guys. I didn't call him out on that, but we both knew it was true. If I needed him to beat the shit out of anyone—I hoped I never did—he'd do it.

"This is where I should offer to make you a coffee—" I started.

Before I could tell him he could think again, he said, "I'd love one, thanks. Strong, like me."

I smiled sweetly. "So lots of sugar and a shit load of milk then?" That would make it as weak as coffee could be.

He snorted a laugh. "Good try, but we both know I meant super strong. And extra thick." His gaze dropped toward his groin.

"I didn't realise we were talking about the head on your shoulders," I said tartly. "Extra thick sounds exactly right."

"And yet, you're thinking about my nice, thick cock right now, aren't you?" He smirked.

Yeah, unfortunately he was right. The idea of slipping and accidentally falling on his cock didn't sound so bad right now. If only he wasn't an arrogant, self-centred, smug asshole. The fact he was made him easier to resist. Kinda.

"Are you studying psychology so you can be a therapist some day?" I asked. "Or just so you can be even more annoying by pretending to read what's going on in people's heads?"

"I don't need to pretend," he said. "Most people wear whatever they're thinking on their faces like a mask."

I knew his choice of words was coincidental, but they still sent a spike of unease up and down my spine.

I went right back to that night.

"They're going to be pissed off I let you go, but don't worry. I'll deal with them. I know just the way to handle them, like I know how to handle you. You're probably thinking I don't have a clue, but I know more than you might imagine. Such a sweet perfume, little mouse. I don't mean the stuff you dabbed on behind your ears and on your wrists. I mean the scent of you. Your pussy. Your arousal. Your fear." He took a long, slow sniff of the air. "Intoxicating."

Without realising, I whimpered softly.

"Holy shit," Ares whispered. "Don't do that."

I slammed right back into the present.

I swallowed and blinked, reorienting myself. I was in the kitchen, making coffee. Not hiding in the bushes.

My eyes found his. "Don't do what?"

"Don't make sounds like that or I might forget to keep my cock out of your pussy." He made a face like he was in pain. My whimper must have turned him on hard. Any other time, I might have found it funny, but right now the memory of a black and red mask lurked in the back of my mind. It chased all thoughts of humour away.

"Right," I said distractedly. I grabbed another cup and started to make him a coffee.

Anything to keep my mind off the memory of that dark, bloody night.

CHAPTER 19

KENNEDY

My laptop slammed shut, narrowly missing squashing my fingers.

I jumped and glanced up to see Mannix, his face centimetres from mine. I hadn't even noticed he was in the room.

Yes I did, I realised after a moment. I felt the air get heavier. Thicker. He had a way of filling a space just by being in it. Owning every centimetre of it. My nipples hardened in response to his presence, even if the rest of me was focused on work. Hussies.

"Time for a break." His hand stayed pressed down on my laptop. The expression on his gorgeous face suggested he'd throw it in the pool if I refused.

I glanced at the clock on the wall. How did it get that late? I hadn't even realised the sun set an hour ago. My stomach rumbled impatiently.

"I guess I could use a short one." I started working on this report three or four hours ago. I wasn't much closer to finishing, but I needed to eat. Maybe then I could focus better.

Every time I tried, my brain went back to that night, distracting me and making my palms sweat. Several times, I found myself scrolling through social media, just to take my thoughts of everything.

I couldn't even remember what I saw, or whose posts I liked. Everything was a blur of random videos, interspersed with a friend's photos of her poodles. Those, I remembered. Her dogs were too cute to forget. Unfortunately, cute wasn't going to get my report finished.

"Yes, you could." He was clearly not taking no for an answer. So what else was new?

"Come on." He grabbed my hand and pulled me with him through the sliding doors that led out the pool. On the grass beside it, a blanket was spread out, covered with pillows and a couple of large baskets.

"You organised a picnic?" When did he have time for that? Not to mention, how did he arrange food when I was working in the kitchen? I must have been very distracted by those poodles.

"I organised it, but one of the staff put it together. Since I can't cook, I ordered all the food in." He tugged me down to the blanket beside him and opened one of the baskets.

"I wasn't sure what you liked, so I got a bunch of stuff."

He drew out a box of spring rolls and one of fried rice. Another box contained everything we needed to put together tacos. Yet another contained pizza. The last one was full of a variety of rolls of sushi. In the other basket, was a couple of glasses and a bottle of wine.

"There's cola too if you don't like wine."

"I've never really had it." I leaned back against the pillows and tried to take in everything. "This is amazing." I was speechless that he did something so thoughtful. So… romantic. In a million years, I wouldn't have guessed he'd be into gestures like this. The unexpected sweetness made my heart flutter.

He flashed a smile. "Of course it is. You're worth it. The hardest part was getting the other guys to fuck off for a while."

"Oh." I glanced around. I wondered where they were. Neither was ever far from Mannix, especially Ice. If I had to, I'd have guessed they were lurking around somewhere, waiting for the food to be opened. Then, like a pair of vultures, they'd descend on it.

"I sent them to deal with some business-related stuff," Mannix supplied. "They'll be gone for hours." He growled like they better not hurry back, or they'd have to answer to him.

Ares might stay away, but we'd probably see Ice the minute he got back. Even if the food didn't draw him in, us being out here having a picnic would. Like the proverbial moth to flame.

"Also, my dad and Helen are having dinner in the city. They do that at least once a month."

"Right." I nodded. Mum mentioned something about that. She seemed disappointed it wasn't once a week, or every night. The woman did like her comforts. Although, since most of our meals were cooked by a Michelin starred chef, I didn't think she had too much to complain about. Honestly, I was happy eating grilled cheese or instant noodles. I was used to that at uni. The food here was a whole new level of decadence for me. One I could get used to, even if my waistline couldn't.

"I gave Francisco the night off," Mannix added.

"You thought of everything." I accepted the glass of wine he handed me and sniffed. It was soft and sweet. 'A delicate bouquet,' I thought wine people would describe it. "This smells good."

"It's a rosé. Apparently it tastes like fruit juice." He took a sip and nodded appreciatively. "Tastes like my childhood, but alcoholic."

I sipped and found he was right. I'd have to be careful. A girl could drink a lot of it without meaning to.

"What do you want to eat? I can order us something else if you don't like any of this?" He'd do it too. If I told him I wanted a triple chocolate cheesecake, he'd have one on its way in moments. That thought alone added at least three kilos to my hips.

"No, this is plenty," I said quickly. There was almost too much to choose from. "Maybe some sushi for starters? None with avocado. I'm allergic." Not deathly so, but my face would resemble a red balloon for a few hours if I ate it.

"None of it has avocado. I checked with your mother before I ordered anything." He piled a plate high with sushi rolls and handed it to me.

"I'm impressed you'd take the time to do that," I admitted. "Most people wouldn't bother."

"I'm not most people." He piled sushi onto his own plate and leaned back on his hand. "I like to do things right the first time.

Besides, I made it my mission to learn everything about you. Your likes, dislikes, pet hates."

I grimaced. "Like most people, one of my biggest pet hates is the expression pet hate. I mean, it sounds so cute, but at the same time not." Was I making any sense? I hadn't had that much wine yet, had I?

He chuckled. "Yeah, it does sound kinda dumb. What else annoys you as much as that?"

I swallowed my mouthful. The sushi was so good. So fresh.

"I don't like pickles on hamburgers. Or beetroot for that matter. I don't like people who park in the middle of two parking spaces."

"Does anyone? The amount of times I've been tempted to…" He shook his head. He finished with, "It's annoying as fuck."

I'd had just enough wine to ask, "Tempted to do what? Key the side of their car?"

"More like key the side of their face," he growled. "The car did nothing wrong."

"Yeah. I guess it's not okay to take it out on the car." I wasn't sure I advocated scraping a piece of metal along someone's face either, but people do things in the heat of the moment.

He huffed out a breath. "What else? How about things you like? Apart from me and Ice that is. And computer shit."

I wasn't sure how I felt about him referring to what I did as 'computer shit'. "I like chocolate covered liquorice. In fact, I like chocolate covered pretty much everything."

"Good to know." He looked sly. "I'm sure you'd love chocolate covered cock."

My face heated. "I might. I'm sure Ice would too."

Mannix leaned closer to me. "You want to see that, Princess? Because I can arrange it. You can have a front row seat to watch Ice suck chocolate sauce off my cock."

His words ignited my core.

"I would like to see that," I said softly. I was about to add, 'But only if you want to do it.'

I remembered what Mannix said about asking for what I wanted, and taking it, so I didn't. Of *course*, they'd only do it if they wanted to. If they did, I'd be into it.

"I'll sort it out." He brushed his lips over mine, then sat up to refill both of our glasses and drag the taco ingredients over closer.

"Let me guess, you like it stuffed as full as you can get." The look he shot me was questioning and heated at the same time.

"That's exactly how I like it," I agreed. My taco and, from my limited experience, my pussy.

"That's my girl." He put every possible ingredient into the taco except the guacamole. "Extra sour cream for you." He smiled like he was putting cum on my taco before he handed it to me.

Either way, I bit into it and closed my eyes in appreciation.

"Tacos are one of my favourite foods."

"Mine too." He leaned over to lick sour cream off the side of my mouth. "Mmm, delicious. And the dinner isn't bad either." He sat back and ate his.

"This is nice." I looked up at the stars while I ate. For a little while, I forgot about everything. Study, the stalker, murder, even Ares' antagonism.

"I spoke to your father the other day."

I didn't expect Mannix to stiffen the way he did. His response was immediate, his whole body alert, wary.

I shrank back slightly, involuntarily. Was that the wrong thing to say? If I ruined our—I guessed I could call this a date—I'd be disappointed in myself. I didn't realise his father was a hot button topic in any way.

"You did?" he asked carefully. "What about?"

"Just about us." I spoke with forced lightness. "I got the impression you talked to him about us too. He seems to approve, as long as things don't get messy."

"Right." Mannix relaxed visibly. "I told him. Assured him things wouldn't get messy. He assured me the same thing about your mother. If *they* do, it's no big deal. We're solid, you and I."

"Are we?" I asked. "What are we, exactly? Step siblings with benefits?"

Something flashed behind his eyes, but it was gone before I could identify it.

"You're my girlfriend," he said. "And Ice's girlfriend. Someday, you'll be Ares' girlfriend too." He made it all sound so simple, so straightforward. Maybe it was that simple. Maybe I was the only one making it complicated.

"And you're my boyfriends. Isn't that a little weird? I know polyamory is nothing new, but I don't know anyone in that kind of relationship. Except the band Wolf Venom."

"There you go then. We can be as cool as they are." He finished his taco and handed me a napkin before wiping his fingers on another one.

"That's a stretch," I said, "that I could ever be as cool as them."

"I've met most of them and let me tell you, you're much cooler than they are." He said it like meeting one of the biggest rock bands in the world was no big deal.

Meanwhile, I gaped at him. "You've met them? How?"

"Daze's boyfriend Ric is the drummer, Asher's, cousin," Mannix explained. "And my father works with the brother of the lead singer, Zeke Brantley. They don't come to Dusk Bay often, but when they do, Ric always throws a party and invites everyone. I'll make sure you come the next time."

Come was the right word for it, because I was so excited at the prospect of meeting them, I might do just that. Aside from Mannix, Ice and Ares, Zeke Brantley was one of the hottest guys on the face of the planet. I might even have photos of him on my phone. And the keyboard player, Penn. And... Okay, they were all hot. Their girlfriend was a lucky woman.

"On the other hand, if you're going to look at them like that, I'm going to tie you to my bed and make sure you stay there." He looked slightly annoyed. Was he actually jealous of me fangirling over famous musicians? I wouldn't have a chance with any of them even if they were single.

"I'm not going to throw myself at them," I argued.

"You better not," he growled. "I'd hate to have to take a hit out on a whole band just to keep them away from you."

I wasn't sure if he was joking or not.

"If you care about me, you won't kill my favourite band." Softly I added, "I know who I belong to. I just like their music, that's all."

He seemed placated by that. "They're just regular guys who happened to be famous at the moment. That's all. When their fifteen minutes of fame are over, you'll forget all about them."

I hoped they didn't stop making music anytime soon, but I didn't want to get into an argument over a rock band, of all things. No doubt he was right, they were just regular guys, and Mannix and the others were so much more than that. They were like no one else I ever met. Intense, intelligent and off the charts hot. How could any rock band compete?

"Why would I want them anyway, when I have you?" I asked.

"Exactly." He started to pack up the picnic. "Let's go for that swim we talked about. After that, I hope you're ready for me to fuck you, because I'm more than ready."

Before I could answer, he rose, scooped me up in his arms and jumped into the pool.

We were both fully dressed.

CHAPTER 20

KENNEDY

I squealed, but snapped my mouth shut right before I slipped under the surface and drank a bunch of salty pool water.

Mannix let go of me when our feet touched the bottom. I paddled wildly until I shot back up and sucked in a gulp of oxygen.

"What the fuck?" I pushed wet hair off my face. My clothes clung to me, heavy as hell. I shot him a dirty look and paddled over to grab hold of the side.

Mannix bobbed up and down in the middle of the pool. He was grinning like the idiot he might just be, since he tried to drown us both.

"You were never in any danger. I'm an excellent swimmer."

"I'm not," I growled. I looked down at myself. My favourite white T-shirt, with the Wolf Venom logo on the front, was practically transparent. My drenched, black bra did nothing to hide my pebbled nipples. My shorts and panties stuck like they were glued on.

"I like you wet." He paddled over and braced himself, one hand on either side of me. "You look like a gift I need to open."

He slammed his mouth down on mine. Wet with pool water, our lips slid against each other. He pinned me to the side of the pool with his body, his full length pressed against me.

On principle, I should have pushed him away. I really wasn't much of a swimmer and drowning was not on my to-do list today. But the moment his mouth met mine, I forgot to be angry, and instead slipped my arms around his neck. My legs went around his waist, partly to get him closer and partly to keep me from sliding under the water again.

"That's my girl," he said against my mouth. He reached down and peeled my T-shirt up and over my head before tossing it onto the pool deck. At least he had the sense not to drop it into the water.

My bra went next.

His lips broke off from my mouth and he leaned me back so he could lavish attention on my nipples with his lips and tongue.

"You're so fucking perfect."

It might have been the wine that made me bold, but I grabbed the hem of his dark grey T-shirt and helped him out of it. I tossed it aside somewhere, maybe the pool deck, and let my hands roam across his chiselled stomach and hips.

"Are you made out of stone or something?" I asked. Every bit of him was so hard, like a statue. Maybe he was a Greek god in a past life. Or some other kind of god. The gorgeous kind.

"I might be," he said, his voice muffled by my nipple. "My cock is hard for you." He unwound my arm from his neck and guided my hand down to his length.

He wasn't wrong. Even through his jeans, he was hard, hot and thick.

After a breathless moment or two, I said, "I'm ready."

Because he was Mannix, he couldn't make it that easy on me.

"Ready for what?" He rolled his hips to press his cock deeper into my hand.

"You know what." My face heated. Would I ever stop blushing at the idea of sex?

"Do I?" He grazed his teeth over my nipple and made me groan.

I managed to say, "I'm ready to be with you. To… let you fuck me."

"That wasn't so hard, was it?"

"Not as hard as you," I agreed.

He chuckled and helped me out of my shorts and panties. He placed his hands on my hips and lifted me up to the side of the pool.

Instinctively, I put my hands over my breasts.

He grabbed my wrists and pulled them away. "No hiding yourself. You're beautiful."

"What if someone sees?" For all I knew, my mother was looking out the window, exactly in our direction. Okay, I knew she and Leo wouldn't be back for hours, and all the staff would have gone home by now.

"Let them see," Mannix said. "The whole world should know how stunning you are and that you're mine. All of this—" he nodded up and down my body "—is glorious."

He let my wrists go and gripped my thighs instead. He opened my legs wide enough to place his face between them. He wasn't gentle when he attacked my clit and folds with his tongue. He was merciless, like he hadn't eaten a crumb of food. Instead, he feasted on me. It was nothing like the first time we were together like this. He was gentle then, considerate of my virginity. Tonight, he wasn't leaving one drop on the table.

Under the onslaught, I forgot to care that I was naked. All I knew was the way his mouth felt on me, his teeth nipping my clit, tongue slipping inside me. He pushed a finger inside, then another one. He hooked his hand around to stroke me from the inside.

I arched my back, thrusting my breasts out further, lost in a world of pleasure.

"Mannix…" I said breathlessly.

He lifted his shining face up enough to say, "I like it when you say my name. Say it again." He lowered his mouth back to me.

I said his name again and again until I came, bucking and groaning against his mouth.

"I'll never get tired of that sound either." He kissed his way down the inside of my thigh to my knee and back up the other leg. "So perfect."

He placed his hands on the side of the pool and in one smooth motion pushed himself up to lie beside me. He shed his jeans and boxers as if they didn't stick hard to his body.

"Maybe we should go somewhere no one can see?" I suggested.

He grabbed my wrists again and pinned me to the hard tile beside the pool. "Let them watch. They might learn something." He nudged my legs open with his knees and knelt between them.

He lifted himself up on his arms like he was doing a push-up and said, "Look how hard I am for you, Princess. My cock is aching for you. Aching for your warm, wet, tight pussy."

He certainly looked hard. And big. His piercing shone in the light that shone up from under the water.

I swallowed hard.

He lowered himself back down until he rested on his knees and elbows, and positioned his cock outside my entrance.

"Usually, I like to fuck from behind, but I want to see your face. I want to watch you watching me fuck you. I want you to remember our first time together for the rest of your life. Let it be seared into your mind like my brand on your skin."

Without another word, he pushed straight into me. Like his tongue, he showed no mercy. He gave me no time to get used to him, not until he was balls deep inside me. Then he stilled, watching me and savouring the way I felt, and the way our bodies joined together.

He made an incoherent sound, somewhere between a gasp, a grunt and a word of some kind.

"Holy shit."

Now *that* I understood.

"You're so fucking tight, Princess. It's like the warmest, wettest vice I ever felt around my cock."

I'd probably forget to ask him how often he put a vice around his cock, but it was still a good question. I suspect he meant it all metaphorically though. Maybe.

When I finally got used to him, let my muscles relax, I savoured the way he felt, filling me so full and deep.

"You feel pretty amazing yourself," I said.

When he started to move inside me, I forgot to worry that we were right beside the pool. The only thing that mattered, was right there, right then, in the moment. His cock slid in and out of me, his piercing massaging my insides.

He hooked his arms under my legs and brought them up over his shoulders. He pulled all the way out and slammed into me so hard I felt like he might rearrange my insides. It hurt, but it same time it felt so fucking good.

I groaned.

"Mannix…"

"Princess…" He thrust harder and faster. "You're mine. This precious pussy is mine. I'm going to fuck you so hard you can't walk for a week. I'm going to shatter your sweet, amazing pussy." He drove into me so hard it bordered on viciousness, but the harder he drove, the more I wanted.

My back slid up and down the tiles made slick by the water still dripping off our bodies. If it wasn't for Mannix's weight holding me in place, I might have flown across the pool deck.

He grunted. His breath was coming in ragged pants now.

"Princess," he breathed. "Kennedy."

It was the first time I remember him saying my name. I liked the way it sounded on his lips. I liked it almost as much as his nickname for me. I wondered what Ares' nickname for me would be. Probably something along the lines of 'spoiled brat.' Or just brat for short. As if he could talk. He was more spoiled than I would ever be.

Still, thinking of him made me wonder how it would feel to have him in my mouth and Mannix in my pussy. And Ice… He could be wherever he wanted to be. I had a feeling he had some creative ideas I'd discover at some point. Hopefully at some point soon.

Mannix pulled one of my legs over his head and faced me while he went on thrusting.

"You have no idea how beautiful you are, do you?" he asked. "Inside and out. Beautiful, and you belong to me. All mine."

I watched his face in fascination while he fucked me. Every expression of concentration and pleasure. He was so gorgeous, this moment couldn't possibly be real. At any moment now, I'd wake up and find myself fucking my vibrator, lost in my own fantasy.

I hoped that *wouldn't* happen soon. This fantasy was incredible. If anyone was around, I hoped they didn't pinch me. I never wanted to come out of this.

"I belong to you," I whispered.

"You definitely do. I'm going to come inside your gorgeous body.

I'm going to fill you up with my cum, so full. So fucking full. And you're going to take every single drop. That's what you were made for. You were made for me to fill you up with my cock and cum. You were born for this moment. You and your tight, wet pussy."

Between his words and his thrusts, I came again, breaking apart into a million pieces, each a drop of throbbing, lava hot blood. I threw back my head and cried out his name, even though I could barely remember my own.

"Good girl, Princess."

He rammed into me harder than ever, faster and faster until he finally stilled and groaned.

"Yes, yes, yes. Princess." He grunted. "Fuck, yes. Ahhh. Fuuuuck." He sagged, panting, his fingers digging into my hip. "You were everything I imagined and more. So much more." He nuzzled his face into my wet hair and sighed near my ear.

"So perfect."

I didn't know about that, but I didn't try to correct him. There was no point, he'd only insist he was right.

"Let's go inside and have a shower," he said after a few minutes of lying there on the tiles. "I'm going to see how many times I can make you come before you beg me to let you sleep. Just so you know, I'm going to make you come one more time after that."

"Don't threaten me with a good time." I searched around and picked up my clothes off the pool deck.

He chuckled. "Princess, you haven't even started to see a good time yet. You can still walk, can't you? When I'm done with you, you won't be able to. And that's not a threat, it's a promise."

CHAPTER 21

KENNEDY

I hung on to the silk with my thighs and one hand. Slowly, the fabric started to unwind. Faster and faster until the gym became a blur. I tipped my head back and laughed. The sensation of spinning out of control was heady, addictive. Like my whole life since I moved to Dusk Bay.

Unlike my life, I was in complete control here. To anyone watching, it looked like a wild ride, but with a snap of my wrists, a slide down the silk, I could stop it.

I didn't want to. I wanted to spin and spin forever. To fly in a blur of motion until I was too dizzy to hold on anymore. Even then, I'd cling and wish to go faster and faster.

Like always, the spinning slowed and everything came back into sharp focus. The well used gym; boxes still scattered from the afternoon's classes; Charlie replenishing the chalk tub. Nicola was in the office for most of the day, doing admin, but she left an hour or so ago.

Reluctantly, I slipped down to the mat.

"Isn't that dangerous?"

I hadn't seen Mannix and Ice enter the gym, but they now stood near the door, arms crossed over their chests.

It was Ice who spoke, but he didn't look concerned. Unlike Mannix, who looked ready to get a ladder, climb it and snip the silks off at the ceiling.

"It's only dangerous if you don't know what you're doing," I said. "I've been doing this for a long time, and I'm careful."

"Isn't it a circus trick?" Mannix asked. "It's not real gymnastics."

"It's not a recognised apparatus," I agreed. "But it's still fun and requires hard work and skill. Do you want to try?" I was goading him. He clearly didn't want to try, but I couldn't resist. Judging silks was like judging pole dancing. Until people tried it, they didn't know how much was involved and how difficult it really was.

"I do." Ice grinned and stepped forward.

Mannix cut him a hard look. "You'll kill yourself."

That only made Ice's grin broaden. "At least I'll die having fun."

Mannix shook his head. "You're insane. Anyway, that's not what we're here for." To me he said, "I have a surprise for you."

"Hey," Ice protested. "I was in on it too."

In my peripheral vision, I saw Charlie looking wide-eyed at both guys. He noticed me watching and hurried into the office. He reminded me of a scared rabbit.

I turned my attention back to the guys, who were in the middle of a brief argument over who was and wasn't involved with whatever the hell they were talking about.

I waited until they realised I was waiting, one eyebrow raised.

"Is one of you going to explain?"

Mannix pulled a piece of paper out of his back pocket and handed it to me. "We did a little something for you."

I eyed the paper before I took it from his hand. "What did you do?" Since the last time he did something for me—aside from the picnic—I ended up with an expensive car, there was reason to be suspicious.

"Open it." He looked more smug than usual.

I gave them both a look, then slowly opened the sheet of paper.

I read it.

Read it again.

What the absolute mother-loving fuck?

"You didn't. You couldn't have."

Both of them smiled. Ice rolled from his heels to his toes and back again.

Mannix looked like the cat that got all the cream. "We could and we did. It took some time to convince Nicola to sell, but she gave in eventually."

I looked up from the deed which had my name on it. "You didn't threaten her did you?"

Mannix shrugged one shoulder. "We didn't need to. Everyone has their price and we finally reached hers. That's all."

"You didn't even want me working here and now you bought me the place? This must have cost a fortune." I couldn't get my head around it.

"It didn't cost as much as the car," Ice said. "This way, we can put in all the security measures we want to take care of you."

"What does Ares think of this?" I asked.

"He said he thinks it's idiotic, but the truth is, we'll all come here and work out. We might also have bought the building next door to put in weights and machines. Think of it as the start of your empire." Mannix spoke as if all of this was perfectly reasonable.

"All of this will help fund your dreams of having a computer security company," Ice said.

I shook my head. "You guys have put way too much thought into this. Honestly, I don't think I can accept a gift this extravagant." Especially knowing what Ares would have to say about it. Something about owing the guys a bajillion blowjobs. I hadn't even given one of them yet.

"It's in your name," Mannix said easily. "You can keep it running or shut it down. It's up to you."

"You don't want to disappoint all those kids, do you?" Ice asked. There was nothing like a bit of emotional blackmail on a Tuesday afternoon.

"Of course not, but I…" I didn't know what else to say. No one had ever done anything like this for me before.

"There is one thing," Mannix said. He strode over to the office, wrenched the door open and said, "You're fired. Get the fuck out."

Charlie turned and stared at him, wide eyed.

"Wait, no," I said quickly. "He's a good coach. The kids love him."

When Mannix turned to argue with me I said, "If this is all really mine, you'll let me hire whoever I want to hire." Nothing was ever that simple when Mannix was involved, but I couldn't let him fire Charlie because he had a problem with him. For one thing, there were laws against it. This whole enterprise wouldn't start very well if I got sued straight off.

"He might not want to stay." Mannix looked at Charlie as if daring him to contradict him.

Charlie looked at me and sat up a bit straighter. "I do want to stay. I have to eat." He looked like he was trying not to wet himself. Still, he managed to stand up to Mannix. That wasn't easy for anyone to do. He must be tougher than he looked. Or desperate.

What did I really know about him anyway? Not much. Trying to engage him in conversation was difficult. After our first meeting, he closed himself off from me.

"Then you can stay." I gave Mannix a challenging look of my own. He couldn't say I owned all of this, and then immediately override me. Well, he could, but if I let him walk all over me now, he always would. The last thing I wanted to do was throw someone out if their financial situation was so tenuous. I'd have to find time to sit down with Charlie and see if he'd open up.

"For now," Mannix said. Apparently that was all the concession he was willing to give. "But if he steps a foot out of line..." He shot Charlie a warning look.

"He won't," I said firmly. "I wouldn't be able to do any of this without him. He knows the gym a lot better than I do."

Charlie looked grateful, but at the same time very much like he wished he was anywhere but here. Or in anyone's company but Mannix.

"He looks harmless to me." Ice looked him up and down like he was assessing a piece of meat and deciding on the best way to cook him.

"I am harmless." Charlie's voice squeaked when he spoke, and his throat bobbed. "Kennedy is right, I know this gym better than anyone, including Nicola and her. I can help."

"Then it's decided. We can keep the roster as it is for now. I don't see any point changing anything, except to upgrade the computer system. I'll make that as easy a transition as I can." There was nothing worse than workplaces changing systems in such a way that staff didn't know what the fuck was going on and how to use it.

"We'll work out the security," Mannix said. "Cameras out the front, for a start. State-of-the-art alarm system."

"This is a gym, not a bank," I pointed out.

"You're more precious than all the money in any bank," he said. "Any time you're here, I want you to be safe."

I could tell he wasn't going to back down on this, so I threw my hands up to either side and dropped them. "Fine, whatever you think we need. Just don't go spending too much money. Please."

"We make no promises," Ice said.

"None at all," Mannix agreed. "If we want to buy you things, then we're going to buy you things. What's money for if I can't use it to buy things for my princess?"

I gave Charlie a tentative smile and followed Mannix out the office door.

"What he said." Ice jerked a thumb in Mannix's direction. "Princess Beautiful deserves all the good things. If we can give it, then we will." He slipped an arm around me. "It doesn't really bother you, does it?"

"It does a bit," I admitted. "Ares said—"

"Don't worry about what Ares says. His bark is worse than his bite. Unfortunately, because a good bite is…" Ice shook his head. "It doesn't matter. The point is, we want you to have these things. And the town needs a really good gym. The other one is all the way on the other side of the city."

"And in Leo's basement," I pointed out. "He has everything you need right there."

"Everything we need," Ice agreed, "but what about the rest of Dusk Bay? We saw a hole in the market and decided to fill it. Actually, it was Mannix who saw it and made that decision."

"It's good business," Mannix said. "Wherever there's something lacking, there's a chance to make money by supplying it. In this case, making you some money. We'll help you with whatever you need, but this is your baby."

I was sure both of them, and Ares, would have a lot to say about the new gym and the old one. Mannix, in particular, liked to control everything way too much to step back from this.

"You've ordered all the equipment already haven't you?" I guessed.

Neither of them flinched or even batted an eye.

"Not all of it," Mannix said. "We need to get a builder in here to fit everything out and do the measurements before we finalise everything. We haven't even agreed on the right shade of blue to paint the inside yet."

"Maybe I don't want blue," I said.

"You don't like blue?" Mannix asked.

"I like blue, I just haven't had a chance to think about anything like that."

He slipped his arm around me. "That's what we're for. To take the stress off your shoulders."

The stress they put there.

"Maybe I should leave the setting up of that side of the business to you," I said. I might as well surrender it now, I had no hope of them stepping back from this. Did I?

"We're happy to help." Ice smiled. "What do you think about an indoor swimming pool?"

"I don't think the space is big enough." I couldn't say he wasn't ambitious. "But before you say it, this space is fine. Don't go running off finding me something bigger. Okay?"

They both looked as cagey as fuck and didn't answer.

Wonderful.

CHAPTER 22
KENNEDY

"Leo and I are thinking about bringing the wedding forward," Mum declared at dinner.

I stopped with my fork halfway to my mouth.

Mannix looked vaguely interested, but Ice and Ares didn't even pause in their eating.

I supposed it wasn't their family, not exactly. Them living here was only supposed to be temporary. No one mentioned when they were moving out again, that I knew of. They both seemed very much at home. Honestly, I was used to having them both around. I was in no hurry for them to go.

I lowered my fork. "I thought you had most of the plans made already?"

"We do, but a lot of them are flexible and those that aren't…" She turned out her hand, unconcerned.

It was only money, after all.

"Can't wait any longer huh?" Mannix asked. He glanced at me like being his step sister sooner would make our relationship spicier.

"We thought we'd waited long enough, so why wait any longer?" Mum said.

"It's only a few months," I pointed out.

"I know," she said lightly. "But look at this man. How could any woman wait any longer?" She gave him a long, loving look. It was adorable, in a sickening kind of way. I mean, she was my mother. I wanted her to be happy, but I didn't want to witness too many PDAs.

Leo, in a dark blue button down shirt with the sleeves rolled up, and a chunky watch on his wrist, looked like an older version of Mannix. The hair at his temples showed a hint of grey, and his eyes were lined in a way that suggested he smiled often. He'd be attractive if he wasn't my boyfriend's father and my mother's fiancé. If Mannix looked half as good as him at his age, we'd all be winning.

"I know I wouldn't wait," Ice said. "Life is way too short to wait for things."

"That's deep, bro," Ares said.

Ice cocked his head at him. "Isn't it? It's true though."

Something passed between them I couldn't identify. I noticed Leo watching them and had the strangest feeling he knew exactly what they were referring to. Of course, he'd known them most of their lives, so he probably had a good idea of what kind of things they got up to.

Would he tell me any of it if I asked? Then again, maybe I should wait for the guys to do that. I bet they could talk for hours about the shit they did as kids. Hell, they probably had stories they could tell about shit they did last week.

I stabbed my fork into a piece of chicken, and said, "When are you thinking of moving the wedding to?" I popped the chicken into my mouth.

"This weekend," Leo said.

I almost choked on my mouthful.

Mannix patted my back while Ares handed me a cup of water.

When I finally managed to stop coughing, I said, "That soon?" It was Monday—no wait, it was Tuesday. Tuesday night, to be specific. That only left three days to plan anything.

You know what they say, what could go wrong? At least a metric fuck ton.

"It doesn't have to be anything fancy," Mum said.

Everyone at the table snorted a laugh.

Leo chuckled. "I'm sorry, Helen, honey, but we all know we prefer fancy. I'm sure we can pull 'fancy' together in three days. Kennedy and the guys will help, won't you?"

I'd rather stick the fork in my eyeball right now, but I said, "Yeah, we will. The dresses are ready anyway." Dark green, thank fuck. Mum wanted pink, but it was Leo who suggested green would look better on everyone, including him in his waistcoat.

Common sense prevailed and Mum agreed. However, while she had made that concession, she wanted my dress and hers covered in crystals and sequins. And of course, a unique design so I could never wear it anywhere else again. Heaven forbid Mum choose something practical.

"Can we wear shorts?" Ice asked.

All eyes turned to him.

He raised his hands in surrender. "I was just asking, that's all. Shorts can be fancy."

Mum closed her eyes, and shook her head, but Leo looked amused.

"I suggested to Helen we all wear shorts or swimwear and have the ceremony beside the pool, but she didn't like the idea for some reason." He gave her a lopsided smile. The fact he genuinely loved her was clear and sweet.

I was happy for them. I wanted them both to be happy. Not just because it made life easier for everyone, but because I loved her. She was crazy at times, but she was a good person.

Mum rolled her eyes. "Like you said, we like fancy. There's nothing fancy about getting married in swimwear."

"That depends on the swimwear," Mannix said.

"And the wearer," Ice added. "I look fancy naked, and in swimwear. I'm very versatile as well as flexible."

"This is dangerously close to too much information territory," Leo said. "Maybe we can figure out how to get a cake done in time."

Ice raised his hand above his head.

"Can you bake?" I asked.

He lowered his hand and grinned. "No, but I can pile TimTams onto a plate. If you like, I can even put strawberry jam in between them." He mimed doing that with a knife.

"I'm not saying that's not fancy," Mannix said slowly.

"You're saying it's fucking nuts," Ares said. "Don't put Ice in charge of the food preparation."

"Hey, I'm really good at carving roast meat." Ice grimaced at him playfully. "But if I can't do that, I'll have to fall back on my usual role." He held both his arms up above his head and posed like a statue. "I'll be the ice sculpture."

"Ba-dum-tish," Mannix said dryly.

"Also don't let Ice think he's a work of art," Ares said. "If anyone around here is a masterpiece, it's me." He actually flexed. For real. He held up his ridiculously muscular arms and flexed. I was surprised he didn't kiss them.

Since he had muscles for days, I stared. It wasn't fair that he was so gorgeous, but such a jerk.

Ice handed me a napkin.

I turned to frown at him. "What's that for?"

"To wipe up your drool. If you stare at Ares any longer, it's going to start dribbling down your chin."

I flicked the napkin at him. "I wasn't staring."

"Yes, you were." Ares looked smug.

"Fine, I was," I said. "I was trying to understand why you think you'd be a masterpiece."

He scoffed. "You know why. You have eyes. And I have biceps as thick as my thighs."

I rolled mine. "If you say so." I turned my attention back to Mum and Leo. "I hope you're having this wedding outside, because inside isn't big enough for Ares' ego."

He flipped me off. He looked as though he wanted to say something about one of his body parts being too big to fit inside, but he glanced at Mum and went back to eating.

Good to know he had a filter after all. Such as it was. No doubt we'd revisit this conversation later.

"The boys and I can organise our suits," Leo said. "Assuming Mannix still wants to be my best man?"

Now Mannix looked smug. "I do. It's accurate."

Ares barked a laugh, but neither Ice nor I disagreed. He was one of the two best men I knew.

"Can we call you the best Man-nix?" Ice teased.

"That's also accurate," Mannix said evenly. "So go ahead."

Ares turned to Ice and asked, "Can we call you Icehole?"

"Only if we can call you Areshead," Ice retorted. "You know, like airhead."

"We get it, Isaac," Mum said. "You boys are so funny. No wonder Kennedy likes spending time with you. You're all so sweet."

It was her turn to get stared at. There were many, many adjectives I could think of to describe the guys, but sweet?

Okay, Mannix was sweet to buy me a car and he and Ice were sweet to buy me a gym. Mannix was sweet to set up that picnic for us. Still, it didn't seem like quite the right word.

"We're funny all right," Ice said.

"Funny looking," Ares told him.

"Speak for yourself." Ice picked up his bottle of beer and took a sip.

"I'd rather speak for you." Ares tore a piece of bread off his roll and ate it. "It's much more fun."

"Don't speak with your mouth open." Ice shook a finger at him.

I frowned. "Don't you mean that he shouldn't speak with his mouth *full?*"

Ice grinned slowly. "Nope, I meant what I said. Ares shouldn't speak with his mouth open. It's much quieter around here like that."

"The only thing Ares has to say to you, I can say with one finger." Ares stuck up his middle finger at Ice.

"That was accompanied by a lot of words," Mannix pointed out. "Way more than just one skinny little finger."

"They are not skinny." Ares flipped him off with both hands.

I turned to Mum and said, "Have you thought about eloping? I hear Vegas is fun for that."

She responded with a tinkly laugh. "I'm sure they'll behave themselves on the day. Won't you boys? I'd hate to have to insist Kennedy not have anything to do with any of you."

It was like she poured oil onto an open fire. All of the guys turned to look at her, including Leo. He seemed irritated.

Mannix's eyes were like twin chips of ice.

Ice's hand went white, he was holding his fork so tightly. He looked like he was trying to contain the urge to jump up and stab her in the forehead with it.

Ares even put a hand on Ice's shoulder like he was holding him back.

"No one will be insisting anything like that." Leo's tone matched his son's eyes. He seemed to be issuing a warning, but it wasn't to Mum. Something in his voice and posture suggested he was telling the guys to stand down.

My eyes flickered from one face to another. What the hell was going on here? I knew the guys had a slightly possessive streak—okay, very possessive streak—but they wouldn't hurt my mother if she tried to get between us. Would they? They must know if they harmed a hair on her head, I'd never speak to any of them again. She wasn't perfect, but she was my mother.

"I'm sure I won't have to," Mum said, but she didn't back down even half a step. Was she so bad at reading the room that she didn't get how annoyed they were, or was she just not easily intimidated?

Or maybe she knew Leo would cut off Mannix's trust fund if he so much as tried to do anything to her. All hell would absolutely break loose either way.

I cleared my throat. "I thought I saw the chef making chocolate mousse for dessert."

The tension didn't evaporate, but my words broke through the mist.

"I could eat chocolate mousse," Ares said.

"We'll get ours and go and sit out near the pool," Mannix said. "I'm sure Dad and Helen have a lot to talk about." He still looked pissed as hell, but either he didn't want to be around my mother anymore or he decided to leave it to his father to deal with.

I didn't much care, as long as we got away from the air of barely contained violence.

Mannix stood. "Kennedy." He nodded at me like he expected to be obeyed.

In this mood, it was better to go along with him until he lightened up.

"I'll see you later," I said to Mum. "We can sit down tomorrow and talk about the rest of the wedding plans."

"Yes, yes." She waved us away. "Go and enjoy yourself." It seemed she couldn't get us away from her fast enough.

Judging by the way the guys hurried into the kitchen, grabbed bowls of mousse and headed out the door, the feeling was mutual.

It was probably nothing more than pre-wedding jitters on behalf of everyone. Even the two guys not involved in the wedding. Weddings were a stressful time for everyone.

That was what I told myself, but I hadn't felt that kind of energy in the air for weeks.

Not since that night at the masked ball.

CHAPTER 23
KENNEDY

"They're a handful, those boys of yours." Mum frowned at her reflection in the mirror and went on brushing her hair.

"I don't think you could call Ares mine." I took the brush from her hand and started working on the back of her hair, running strokes slowly from the roots down to the ends.

Her hair was a couple of shades darker than mine, closer to brown than bright red.

"I've seen the way he looks at you." She smiled knowingly. "You could do worse than those three. If you can keep them in line. Leo is enough for me."

"That's good to know, because he doesn't seem like the sharing type," I said. "Except his money. He seems happy to spend that on people he cares about."

"He's very generous," Mum said. "But he's also very careful about where he invests his money. He's the kind of man who only bets on a sure thing. Like his son."

I paused my brushing for a moment. "You think my gym is a sure thing?"

"With you in charge of it, how could it not be?" she said in a way only a mother could. With faith that I'd succeed, even if that faith wasn't based on anything more than maternal love.

"Right." I swiped the brush through her hair a couple more times before I put it aside. "Do you have any idea how you want your hair for the wedding?"

In place of any kind of bachelorette party, she suggested a mother-daughter bonding evening, involving doing each other's make-up and hair and eating ice cream while watching a romcom. I interpreted that as practice for her wedding hair and make up, but it was nice to spend some time with her.

"I was thinking I could just put it up in a ponytail." She swept her hair back and looked at herself this way and that in the mirror.

I didn't know who she was trying to kid, because she wasn't kidding me. My mother wouldn't leave the house with a hairdo so simple, much less get married like that.

"How about I try a couple of things?" I suggested.

She lowered her hands and let her hair tumble to her shoulders. "You always were better at doing my hair than I was, so have at it."

I started to braid her hair from the front, drawing in pieces from the sides.

"So what does Leo invest in?" I asked.

Her body stiffened just slightly. "All sorts of things."

"Like what?" She should know that giving me a vague answer would only pique my boundless curiosity.

"Like transport and logistics. Things like that." That was only slightly less vague.

"What does he transport?" I pressed. "Ice cream? Chocolate? Dead bodies?"

I said the last without thinking, but the moment I did, memories of that night crashed back into my brain, very much unwelcome and no less terrible than they were at the time.

I was so caught up in them, I almost missed my mother's awkward laugh.

"Dead bodies? You always did have a good imagination." There was something in her tone that put me on edge.

It's my imagination, I told myself. I was jumping at shadows because I was thinking about what I saw. This might be a good chance to tell my mother about it, but something stopped me from saying the words. I couldn't put my finger on what it was, but they were stuck in my throat.

I realised I'd stopped braiding. I had to check to see which side I needed to take hair from next before I kept going.

"Someone needs to transport dead bodies," I said. "As much as they need to transport ice cream and chocolate."

"I suppose so," she said. "That looks nice, but I'm not sure that's what I want."

It took me a moment to realise she was referring to her hair.

"Oh." I stopped mid-braid and started to tease the hair loose again. "What about a bun?"

"What about curls all over?" She swept her hands through the ends of her hair and lifted them up before dropping them again. "I have a curling iron in the drawer over there." She gestured with a wave of her fingers.

Curls would take ages, but it *was* for her wedding. I headed over to the drawer and pulled out the iron. I plugged it into the wall and waited for it to heat up.

"You never told me how you and Leo met." I held the iron near my hand and decided it was hot enough. I gripped a section of hair between my thumb and forefinger and fed it through before twisting the iron and waiting for the hair to curl around it.

"Didn't I?" She frowned at her reflection. "We met through mutual friends. More… business associates really. Reuben and Caleb Brantley. I was doing some work for them and Leo was doing some business with them. We had a few business meetings and then a few dates. The rest is history."

"Brantley? As in Zeke Brantley?" I slid the iron of her hair and let the newly formed curl bounce. Satisfied it looked good, I started on another section of hair.

"Is that their brother, the musician?" She turned her head to inspect the curl. She seemed to like what she saw.

"Musician? He's only the hottest rock star in the whole world." I rolled my eyes at myself for sounding like a fangirl.

"Good looks must run in the family then," Mum said. "For a while there I had dreams of setting you up with one of their two youngest brothers, Hunter or Parker. They're both a couple of years younger than you though."

"Yeah, hard pass on younger guys." I wrinkled my nose. Although, if they were half as hot as Zeke, they'd be a fun package deal for some girl someday. But not for me. Not to mention two and a half guys was enough. Five might be way too much.

"There's always Joshua," Mum said. "He's a few years older than you, but he's a very successful lawyer."

"Thank you, but I have my hands full, like you said." I finished another curl and started on another.

"I'm thinking ahead, in case it doesn't work out with those boys. It's always good for a girl to have her options open."

"Do you have your options open?" I asked teasingly.

She laughed. "Of course not. I have my one and only option, but I'm not twenty-one, with my whole life in front of me. You might decide you'd prefer to look around. Sow your wild oats, whatever that means."

"I think it has something to do with farming." In particular, ploughing, but I wasn't going to have that conversation with my mother.

"I didn't think it had to do with porridge," she said sarcastically. "Although, that's probably a euphemism for something."

"Everything is a euphemism or an innuendo if you think about it hard enough." I stepped back to inspect her hair. "How's that?" I'd only done one side so far, to see if she liked it. If she didn't, I'd try something else.

She turned her face to get a better look at my work. "That's perfect. If you can do it like that on Saturday, I might even look presentable."

"When have you ever looked anything other than presentable?" I stepped around to the other side and started to curl that.

"Never," she conceded. "But there's a first time for everything." She sighed and added, "I have to admit, I'm nervous. I know it's normal to feel that way before my wedding, I'm more jittery than usual. That was one reason I wanted to bring the wedding forward. If we waited months and months, my nerves would have gotten the better of me."

"I can't imagine anything getting the better of you, including your nerves," I said easily. Mum was the kind of person who pushed through and landed on her feet, no matter what was thrown at her, or what she went through.

"I'm good at hiding it," she said with a laugh. "Don't get me wrong, I'm excited. I can't wait to marry Leo. He's the most amazing, handsome, intelligent man I've ever met. I'm a lucky woman to have found him."

I scoffed. "He's lucky to have you. You're beautiful, smart and have the best daughter in the whole wide world." I grinned at her in the mirror.

She cocked her head, pulling against the iron slightly. "I didn't realise I had two daughters."

I laughed. "Do you really want to say that when I have a hot iron next to your head and your hair in my hand?"

"You would never hurt me," she said. "You're right, I do have the one, best daughter in the whole world. Those boys better do right by you. If they break your heart, they'll have me to deal with." Her eyes were steely. They always were when she was in full tiger mother mode. Since most of my life, it was just her and I, she had always been super protective of me. And I'd always been protective of her. Mum and Kennedy against the world. Just because Leo was in the picture now didn't mean we wouldn't look out for each other.

"If that doesn't make them shake in their boots, nothing will," I teased. I doubted those guys would be intimidated by Mum, unless Leo took her side. Things might get ugly then.

"Of course it will, I'm terrifying." She bared her teeth, but the effect was ruined when she smiled. "Okay, maybe not, but I know people who are." She looked surprised she said that out loud.

I decided a change of subject might be a good idea right about now. "I think your hair looks great like this. It's going to look perfect with your dress. Do you want my hair to look the same?" I was good at curling her hair, but I sucked hairy donkey balls at doing my own. Just like she struggled doing her own.

She looked both thoughtful and glad to be on a different topic. "I think having your hair up would suit your dress better. Don't you? I could braid your hair when you're done with mine and see how it looks. And then after that, ice cream and *Sleepless in Seattle*. Maybe some vodka."

I snapped my fingers. "I knew I forgot something." Before she looked too worried, I added, "I forgot to book the strippers." I watched the expression on her face as she went from slightly freaked out to realising I was joking.

The relief on her face was obvious.

She laughed. "Can you imagine Leo's face if strippers turned up here? Like he said, he's not into sharing. That includes me looking at half-naked men, and them grinding on me."

"Yeah, I see why he might be uncomfortable with that." The idea made my face heat. The last thing I wanted to see was some guy grinding onto my mother.

I pictured the guy's faces if they saw a stripper anywhere near me. They'd kick them straight out the door, if strippers even got in the door to start with.

Honestly, I'd feel the same way if the tables were turned. I didn't want the guys, including Ares, looking at other women dancing around and taking their clothes off. The idea gave me an irrational worm of jealousy in my stomach. It wasn't just about them looking, and maybe touching, but also about my lack of body confidence and confidence in general. I was fit enough and strong enough that my body should compete with a professional dancer, but when I looked in the mirror, I wondered what if. What if my breasts were bigger? What if I had fewer freckles? What if…

"You didn't forget the ice cream did you?" she asked.

Her words brought me back to the present.

"I'm not perfect, but I would never, ever forget the ice cream."

CHAPTER 24

KENNEDY

"Hey." Charlie stuck his head in the office door.

I glanced over my shoulder. "Hey. I'm almost finished updating the system. Give me a couple of minutes and I'll talk you through it."

"Okay, but I have coffee." He moved so I could see his hands, a takeaway cup in each. "Kind of a thank you for not firing me. Or letting what's his name fire me."

"You should have led with coffee," I teased. "Come on in." I took the coffee he handed me and shot him a grateful smile. The one I had sitting on the desk went cold about two hours ago. The milk was probably a bunch of hardening lumps. Not even my coffee addiction could deal with that.

He leaned against the doorframe and sipped in silence for a couple of minutes. "Can I ask you something?" he asked eventually.

"That depends on what it is." I sat back and waited for the changes to update. The Internet in Dusk Bay was so fast it should be illegal. Or better yet, rolled out to the rest of Australia.

Yeah, like that would happen. Either way, the update wouldn't take long.

"What do you see in a guy like those? They both look like they want to put a collar on you and keep you on a short leash."

I tried not to bristle, because at least to some extent he was right. Mannix was a control freak who'd control every aspect of my life if I let him. Ice was... He wasn't as bad but he was protective. Ares— I suspected he might be the worst of all, if we got together. I knew from his interactions with the other guys, he'd always give me hell. But he'd bring down hell on anyone who did anything *to* me. I already felt sorry for the imaginary perpetrators.

"They like to watch out for me," I said carefully. "They care about me. It's complicated, I guess. They want the best for me."

"I want the best for you too," Charlie said. "Especially now you're my boss." He didn't seem entirely happy about that.

I sighed. "If I say I want you to just think about me as Kennedy, would you? Just because my name is on a piece of paper doesn't mean I'm not another coach. And new here too. It would be nice if we could be friends."

"That depends if your boyfriends let us be friends." He looked at me intently.

"I get to decide who I'm friends with and who I'm not," I said firmly. "I'd like to be friends with you. I don't want you thinking of me as the boss, or as someone you can't come to when you have a problem, or if you think we could be doing something differently."

After a moment I added, "Do you think there are things we can do differently?" I had a sudden mental image of him pulling a giant scroll out of his back pocket and unrolling it, before reading a list of three thousand, two hundred and twenty-four suggestions. All of which would make perfect sense, but not be free.

"There's always room for improvement," he said. "New equipment. Cappuccino machine in the staff room..."

"We don't have a staff room," I pointed out. "Oh. That's your point, isn't it? That we need a staff room?" I pinched the bridge of my nose and thought about that for a moment.

There was nowhere in the old space for it, but if we considered the space next door, maybe we could steal a few metres, even if it was shared between the gymnastics and the workout gym.

"I'll see what I can fit into the plans, but a cappuccino machine is a must." What? I wasn't exaggerating *that* much.

I sipped my coffee and made a face. It wasn't that it tasted funny, exactly, but after the coffee at home, takeaway coffee was nowhere near as tasty.

Oh good, I really was becoming spoiled.

"That bad, huh?" he asked.

"It's fine," I said quickly. To show I meant it, I gulped down the rest of it and put the empty cup on the desk. "Thank you for the coffee." Even bad coffee was better than no coffee at all.

"Any time. Especially if we really get that cappuccino machine." After Mannix almost fired him, it was awkward enough already. Strained. If I wasn't careful, that would start to impact the business and the kids. Kids, especially, were good for noticing tension, and feeding off bad energy. This place was supposed to be fun. I wanted to keep it that way.

"Okay, let me walk you through this system." I waved at the screen and moved my chair over so we could both sit in front of it. He pulled over a chair and sat. His arm brushed mine. He jumped, moving the chair away quickly before he sat back down.

He gave me a look, but didn't say anything.

I cleared my throat and started to explain, although the new system was straightforward and a lot simpler than the old one. To me anyway.

"Does that make sense?" I asked when I finished.

I realised he'd been staring at me for the last couple of minutes. Had he heard anything I said?

I turned my face to look at him. "Did I lose you?"

He blinked. "Sorry, what? Oh. No, you make perfect sense. I mean, the system. You're right, that looks a lot easier than what Nicola had set up. Quicker too. I'd much rather spend time coaching than doing paperwork."

"I'd rather be coaching, practising or drinking cappuccino than doing paperwork," I agreed. "If we do well enough, I'll hire someone to do all of this. We can focus on the things that matter. Helping make kids better gymnasts and have fun."

"I'm a big fan of both of those things," Charlie said. His expression was unreadable. He might be more like Mannix than he'd like to know, or admit. I decided against telling him that. The situation was tense enough already.

"Anyway, that's it." I turned away quickly. "The first class should be here soon."

"Right." Clearly relieved, he stood and picked up both of our empty cups to throw them in the rubbish bin.

"Just so you know, construction next door will start next week," I said before he left the office. "They know not to work while we have a class, but there's going to be some disturbance. Apparently they need to break up part of the floor and put down new concrete. After that, it shouldn't take long."

No doubt the guys would turn up at least once a day to check on the progress. And to make sure none of the tradies working next door tried anything inappropriate with me. Like smiling. Or breathing the same air.

"Great," Charlie said. "Any chance I can expand my skills by giving classes in there too? I could use the extra hours."

"I don't see why not," I said. "Let's revisit that closer to opening." I didn't even know what skills or qualifications a person needed in order to teach things like spin classes, or circuits. Or aqua aerobics, if Ice got his way. I added that to the long list of things I needed to look up or think about when I got the chance.

"Okay, boss," he said, his expression grim.

I smiled wryly. "I did sound like the boss, didn't I?" I clapped a hand to my forehead. "It's happening already." I grinned past my hand.

Charlie almost smiled before he moved away from the door to welcome the kids into the gym.

I sighed. Was the guys' buying this place a gift or a curse? On one hand, it was amazing. On the other, it was a lot of work. At least, it would be until I could hire a manager to take over the administrative stuff. All of this could very easily overwhelm me. What the hell did I know about running a business anyway?

The guys were crazy for wanting to get rid of Charlie, I decided. The only way this place was staying afloat was if I had help from someone who understood the business. He could give me a list of things needed to be changed and every single one of them would be right.

I watched through the window as he greeted the kids with a smile and a high-five.

They all grinned, clearly happy to see him. There wasn't a single one who didn't adore him. Should I make him the manager? Would he even want that? He loved what he did, but if he needed the hours, running the place would give him that.

It was another thing I would have to revisit later. I wasn't going to ask the guys for more money, so I'd have to wait until the gym was making it for me. They might try to put a collar and a short leash on me, but I wouldn't let them. I was determined to do things my way, even if I fell on my face in the process.

I caught Charlie glancing at me and looked back towards my computer screen. I hoped like hell he'd lighten up, sooner rather than later, before it made working together difficult, or even impossible.

I turned off the computer and slipped out of my chair. I should be excited. My mother was getting married tomorrow and today was the first silks class I was teaching in the gym. I finally had that report finished and only had one exam to do before my semester was done. One more semester and I could graduate.

I *should* be excited, but the nightmares persisted, even when I slept beside one or two guys every night. Even when I woke with Mannix holding me, and Ice rubbing my back. Even when we fucked until I was exhausted.

I couldn't shake the feeling they were out there and they were getting close. More than that, I felt like I was missing something. Something important.

Something in the back of my mind I didn't want to think about, or acknowledge, because the truth might be more than I could handle. Even touching it with the corner of my mind, I recoiled from it.

There was no way. I couldn't even let myself think it, not even for a nanosecond. If I thought about it, I might put together pieces I didn't want to put together.

Denial isn't just a river in Egypt. It was a wide expanse of my brain.

I wished I could erase it entirely. I wished I could go back and do that night over again. I would have stayed inside the ballroom and suffered the stifling heat, press of bodies and smell of sweat. All of that was better than this. I could have lived my life in blissful ignorance of what happened to that man that night. He still would have died, but I wouldn't have seen it. I wouldn't have known.

I shuddered.

I forced a smile onto my face and stepped out of the office, closing the door behind me. I had to stop thinking about it, at least for a while. Focus on my class and enjoying myself.

The memory would come crashing back in soon enough.

CHAPTER 25

KENNEDY

"This is insanity," Ares commented. He leaned against the door frame, arms crossed.

He looked good in a suit. Too good. The earthy, leather and spice smell of him flooded my senses and heated my core.

"That's one name for it." My bridesmaid dress brushed the top of my feet. The neckline plunged down between my breasts, showing off a bunch of cleavage. The back was lace, decorated with tiny green flowers.

We stood back and watched as a team of chefs and other staff prepared food for the handful of guests. Every so often, someone would run in looking for something and run back out again.

"Do you think we should help?" I asked.

"Nope," he said simply. "It's more fun to watch. Besides, if you try to help you going to trip the fuck over that dress."

I glanced down. "Yeah, you're right, I would." Before he could say anything I quickly added, "That's the one and only time I'll ever admit you're right about anything."

"No, it won't be." He smirked at me.

I rolled my eyes.

"I'm going upstairs to make sure Mum is doing okay." I carefully picked up my skirt in both hands and stepped lightly up the stairs. I didn't need to look back to know Ares watched my ass the whole way up. I didn't give him the satisfaction of glancing back to check.

I reached the top of the stairs without tripping the fuck over my dress and headed over to the room where Mum was getting ready.

Before I could knock on the door, the one on the opposite side of the wide hallway opened. Ice stuck his head out.

"Hey, Beautiful, can you do Mannix a favour and grab his bowtie? He forgot to bring it in here." He made a playful face and shrugged. "It's in the top drawer in his walk-in wardrobe. He's currently in his underwear and doesn't want your mother to see him, or he'd get it himself."

"Of course," I said before Ice disappeared and shut the door behind him. Chaos might be a better word than insanity. It seemed like Ares and I were the only ones ready.

I shook my head to myself and hurried into Mannix's room.

Like all the other rooms here, his wardrobe was enormous. Almost as big as the bedroom itself. It was stuffed full of clothes and random items, like a snowboard, which leaned against the wall. What looked like the end of a snorkel stuck out from under a pile of dirty clothes. Or were they clean clothes he hadn't put away yet? Either way, I wasn't going to start tidying up after him.

There was only one set of drawers in the wardrobe. A stack of four long ones that stretched almost from one wall to the other. Any longer and the snowboard would fit inside it. If the drawer wasn't crammed full of stuff, that was. If the floor was any indication, there wouldn't be a spare centimetre, much less a metre and a half or so.

I stepped over to the drawers and opened the top one. Just as I suspected, it was jammed full.

"In the top drawer," I muttered to myself. Ice made it sound as though it should be easy to find. Instead, I was forced to rummage around for anything that looked like a bowtie.

I moved some superhero boxer shorts aside and froze.

A face looked back at me.

No, not a face.

A mask.

A red and black mask.

My mind skipped back to the first time I saw it.

Whatever he was going to say was cut off by the slice of the knife across his throat. He let out a gurgle. Light reflected off a gush of blood which poured from his open neck. His eyes opened wide and he sagged.

Shit.

I caught a glimpse of the mask he wore on his face. Black with splashes of red here and there. A black feather slanted from the top of either side of the mask, across his forehead. Simple, but menacing.

The denial I'd embraced so soundly, shattered. The reality came crashing into my brain. I don't know how long I'd known the truth. Maybe I'd known it all along.

The guys I'd fucked, and were falling for, and the guys I'd seen murder that man were the same people.

Hands trembling, I touched the mask. Maybe my hand would go right through it. Maybe this was some stress induced hallucination.

My fingers bumped against plastic covered with black fabric, red fabric and feathers.

It was real.

The nightmare had found me.

PREY

DARK MASQUE 2

CHAPTER 1

KENNEDY

I stood frozen, staring down at it.

The mask.

The mask.

It stared back at me. Taunted me. Dared me to touch it.

It was nothing more than a piece of plastic covered with black and red fabric, a black feather attached to it.

At the same time, it was so much more than that. This was the mask I saw in my nightmares.

In those, dark eyes peered out, watching me. Knowing what I knew. Searching for me in the darkness. The mask sat over a mouth that was now so familiar to me.

A mouth that had kissed me, licked me, and claimed me.

Mannix's mouth.

Now, the mask lay in a drawer, discarded, maybe forgotten. Did he know I'd find it here, or was that an accident?

They didn't know I saw them that night. Mannix, Ice and Ares. They killed a man while I hid in the bushes, watching. They knew someone saw them but one of them—I now realised it was Ice—let me go without seeing me.

It was his words I replayed in my head over and over.

"I could turn on my phone and find you," he said easily. "But where's the fun in that? The thrill of the chase is much more entertaining. Then when I catch you, I'll know I've earned my trophy."

I put a hand over my mouth.

I wanted to scream. I had to force down the urge.

I gave myself to him. Gave him my virginity.

Had he known who I was? How could he? I'd heard their voices and I hadn't known it was them when I met them.

Only, in the back of my mind, in a way I had. I'd recognised them the moment I saw them get out of the car on the day they supposedly arrived in Dusk Bay. I convinced myself that was really the first time they stepped foot in town after coming home from Brutham Academy. I couldn't prove it wasn't.

Until now.

I sucked in a breath and let it out through pursed lips. I needed to think critically. Calmly. This might not mean what I thought it meant. There had to be thousands of identical masks in Australia alone. They probably sold them in that dollar shop in the mall in Dusk Bay.

If you were going to murder someone, you'd wear something generic, popular. Wouldn't you?

That was rational, but I knew it wasn't true. I had absolutely no doubt in my mind Mannix was the one who cut that man's throat. Ice stabbed him in the eye and joked about writing a book on killing people. Ares held the man in place while they did it.

And me, I was the one who saw it all.

I'd fucked two killers. What would they do to me if they knew I was the one there that night?

I'd be fucked, in a whole different way. A much less pleasant way.

I glanced towards the door. I was supposed to be getting Mannix's bowtie out of the drawer. He was best man at the wedding of his father and my mother. Helen Knight was supposed to marry Leo Cassani in under an hour.

Leo. Did he know what his son was up to?

The chill already curling through me grew.

Mannix worked for Leo. If the killing was anything to do with business, then Leo did know.

And my mother met Leo through work. It explained everything and at the same time, it explained nothing. Why did they kill the man in the first place?

That, I realised, might be a question I'd never get an answer to. I couldn't let them know I saw them. I couldn't stay here either.

I found Mannix's bowtie and snatched it up before slamming the drawer shut.

I hurried over to the room where he and the other guys were getting dressed for the wedding. I barely touched the door to knock when it opened and Ice stuck his head out.

He was still the same, gorgeous, easy-going guy. His hair was tied back in a neat bun and he wore a perfectly tailored suit.

Any other time, I would have melted looking at him.

But now, all I could see was him with his mask on, stabbing that man in the eye. Him walking towards me in the dark, taunting me.

"Hey Beautiful, you found it?" The smile he gave me was warm, sensual. Like he wanted that one expression to wrap around me and keep me close.

It gave me shivers somewhere between fear and desire.

"Yeah." I held up the bowtie. His fingers brushed against mine as he reached for it.

The touch was barely more than the pressure of a butterfly wing, but it sent a flight of them through my stomach.

"It was right you said it would be." Right next to that mask. If this was a test, I couldn't let on what I found. The bowtie was long enough to fit around my throat. To be pulled tight to cut off my air.

It was suddenly incredibly difficult to breathe.

"You're the best, Beautiful." Ice leaned out further and pressed a lingering kiss to my lips.

Hopefully he'd put my trembling down to nerves over my mother's wedding, or my body's response to his touch. In spite of what I now knew, the kiss was enough to make me wet. A coil of need twisted inside me.

Treacherous body.

"I should let you go and take that to Mannix. I think I'm going to get some air."

Before I could leave he whispered, "I wish I could bury my face between your thighs, rather than getting all dressed up. We can save that for later." He winked and smiled before closing the door.

My body throbbing, I hurried to my room and pulled off my bridesmaid dress. I rolled it up and stuffed it into a draw, then changed into shorts and a t-shirt.

I thought about throwing a few things into a bag, but decided against it. I needed to get the hell out of here and I needed to go *now*.

I grabbed up my phone, card and what little cash I had in my purse and stuffed them into my pockets. I thought about taking my car keys, but dismissed it. A black Porsche Traycan would stand out like an elephant in a mob of roos.

Trying not to look like I was hurrying, I walked down the stairs and skirted around the busy kitchen. Everyone in there was getting ready for the wedding. If they saw me, they wouldn't think twice until later. But the fewer people that saw me, the better.

I slipped out a side door and headed for a small gate toward the back of the house. It was locked, but I knew the code. I keyed it in and hoped like hell it hadn't been changed since Leo told me what it was. For several heart stopping seconds, I waited for an alarm, for people to come running. Something.

Or worse, for the gate to stay stubbornly shut.

The lock clicked agreeably and I was able to push the gate open. Forcing myself to look ahead and not back over my shoulder, I slipped through and shut the gate behind me.

A track and steps directly in front of me led to the beach, but I went the other way, skirting around some massive rocks and stepping carefully along the cliff face.

I saw the drop, and the surf in the corner of my eye. Falling would suck. Landing on the rocks below would suck even harder. I probably wouldn't die, but I'd brake a few bones, and the guys would find me.

Broken bones might not be so bad compared to what they might do to me.

Don't panic, I told myself. *Just because everyone knew but you, isn't a good reason to freak out.* Okay, maybe it was, but I needed to save that for later. When I was away from here.

I made it around the edge safely and headed for the road.

The direct route would have been quicker, but opening the big iron gates wouldn't have gone unnoticed. Especially with everyone on edge after I was followed home from work the other night. The guys had increased security at the house, but now I wondered if it was to protect me or them. If they'd kill, then what else would they do? Killing seemed like a game to Ice. Like something he enjoyed doing. That was as twisted as fuck.

In the distance, someone shouted.

I startled and ducked behind a tree.

It wasn't much of a tree, just one trying to live its best life on the side of a cliff next to the ocean. It was all I had for now.

I waited, frozen in place. Crouched down as low as I could. My heart thundered harder than high tide smashed on the rocks during a storm. I couldn't stop a soft whimper from escaping my lips. Little mouse, Ice called me that night. I felt like one now. A tiny creature running, scared, waiting for the trap to snap around me at any moment. Hapless, helpless prey.

No one came running. No alarms sounded.

I managed to slow my pulse and racing mind. *Chill, Kennedy.*

Whatever or whoever they were shouting at or about, it probably had nothing to do with me. I doubted they even noticed I was gone yet.

Before I stood again, I pulled out my phone and shot off a text.

The answer was almost immediate.

I replied, then put my phone back and kept moving slowly. If I stood on my toes, I could see the road past the long grass. Grass that was tall, but not thick enough.

I trotted to a tree only slightly better than the last one. I grasped the lowest branch and pulled myself up. Sweat slid down my back. It coated my palms, making them slick. They slipped on the next bough, but I climbed higher, to where the leaves were thicker, the branches more solid. I chose one that didn't bend so violently under my weight.

A hand on the trunk, I crouched down and waited.

I didn't have to wait long. A small, faded red hatchback appeared around the bend. It slowed as it neared the gates. It slid past and came to a stop about a hundred metres from the driveway that led to the house.

I dropped out of the tree and landed with a soft thud on the leafy ground. My knees bent to absorb the impact, almost giving out and dumping me hard on my ass. The ground was no gymnastics mat.

I straightened and ran through the grass, hoping like hell I didn't step on a snake along the way. That wouldn't end well for either of us, especially if it was a brown snake or a death adder. Hard pass.

I reached the road and bolted to the car. I took one, quick look inside and wrenched open the passenger door. I threw myself in and dragged the door behind me.

Charlie pulled the car away from the side of the road. "You're as white as a sheet. Did something happen?"

"Kinda. Thanks for coming. I know you must have been busy but..." I didn't know who else to call. Everyone I cared about, or thought I cared about, was back at the house getting ready for the wedding.

"Your text sounded frantic," he said. "You look like you've seen a ghost. What did those guys do?" Of course he would assume it was them. They had a history of animosity towards him because we worked together. Mannix, in particular, was possessive, and hated the idea of anyone touching me. Which Charlie had, but only in his capacity as gymnastics coach. Mannix hadn't seen it that way.

"I... I'm not really sure." I wasn't ready to talk about it. How did you explain something like that? How did I explain not coming forward and telling the police? What if they killed someone else because I stood by and didn't say anything?

I could have a metric, if figurative, shit ton of blood on my hands.

I pinched the bridge of my nose. This was all so complicated and ugly, and terrifying. I shouldn't have dragged Charlie into this. As soon as we got to town, I'd figure something out. I'd go to the bank, take out all my money, and disappear.

What was Mum going to think? I skipped out on her wedding day. Of all the days.

Should I have stuck around until after that? I could have waited till everyone got drunk and slipped away. Should I ask Charlie to take me back?

Even if I tried, I couldn't get my mouth to say those words. The idea made my blood cold with fear.

I needed time to think and process everything. Around the guys, I was vulnerable, not only to them killing me, but to their touch. The way I felt when Ice kissed me was proof of that. I was scared as hell of him, but at this same time, I wanted to let him touch me and taste me all over. I wanted to feel him sink his cock into my body.

Maybe I was the one who was all kinds of fucked up.

"You don't have to tell me until you're ready," Charlie said. "I'll be the model employee and drive you wherever you need to go. Let's start with my place. You can get your thoughts together there."

I couldn't do anything but nod. Right now, I couldn't trust anyone, including myself. And I couldn't trust myself not to tell him everything. The last thing I wanted to do was to get him as involved in this as I was. If that happened, I wasn't sure he'd get out.

Hell, I wasn't sure if *I* could get out.

CHAPTER 2

KENNEDY

Charlie's place was a small townhouse on the other side of Dusk Bay.

"I was meeting up with a friend when you texted. That's why I got there so quick." There was no off-street parking, so he pulled up next to the curb.

"That was lucky," I said. My tone was flat, but I'd spent most of the drive here looking out the back window to see if anyone was following. If they were, they did a better job of it than the driver of the car that followed me home from work the other night. As far as I could tell, all I saw were people going about their daily lives. What the fuck did I know though? I wasn't trained to detect people following me if they didn't want to be detected.

Charlie gave me a long look, but I didn't meet his eyes. I couldn't.

With fake cheer, he killed the engine and said, "This is the place. It's not as nice as the place you came from, but it's a roof over my head."

He pushed his door open and got out.

I checked again before doing the same.

"It's nice," I said politely. It was nothing special, but it was somewhere to be while I got my thoughts back together. For that, I was as grateful as hell. He could have ignored my text altogether. The fact he didn't, showed he had some balls at least.

"Yeah." He looked back down the street too, before he unlocked the door and let us both in.

The worn out front door was a good indication of what the inside would look like. Tired carpet in the living room led to tired linoleum in the small kitchen. Apricot coloured Formica bench tops were the perfect complement to apricot and white tiles with diagonal stripes. The oven looked older than me.

"Look… Thank you for helping me out." I turned to face him. "I know you're no fan of the guys."

If he knew what they did, he might not have helped me at all. If they figured out he helped me, that could put his life at risk. I'd have to figure things out quickly and be gone before that happened. I'd never forgive myself if I had Charlie's blood on my hands. Or anyone else's, for that matter.

"Anything for my boss," he said lightly. "Sit down, I'll make us both a coffee. Apologies in advance for it not being anything fancy." He flashed me a smile and stepped into the kitchen.

"It's okay." I stepped over to the couch which sat under the window, facing a small TV. I perched on the brown cushions and propped my arm on the armrest. It was covered with the same brown fabric, a hint of formerly shiny metal peeking out through a tear near the backrest. Pea green blinds rattled against the window when I sat.

The whole place was a testament to the truth in the belief that if you hang on to something for long enough, it would come back in style. Everything here screamed late-1970s. Some of it was probably worth a small fortune to antique collectors.

My mother would have hated it.

"I'll take any coffee right now." I'd settle for hot chocolate or tea right now too. Although, I could really use a double shot of something a hell of a lot stronger.

He filled up the electric kettle, set it down on the base and flicked it on. He turned and leaned his back against the bench.

"Are you ready to talk about what happened? Did they hurt you?"

"No," I said quickly. "They didn't do anything to me. It's—" I sighed out my nose. "It's complicated."

He looked like he really wished I'd give him more than that, but I couldn't.

What would I say? The guys aren't who I thought they were? We both knew that wouldn't fly. Not really. Apart from the bit about killing people, the guys didn't hold much back. Mannix was every bit as controlling and possessive as he displayed in front of Charlie.

I could honestly not say I was oblivious. I hadn't wanted to believe it. I wasn't ready to admit that, any more than I wanted to admit to liking how Mannix was.

There was something surprisingly hot about a man who knew exactly what he wanted and didn't hold back in telling people that. There was also something very hot about being wanted in the first place. I was used to being the nerdy girl in the corner who no one paid any notice to. To go from that to getting attention from three guys who basically looked like gods was heady.

No wonder I ignored my own instincts.

"It's always going to be complicated with people like them," Charlie said. "People like us are better off staying away from people like them."

It was easy to say, but doing it…

The kettle whistled and clicked off. He turned away to pour water into two cups. He added milk and sugar, just the way I liked it.

"Thanks." I took the cup he handed me and held it for a while to let it cool. I might have a masochistic streak that included liking controlling men and assholes, but I didn't want to burn my mouth.

He nodded and went to get his own coffee. "Isn't your mother getting married today?"

That was the most conflicting part about all of this.

"Yes, but she doesn't need me there." If she knew everything, like I was certain she did, then I didn't wouldn't feel bad about missing her big day. She could have told me.

Better yet, she could have insisted I stay in Sydney. Far away from Dusk Bay and all the darkness and violence. I had a feeling I hadn't even scratched the surface of what went on here.

"Do you know Reuben Brantley? Or Caleb Brantley?" I blew softly on the surface of my coffee.

"I know *of* them," Charlie said carefully. "If the rumours are true, they're up to their eyeballs in some shady shit."

That was what I was worried about.

"What kind of shady shit?"

"I dunno," he admitted. "Illegal stuff. Stuff I don't want to know about, because it would shorten my life expectancy. Why? Do you think those guys are involved with them?"

"Maybe." And by that I meant it seemed highly likely. His confirmation also shone a light on my mother and Leo. Men like the Brantleys usually dealt in legal stuff too, to cover their tracks and look legit. For all I knew, Mum was only involved in that.

I remembered what Mannix said about Daisy Lasalle and her boyfriends being friends with the Brantley family. Did that mean they were also into shady shit?

Wait, did that also mean Zeke Brantley, lead singer of my favourite band, Wolf Venom, was also into shady shit? And the drummer, Asher. He was Ric DiMarco's cousin. If Daze and Ric were into shady shit, then Asher might be too. Hell, the whole band might.

Or maybe I was putting sixty-nine and sixty-nine together and getting six hundred and sixty-six. Just because they were related, didn't mean they shared the same interests, much less crimes. I was my mother's daughter and I'd never even had a speeding ticket.

My head spun so hard it hurt. All I was doing right now was jumping to conclusions. What did I do about that though? Should I go back, sit down with my mother and ask her for the truth? Would she give it to me? Would the guys let me leave again if I stepped foot back inside the gates?

Would they let me live, now I knew what I knew? A cold shiver of fear passed right through me. They hadn't given the man they killed any mercy. They wouldn't give me any if they decided I had to die.

My cup shook and I realised I was trembling. I managed to push the fear aside just enough to still my hands. That was all. I was half a thought away from full-blown terror. I should probably get some hair colour, dye my hair, and then get the hell out of Dusk Bay.

I realised my coffee was cool enough to drink and took a sip. I managed not to make a face at the taste. Go me. Since he'd gone out of his way to pick me up, the least I could do was not insult his coffee.

"What are you going to do about the gym?" Charlie asked. "If you're worried about them being into the wrong things, then them buying the gym might be suspect."

There was no, 'might be,' about it. Although the gym was probably one of those legal businesses they liked to have to cover their tracks. If it wasn't, did that mean I was some sort of accessory to something? In situations like these, often ignorance was no excuse. Especially if the guys had the resources to make it look like I was in deeper than I was.

Fuck in a plastic bucket.

On a scale of one to one hundred, how fucked was I? Any hint of suspicion could destroy any chance I ever had of running my own cybersecurity business. Or getting any kind of job working in my field. Or even one making coffee in a small café.

I pinched the bridge of my nose. "I don't know. It's probably the first place they'll look for me. Once they don't find me there…" It might not be safe for Charlie to go back to work, but what else would he do?

"I'll try to figure it out so you can keep it running," I said finally. It wasn't much, but it was all I could do right now. Vague promises were all I could manage.

"I'm sure everything will work out," he said with more certainty than I had. "Even if they are assholes, they won't want to disappoint the kids."

"I'm sure." I wasn't sure. Not at all.

I didn't think the kids were the guys' reason for buying the gym, or even in their top one hundred of their priorities. If they found out Charlie helped me, they may just as easily blow the entire gym up. That would be an enormous waste of money, but I doubted they'd feel it, in the scheme of things.

"I'm sorry I dragged you into all of this." I regretted the day I stepped foot in the gym and met him. If I hadn't, he and Nicola could have gone on living their lives, never knowing I existed. Charlie should have been the last person I texted to help me out. This could all end so badly for him. For us both.

"I don't mind," he said. "I like you. If it wasn't for those guys, I would have asked you out."

I sighed again, deeper than before. "If it wasn't for them, I might have gone." I didn't think I'd ever have seen Charlie as more than a friend, but a date didn't hurt to find out.

"Of course you would, I'm awesome." He grinned.

His attempt to lighten the mood fell flat. All I could rustle up was a faint half-smile.

"Yeah, you are. You're a nice guy."

He winced. "Nice. You know what they say about nice guys."

"They say they always finish last, but isn't that what a gentleman does anyway?" I asked, joking weakly.

He snapped his fingers.

"That's right. Finishing last is a good thing." He gave me a lopsided grin like he had it all worked out.

I hoped I hadn't encouraged him too much by bringing sex into the conversation. I didn't want him thinking there was any chance of something happening between us.

If I thought about anything intimate, my mind immediately went to Mannix and Ice. Ice in particular, since he was my first. He'd always have a special place in my mind, if not in my life. Both of them, and Ares, changed me. I wasn't sure if that was a good thing.

I thought Charlie might say more or even invite me to find out what it would be like to sleep with him. Thankfully, he didn't. He must have known I'd refuse. I was in no state to fuck, even if I'd do it with him. Basic functions were difficult enough just now.

Instead, he put his empty cup in the kitchen and stepped over to take mine. He set it beside his and came to crouch down in front of me.

"I know you must have had a long day," he said softly. "You're asking yourself all kinds of questions." His eyes searched mine, his gaze laced with genuine, platonic concern. He was a better friend than I deserved right now.

"I hope you get the answers."

Before I realised what he was doing, he grabbed my hand and snapped something over my wrist.

CHAPTER 3

KENNEDY

What the fuck?

"What the fuck?" I tried to lift my arm, but couldn't. My wrist was handcuffed to the arm of the chair. I tugged against it, but it was locked fast, the chain strong. It was in better condition than anything else in the place. Of course it fucking was.

I hadn't noticed the cuff before. It must have been hidden behind the couch cushions. To be honest, I wasn't looking for anything like that. Not from Charlie. I should have known better than to trust anyone. My track record was zero. To think I'd just finished thinking he was a good guy. A good friend. He was a motherfucker, like the rest of them.

Ugh, Kennedy, you shouldn't be allowed out unsupervised. Look where it gets you.

Angry, that was where it got me. Blazing furious.

I jerked my arm up hard and fast. If I couldn't break the cuffs, maybe I could break the arm of the chair. It didn't budge. Evidently, it was stronger than it looked. There was absolutely no give in it at all.

"You asshole." I kicked out at Charlie. "If you think I'm going to—" I wasn't going to let him touch me. Being restrained didn't mean he could do a damn thing to me. If he so much as took a step closer, I'd kick him in the nuts.

Okay, being angry gave me bravado. The fact was, I was restrained and he was a lot bigger than me. If he wanted to hold me down, he could do it with one hand. I could fight, I *would* fight, but it wasn't a fight I could hope to win.

Don't panic, I told myself. *Whatever you do, don't freak out. That's what guys like him want.*

Icy fingers of fear slid up my spine. An hour ago, I thought dying was the worst thing that could happen to me. Now…

Tears spiked the corners of my eyes.

"I'm not gonna touch you," he said.

Yeah, like I'd buy that. Asshole.

He stepped back and pulled out his phone. He tapped the screen and put it to his ear. After a couple of moments he said, "She's right here. She came straight to me like you said she would."

I blinked away hot tears and stared. What the—

Who the hell was he talking to?

"Don't worry, she's not going anywhere. Yep, I'll see you soon." He slipped his phone back into his pocket.

"What did you do?" I hissed.

"I covered my own ass," he said with an absolute lack of apology. "The minute they realised you were missing, Mannix knew where you'd go. He told me to keep you safe and let him know where you were." He scratched the back of his neck and shrugged. "If I told you sooner, you would have run."

As if that justified any of that. I was right back to dying being the worst thing that might happen to me. The fact he didn't plan to rape me was a small mercy, I supposed. Very small in the scheme of things. I bet his cock was just as small.

Yeah, it was a petty thought, but whatever right now. I was still pissed and scared.

I gritted my teeth and pulled at the handcuff again. "Of course I would have run," I growled. "Do you have any idea what they're capable of?"

"Probably more than you." He sat down in an armchair opposite the couch, but kept his eyes on me. "After I spotted you on the uneven bars, your dear Mannix paid me a visit. He told me if I touched you again, I'd die choking on my own balls. He wasn't joking."

His mouth twisted to the side. "After you stopped him from firing me, he dropped in again. Him and that Ice guy. He told me he didn't like the way I looked at you, and the way you were nice to me. He said the only reason he was letting me live was because you wanted me to work at the gym."

"And yet, you were quick enough to call him and tell him where I was." I gave up trying to break the armrest, but stayed on alert. What the fuck I'd do was another thing, but I wasn't going to let anyone take me by surprise again.

"You said it yourself, the first place they'd look is at the gym. The second place would be here. How long did you think it would be before they turned up? And how long after that would I still be breathing? What choice did I have?" He almost sounded reasonable.

"You could have ignored my text." I gritted my teeth in frustration. "They would have come looking, but they wouldn't have found me if I wasn't here."

"They would have killed me anyway, to keep me from helping you in the future. The moment you texted me, you dragged me right into the middle of this shit storm. At least this way, I have them grateful to me. That might work in my favour someday."

"You're so fired." I was half tempted to stand up and drag the couch over to him so I could kick the crap out of him. I should have sat in an armchair. They had the same armrests, but I could have picked it up and high-fived him in the face with it.

What was I thinking? I wasn't usually given to violence. Then again, I wasn't usually running from killers either.

Charlie shrugged. "I'd rather be fired than dead. Maybe Mannix will give me a job. Or his father."

"They can give you the perfect job of having your head decorate one of the spikes beside the gate," I said with extra added vindictiveness. "You could serve as a warning to their enemies."

"No wonder you were drawn to those guys." Charlie looked down his nose at me. "You're as bloodthirsty as they are."

"You have no idea," I said softly.

I took several slow breaths to compose myself, then said, "I saw them kill a man. They didn't know I was watching. I didn't even realise it was them until a couple of hours ago. It was dark and their faces were covered. It was…" I shuddered.

"Probably not their first or their last," Charlie finished for me. "That was why you ran? You figured you might be next if they knew?"

"I probably will be, which is why you need to let me go." I tugged at the handcuff again. "Please, before they get here. We could get out of here together."

"And go where?" He almost seemed to be considering it.

"Anywhere," I said. "We have to get out of Dusk Bay first. Unlock this thing and we can go."

Charlie pressed his finger to his top lip and appeared to be thinking. When he lowered his hand, he said, "If I unlock that, what guarantee do I have that you won't cut and run? I'm dead if you leave me behind."

I won't lie, I was thinking exactly that. Maybe kick him in the balls and the way past, but then grab his car keys and bolt.

"I won't," I said, trying to sound as convincing as I could. "We're wasting time. We need to leave now." How much time did we have before the guys turned up? It couldn't be much longer, especially the way Mannix drove.

He shook his head slowly. "No. I think my best bet is to leave you right where you are until those guys arrive. They can decide what to do with you."

I gave him a dark look. Hopefully I conveyed all my loathing to him. I'd hate for him to miss out on knowing how much I thought he sucked right now. Asshole.

"I was wrong, you're not a nice guy. You're a self-serving son of a bitch. I'm not sure I'd even try to stop Mannix or the other guys if they wanted to kill you." Right now, I could happily stand by and cheer.

"If that's supposed to change my mind, it hasn't," Charlie said. He frowned at me. He seemed to be considering something.

"What?" He was giving me the creeps.

"I was just thinking if putting duct tape over your mouth to shut you up would constitute touching you, or if they'd understand." He eyed my mouth speculatively.

I bristled. Being handcuffed was bad enough, I didn't want to be gagged as well. Especially with something as sticky as duct tape. I wasn't due for a waxing, especially on my face.

"It would definitely require touching me," I assured him. I'd scream my head off, but if anyone came running to help me, they'd be sucked into this insanity as well. I didn't want any more blood on my hands. Especially from someone who was actually innocent. If there were such people in this city.

"You didn't look that surprised when I told you about what I saw." Slightly disturbed, but not surprised.

"Dusk Bay is..." He searched for the right words. "Shady shit central. People like Caleb Brantley run the place and him and his family are the worst. If it's illegal, they're doing it. Lots of it. Running guns, extortion, smuggling diamonds, prostitution, human trafficking. And that's just what I can think of, off the top of my head. Everyone in town either knows about it and turns a blind eye, or is involved in it. So when I said they weren't joking about killing me, I meant exactly that. They wouldn't bat an eye. In fact, I wouldn't be surprised if the newly poured concrete in the gym contained the remains of someone."

"And how do you know all of this?" I wasn't even sure I believed half of what he said.

And yet, there was obviously at least several grains of truth in it. Criminals running around a city, getting way with everything from murder to blackmail to fuck knows what else, was nothing new. Why wouldn't it happen here, in Dusk Bay?

He shrugged one shoulder. "I was born and raised here. I went to school with guys like Mannix Cassani, Ice Miller and Ares Turner. I did my best to try to stay out of trouble, but it was inevitable trouble would find me. And it did the moment you walked through the door. But maybe it's not a bad thing. Being a gymnastics coach doesn't pay very well, and honestly, I'm sick of teaching those little shits."

I was starting to feel like an even worse judge of character right about now. Where he was concerned in particular. He'd done a better job of fooling me and hiding the real him from me than Mannix, Ice and Ares put together.

Where they were concerned, I knew there was some capacity for violence, even if I hadn't admitted that fact to myself.

Charlie, he was an asshole, hiding behind the façade of a nice, gentle guy. Judging by the way he was looking at me, if he didn't know the guys would kill him, he'd try something with me. He could have slipped something into my coffee. He could use his bigger size and weight to try to pin me down. Something. If it wasn't for the threat of death, he wouldn't have held back.

The coffee curdled in my stomach and threatened to come back up. In spite of everything, I felt safer with the other guys than I did with this one. They might kill me, but they wouldn't force themselves on me.

Yeah, that wasn't a whole lot of consolation.

"Maybe they'll give you a job as hired muscle," I said. "How do you feel about beating the snot out of people?"

He stiffened slightly. "Whatever it takes. I'm ready to get out of this shit hole." He gestured around him with one hand.

Okay, I got that. This place was tired, dark and depressing. Only one wall was painted white. The others were exposed, dark brown brick. Every one of them sucked in the light and gave back depression in return. The dark carpet was no better. The whole effect was unloved, dated and miserable.

"You live here alone?" The place was big for one person.

He visibly debated whether or not to answer that question. Finally, he nodded. "I have a sister. She's at a friend's house. You didn't think I'd let her stick around with this going on, did you? The moment you texted me, I sent her off to play."

"What would she think of this?" I jerked my head toward the handcuff. "Most people don't keep a handcuff attached to the couch." The bed, yes, but not the couch. Not that I would knock anyone's kink. If this was what got him off, then whatever. As long as he didn't expect me to take part, then I didn't care.

"She knows I'll do anything to take care of her," he said earnestly. "I made that promise to her after our parents died. They wanted to send her to live with our aunt. I had to work my ass off to make sure that didn't happen. We belong together."

This, right here, was the real Charlie. Maybe not the nice guy he made himself out to be, but not a monster either. Just a desperate big brother who wanted to keep his family together when the system wanted to tear them apart. He still sucked.

"Is that what happens to her if you die?" I asked. "She gets sent off to your aunt?"

"She gets sent off to Brisbane. A long way from everything and everyone she knows. She's only eleven. She deserves better than that."

If Dusk Bay was as bad as he said it was, he might be better off to grab his sister and take off to Brisbane, but obviously that wasn't my call. No doubt he would have done that if he thought that was the answer. For some reason, he didn't.

That wasn't really my problem. Any temptation I had to ask was cut off at the knees by a brisk knock on the door.

"Open the fuck up."

CHAPTER 4

ICE

Say whatever the fuck you want about me, but never say the Iceman was born yesterday.

I asked Kennedy if she could get Mannix's bowtie for him, because he was a hot mess running around in his underwear, trying to help his father. We've all seen him naked, including most of the staff. He's fucked half of them. For some reason he felt uncomfortable with the idea of Kennedy's mother seeing him in his boxer shorts. Maybe if he didn't wear ones with action heroes on them, he wouldn't feel like he had anything to be embarrassed about.

Whatever though. Me, I preferred to go commando.

Anyway, so I asked her to get that tie, and she was happy to do it, although I was ninety-nine percent sure she'd rather sneak away somewhere with me. Yeah, me too, Beautiful, me too.

When she got back with the tie, her face was white. More so than usual. She looked rattled. Scared even.

I'd like to think she found some of Mannix's old underwear that he hadn't thrown away. Or a pair of used panties from an old girlfriend. Who knows what Mannix keeps in his drawers? For all I know, he had a collection of cocks from his enemies.

I got the impression it wasn't any of those things. Whatever she saw had her spooked.

After I gave Mannix his tie, I waited a few minutes and went to her room.

The door was open, but she wasn't in there. Rationally, I knew she was probably helping her mother.

Not wanting to disturb them and blessed, or cursed, with boundless curiosity, I stepped over to her walk-in wardrobe and took a peek in her top drawer.

I picked up a pair of black, lacy panties and took note of the size. A good boyfriend always knows his girlfriend's underwear size, so he can buy her all the pretty things and get them right. Right?

Stashed in a corner of the drawer, was a small bottle of perfume. I pulled it out and popped off the lid. I raised it to my nose and inhaled the soft, floral scent. It wasn't Kennedy's usual one, but it was nice enough. Perfume always smelled better on a person than it did in the bottle.

I decided she wouldn't miss it, so I put the lid back on before sliding the bottle into my pocket. I did the same with a pair of white, floral panties. Just in case I forgot her size.

That would be lame, wouldn't it?

I turned around and that was when I noticed a puddle of green in the corner. Her bridesmaid dress. From the look of it, she'd taken it off in a hurry and stuffed it down where she thought no one would see. And no one would have if I wasn't sniffing around her stuff.

I picked it up and smelled it. Definitely a different perfume from the one in the bottle in my pocket.

I shook out the dress and placed it up on a hanger. Kennedy wouldn't want it wrinkled. She must have been in a hurry or she would have thought of that. She wasn't the messy type by nature, as far as I could tell. Her room was always neat, with everything put away in its right place.

I organised her hangers so there was a precise finger space between each one. I used my little finger, because if she wanted to keep everything hanging as tidily as this, she'd have to use her own finger. My little finger might be bigger than any of hers, but it was close enough. I was nothing if not thoughtful.

Once it was done, I stepped back to take a look and nod. Much better.

I thought about taking everything out of her drawers and rearranging them, but figured I'd leave that until she got back. In case she preferred it a different way.

I strolled back over to the room where the other guys were getting changed and stepped inside.

I jerked my head to the side to indicate to Mannix and Ares that I wanted to talk to them. Mannix managed to be wearing suit pants, shoes and his white button down shirt.

Judging by the bulge in his pants pocket, he was leaving his bowtie until the last minute. Or he was happy to see me.

Sadly, since his cock wasn't as slanted as mine, it must be the tie.

Relatable. I hated the things too, even though we looked pretty fucking hot dressed up all fancy. Mannix in particular.

Although, let's be real here, he looks smoking hot in anything. Or nothing.

I once tried to figure out who was hotter between him, Kennedy and Ares. They all did it for me, although I suspected it would only ever be one way with Ares. His loss.

Ares and Mannix both gave me a funny look, but followed me over to the side of the room.

"Kennedy seems to be gone," I said casually.

Mannix was the first to stop staring and speak. "What the fuck? Gone where? Why?"

"My guess is that she saw something she didn't like," I said. "As to where she went—"

My words were interrupted by the sound of Mannix's phone ringing.

He scowled, but snatched it up from the table and put it to his ear.

"What the fuck did you do?"

Apparently that was the new version of 'hello.' People worried about the handwritten letter becoming a lost art form, but maybe they should be concerned about people not knowing how to answer the phone and talk on it. Young people these days.

"Wild guess, that's not Kennedy," Ares remarked.

I snorted softly. That sounded about right. Mannix might have growled at her like that, but he would have called her Princess. He could be sweet when he wanted to.

"Where is she?" Mannix demanded. He shut up long enough to let whoever was on the other end of the line speak.

It sounded like that Charlie guy from the gym. No wonder Mannix was pissed. He'd be lucky not to have his cock added to the cock collection. If that was such a thing.

Honestly, I could picture it now. I could get one of those shadowbox things and hang it on the wall in my workroom. I could pin and label each cock. Of course, I'd have to leave a space or two to imply I was ready to add more to the collection at a moment's notice. I bet that would make people talk much more quickly.

On the other hand, that would spoil my fun. I put that on my mental *maybe* list. I'd revisit it later.

"Take her there and keep her there," Mannix was saying. "We'll be right there. You know what will happen to you if you touch her." He hung up without waiting for a reply.

If that wasn't confirmation speaking on the phone was a dying art form, I didn't know what was.

"That was that Charlie prick. Kennedy texted him. He's going to pick her up and take her to his place. We're going there to get her. *Now.*"

Leo stepped out of the bathroom in time to hear that last sentence. He adjusted the sleeves of his tuxedo and asked, "Is everything all right?"

"It will be," Mannix said curtly. "We won't be long. Helen probably isn't ready yet anyway."

If Leo was tempted to tell us we couldn't go, Mannix marched out the door before he could.

I glanced at Leo and shrugged before I followed Mannix.

Ares was a few steps behind me, moving with an aura of reluctance. He was still in his, 'pretending to hate Kennedy,' mode. I had no idea who he thought he was fooling. He didn't fool me for a minute. Like I said, the Iceman wasn't born yesterday. Not even the day before that.

We didn't question Mannix when he stomped over to his car and slipped into the driver's seat. There was no point arguing with him most of the time, but not when he was in the mood he was in right now. He was like a hibernating bear who got woken up in the middle of a good dream. Try to get in the way and you may get a claw in your face.

While I didn't mind a few good scratch marks, and some pain, we didn't have time for that right now. Later though, I was there for it.

Ares climbed into the front passenger seat like he was taking the job of shotgun seriously.

I suspected he liked to pretend he was actually the god of war, but drive-by shootings weren't our style. They were messy, tacky and impersonal. If we went after someone, we wanted them to see us.

Seeing the fear in people's eyes and smelling it on them was almost as arousing as Kennedy. In spite of what the guys thought, I didn't kill my pet rabbit, Mr Flopsy, but I'd killed lots of other things just to see what would happen, and because I enjoyed the way it felt.

People were the most satisfying. Animals had no idea why you were doing it. Humans always did.

For the record, I've never killed a dog. Or a cat. I might be slightly unhinged, but I'm not a monster.

Mannix all but flew his black SUV through the big iron gates and along the streets of Dusk Bay.

I sat sideways across the back seat and enjoyed the ride. His driving was the closest thing to a rollercoaster I could get without going on an actual roller coaster. If he got pulled up and booked as often as regular people, he would have lost his license several times over by now. Typical young male driver.

It was the adrenaline rush I needed right now. The idea that he might lose control at any moment and smash the car into a tree, killing us all. It had yet to happen, obviously, but that didn't lessen the fun.

I leaned my head against the back of the seat and wondered if Mannix would let me pull out Charlie's toenails, one by one. I didn't need his permission, but there was some kind of chain of command when it came to work stuff. Sometimes I didn't listen. Usually I did. In our line of work and lifestyle, not listening tended to shorten our life expectancy.

If Leo ordered Mannix to kill me, he'd have to. I might even let him, as long as he made it interesting.

Better not to let it get to that point though. Death was a bit too permanent for my liking.

"What the hell did you say to her to make her run off?" Mannix asked over his shoulder.

"I asked her to get your bowtie for you," I said. "If I had a clue the experience would be so traumatic, I wouldn't have asked."

Mannix grunted.

"We've all seen Mannix's room," Ares said. "If it doesn't scare people off, nowhere will."

"Fuck off," Mannix growled. "You want to walk the rest of the way to town?"

"No, but it would be safer than your driving," Ares said. "We both know we don't have time to stop and drop me off," he added before Mannix could slow down.

Mannix muttered something about investing in ejector seats, and took a corner so fast I'd almost swear the right-hand tires left the road.

I grinned. "Do we have time to go around and do that again?"

For some reason, Mannix ignored me. I guessed he wasn't having as much fun as I was. Shame.

We finally pulled up in front of an address in a less affluent part of the city. I knew I didn't imagine the stiffening of Ares' back. He never liked this part of Dusk Bay, for some reason.

Me, I liked it. It was gritty and real. The people here were regular people. A lot of them worked for us. Those who didn't usually had a fair idea of who we were and why it was a good idea to give us a wide berth. Once in a while they'd give us trouble and try to upset the status quo, but it never lasted very long. A few deaths here and there took care of that.

Good times.

Ares and I walked a couple of steps behind Mannix as he strode up to Charlie's front door. We probably looked like the mafia boss and his underlings that Mannix aspired to be. Would be some day, when Leo handed over the reins. This was good practice for when that happened.

Mannix hammered on the door so hard I was surprised he didn't knock it in.

"Open the fuck up."

CHAPTER 5

KENNEDY

I gave Charlie a last pleading look, which he ignored.

Half an eye on me, he hurried to the door, unlocked and opened it.

Mannix shoved past him and strode inside. He looked way too good in his tuxedo pants and white button down. The fabric was taut over his broad chest and shoulders. His pants were a snug fit, defining the muscles in his thighs.

Ice followed him in, no less panty-melting in his full suit. His shirt was dark grey, but the rest of his outfit was black. He looked mysterious and sleek, in a terrifying kind of way.

Ares followed the others in like an afterthought. He also wore a suit, but his was grey and he wasn't wearing a tie. He looked like he'd come straight from the pages of a magazine. They all did.

While Mannix stopped to give Charlie a dark look, Ice slid past him and came to sit down beside me.

He eyed the handcuff and gave me a knowing smile.

"Well this is interesting."

It shouldn't surprise me his thoughts would immediately be sexual. He was a guy, after all.

My insides might have been trembling, but I managed to raise my chin and stare him down.

"We're not going to hurt you," he said as though he saw right through the brave façade. "No matter what happens, that's the last thing any of us wants."

I held his gaze as long as I could, but I was the first to blink and look away.

Ice placed his knuckle under my chin and turned my face back towards him.

"Hey, Beautiful," he said softly. "It's okay, I promise."

I swallowed, but managed to look him right in his face. I didn't know how, but I got the feeling he knew exactly why I ran. If he did, how could he promise not to hurt me?

"I don't know what the fuck is going on," Mannix started. "But we're going home. Now." He gestured for Charlie to give him the key to the handcuffs. "We're going to watch our parents get married and then we'll sort this out." His tone left no room for argument.

Charlie walked over to the kitchen and took the key out of the drawer. He handed it to Mannix who tossed it to Ice. Ice caught it with one hand and crouched down to unlock the handcuff from the couch.

I started to jerk my wrist away and stand, but before I could, Ice snapped the cuff around his own wrist.

I dropped back down with a plop.

Fuck.

"I've always wanted to know how it felt to be handcuffed to someone." Ice smiled like he was playing some kind of fun game and not a terrifying one of cat and mouse. I was a tiny mouse and they were the three, hungry lions.

He slipped the key into his pocket and stood, pulling me to my feet in the process.

"This could be fun, don't you think?" He grinned.

"Not as much fun as it would be if you took this off." I raised my hand and looked pointedly at the handcuff.

His mouth curled up further. He leaned in and said, "I'll happily take everything off you but that."

"I can't go to my mother's wedding handcuffed to you, or anyone else," I pointed out.

He looked thoughtful. "It is more of a bachelor party thing, but we'll make it work. Don't worry. It'll be fun."

"Let's go," Mannix said. He nodded at Ares to step out the door first and moved around so he was behind us.

I felt like I was being marched to my execution.

I gave Charlie a dirty look before I reluctantly walked outside. It did nothing to make me feel better. He was still fired. Unless the guys let him manage the place after they did away with me. In spite of Ice's assurances, I couldn't see how this would end any other way. I was a witness to a crime they committed, how could they possibly let me live, even if they gave a shit about me like they claimed to?

Ice opened the back door to the SUV and gave a sweeping gesture for me to climb in first. He followed close behind, his arm outstretched so the chain of the handcuffs was never taut.

"Can you get your seatbelt on?" He genuinely looked concerned for my safety. Maybe he didn't want me ruining his fun later.

"I can manage," I said quickly. I grabbed it and clicked it into place.

Ice did the same with his and said, "Are you comfortable, Beautiful? You look as though you think I'm about to eat you whole."

"Aren't you?" I asked.

He placed a hand on my knee. "If you want me to. I've never gone down on someone in the back of a car while handcuffed to them. I'm guessing you haven't either."

I snorted softly and moved over, away from him. As far as I could get with the fucking handcuff on anyway.

"I'll take that as a no." But his smile faded. The look he gave me all but confirmed I was right. He knew what I saw that night. The congenial, friendly Ice was one of the masks he showed the world. Underneath that was a stone cold killer. A man who took pleasure at sticking a knife in another man's eye, then joking about it.

I swallowed hard.

"I didn't mean to—" I wasn't even sure what I was going to say, but he cut it off with a shake of his head.

"When we get back. We'll talk and you'll understand." It didn't sound like he was giving me any choice. Of course he wasn't. He could have unlocked my handcuff and asked me if I wanted to come back with them, but he didn't. Instead, I was restrained like an animal. Or a criminal.

The irony wasn't lost on me.

My mouth moved but no coherent sound came out. I knew the expression on my face clearly said I understood what he was referring to.

Every now and then, Mannix would look back over his shoulder, but he didn't say anything. Neither he nor Ares seemed to have a clue what was going on.

Mannix had gone to Charlie's house to get back what was his. I could only guess at why Ares came along. Presumably because whatever the other guys did, he took part. Or maybe he'd thought he could talk the other guys into leaving me there.

I looked back at Ice.

I should have been more scared of him than I was. More scared of all of them. Rationally, I wasn't getting out of this alive. My heart and body said otherwise. Maybe the message here was to listen to your brain, not the rest of you, but I couldn't help myself. Even now, I wanted all of them. I wanted Ice to tear off my shorts and panties and bury his face between my thighs. I wanted to feel his cock slide into my pussy.

What the fuck was wrong with me? Normal people didn't lust after murderers. Did they? Did I have an actual clue how normal people behaved? I was starting to think I had none. None at all. No wonder I was a terrible judge of character, I couldn't even figure myself out.

"I won't say anything," I said softly.

Ice closed the distance between us. He twisted at what looked like an uncomfortable angle, and put his hand on my shoulder.

"I know you're confused, but you have nothing to worry about. I promise. Let's just get through this wedding and we'll sort everything out."

I wanted to believe him, but I saw what I saw.

There was one thing I needed to know.

"Does my mother know? Does Leo?"

"Leo definitely." Ice nodded. "Your mother, more or less. But don't freak out," he added as I was about to freak out. "Everything will make complete sense. If we had time..." He glanced at the window. "You'll have questions and we want to answer every single one of them."

"Do we?" Ares asked. He glanced over the back of the seat and glared at me. He curled his lip like he wished I was back at Charlie's place. Or anywhere but here.

I looked back at him with the same expression. Did he think I wanted to be here? I wouldn't have run away in the first place if I did. But now I was back, they owed me some kind of explanation.

"Of course we do," Ice said. "Our girl deserves all the answers."

"That depends what the fucking questions are," Ares growled.

"It doesn't matter what the fucking questions are," Mannix snarled. "We'll get this shit figured out and then there will be no more secrets between any of us." Like always, he left no room for argument.

"See?" Ice asked. "There's nothing to be worried about. Except that if we don't hurry, we'll be late. If there's anything Leo hates, it's people who are late."

That didn't bode well for me, since it was my fault they were late. Well, in as much as they felt the need to come and get me. They could have stayed back at the house and come for me afterwards. Or not at all.

This hole I was in seemed to get deeper and deeper.

"We'll get there in time," Mannix declared. He gunned the engine and the SUV flew down the road. He swerved around a couple of smaller vehicles, and took a corner like he was driving a racecar.

How the hell we didn't crash, I didn't know. Maybe that was how they were going to kill me. We'd all end up in a fireball, all of us together.

We skidded to a stop outside the iron gates.

The way they opened was both slow and ominous. The feeling I was going to my execution got stronger.

I should have tried harder to run after Ice unlocked the handcuff from the couch. When he didn't unlock the one from my wrist, I should have realised he intended something. I let fear and my feelings for these guys get in the way. Since those two things were in direct conflict with each other, it was no wonder I was caught out.

"You're shaking," Ice said in my ear. "If it wasn't your mother's wedding, I'd take you away and get straight to the part where we enjoy being handcuffed together."

His words should *not* have sent heat through my body. They definitely shouldn't have made me wet. They should have horrified me. What was happening to me? Had I been hit in the head and forgot about it? Because these thoughts were not normal. Not even close.

"Is that before or after you explain everything?" I found myself asking.

"I think after would be best," he said. "I don't think I could perform with you looking at me like that. Like you're not sure of me. Not sure if you can trust me." He looked like he wanted to say more, but he didn't. I presumed that was part of the conversation later.

Mannix drove the car through the gates and they clanged shut behind us.

The moment they met, it was difficult to breathe. It was like metal meeting metal cut off my oxygen. Like the full weight of the gates pressed down on my lungs.

Mannix parked the car in the garage and Ice helped me out.

Mannix gave me a long, unreadable look before he led us back toward the house.

CHAPTER 6

KENNEDY

"The gate code has been changed," Mannix said. "I need to get my jacket and tie on and see if Dad is ready. Ice, take that handcuff off her. Help her get changed into her bridesmaid dress. Don't get distracted."

Clearly he saw the way Ice looked at me. Like maybe the wedding could go ahead without us. That maybe people wouldn't notice if we didn't show. As if somehow I could think about anything like fucking right now.

All I felt at this moment was trapped, confused, and worried about what Mum and Leo would say. After the conversation the other day where Mum threatened to keep me away from the guys, things were a little tense between them. If she blamed them for me taking off, the situation could get a whole shit load worse.

What was that quote about tangled webs? This one was getting tangled tighter and tighter. The more I struggled against the strands, the worse it got.

"Ares, stand guard," Mannix snapped before he left the room.

Ares glared after his back, but closed the door and stood in front of it, arms crossed over his chest.

I tried my best to ignore him, because the aura of dominance and masculinity rolled off him in heavy waves. I wanted to drink it in; at the same time, I wanted to punch him.

Ice looked regretful, but took the key out of his pocket and unlocked his handcuff, then mine. He pushed both of them into his pocket and smiled.

"Something for later." He waved in the direction of my walk-in wardrobe. "I tidied up in there a bit for you. I'm sure you'll like it." He wasn't even slightly apologetic for going through my stuff. Why was he even in there at all? Maybe I was better off not knowing.

"Um, thanks." Okay, everything was hung there nicely, but it was so nice it was weird. I grabbed the dress off the hanger and shoved a couple of things apart, and a couple of other things closer together. As acts of defiance went, it was juvenile. Whatever, it made me feel better.

"Turn around." I took the dress off the hanger and held it in one hand.

Both guys looked at me and frowned.

"What?" Ares asked.

"I said, turn around." I made a turning gesture with one raised finger. "I'm getting changed and if you insist on being in the room with me, you can turn around and look the other way. What do you think I'm going to do? Jump out the window?"

"I wouldn't be that lucky." Ares turned around to face the door.

I smirked at his back. I might even have mouthed, "Fuck off." At this point, it couldn't make things much worse for me.

Ice was more reluctant to turn around, but he eventually did.

It took me approximately ten seconds to realise he could see my reflection in the mirror.

I moved deeper into my wardrobe and turned my back. Maybe it was silly. It wasn't as though Ice hadn't seen me naked, but I wanted some control over my existence. Even if it was only this tiny amount.

I stepped back into the dress and pulled the straps over my shoulders.

"Can you zip me up?" I tried to do it myself, but couldn't quite reach.

"Do I have to keep my eyes closed?" Ice asked. When he turned back around, his face was scrunched up, eyes squeezed tight.

Although he couldn't see it, I shrugged. "Works for me." I put my back to him and watched over my shoulder as he put out his hands, trying to find me.

I guess you can't hunt me down that easily after all, I thought. Although, they'd found me quickly enough at Charlie's house, thanks to that asshole. I made a note to myself that if I ever ran again, I should be a lot less predictable. Maybe even prepared. I couldn't blame myself for not being ready. How could I predict I'd find that mask in Mannix's drawer? I couldn't. The guys had sucked me in, in every way possible. I was so fucked, I wasn't sure there was a way out.

Ice finally bumped into me with his hands and felt around for the zip. His knuckles slid up my back as he did it up.

His cool hand set my skin on fire, all the way from the top of my panties to the back of my neck. My whole spine wanted to curl around him and never let him go. The rest of me wasn't far behind.

"You want me to take it back off again, don't you?" His breath caressed my ear and his words massaged the rest of me, sending tingles all the way down to my toes. "You want me to run my tongue all the way from your throat, over your nipples and down to your clit."

I hated the way my breath hitched.

He laughed softly in response. "I thought so. I want to do that to you. And a lot more things too. All the things. Remember how my cock felt deep inside you? How my magic cross made you feel? How my cum was sticky against your thighs when I slid out of you."

I didn't realise he put his arms around me until his feather light touch danced across my chest. He teased the top of my dress down and pressed two fingers inside, one on either side of one of my nipples. He slid them up and down slowly until my traitorous nipples pebbled hard. My breath caught in my throat. This was so wrong, but I wanted more. So much more.

"Ares, how long do we have until the ceremony?" Ice asked over his shoulder.

Ares had turned back around, and now said, "About ten minutes."

"That's enough time," Ice said. He pulled his hands out of the front of my dress and tugged up my hem.

"What are you—" I wanted to protest, but my blood was on fire. I wanted all the things he talked about. I wanted him, needed him.

"You're going to stand beside your mother while she marries Mannix's father, with my cum trickling down your thighs and sticking to your skin."

Fuck.

No.

Yes.

Please.

He grabbed the top of my panties and tore them off. He bent me over the top of a low chest of drawers.

I leaned on my elbows and lowered my head, sticking my ass out with need. Then his hands were on my clit, fingers inside my pussy. Every movement was deliberate, frantic, needing me to come, driving me hard.

I told myself this was crazy even as I plunged over the edge, stars dancing in front of my eyes. He was one of the three last people in the world who I should be fucking, but the only one I wanted right now. My whole body ached. I'd never before in my life felt so empty, my pussy so hungry.

I rocked back and forth on my elbows, grinding myself against his hand. I tried to remind myself what he did, what I saw that night, but all I knew was here and now. A moment of perfect, exquisite bliss. Hot, wet and irresistible.

In that moment, my body was one hundred percent his, to do whatever he wanted with. He could have asked me to do anything and I would have done it. In this frenzied rush, he owned me.

I was still coming down when I heard him undo his pants and push them down to his hips.

I wanted to plead with him to hurry, to bury himself deep, but I had no words. All I could do was stand with my legs apart a little more, inviting him, insisting.

Then he was slamming into me, urgent, driving hard. I cried out with a combination of pleasure, pain and surprise at suddenly having all of him inside me.

He gripped my hips with bruising fingers and drove harder still.

"Fuck, Beautiful, I'll never get enough of your pussy. It's like it was made just for me. So tight, so perfect. I'm going to come so hard in your beautiful body. You're going to feel me for the rest of the night, aching and dripping."

The tiniest whimper slipped from between my lips and I heard Ares groan. He had once told me not to make sounds like that or he wouldn't be able to keep himself from fucking me. With that in mind, I deliberately did it again. If he was aroused by it, that was his problem. He could have left the room.

"I'm going to come," Ice panted. "I'm going to spill myself into you. I can't wait to spend the rest of the night knowing you're going to feel me between your legs the entire time."

I moaned his name. "I want that," I whispered. "I want you to come inside me."

He promised not to hurt me. This was an extension of that promise. I had no idea if whatever they were going to tell me would make me understand why they did what they did, why they killed someone, but I had this. If they killed me once I told them what I saw, then at least I had this.

Ice grunted and fell still as he came. He made a series of unintelligible sounds that might or might not have been words, then he sagged.

"You are incredible," he whispered. "Just incredible." He stood like that for a minute or two, then slid out of me and tugged my dress back into place.

"How do you feel?"

I pushed myself up off the chest of drawers and stood up straight. "Warm, wet and sticky." I would have liked a shower, but there was no time for that. He'd definitely get his wish. My thighs were quickly smeared with his pearly cum.

He grinned. "Perfect." He patted some of my hair back into place and then offered me his arm. "We should go and watch your mother get married."

Still somewhat wary, I took his arm.

Ares was tucking his cock back into his pants. He disappeared into my bathroom long enough to wash his hands. Shame. He should have left cum on his fingers. Why should I be the only sticky one?

"Liked what you saw?" Ice asked him. "Maybe you should join in next time."

Ares grunted and yanked the door open before stepping out ahead of us.

Ice glanced at me and shrugged. "I guess there wasn't much time." His easy smile tugged at the corners of his mouth.

"I guess not," I said. I hoped this wedding would be over quickly because I needed some answers. Nothing in my life was making sense right now, and it was threatening to drive me crazy.

I'd just knowingly fucked a killer. What did that make me?

The worst part about it was that I'd do it again. Not just with him, but with Mannix as well. And Ares. This whole thing was at least several thousand times fucked up.

"I don't regret what we just did." Ice led me down the stairs and toward the door that led out to the pool.

The sun was starting to set. The whole scene was beautiful. Flowers decorated the space, looking gorgeous and smelling fragrant.

"You shouldn't either," he added.

"That's easy for you to say." Dryness crept into my tone. "You know what's going on."

"If you think about it long enough, you'll realise you do too," he said. "But all of this will be figured out soon enough. When it is, you won't have any regrets or doubts."

"You make it sound so simple."

"It really is simple, but we should stop talking about it now." He looked meaningfully towards some staff as they bustled around the kitchen, finalising a few details.

I wanted to insist we keep talking about it. Did these people have a clue who they were working for? If they had known, they might have run away screaming. On the other hand, would the guys let them leave? Specifically, would they let them leave alive?

I pressed my lips together when I saw Leo in his tuxedo, Mannix right behind him. They wore matching, unreadable expressions.

CHAPTER 7

KENNEDY

"Do I look all right?" Mum peered into the mirror. She frowned at her reflection, this way and that. She bared her teeth to check for lipstick. There was none there, but she ran her tongue over them anyway.

"You look stunning," I said honestly.

Simple, elegant, ivory silk brushed the top of her heels. Her hair hung past her shoulders in curls that somehow held their shape after all my work putting them in. That was a miracle in itself. Or an entire bottle of hairspray.

She glanced at me and frowned slightly at my own hair. I brushed it quickly and plaited it. That was all I had time for, before Mannix told me she was waiting for me. It was better than the freshly fucked look I'd had before that.

"Are you okay?" she asked. "You looked flushed."

I glanced over her shoulder. The mirror showed my cheeks were pink, brow crinkled, and a slightly wide-eyed expression.

"I'm fine. Just… excited for you." So my hair didn't look freshly fucked, but my face did.

She didn't look like she believed me, but she patted her hair and smiled. "I think we've kept Leo waiting for long enough. We wouldn't want him to think I've changed my mind."

"Yeah, wouldn't want that." I looked away from my reflection and followed her down the stairs in heels so tall I needed to hold onto the bannister to keep from toppling the rest of the way. No one could accuse my mother of choosing practical footwear.

She gave me a nervous smile at the bottom of the stairs, and blew out a breath through pursed lips.

"You've got this," I said, because it seemed like the thing to say.

That earned me a grateful smile, and a nod. "I know, I just can't believe the day here. It feels like I've waited…" She shook her head.

"You haven't changed your mind have you?" I asked teasingly.

"Of course not," she laughed, slightly higher than normal. "Let's do this."

One of the staff hovered, holding a bouquet of flowers in each hand. She handed the smaller one to me, the bigger to Mum.

Red and white roses. They reminded me of blood on pale skin.

A thick green ribbon wound around the stems and poured down my hand, the exact shade of my dress. Whatever else might be said about Leo, he could pick a good shade of green. Thank fuck there was no risk of me dying while wearing pink. It's the little things.

I nodded my thanks and she hurried away. Lucky her, she could escape this chaos.

From hidden speakers out near the pool, music started to play. Some cheesy love song by Mum's favourite singer.

For some reason, she'd said no to my suggestion to walk down the aisle to something by Bliss n Eso. Something about not liking their music. There was no accounting for taste. Especially since she also said no to Wolf Venom, Abbie Hart and Blazing Violet.

"You walk in first," she reminded me. I hadn't even noticed I stopped on the threshold. She must have assumed I was nervous, because she didn't look concerned.

We'd rehearsed all this, but that seemed like years ago. My whole world changed since this morning, much less yesterday when we ran through every step of the ceremony. Did she know I ran away and the guys brought me back? If I didn't know better, I'd think she was oblivious.

"Right." I gripped the flowers and tried not to grimace at the sticky slickness between my thighs. Ice was right, I was going to feel him there during the whole ceremony. It was equal parts hot and messy. Hopefully no one would wonder too much at my expression. I was just as hopeful the trickle wouldn't reach my feet.

I took a breath and started to walk slowly up the aisle towards Leo and Mannix.

Their faces were expressionless, until Leo saw Mum. Then his face melted into an adoring smile.

If there was anything I was sure of right now, it was that he loved my mother. Honestly, that wasn't a whole lot of consolation, since he was potentially an accessory to at least one murder. Fucked up was putting it mildly.

I dropped my gaze and looked at the long, red carpet I walked up. I couldn't meet Mannix's eyes. Not now. If I did, I might forget I needed answers from him. One heated look and I'd be lost. His all over again. I couldn't let him get to me that easily.

I reached the end of the carpet and stepped aside to let the bride stand beside her groom.

The ceremony itself passed in a blur. I only half listened. Most of the time, I kept my eyes down. Once in a while I glanced up at Mannix, or Ice, who sat in the front row.

Every time I did, they were looking at me. Ice with a smug expression, Mannix with an intense one.

I resisted the urge to speak out when the celebrant asked if anyone objected, but it was a close-run thing. I was sorely tempted to interrupt and demand answers instead.

I bit my tongue, literally, to keep from saying anything.

This would be over soon enough, I told myself over and over.

"Do you have rings?" the celebrant asked, bringing my mind back to the wedding.

"Yeah." Mannix dipped into his pocket and pulled them out. There were no jokes about misplacing them. No pretending to drop them. He handed them to the celebrant and stepped back again.

The celebrant nodded his thanks and gave the rings to the bride and groom.

Mum handed me her bouquet and raised her hand for Leo to slip an ornate ring on her finger. She slipped a simpler ring onto his.

"You may kiss the bride," the minister told them.

Leo leaned forward and kissed Mum gently. They were both clearly holding back, but neither of them were given to overt PDAs. Thank fuck for small mercies.

Leo pulled away, looked at her and said, "I've never seen anyone so beautiful."

Mannix moved to stand beside me and whispered in my ear, "I have."

I made a face and whispered back, "Yeah? Where is she?"

He slipped his hand into mine. "She's right here."

I wasn't sure if I should pull my hand away or not, but I had the sudden feeling that all eyes were on us.

The least I could do on my mother's wedding day was to not make a scene. At least not in front of the few guests she and Leo invited. Mostly Daisy Lasalle, her boyfriends and a handful of other people Leo worked with.

Just ordinary people to look at them. Friends and family. At some point the lines got blurred, and it was difficult to separate these people from that night. Part of me even wondered if I'd dreamt it.

We quickly signed the register to formally, legally marry Mannix's father to my mother, then the photographer whipped them away for post-wedding photographs.

The staff started to bring out food, and move the chairs, scattering them around the pool area for guests to sit and chat. Or plan more murders, or whatever people like these did.

"This looks like, 'after the wedding,' to me." I gave Mannix a meaningful look. In spite of his assurances, I had no guarantee he would tell me anything. If he didn't, I might be tempted to pick up one of the cocktail forks and stick it in his balls. I might just do that anyway.

Lucky for both of us, he nodded. He gestured for the other guys to join us and led me inside and back up the stairs. We all headed into my room and Ares closed the door behind us.

Ice flopped down on my bed on his stomach, but the rest of us stayed standing.

Mannix crossed his arms over his chest and regarded me for a minute or two. "What do you think you know?"

"It's not what she thinks she knows," Ice said before I could respond. "She saw us kill Eric Parcell." He said it like it was no big deal. Like I saw them do nothing more terrible than walking down the street.

Ares and Mannix both stiffened.

"What the fuck?" Mannix dropped his arms to his sides. His eyes narrowed and he looked at me. Then at Ice. "Bro, what are you talking about?"

"The person who saw us kill Eric," Ice said slowly. "It was Kennedy."

All eyes turned to me.

"You called me little mouse," I whispered. "You said you'd find me." Ice's words had tumbled around in my head over and over, but suddenly I couldn't remember them all. It was as though knowing they did it, my mind wanted, needed, to block it out.

Ice grinned. "And so we did."

"How?" Ares demanded.

"I found the mask Mannix wore that night in his drawer, along with his bowtie," I said. "I thought maybe it was a coincidence, but I panicked and ran. When you came to find me, Ice knew what I saw. That was when I knew it was true."

"So how did Ice know?" Mannix asked Ice.

"With this." Ice dug into his pocket and pulled out a bottle. "She was wearing this perfume that night."

My lips dropped apart when I saw it. "That was in the bottom of my drawer." He'd gone through my stuff?

"Yeah, and now it's in my hand," Ice said lightly, unapologetically. "You should wear it more often. It smells nice on you. If you had, I would have worked out who you were sooner."

That didn't sound like a good idea to me.

"It would have been easier if we'd worked it out earlier." Mannix took a step towards me.

I took a step back, eye wide, hands raised.

He kept walking until my back hit the wall, then pressed me against it, his chest on mine, thigh holding my legs.

My heart raced. I barely contained a whimper. This was it. He was going to kill me.

He raised his hand and wrapped it around my throat. He applied a slight amount of pressure. A little more.

My head spun. I started to run out of air. Panic rushed through me.

"We're going to explain who and what Eric Parcell was." His breath brushed my cheek.

I was both scared and aroused at the same time.

"And," he continued, "who we are and what we do." His lips brushed over mine, barely more than a touch before he stepped back and undid his tie. He let it hang around his neck and worked at the top couple of buttons of his shirt loose.

"My family is connected to the people who run this city."

I rubbed my throat. I already missed the way the pressure felt. The perfect combination of terrifying and arousing as fuck. Every moment was more conflicting than the last.

"Reuben and Caleb Brantley," I said. When he looked surprised, I added, "Charlie told me. He said they were... Mobsters?" He hadn't said that in so many words, but that was what he implied.

"That's basically accurate," Ice said with a smile.

I frowned. "So your family is connected to the mafia?"

"Not just connected, we're part of it," Ice said. "Mannix's dad is pretty high up. He answers to Ric DiMarco and Hilton Blake. And Daze Lasalle. In turn, they answer to Caleb Brantley. Reuben Brantley is at the top of the food chain."

"And you three answer to Leo." It was a statement not a question.

"For now," Mannix said. "Until I take his place."

"Are you in competition with your brother, Gunnar?" I asked. Talking about all this so casually was surreal, but I needed to know if I was going to get stuck in the middle of a gang war. Wait, was I actually thinking about sticking around?

Yeah, the jury was out on that one.

"No, he's happy to be an enforcer." Mannix looked indifferent.

"An enforcer?" I echoed.

"Yeah, he beats the crap out of people to keep them in line," Ice said. "Although, mostly, he just threatens people. Most of them don't like the idea of having their kneecaps broken, so they do what they're told."

"Right," I said. That wasn't fucked up at all. Only a lot. "Is that what you guys are? Enforcers?"

Mannix bristled, but Ice said, "We do some of that, when we have to. When Leo needs us to. But we have other roles."

"What about this Eric guy?" My head was swimming, but I really wanted to get down to why they killed someone. The rest of it, I'd figure out later.

"He worked for a rival." It was the first time Ares said anything for a while. "He was in town trying to stir up some shit for ages. He'd been told not to."

Ice nodded. "He'd had several warnings to get out of Dusk Bay, but he wore down Leo's patience."

"So because he wouldn't leave, he got killed?" That seemed like a flimsy excuse to murder someone to me.

"No, he was killed because he was trying to take business from Leo, and because he was harassing some of the girls in town." Ice had an unusually angry expression on his face.

"One night, it went beyond harassment. She spent two weeks in hospital, recovering from what he did to her. Leo called us home from Brutham early to deal with him. He doesn't tolerate men who assault women."

It wasn't difficult to put one and one together, but I wasn't sure if I was getting four or five.

"You killed him because he raped a woman?"

"I wanted to do it slower, starting with his balls, but Mannix over here wouldn't let me." Ice jerked his thumb towards Mannix.

Mannix shrugged. "He deserved a slow, painful death as a message to anyone else who might think about doing that, but we didn't have time. Eric was getting slippery, and harder to pin down. If we'd tried to drag him away, it would have been difficult to do without being seen by someone from the ball. It was difficult enough to get rid of his remains."

I decided against asking for specifics about that. I'd never unhear it.

"If Leo tells you to kill someone, you do it?" I asked tentatively.

"Are you asking if we'd done it before?" Ice cocked his head at me. "Yes, we have, and we've done it since. We think someone is coming after us. Eric was part of it, but it's going to escalate."

"It's them or us." Mannix slipped out of his tuxedo jacket and tossed it over the back of a chair.

I was silent for a long while, trying to process at least part of this. I wasn't sure if it wouldn't be better to leave people like Eric to the police, but I knew the legal system often didn't work in favour of victims. That would leave him free to do it again. So yeah, I got why they did what they did. But that wasn't the whole of it.

"You seemed to enjoy killing him," I said to Ice.

"Ice is fucked in the head," Ares said.

I was starting to figure that out for myself.

"Don't feel bad for his victims," Ares said. "If they're coming after us, they're coming after you too. This goes beyond one thug. This is war."

CHAPTER 8

KENNEDY

Their words went around and around in my head for hours while we drank, danced and ate. I tried to act naturally, but everything had changed.

I now had a stepfather and a stepbrother, and knew a lot more about the people around me. Too much, maybe.

I spent some time chatting to Daze like we were old friends. I got the distinct impression she knew a lot more about me than I knew about her. That was undoubtedly true. People like her didn't let other people into their circle without knowing all about them.

I also sensed she was aware I knew more than I had the first time we met. Did someone tell her, or was she that astute? She seemed like the type of person who was good at reading other people.

Me, on the other hand, I was someone who hadn't had to hide before. Not really.

I even danced with Ric, but for only half a dance before Mannix interrupted. He gave Ric a death stare, while smiling at the same time. Apparently there was a fine line between threatening upper management and claiming what's yours. A line Mannix wasn't scared to step on, if not over.

He whisked me away, put his arms around me and spoke into my ear. "Don't make me kill him for touching you."

"Wouldn't you get in trouble for doing that to the boss?" I asked.

He gave me a look like he'd do it anyway, regardless of the consequences.

Oh boy.

"I've been thinking about your punishment," he said. His hands slipped down to my ass. He squeezed my flesh hard enough to hurt.

I winced, but I liked the way it felt. It was his words that concerned me.

"Punishment? I understood why you did what you did. I'm not planning to tell—"

He interrupted me. "I know you're not going to tell anyone. Firstly because of the way it would look to the police if you did. You didn't tell them sooner, and you've been living with us. That makes you an accessory. If we get arrested for it, you'll be arrested alongside us."

That was a cheery fucking thought.

"Secondly," he continued before I could speak, "you're one of us. You got scared. It happens, but you belong here with us. If—*when*, someone like Eric turns up again, you'll be there with us dealing with them, the way we dealt with him." He leaned back just far enough to give me a challenging look.

I felt as though he was looking into my soul. Like he knew there was darkness in me that would speak to the darkness in him.

"I guess so," I said finally. "If it keeps people like that off the streets." After a moment I added, "Was Ares right? Is it really war between you… us, and whoever Eric was working for?"

He looked approvingly at my correction, and nodded. "Whoever followed you home that night, that was part of it. If they caught up to you…" He was obviously thinking murderous thoughts.

My blood filled with ice and I shivered. That night was disconcerting as fuck, but I hadn't thought about what might have happened.

"They could have caught up to you when you ran," Mannix continued. "Charlie is a dickhead, but if someone found you before he did, or someone got to you before we picked you up…" Again with the murderous-thought-face.

"Did it cross your mind to tell me all of this before now?" I asked. "I've been living here for weeks, not knowing any of this." That explained the increased security at the gym, and the way they hated to let me out of their sight. It went beyond being possessive, although that certainly was a big part of it. They were also trying to keep me safe from people even more unscrupulous than they were.

"We were going to tell you when I decided the time was right," he stated. "You forced my hand. Next time, come to me instead of sneaking away."

"I thought there was a good chance I would end up the same way Eric did," I admitted.

He stared at me for a moment, then sighed. "That's why you have nightmares, isn't it? Because of what you saw? Fuck."

"Yeah, and because Ice's words were as scary as hell. I thought you were going to spend your days hunting me down so he could kill me. Would you have killed me if you caught me that night?" Did I want to know the answer to that?

"Only if you worked for them," he said easily.

"Who are they?" If someone was coming after me, then I should know who they were.

"Most likely the Bell family, or someone who works with them and is trying to flex their muscles." He scowled. "They're one of the three most powerful families in Australia. The Bells, the Brantleys and to a lesser extent the Fiorellis. Although, the Fiorellis are too disorganised to get much done. Rumour has it they're fractured, which works perfectly for us. They're less likely to come after us if they can't get their own shit together."

I nodded. "So this is a turf war? Like rival gangs trying to elbow into the space of other gangs?"

"Yeah, kinda, but we're more sophisticated than a pack of street thugs." He'd put his tuxedo jacket back on, but he still had his shirt unbuttoned and his tie hanging around his neck. He looked like the opposite of a street thug. He looked more like a billionaire apprentice. Which was precisely accurate.

"What does that make me?" I raised a perfectly shaped eyebrow at him. Mum and I had spent the morning getting waxed and plucked in all the right places, so I knew I looked somewhat respectable.

He pulled me closer and blew softly on my earlobe. "It makes you my very fuckable, gorgeous step sister. Who now understands what's at stake."

"I guess I do," I agreed. "What does that mean for me though? Are you going to let me keep running the gym?" Could I do it without Charlie?

"Could I stop you?" he asked.

"You could lock me in behind the gates until I'm old and grey," I said.

"I don't think you would tolerate that for long," he said. "And unless I take every device and computer away from you, you'd find a way to get out. Changing the code will only hold you for so long."

"Damn right." I gave him a short nod. "I like that you care, but I don't need you controlling every little thing I do."

He gave me a look that suggested he'd do that anyway, at least as much as he was able to.

"You can keep running the gym, but I'll be vetting any new staff you hire. And any families who put their kids there. And the kids themselves." He was deadly serious.

"Good, because I don't want to let the kids down." I had some idea how it would feel to have the place close with no warning. For a lot of kids, the gym became a sanctuary away from their regular lives. It wasn't just great exercise, it was a great way to burn off frustration and anxiety. That was one of the things I liked the most about it.

"But once you can pass it on to a manager, Leo agrees there is a role for you in our business." He was blasé about talking about me behind my back.

"Oh really?" It shouldn't surprise me he'd done that. It wouldn't even surprise me if he told me he had the rest of my life planned out. For at least a second or two, while standing beside Mum, I thought he'd tell me he'd arranged for us to get married too. I wouldn't put it past him.

I sure as hell wasn't going to say that out loud, in case he got any ideas. I was definitely *not* ready to get married.

"More and more, we're moving into digital methods to do what we do," he said slowly.

"Cybercrime," I said flatly.

"Something like that," he said, not looking even slightly ruffled. "It wouldn't hurt to have someone like you to keep our rivals from hacking us. If you wanted to take it a little further…"

"Mannix Cassani, are you suggesting I use my degree to become a cyber criminal?" I asked. I wasn't sure if I was amused or offended at the suggestion. "Do I look like a hacker?"

He grinned. "Kennedy Knight, I'm certain you can be whatever you want to be. You're smart enough to get into any bank in the world and make yourself a billionaire if you wanted to."

"I think you might be giving me a bit too much credit, but thank you." It was one thing to create security systems and another to get past those created by someone else. Although, with the resources Mannix and his family had, I could probably do it with a bit of time.

"What would I do with a billion dollars anyway?" I asked.

"Anything you want," he replied. "Haven't you always wanted a private jet?"

"Not really," I admitted. "I'd prefer a private helicopter. Much easier to take off and land wherever you want."

He looked proud at my answer. "I was thinking luxury travel, and you're thinking quick getaway. You're more suited to this lifestyle than you might have realised."

"I was thinking quick getaway to a tropical island for a holiday, not running away from a crime," I argued.

"It's a fine line," he teased.

"I'm sure it is." I was about to find out, from the sound of it. "And what if I want to stay on this side of the law?" Knowing what they did and agreeing to take part in it were two very different things. Or were they? He was right about me being an accessory. The longer I stuck around with them, the deeper I got into an even more tangled web. The strands of this were stickier than Ice's cum on my thighs.

"Like I said, we could use help keeping our rivals out of our computer systems. If that's all you want to do, then that's all we'll ask of you, but I guarantee once you get a little taste for the illicit, you'll get addicted. Apart from our rivals, no one can touch us. We can do whatever we want, whenever we want, to whomever we want. We can go anywhere in the world and see things other people can only dream of. If you want front row tickets to Wolf Venom, you only have to ask."

"Is this where you tell me you kill people who have front row tickets and take it from them?" I asked. Wait, did I really want to know the answer to that?

He laughed and squeezed my ass a little tighter. "No, they're friends, remember? If it's another band you want to see, we can buy the label and make sure you get all the tickets you want. Or, you can hack in and get them yourself."

He made it all sound so easy and enticing.

I admit, front row tickets to any act, anywhere in the world did sound pretty fucking amazing.

"It's a lot to think about," I said. One minute I was a law-abiding citizen, the next I was contemplating breaking a bunch of laws just so I could go and see some good music. It would take more than a minute or two to decide if that was something I was going to do.

"There's no hurry," he said.

"Did you just study business to work for your father?" I asked.

"That, and so I can work for myself some day," he said. "Ares studied psychology so he can understand our rivals and how to manipulate people into doing what we want."

That was both disturbing and hot as fuck.

"And Ice? Didn't he study forensic pathology?" Did I really want to know about that?

"That's something you should talk to Ice about," Mannix said. "His kind of fucked up is better coming from his mouth than mine."

CHAPTER 9
ICE

"Have you ever done tequila shots?" I had a bottle of tequila in one hand, some salt and a couple of limes in the other.

Kennedy gave me a dubious look, like I probably deserved, but shook her head.

"That sounds dangerous."

I grinned. "We like dangerous around here." I turned to Mannix and Ares. "Are you guys in?"

Mannix grinned. "If you're talking about what I think you're talking about, I'm definitely in. Let's go."

Ares had his, 'I might dig my heels in,' expression on his face. I don't know if mules are as stubborn as people say they are, but he was definitely worse than one of those.

"You don't have to take part, you can just drink if you want." Without stopping to see if he answered, I led the way up the stairs to Kennedy's bedroom.

This was fast becoming my favourite part of the house. I wondered if she'd let me move in with her, instead of sleeping in the room across the hall. Maybe I wouldn't ask, I'd just gradually bring more and more of my stuff over here.

How long would it take before the guys cottoned on and tried to do the same thing? The room was big enough. We might need a bigger bed though.

I made a mental note to buy one in the morning.

Ares grumbled something, but followed the rest of us.

"Do we need glasses?" Kennedy asked cutely.

I chuckled. "No need. We have everything we need right here."

She gave me that dubious look again, but shrugged.

I closed the door behind us all and pulled a knife out of my pocket. On that same chest of drawers where I'd fucked Kennedy a few hours ago, I sliced the lime. Fruit isn't as much fun as slicing people, but I took care to make each wedge look pretty and the same thickness as the one before. A guy had to have some pride in his knife skills.

"Let me help you out of that," Mannix said to Kennedy. He moved around behind her to unzip her dress.

Judging by the expression on her face, she realised what we were suggesting. For a moment, I worried she wouldn't go for it. If she didn't, then we'd just drink.

She gave me a warm, fuzzy feeling inside when she smiled.

Yep, she was down for it. That's our girl.

The moment I finished slicing up the lime, Ares grabbed the bottle of tequila and took a swig. He tipped up the salt shaker, letting a bunch of grains pour out onto his tongue. He snatched a lime wedge and bit down onto it.

"Fuck yeah."

I grinned and took the bottle from his hand. I walked over to the bed where Mannix had already laid Kennedy down.

She watched me carefully as I tipped the tequila bottle, pouring a decent amount into the concave of her belly and her navel.

I sprinkled a line of salt beside it and placed a wedge next to that.

I sat back and smiled. "You're a beautiful work of art."

"Thank you," Mannix said, as if I was talking about him.

I snorted and bent down to lick and suck the tequila off Kennedy's stomach. It tasted even more delicious mixed with her skin.

I smacked my lips, then carefully licked up every grain of salt while she writhed.

"That tickles."

I grinned and picked up the lime wedge with my teeth before biting into it.

Around the wedge I said, "Best tequila shot ever."

Apparently done waiting for his turn, Mannix snatched the bottle from my hand and refilled Kennedy's belly. He had just enough patience to wait while I put down another line of salt and another wedge.

I sat back and watched him lick and suck, and she rolled her hips with the most sensual rhythm I ever saw. She made my cock harder than any of my knives.

"Kennedy's turn," I said. I handed her the bottle, and the salt shaker, along with my best lime wedge.

She looked from me to Mannix and back again, and even glanced at Ares.

"We'd all be receptive, Princess," Mannix said.

He was right. Even Ares would have gone along with it right now. He looked as caught up in the moment as the rest of us.

Kennedy obviously noticed that, and knew she may regret asking him to do anything he didn't want to do when he was sober.

Finally she said, "Why choose? Can I get another lime wedge?"

"Of course," I said. I stripped off all my clothes on the way to grab one. By the time I got back to the bed, Mannix was also wonderfully naked.

"Both of you lie down," Kennedy said.

With a fair idea of what she wanted to do, we glanced at each other and lay down with enough space between us for her to kneel. Confirming what I suspected, she tipped tequila into Mannix's navel, then mine. With as much care as I had used on her, she sprinkled a line of salt on either of us, then placed a lime wedge beside that.

She looked around for somewhere to put the tequila bottle, but Ares helped out by grabbing it and taking a huge swig. He'd taken off his shirt and tie, but left on his pants. That might not be the wisest course of action for him, because his cock was trying hard to break the zipper apart. Oh well, he could buy more pants.

Kennedy started with me, licking and sucking the tequila from my belly button.

She was right, it did tickle, but I managed to keep still and grinned at her.

She grinned back and licked up the salt before grabbing the lime.

By now, my cock was so hard, he was pointing straight at the ceiling. A glance over at Mannix showed his was doing the same.

While Kennedy licked the tequila from him, I rolled over and lowered my mouth onto his cock.

He groaned.

I had a mouthful of him. Kennedy had a mouthful of lime. Ares had a mouthful of tequila bottle. I guessed that meant everyone was winning.

Kennedy tossed the lime peel aside and crawled down the bed. She stopped with her mouth right in front of my cock.

"I've never…" Her face turned a glorious shade of pink.

I lifted my face off Mannix and said, "There's no wrong way to do it. Just do whatever feels right. I guarantee it will feel amazing."

I went back to sucking and tracing my tongue up and down Mannix's cock, demonstrating one way to blow a guy off.

Her lips were so soft and delightfully tentative at first. It was almost as though she thought my cock would eat her, or she might choke on me.

She started with a series of little licks and kisses, which felt like pure heaven to me. Her hand wandered up so her fingers could lightly touch the base and my balls.

Inspired, I massaged Mannix's balls with one of my hands, while the other lightly traced lines up and down his hip and over his ass. He started to buck into my mouth, slowly at first, then gradually deep down to the back of my throat.

His breath became a series of grunts. Then, so did mine as Kennedy fastened her lips around me and started to suck, and graze her teeth over my sensitive skin.

If I died right now, I would die in absolute, perfect bliss.

I caught a glimpse of Ares. He'd pushed his pants down and had his hand around his thick cock.

I'm not gonna lie, I'd love to know how he'd feel in my mouth. I'd bet anything he was tasty.

Right before he came, Mannix slipped himself out of my mouth. He walked on his knees over behind Kennedy and pried her legs apart with his hands. His cock still glistening, he positioned it outside her pussy, then pressed himself into her body.

She groaned around my cock, but didn't stop sucking.

"Good girl," I told her. "You're so good at this already. I can hardly believe this is your first time sucking a cock. Your mouth and tongue are just perfect." I rolled my hips and half closed my eyes. I wanted to savour every moment of this. To make it last forever. At the same time, I wanted to come down her throat right now.

The sound of Mannix's hips slapping against her ass drove me closer and closer to the edge. Watching him drive into her, his face a mask of concentration, incredible sounds slipping from his mouth… I loved everything about it.

She cried out and ground her hips into the mattress as she came.

I grabbed onto the back of her head, and tangled my fingers in her hair as she took her mouth off my cock. I grabbed my length in one hand and pumped it until I came, squirting my pearly juices all over her cheek and into her hair. Ice cream at its finest.

"I want you to taste it." I slowly, carefully, scraped the side of my finger down her cheek and pressed it into her mouth.

She sucked my finger like a baby animal seeking a teat. This woman was going to kill me with how incredible, curious and willing she was. I had so much to teach her. I knew she'd want to learn all of it. Even the darkest, most disturbing stuff.

"That tastes even better than the shot."

"Next time, I'll put it right in your mouth," I told her. But she did look adorable with strings of cum in her hair.

"Fuck," Mannix grunted. He pounded harder, his balls slapping and slapping against her ass. "This is—"

I never found out what this was, because he stopped talking, thrust frantically into her body and then stilled as he came. He dropped his head back and cried out his nickname for her.

"Beautiful, fucking Princess," he panted.

Well, a variation of his nickname for her. Nothing about that was wrong. She was beautiful, they were fucking and she was definitely a princess. One who was quickly becoming a queen.

He scrunched up his face, trying to make his orgasm last as long as he could, milking himself every drop in her wonderful pussy.

Finally he sagged, panting over her, his face nearly touching her bare back.

Over to the side of the room, Ares was the last to come, his eyes on us.

I watched intently as he pumped his engorged cock. Full of blood, it was red and purple and looked ready to burst. Then it did, exploding a river of cum out over his hand and onto the carpet.

What a waste, I would have drunk that.

Some day.

Then he too sagged, before he grabbed the bottle for another drink.

"I don't know about anyone else, but I could use a shower," he said lightly.

Kennedy touched the side of her face and found her hair all wet. I was getting good at decorating her. I'd have to think of more, interesting ways to do it.

"I could use a shower." I rolled off the bed and onto the floor. "Last one in there has to wash my back." I noticed neither Kennedy nor Mannix rushed. If they both wanted to be last, I was one hundred percent okay with that. In fact, they could both wash my back at the same time if they wanted to.

And then maybe I could fuck one or both of them again.

CHAPTER 10

KENNEDY

"What did you want to know?" Ice set down his coffee and slipped into the stool next to me.

When I glanced over at him questioningly, he added, "Mannix said you might want me to explain my special brand of fucked up." He didn't look worried about referring to himself that way.

I cleared my throat and swallowed my mouthful of toast. "I was curious why you studied forensic pathology. I thought you'd do autopsies, and stuff like that."

"What makes you think I don't?" The smile he offered me was somehow sweet and sinister at the same time.

"Do you?" I nibbled on the corner of toast while he watched my mouth.

"Sometimes," he said lightly. "At uni I did. If I got a job with the local morgue, I might." He looked thoughtful as he sipped his coffee.

"And if you don't? What else are you going to do with a degree like that?" I remembered him shoving the knife into Eric Parcell's eyeball and suppressed a shiver. I bet they didn't teach that at university.

"I can show you if you want?" he offered. He chuckled at the suspicious look I gave him. "I wasn't suggesting I practice on you. I was just gonna show you my workroom. You might find it interesting and... Educational."

I had the distinct impression I'd find it disturbing as hell. At the same time, I was curious. Yeah, I knew what curiosity did to the cat, but I remembered his promise not to hurt me.

"Okay," I said finally. I hoped like hell I didn't regret agreeing to go.

"Do you trust me?" He cocked his head at me. He reminded me of a dog. Adorable when they lie on their back and let you rub their tummy, but if they wanted to tear you apart, they would. I'd only ever seen the tummy side of Ice. Unless you counted that night.

Now I knew the context, I was a lot less scared, but it was still disturbing as fuck.

My tongue flicked over my lips and gathered a few stray crumbs. I drew them in and swallowed them.

"I... I want to," I said slowly.

"But?" he prompted.

"But I hardly know you," I admitted. "Everything I learned yesterday really brought that home. It's one thing to care about someone and another to learn their whole life is—" I stopped to compose my thoughts. "Not what you thought it was."

"It's not everyday you learn your boyfriends are involved with organised crime." It was a statement, not a question.

"Exactly," I agreed.

"You understand why we didn't tell you straight away?" He looked anxious now. Worried I harboured resentment toward the guys for keeping something so important from me.

Did I?

"I do understand, but is there anything else I should know?" If they had any more enormous truth bombs, I wanted to know about them now. I'd had enough surprises to last for a long time. Unless they were pleasant ones, then I'd just as soon skip them.

"Yeah, that's why I want to show you my workroom." He downed the last of his coffee and hopped up off the stool. "If you can handle what you see there, then you can handle anything."

"I'm starting to think I should run away right now." But when he offered his hand, I accepted it.

"You'll be fine. I'm a better driver than Mannix. If you can survive his driving, then everything else after that should be easy."

"Those sound like famous last words if I ever heard them," I said.

He grinned. "Ares always says I should work in a funeral home, because I drive like I'm driving a hearse. Does that make you feel any better?"

"A little bit," I said. "As long as you don't expect me to ride in the back."

"The only way you'll be in the back is if I'm there too." He smiled suggestively.

I glanced back as we walked towards the garage. "Are the other guys coming too?"

"No, they left half an hour ago to go and do some stuff." He pressed the button on his fob and the garage door slowly slid open.

"Illegal stuff?" I couldn't resist asking.

He grinned. "Probably. They'll fill you in on all the details later."

"Are you sure about that?" I slipped into the passenger seat of his white, classic Corvette. Telling me about their lifestyle and giving me blow by blow descriptions were different things. Neither of them seemed inclined to share their shoe size, much less what they got up to when I wasn't around.

"Maybe not all the details," Ice conceded. "The important ones."

"Are those the ones they think I should know?" I clicked my seat-belt into place and sat back as he drove the Corvette out of the garage.

"Probably," he agreed. "But you know them. They're not the chatty type like me."

"It's probably best I don't know everything anyway," I said. "I'm still not sure what I think about all of this. Part of me is sure I should wait until you stop at a red light and jump out and run." How far would I get if I did? I suspected it wouldn't be far.

He glanced over and flashed me a smile. "If you're thinking of doing that, then I better not stop at any red lights. I hope there aren't any big trucks going through at the same time we are." He made a sound like squealing tires followed by a loud impact.

A beat later, he added, "I'm curious what it's like to be dead, but I don't want to find out today."

"Me either," I agreed. "Mostly I don't want to get out at a red light, so please stop when you get to one." That led me to ask, "Have you always been involved in, you know, illegal stuff? Were your parents involved in it too?"

"No idea about my father," he said lightly. "I was raised by my mother. He took off when I was a baby. I never knew him, or much about him. Just who he was. For all I know, you and I could be half brother and sister."

He glanced over and grinned.

I grimaced back at him. "Ewww, I hope not." Fucking my step-brother was one thing. Doing it with an actual blood relative was something else entirely.

He chuckled at my reaction. "It wouldn't change anything between us for me. I'd still want to bury my cock as deep into your pussy as I can. But just to be sure, we can do a DNA test."

I didn't doubt him for a moment. If we discovered we were blood siblings, he'd still want to be with me. I should be grossed out, but for some reason I was slightly turned on.

Maybe we were related, because apparently I was fucked up in the head too.

"A DNA test might be a good idea," I said finally. "Apparently my father was a serial cheater, and if my mother was connected to this place all along, then who knows what might have happened."

"I can take some samples at my workshop and send them off, but I'm sure they'll come back saying we're not related at all."

I wasn't sure if he was disappointed at the idea or pleased. Maybe a little of both. I didn't think it was because he actually wanted to screw his biological sister, but because he liked to push the envelope, and get away with things he shouldn't. Forbidden fruit and all that.

"While I'm there, I'll check Mannix and Ares too. How wild would it be if you were half sister to all three of us?" He chuckled to himself.

"I'm starting to see what Mannix means when he says you're fucked in the head," I said lightly. "Who thinks things like that?" Maybe I shouldn't *say* things like that, in case he was offended. He was driving after all.

He gave no sign of offence. Rather, he grinned. When he did that, he was too fucking cute for his own good, or mine. Or Mannix's, for that matter. The memory of him with his mouth around Mannix's cock, then my mouth around Ice's, made me hot all over.

For a little while there, I thought Ares was going to join in, but then he was getting himself off and Mannix was thrusting hard into me. It wasn't that long ago I was a virgin and now I'd been with two guys at once, while another watched.

I would never have dreamt it was possible, but I was one hundred percent here for every second of it.

"Just the Iceman," he said unapologetically. "I have a vivid imagination and a twisted sense of humour. I don't regret either of them."

"I'm sure you don't," I said. "There's nothing wrong with that. I have a pretty twisted sense of humour myself. As for my imagination, you don't want to know."

"I absolutely want to know, but we're here, so it may have to wait for a little while."

He pulled up the Corvette in front of a nondescript building. It looked like a derelict warehouse, but none of the windows were broken.

I climbed out of the low-slung car and looked more closely.

No, they weren't just broken, they were boarded up from the inside. Like whatever went on wasn't meant to be seen by the casual passerby.

The state-of-the-art keypad beside the door was at odds with the rest of the building. It looked relatively new. Dirty, like someone smeared soil or grease over it to make it look older, but free of rust, dents or worn out numbers.

Ice tapped in the combination and turned the knob to open the door.

"Let me say before we go in there that you can leave at any time. The combination is seven-five-nine-two. That will get you in or out. Obviously, don't share that with anyone."

He waved me inside and closed the door behind me.

I ran the combination over in my head a few times so I wouldn't forget. I doubted he shared the combination with anyone but Mannix and Ares. And now me. If he was trying to earn my trust, he was doing a good job of it.

Assuming he was telling the truth about the code letting me back out. And that it was the right code in the first place.

I found myself in a virtually empty room that looked as worn as the outside of the building. Only a table and a few chairs sat against one wall. A few hooks hung on the opposite wall. Right now they were empty, but they looked like the kind you'd hang a jacket on. A single bulb hung from the ceiling.

"This is... Cosy," I said. It looked like the kind of place you'd see on TV, where the bad guy took the innocent victim to be horribly murdered. I swallowed hard and repeated the code over and over again in my head.

"This is just the reception area. In case anyone does break in, we make it look as harmless as possible." He walked over to a doorway at the end of the room and pushed down the handle.

Instead of the door opening, a hatch in the floor slid back.

"Lucky I wasn't standing right there." I stared at the sudden hole with wide eyes.

"I wouldn't have let you stand *right there*," he said. "I save that for my enemies."

I couldn't tell from the expression on his face whether he was joking or not, so I decided he wasn't. Although, since the hole led to a set of stairs, I decided his enemies wouldn't get too badly hurt from the drop anyway.

I decided not to think too hard about him having enemies in the first place. I guessed that came with the territory of being a mobster.

"Your workshop is down there?" I peered into the darkness.

"Cool, isn't it?" he asked. "No one knows it's here but us and the occasional special guest."

Special guest? Did he actually mean—

He started down the stairs. Not wanting to be left behind in the dingy space, I quickly followed.

CHAPTER 11

KENNEDY

The first thing I noticed when we reached the bottom was the tang of what smelled like blood.

Yeah, it probably was blood.

I stepped into what looked like a horror movie.

Or a nightmare.

A couple of large hooks were bolted to the ceiling. The chains that hung from them were stained with something dark. The concrete floor underneath was similarly stained.

A long, wooden work table like the ones we had in art class at school sat a couple of metres from the chains. At the moment, there was nothing on it. Nothing but the same stains as the rest of the room. And other stains, it looked like someone tried to bleach the surface of the wood. Long scratches and gouges were embedded in the timber.

To the side of the room, a metal chair was bolted to the floor. Restraints were attached to the arms and legs, reminiscent of Charlie's couch, but a lot less comfortable.

Beside that, was a small table, pliers and scalpels laid out in a menacing display. Ready for… Whatever Ice would use them for.

"What is this place?" I asked. I turned around slowly, taking in the exposed, grey brick walls and the dim light. We were underground, so there were no windows. It was the kind of place someone came to die a horrible death.

"It's just my workroom," he said like it was no big deal. "Sometimes we find people who don't want to be forthcoming with information that we need. It's my job to get them to share."

I stopped to look at him.

"You torture people for information?" Of course he did, what else would go on in a place like this?

"I prefer to think of it as persuasion, but yes," he agreed. "I extensively studied human anatomy so I knew exactly where to work on people. Where it hurts the most and how to keep them alive. It's a last resort, but sometimes a necessary one."

My heart thundered in my chest. "How many people have you…"

"Enough," he said vaguely. "I'll spare you the specifics." He stepped over to me and slipped his arms around me. "You haven't run away yet."

I was resistant to embracing him for a few moments. "Will I end up restrained to that chair if I do?"

He looked over to it and chuckled. "Not unless you want me to. If it'll make you feel better, I'll let you restrain me."

Before I could answer or melt against him, voices and the sound of scuffling came from the top of the stairs.

"Things might just get interesting. " Ice tipped his head back and looked up to the upper level.

Mannix and Ares carried someone between them. A man, judging by the height and physique.

When they reached the bottom of the stairs, I saw the man's mouth was duct taped shut. His eyes were wide with fear and defiance.

He kicked out, but they dragged him over to the chains. All three guys attached them to him. Manacles snapped around his wrists, forcing him to hold them up over his head.

"Well, well, what do we have here?" Ice stood back and crossed his arms over his chest. He looked appraisingly at the struggling man.

"We did a bit of digging into this asshole," Mannix said. He turned to me. "You recognise him?"

I frowned. "Now you mention it, he's the father of one of my newer students. What is he doing down here?" I'd only seen him once or twice, but he gave me the creeps both times. What was his name?

Nixon.

Frank Nixon.

"The cameras caught him getting into his car the night you were followed," Ares said, his eyes firmly on Nixon. "The same kind of car that followed you."

"That doesn't necessarily mean anything," I pointed out.

Nixon nodded vigourously. He made an incoherent sound of agreement through the tape.

"It might not," Mannix agreed. "Except he works for the Bell family, as an enforcer. He and his family have only been in Dusk Bay for a couple of months. The same amount of time we've been having trouble with people like him. I want to know why he followed you. Unfortunately, Mr Nixon here hasn't been forthcoming with any information."

Ice was wearing a sleeveless T-shirt, muscular biceps on display, but he pretended to roll up his sleeves. At the same time, he smiled. The whole look was adorably sinister.

"Perfect. Anyone who comes after my Beautiful gets special treatment."

Nixon struggled harder and tried to speak. Or maybe to scream.

Mannix curled his hand into my hair. "You don't have to be here for this, Princess. One of us can take you home."

A normal person would take him up on his offer, but I realised by now that I wasn't as normal as I thought I was. If anything, I was intrigued. The man followed me. Who knows what he would have done if he caught up with me?

What had Ice said about Mannix's brother Gunnar? He beat the crap out of people to keep them in line. Would Nixon have done that to me?

"I want to stay," I said finally.

"That's our girl," Ice said approvingly. He grabbed hold of a corner of the piece of duct tape and yanked it off in one go.

I winced. That had to hurt.

Nixon groaned and swore. "You assholes have the wrong guy. I work in a bottle-shop. I've never followed anyone home in my life."

"Then why do you have regular payments from Samuel Bell in your bank account?" Mannix asked.

"I've never heard of him," Nixon said, but he was clearly rattled. He knew he was fucked.

Not in a good way.

Ice looked over to his small table and picked up the pliers.

"You want to try again?" He did nothing with them, he just stood tapping them against his opposite hand. It was enough to make Nixon scared, and send a jolt of heat right to my core.

Holy fucked up shit, Iceman.

Nixon looked around at us frantically. His eyes locked on me as though he thought I'd be his way out.

"Why did you follow me?" I asked coldly. I was surprised by the calm steel in my own voice. The lack of a waiver; of hesitation.

You don't choose the thug life, I thought.

Nixon said nothing.

Ice grabbed one of his hands and clamped the pliers onto his ring finger. He squeezed tight.

Nixon's eyes widened. He was obviously in a shit load of pain, but he didn't make a sound.

"High pain threshold," Ice said, "my favourite." He squeezed harder.

Nixon's finger crunched as his bone was broken.

Now he cried out.

I really shouldn't have been turned on, but I was.

"Our Princess is enjoying this," Mannix said. "Let's make the most of it."

"Another finger it is." Ice pressed the pliers down onto another of Nixon's fingers, squeezing so hard the bone must have shattered. Both fingers were a bloodied mess.

Nixon gritted his teeth and grunted through the pain. "I was only doing my job."

"Now we're getting somewhere." Ice applied the pliers to a third finger. "What exactly was your job?"

Nixon groaned. "I was supposed to send a message to your family."

"Ever tried texting?" Ice asked.

Nixon responded with a humourless snort.

"What was the message?" Mannix tightened his grip on my hair.

"The message was that you're vulnerable," Nixon said. "They wanted me to take out Leo's stepdaughter to show they could get to you."

I blinked. "Your job was to kill me?"

"Scare you, then wait until after they tightened security, and then kill you. They wanted Leo to know it didn't matter what he did, they could get to him and anyone affiliated with the Brantleys."

"Why me?" That should have scared me, and it did, really, but mostly it pissed me off.

"They probably thought you were an easy target," Ares said. "They misjudged. They sent someone who lacks the skills to carry out something like that."

"Right. If they wanted to take out Kennedy, they needed to send an assassin," Ice said. "Not a third rate thug." He squeezed the pliers down on Nixon's thumb.

Nixon howled in pain.

I couldn't bring myself to conjure up even a little bit of sympathy for him. He would have killed me and not given it a second thought. I didn't want to spare too much thought for what he might have done to me *before* he killed me.

If his boss wanted to send a message, it might include, 'P.S. We can toy with Leo's people as much as we want.'

"How would you have killed me?" I didn't know why it mattered, but it did. Some part of me needed, wanted, to know what I was up against. If nothing else, it served to further justify the guy's killing Eric Parcell. If this was the war they claimed it was, what or who else might come at me?

"Answer the woman." Ice moved the pliers to Nixon's pinky finger, but didn't squeeze yet. It was the only finger on his hand that wasn't shattered and covered in blood. If he got out of here alive, he wouldn't be using his hand again.

Yeah, boo fucking hoo.

"The boss wanted it done in a personal way." Nixon's voice was weaker now as the pain closed in harder on him. "He wanted you to know he could get to any of you as much as he wanted to."

"That's fucked up," I remarked. "You would have, what? Strangled me?" The thought of his hands around my throat robbed me of air for a few moments.

He gasped out the word, "Yeah."

Ice nodded towards the pliers. "Do you want a turn?"

"It's okay if you do." Mannix turned my face and pressed his lips to mine. "He would have wrapped his fingers around your neck and squeezed. He would have watched while you struggled for air. He would have held you down while you fought back. He would have watched the light leave your eyes and felt your body become lifeless. People like him, they enjoy every minute of it. Don't think you would have been his first. Or his last."

His words set my blood on fire.

"Have you killed women before?" I needed the answer to that, even knowing how horrifying it might be. My stomach twisted, rebelled.

"Yeah," Nixon said. "When the boss wanted me to." Any hint of his former denial was gone, replaced by a sickening sense of pride in the horrible things he'd done.

I stepped towards him.

He tried to step back, but the chains held him in place.

"Did you enjoy it?" I locked my gaze on his, unflinching, even as a small part of me protested my being here in doing this.

Shut up, I told it. *This is your life now. You can't unknow or unsee anything. You might as well enjoy it.*

The power of standing in front of someone twice my size, knowing he couldn't fight back, knowing he deserved what was coming to him, was heady as fuck. Mannix was right. This was addictive. No one but us would ever know exactly what went on here today. Not the police, no one.

The smile Nixon gave me was chilling and vicious. "Yeah, I enjoyed it. I would have enjoyed strangling you. I bet you would have put up a fight, but you wouldn't have won. Your life would have been mine to end."

Yeah, he wasn't unhinged at all, was he? I saw it in his eyes that he was imagining what it would be like to hold me down with the weight of his body and watch my life end. He would have gotten off on killing me. The experience would have been orgasmic for him.

That same small part of me I just told to shut up, reminded me I was getting off on this too. That it made me almost as bad as him.

Not as bad, I reasoned, because I did nothing to warrant his boss sending him after me. I did nothing but be Leo's stepdaughter. As far as I knew, that wasn't a crime anywhere in the world.

I reached my hand out for the pliers.

Without a word, Ice lay them across my palm. They felt warm from his touch, slick with Nixon's blood.

I gripped the handle and held Nixon's pinky finger with the end of the pliers before I squeezed.

"This is for the women you killed. You won't be killing any more of us." Flesh and bone gave way under the pressure, like squashing a chicken bone. The crack and crunch, and his howl of pain were the most satisfying sounds I've heard apart from the guys' grunts when they came.

"Do you want to start on his other hand?" Ice offered.

I shook my head. "No." I handed him the pliers before I turned and trotted up the stairs. I managed to key in the passcode and step outside into the fresh air before I threw up every bit of my breakfast.

CHAPTER 12

KENNEDY

Mannix found me a couple of minutes later, sitting on the sidewalk with my back against the building. I'd pulled my knees up to my chest and wrapped my arms around my legs.

"You shouldn't be out here by yourself." He sat down beside me and placed his arm over my shoulders.

"I'm not by myself," I said faintly. "You're here too."

He chuckled. "I am now, but fuck knows what might have happened before I got here."

This part of town was all but deserted, which made it perfect for Ice's workroom, and for me to sit outside for two or three minutes by myself.

I understood the reason for his warning and concern. Of course I did. I wasn't going to quickly forget what I heard inside. And what I did. I swallowed hard.

"It's always confronting the first time," he said. "I threw my guts up too, but I did it in front of everyone. It wasn't my finest hour. You become used to it after a while." He nuzzled his face into my hair. "You don't have to come back here again if you don't want to."

I shook my head slightly. "That's not it. I should have found that...

disgusting, or terrifying, or something." It was all of those things, but it was more than that.

"You're surprised by how much you enjoyed it?" he guessed. "You're worried about what it says about you and what we'll think."

"Is it sick to enjoy getting revenge for those women?" I asked. "Is it even sicker that I'm not sure it was about getting revenge? I think maybe I did it because I wanted to. What does that make me?"

He kissed my temple. "It makes you one of us. Neither Ares nor I get as much of a kick out of it as Ice, so we leave him to it, but we could do all that shit too if we wanted to. If you hadn't broken his pinky finger, I would have. No one goes after my princess and gets away with it. But you know what, when we let him go, he'll go crawling back to his boss with a message from us. Don't fuck with our girl."

"What if he sends someone else?" I asked. "Like an actual assassin." From what I knew about them, I wouldn't see them coming. I'd be dead and that was it.

No thanks.

"If he does, we'll deal with it." Mannix's tone was firm, confident, reassuring. "But I don't think Samuel Bell will send an assassin after you. He'd send one after Dad. If you're going to spend that much on a hit, you go after the big dog. If not Dad, then he'd go after Daisy Lasalle, or one of her boyfriends. Or maybe even Caleb or Reuben Brantley themselves, if he's feeling like he's got bigger balls than usual."

I wasn't sure if I should be relieved or offended that I wasn't important enough to send an assassin to kill me. Maybe a bit of both. But a whole lot of the first one.

I put that aside for now. "So you don't think I'm sick for what I did?"

"Not even a little bit," he assured me. "And none of us will think you're sick if you want to go in there and pull off some of Nixon's toenails. Or cut off his balls with Ice's scalpel. Or whatever you and Ice come up with to teach him not to come after you."

None of that should have made me hot, but it all did. Every last word.

"Last night when we were dancing, you mentioned punishment for running away," I said slowly. "You didn't mean this, did you?" I jerked my head toward the building behind us.

"I meant spanking, but if you want to take it further than that, I'm game." He grinned.

"What do you have in mind?" I asked carefully.

He stood and pulled me to my feet. "Do you trust me?"

That was the second time today one of the guys asked me that and I answered him the way I answered Ice.

"I trust you."

"Excellent. Just remember, if you want to stop, you only have to say so."

Now I was somewhere between nervous and excited. Both of those built when he led me back into the building and down the stairs.

Nixon was still hanging by his wrists. Blood trickled down one arm.

Ares was leaning against the wall, arms crossed over his chest, eyes half closed. He actually managed to look bored.

Ice stood over at the sink, washing blood off the pliers.

"You're just in time for round two. I was about to start decorating him with my scalpel, for shits and giggles. And in case he has more information he'd like to share." He put the pliers aside on the edge of the sink and grabbed up the scalpel.

"I thought we might have some fun at the same time," Mannix said. He gave me a look to remind me I could opt out at any time, but took me over to the set of chains that hung parallel to the ones around Nixon's wrists.

I eyed him doubtfully for a moment, but let him fasten the ends of the chain to my wrists. I was maybe a metre away from Nixon but while he looked defeated I felt elated. And curious. And a little terrified.

Mannix nodded to Ice.

Ice raised the scalpel and sliced it down the side of Nixon's cheek.

"I know you're wondering how I came to have such neat work," Ice said to the man, "it's from years of practice. When I first started out, my cuts were much messier than this."

"He's not joking." Mannix walked over to a set of drawers beside the sink and pulled out another scalpel. "His cuts looked more like chew marks."

Ares snorted a laugh.

Ice pretended to look offended. "They weren't *that* bad."

"Says you." Mannix stepped back over to me and held the scalpel a centimetre from my throat.

I held my breath and struggled to keep from swallowing or freaking out.

"That's my brave girl." He moved the scalpel down slowly, slicing the fabric of my T-shirt as he went.

"Wait a sec," Ice said. "If our girl is going to be naked, he doesn't get to look."

He went over to the same draw Mannix got the scalpel and pulled out what looked like a thick nail and a small mallet.

Nixon started to struggle against his chains. "Nonononono! I'll keep my eyes closed. I swear! Fuck… No!"

Ice placed the nail in front of his eyeball and tapped it with the mallet. Once. Twice.

"Don't want to kill the guy."

Nixon screamed.

And again when Ice took out his other eye.

Ice set the implements aside. "There we go. You can all be as naked as you want to."

Mannix nodded his thanks and went back to slicing through my clothes, until they all lay on the floor at my feet.

My nipples pebbled harder than rocks when Ice made a neat incision in Nixon's other cheek. Blood poured down Nixon's face and trickled onto his shirt. Stains spread where it landed.

Mannix put the scalpel down and parted my thighs with his hands. He slipped his fingers between my legs, brought them up to my pussy. His eyes widened.

"Princess, you're drenched. You really do get off on this." He started to trace light circles around my clit with one hand and around one nipple with the other. "Keep your eyes on Nixon. Watch what Ice is doing to him. Enjoy it."

I *was* enjoying it. The sight of all that blood and pain, and the feel of Mannix's touch.

Ice stopped his slicing for a moment to lean over and lick and suck my other nipple. "Mmmm, you taste extra delicious today." He smiled adorably at me. How could he be so cute and yet so bloodthirsty at the same time?

Mannix knelt on the stained floor, parted my legs wider and dove in between my thighs with his lips and tongue.

He muttered something that sounded like, "Definitely delicious."

To my surprise, Ares stepped over to me. He moved around behind me, put his arms around me and started to knead my breasts. He wasn't gentle, but his touch was pure electricity. Like he was finally giving in to the attraction between us, and it pissed him off, but he was going to throw all of himself into it anyway.

I leaned back into him, so my back was pressed against his chest. With my hands chained above my head, I couldn't touch him the way I wanted to, but that only turned me on harder. The guys had all the control. All I could do was enjoy it.

I groaned as Mannix slipped a couple of fingers inside me. He started to fuck me with his hand and his tongue.

At the same time, Ares' fingers became bruising on my delicate skin.

"I'm going to leave my mark on you, Firecracker," he said in my ear. "Lots of them."

Fuck, yes, please.

He moved around to the side of me and leaned over my breast. He traced patterns over my skin with his tongue, then gripped it hard between his teeth and bit me.

I let out the little whimper I knew he liked so much. If he was trying to keep his cock out of my pussy, he wasn't trying very hard.

He bit me again in another spot, hard enough to draw blood. "All the marks."

I cried out in a combination of pleasure and pain, overwhelmed by all of my senses. At some point, the smell of blood became the scent of sex. I couldn't differentiate between the two.

Letting the chain bear my weight, I rocked against Mannix's mouth.

I was so turned on right now I must be dribbling down my own thighs.

I came suddenly, hard and fast, my scream mingling with Nixon's as Ice cut off a good chunk of his left ear. Not so much that he couldn't hear, but it would have hurt like a bitch.

I'd barely come down when Mannix leaned me back against Ares's chest. He undid the front of his jeans and pushed them down far enough to free his erection. He placed his hands behind my knees and lifted my legs up to his waist. With a grunt, he pulled me onto his cock.

I moaned. I may never get enough of being filled by one of their cocks. It was like pure, thick bliss.

Somewhere in the back of my mind, I was aware of Ares also undoing and pushing down his jeans. He fitted his cock into the crease of my ass and thrust against me at the same time Mannix thrust into me.

"It's a shame you're missing this, Nixon," Ice said conversationally. "It's really hot. I know, I know, you can't see. I'm sure you can imagine it. But don't imagine it, because I might need to stab your brain if you're thinking about our girlfriend like that."

Nixon grunted something unintelligible. It was likely all he was thinking about was his pain, and wishing Ice would hurry up and kill him.

"The more I get to know you, the more perfect you are," Mannix told me. "So perfect."

It figured that most girls wouldn't get turned on or want to be fucked while someone was chained up beside her been tortured. Right now, I didn't care if it was wrong. It felt right. Good.

Mannix thrust harder and faster, his sweated skin sliding on mine.

Ares ground into me, rubbing himself and grunting near my ear. At the same time, his hands gripped my breasts so tight it brought tears to my eyes. I didn't want him to stop.

Both guys came nearly in unison, a beat after I came for a second time. Our cries eventually dwindled down to silence.

"What a shame," Ice said with a sigh. "He passed out."

CHAPTER 13

ICE

I pushed open the door to Kennedy's room without knocking. It was already ajar, so I figured she wouldn't mind. Besides, I was kinda hoping to catch her off guard, or asleep. I would have woken her up.

I found her lying on her bed on her stomach, her laptop open in front of her. Her mesmerising eyes were focused on the screen. The colours in front of her lit her face. They made her look ethereal, like the goddess she was.

I lay down beside her and looked at her laptop.

"Studying again, I see." I overlapped my hands in front of me and rested my chin on them.

"Unless you've got some method to deliver information into my brain without me reading it, and then outputting it just from my thoughts, then yeah." She glanced over at me and smiled ruefully.

"I'll get on that." I grinned back at her. "But I warn you, it might not be ready until after you finish your degree."

"Figures." She closed the laptop and rolled over onto her back. Her eyes toward the ceiling, she let out a soft breath. "What happened the other day, in your workroom…"

"I'm an open book about all of it. Anything you want to ask me, go ahead and ask." I long ago got past any reservations I had about the things I did. I wasn't going to apologise for a drop of blood spilt, or scream of pain I drew from the people I worked with.

"You've done it a lot?"

"You could say that," I agreed. "I haven't lost count, but you probably don't want to know the particulars." It was like sexual partners. It was enough to know whether or not someone had experience. The exact details didn't matter. Not to me anyway.

She looked over at me now. "Does it ever make you feel, I don't know, grossed out?"

I answered her question with one of my own. "Regrets? It's easy to get caught up in the moment and then later on wish you hadn't."

"Not regrets exactly," she said. Her brow creased adorably. "I feel like I should have regrets or be sickened. Or something. But then I think about what he would have done to me and I don't feel bad about it at all. I feel—"

"Vindicated? Turned on?" I guessed.

She let out a grunt so soft I almost missed hearing it.

"A bit of those too. Mostly I feel… I don't know if powerful is the right word. I mean, we could have done anything to him and no one could stop us. It's so wrong, but at the same time…"

"Fucking awesome," I finished for her. "I started because I was fascinated with how bodies worked, but inflicting pain on people who have, or would, inflict it on other people is a rush. I was pissed that I didn't get to do that with Eric Parcell. Mannix was in a hurry. Our friend, Mr Nixon, made up for it."

"Is he…" she asked tentatively.

"Dead? No. Not yet." He wished he was. He'd begged me to kill him, but for what he would have done to Kennedy, he was getting what he deserved. It would have been a lot worse for him if he'd actually touched her. I could work slower and a lot more painfully if I needed to. Only three people got to touch her: me, Mannix and Ares. I didn't even want her touching herself. There was no need for her to get herself off when we could do that for her.

I rolled onto my side. "Do you want me to kill him? Because I can do that if that's what you want." I would do anything, or kill almost anyone, for her. If she wanted me to kill Mannix or Ares, I'd have to think twice about that. They were my brothers and they accepted me when the rest of the world didn't, or wouldn't. I'd do or kill anything or anyone for them too.

Her throat bobbed up and down as she swallowed. "Do you think he's suffered enough? I know what he would have done, but he didn't get to do it."

I kissed the tip of her nose. "You're so adorably big-hearted. If it means that much to you, I'll put him out of his misery in the morning." He was starting to get smelly and was making my workroom messy anyway.

"Thank you," she said softly. She looked like she wanted to ask something, but wasn't sure if she should.

"You want to come and watch?" I offered.

"Is it wrong that I do?" she asked.

"First of all, no, it's not wrong at all," I said firmly. "Second of all, you don't need validation from anyone but yourself. If the idea of pain, blood and death turns you on, that's completely okay. It gives me a raging hard-on every time. Are we normal? Maybe not. Do I give a fuck? Not even a small one. And neither should you. I'll bet you a million dollars Mannix told you the same thing."

"Yeah, he did, I just—" She exhaled softly out her nose. "Being told it's okay and accepting it myself are different things. You know?"

"I do know," I said. "I've been through all of the same feelings you're going through now. We all have. But you know the other guys got off as much as you did. We're all a twisted, dysfunctional, fucked up family. Which, in my opinion, is the best kind."

She was silent for a moment. When she spoke again it was to ask, "Has my mother been to your workroom?"

I pretended to misunderstand the meaning of her question. "Do you think she should?"

Kennedy batted me on the arm. "No, I don't. "I just thought if she knew about all the things then maybe she'd gone there and saw the things you do."

"Your mother has yet to grace my workroom with her presence," I said grandly. "In case you're curious, Leo has, but only once or twice. He's generally the kind of guy who orders a thing to be done and expects it to get done, but doesn't necessarily want to know or see the details. The only time he drops by is to see if we're spending his money the way he expects us to. He gets pissy about waste."

That was unfortunate. I'd be more than happy to have him sit in on the fun and games more often.

On the other hand, Mannix preferred his father to leave things like that to him. It helped to grow his influence in the business, and his ego. It wouldn't hurt Mannix when he took over his father's business if he had influence his father didn't.

If it was me, I'd have my eyes on every aspect, no matter how messy. That way, it was easier to discern if someone was trying to screw you over. We wouldn't, but Leo couldn't know that if he stayed away.

Telling him how to run his business was the top of a long list of things I would never do. I kept my nose out of it and did what was asked of me.

"Does this Samuel Bell have people who do for him what you do for Leo?" she asked.

"Without doubt," I said. "I've heard his stepson, Zachary, has a taste for blood. And possibly for his stepsister Chloe. From what I've heard, she and her twin sister, Lila are as nasty as two people can be. Before I met you, I would have happily been the meat in a Bell sister sandwich."

"What does it say about me if you have a thing for nasty people?" She raised her eyebrows at me.

"Either it says you're nastier than you think you are, or it says I'm reformed," I replied. "I'll leave that for you to decide." I kissed her forehead.

"I'm guessing it's the first one." Her freckled brow wrinkled cutely. "Not more than five minutes ago, I asked to come along and see a man die."

"Unfortunately, nastiness is wildly underrated as a positive character trait." I curled a section of her hair around my fingers. "The best people in the world are the nastiest. I can think of four straight off the top of my head."

She responded by speaking slowly. "You, Mannix, my mother, and Leo?"

I laughed. "You, Mannix, Ares and me," I corrected. "No offence to your mother or Leo, but I don't think either of them could be called nasty. Not the way the rest of us are."

"I didn't realise there was a measurement scale for something like that." She rolled back onto her stomach and lay on her arms. Her breasts were pushed forward enticingly.

"Sweet girl, there's a measurement scale for everything. It doesn't matter what it is, someone will rate it. People love to organise and quantify everything."

"Is that your professional observation, Doctor Miller?" she teased.

"Definitely." I liked the way that sounded, coming from her lips. I was a long way off being able to call myself that, but if she kept saying that, I might just be driven to keep on studying.

"Are you planning to do a PhD too?" I ask her. "Doctor Knight has a ring to it."

She snorted softly. "I'd sound like a supervillain. If I did that, I have to get myself a cat."

I grinned. "We could all be doctors except Mannix. Although, knowing him, if we all went and did our PhDs, he'd feel left out if he didn't do it too."

"Or he could just buy himself one." Her expression was wry.

I snapped my fingers. "Or you could hack into whichever university you like and give us all PhDs."

I frowned and quickly corrected myself. "Don't hack into Brutham Academy. Doing that would shorten your life expectancy by a large amount."

"Is it really that bad?" She didn't look as alarmed as I might have expected. If anything, she looked curious. Hopefully not too curious to try it, because I wasn't exaggerating. Brutham Academy was as possessive of its digital data as me and the other guys were of Kennedy.

"At the end of first year, they let third and fourth years hunt us down," I said. "If we've made the right alliances and haven't pissed off the wrong people, we might just survive. Obviously, the three of us did."

Her eyes widened. "Wait a minute. By hunt you down you mean—"

"Exactly that. We're given a starting position and a location we need to get to. If we get there without anyone catching up with us, we pass. If we didn't, I wouldn't be here telling you this."

Her lips dropped apart. "They're literally allowed to kill students if they catch up with them?"

"They're not just allowed to, they're *encouraged* to. This life is tough. Only the strongest, best connected and smartest, survive. On the upside, we got to do the same to the first years when it was our turn. It was... exhilarating. But we weren't killing for the fun of it. The first years who weren't connected, and allied with other powerful students, were often ones who were ostracised for a reason."

"They touched the wrong guy's girlfriend?" Kennedy guessed.

"That's certainly been a reason for someone to be targeted in the past." And would be a reason for it in the future. Most of the guys in this life were brought up to understand that they protect their woman at all costs. I couldn't think of a single one who wasn't the, 'touch her and you die,' type.

"I'm starting to think the world is a different place than what I thought it was." She sighed.

"In a good way, or in a bad way?" I tangled my fingers tighter in her hair.

"I don't know yet. Maybe a bit of both." She looked thoughtful for a moment. "How reliant is Samuel Bell on his computer systems?"

I smiled. "Very. Do you have something in mind?"

CHAPTER 14
KENNEDY

I'd needed to have this conversation for ages, but now the moment was here, I didn't know how to start it.

"Coffee?" I asked as I added water to the coffee machine. If in doubt, lead with caffeine.

"I'll never say no to coffee." Mum slipped into a stool and rested her elbows on the marble countertop. Her engagement and wedding rings were so chunky and ornate, they took up most of her finger between her knuckle and the first joint. Any bigger and she wouldn't have been able to bend the digit.

"So… Nice honeymoon?" We might as well continue with small talk.

"It was lovely." She smiled like a woman head over heels in love. It was adorable in an, 'ewww, mushy stuff with my parent,' kind of way.

"New Zealand is beautiful at this time of year. Any time of year really. We went on a helicopter ride in Rotorua and landed on the side of Mount Tarawera. The view was incredible. And the dormant volcano wasn't bad either." She gave me an exaggerated wink.

My mother's attempt at winking left a lot to be desired at the best of times.

"I thought about asking the pilot to fly us back home so he could meet you, but you seem somewhat busy right now." She didn't even try to hide the fact she was fishing. She clearly wanted an update on me and the guys.

I might give her one, once she was forthcoming with what I wanted to know.

"Did you know Leo was involved in organised crime?" Shit, I hadn't intended to be that blunt, but when the words were out, they were out.

The coffee machine bubbled and started to pour out an espresso.

Such an ordinary sound as the counterpoint to an extraordinary question.

She didn't flinch. She didn't even blink. Not even one drop of surprise showed on her face.

"Yes," she said simply. "I've known since before I met him. How do you think we were able to afford the lifestyle we had before Leo?"

Yeah, I suspected that, but to hear the words coming from her mouth was a different thing altogether. Especially with no attempt to deny anything. I thought she'd at least hesitate.

She placed a palm on the countertop and leaned over closer.

"Before you get all worked up, I didn't tell you because you didn't need to know at the time. I wanted to keep you out of that life for as long as possible."

I stepped back until I was pressed against the bench in front of the coffee maker, physically as far as I could get while being in the same kitchen.

"Not forever?" I asked. "Why would you want me involved in it at all?"

She raised her hand briefly to gesture around the kitchen. "Because most people can't afford places like this. I want the best for you. I want you to have everything you need and want, without having to worry about where the next meal is coming from. If that means stepping into morally grey territory, so be it."

"So you made that choice for me when you asked me to come to Dusk Bay?" I asked. "You knew what would happen?"

"Not really." She sat back. "The most I expected was that you would finish your degree and leave to get on with your life. I didn't realise you'd let those boys drag you in so deep or so quick." That was definitely a look of disapproval on her face.

It was a bit fucking late for that.

"Why does that bother you?" I handed her the coffee, then put my cup in place in the coffee machine to let it fill.

"Because there's morally grey, and then there's those three boys." She curled her hands around her cup. "Mannix seems very ambitious. I'm not sure Isaac is all there, and Ares is downright grumpy and unpleasant."

I couldn't help my body from stiffening the way it did when she spoke.

None of what she said was wrong, not exactly, but there was so much more to them than that.

"I like them," I said, my voice tight. "Leo doesn't seem to mind Mannix and I being together." If there was anyone's opinion Mum cared about, it was Leo's.

"Leo might be slightly shortsighted where his son is concerned." She sipped her coffee. "Maybe I should talk to him."

Maybe I should fling my hot coffee in her face and see how it sounded when she screamed.

Where the fuck did that thought come from? I should try to get some more sleep. Clearly I wasn't getting enough right now.

The coffee machine finished and I picked up my cup, but held onto it carefully. Just in case it jumped out of my hands and threw itself at her.

"There's no need for that." I tried to keep my voice light, but this whole conversation had me on edge. "I'm an adult and I can make my own choices. You wanted me to come here and get involved with this lifestyle. You don't get to choose how that happens."

Her expression changed to one I'd never seen before. Dangerous, a clear warning.

"If Leo orders Mannix to stay away from you, Mannix will have no choice but to obey him. Same with the other two. If that happens, it will only be because we have your best interests at heart. Those boys are trouble."

"Only because Leo tells them to be," I said coldly.

"Right up until Mannix's ambition gets too big for him to listen to his father anymore."

"Is that what this is about?" I asked. "Leo is worried Mannix is going to step on his toes?" To hear Mannix talk, Leo might be justified in those concerns, but no time soon. "It seems to me like we all have bigger fish to fry. Like Samuel Bell."

Now she looked surprised. "How do you know about him?"

I snorted a bitter laugh and told her everything, except what happened in the workroom. No doubt she knew the details of what went on down there, but if she didn't, she wasn't going to hear it from me. Especially the bit about me using pliers on Frank Nixon. I suspected that was the kind of thing she meant when she said the guys were dragging me down into the dark.

Personally, I wondered if I was there all along, it just took time for my life to catch up with my proclivities.

"So it was Samuel Bell who had you followed?" She looked furious. "You didn't think to tell me this sooner?"

"You were busy getting married," I reminded her. "And then you were on your honeymoon. Besides, you seem to know more about all of this than I do. I'm surprised you didn't know already."

Had Mannix not told Leo? The last thing I wanted to do was throw Mannix under the bus with his father. That would only create more tension, and right now there was enough of that going around.

"Besides, I know nothing about Samuel Bell except he seems to have taken a dislike to me."

Mum hopped off her stool and came around the island to me.

"I'll never let anything happen to you."

I was taller than her when she didn't wear heels, but she still had that fierce, tiger mother thing going on. I could almost imagine her with a set of pliers in her hand, ready to pull off the eyelids of anyone who dared to think about hurting her baby.

Almost.

I might be projecting, because that sounded like something I'd be tempted to do if anyone came after a child of mine. That included the students from the gym. Hurting children was the worst crime I could think of. Stealing their innocence, scarring their small bodies. Anyone who did that got exactly what they deserved.

She closed her eyes and rubbed the tip of her fingers across her forehead. Her fingernails were blood red, like she needed the camouflage if she ever scratched anyone's eyes out.

"I'm starting to think I should have let you stay in Sydney. You were safer there." She sounded tired. Frustrated. Like all she wanted to do was keep me safe, but instead she'd dragged me straight into the lion's den. Dangerous though it might be, it was also secure.

"Was I? I'm still Leo's stepdaughter. This place is much more secure than uni ever was. I would have been a sitting duck up there." No one would have stopped Frank Nixon from getting to me on or around campus.

"There are other places," she said.

"Brutham Academy?" I suggested, half-joking. I doubted I would have made it to the end of first year. Or would I? My mother's relationship with Leo might have given me connections that saw me get past the trial Ice told me about. Added to that, I was fit, athletic and quick. I should give myself more credit for being a badass.

"That would be one good option," she agreed. "I went there. They would have updated the security several times since then."

I shook my head. What the fuck did she just say?

"You went there?" Just when I thought she couldn't surprise me anymore, she came out with that little gem. Had she killed anyone?

No, I did *not* want to know the answer to that. Not in this lifetime or the next. Some secrets were better kept hidden.

I was starting to wonder who this woman standing in front of me really was. She looked like my mother, she sounded like her, but the things she said blew my mind.

I lightly touched her arm. "Just checking I'm not dreaming." I put my cup down and leaned over the counter on my elbows.

"I feel like I've entered some kind of alternate reality. Or an episode of a superhero TV show where they're all bad guys for that forty minutes. Only, this seems to be my life."

She laughed. "None of us are bad guys. Not exactly. We just like to get what we want and, unlike the average person, we've found a way to do it. Sometimes it's slightly illegal—"

I snorted a laugh. "Sometimes?" As far as I could tell, it was more than slightly illegal a lot of the time. Bad guys was both a relative and a subjective term.

She was right about one thing, there was an awful lot of grey involved in all of this. I couldn't remember the last time I saw the world in black and white, but things were more and more complicated and convoluted the longer I was here in Dusk Bay.

"Yes, only sometimes," she agreed. "Only when it's completely necessary. Otherwise, people like Leo are nothing more than savvy business people. He sees an opportunity and he grabs it. And he has enough money to make it happen. There's nothing wrong with that."

"That depends who gets stepped on along the way." My expression was wry. "I suspect a few people wouldn't agree with that assumption."

"Of course not. You can't please everyone. At the end of the day, the best thing you can do is please yourself and those you care about. No one else really matters."

"You sound like Leo," I remarked. "Actually, you sound like Mannix and Ice. They're passionately dedicated to taking care of people they care about. Including me and each other. Maybe if you got to know them—"

"I'd still know they're trouble," she interrupted. "It's easy to get blinded by your feelings, and your hormones. I'm not denying they're good-looking boys, but mark my words. They'll lead you down a path you may not want to go on, and once you're down there, there may be no coming back from it. And if there isn't, I might not be able to save you."

I straightened up and looked her right in the eyes. "Maybe I don't want saving."

She looked at me sadly. "Then it might be too late already."

CHAPTER 15

KENNEDY

"Ice said you had an idea of how we might be able to deal with Samuel Bell." Mannix wore a pair of shorts and nothing else. His chiselled chest and stomach were slick with sweat. His hair was damp, stuck to his forehead. His face was slightly red, suggesting he'd come from the gym in the back of the house. The one in town was weeks away yet. Maybe longer.

Before I could answer, he grinned and walked over to the side of the pool. He jumped, his knees tucked up to his body, arms around his legs. He landed with a splash so big it threatened to flood over me, even though I was leaning against the far end of the pool.

He surged up to the surface, exploding out of the water like he was the son of Neptune. He shook his hair and face, sending droplets flying. Water cascaded down his chest like a stone waterfall, or something from a movie. If I had a phone in my hand, he'd be my next lockscreen.

He gave me a knowing look and slowly swam over to me, chin bobbing just above the water.

The expression on his face was going to make me flood in a whole different way. He looked like he wanted to bend me over, slam his cock into me and fuck me silly.

My tongue slid over my lips.

"Not so much him as his computer systems." I forced myself to focus in spite of the blood thundering through my brain. Not to mention the rest of my body. Meeting these guys awakened something in me I had no idea existed. I didn't care what Mum said, I couldn't stay away from them if I wanted to.

"I was thinking, I could create a virus that would corrupt all his files. Or better yet, erase them." The headache that would cause him would almost make up for wanting me dead.

Almost.

Mannix smiled and cupped my cheeks in his hands. He wore a massive watch which must have been waterproof, because water dripped off it and he didn't look concerned. If I had to guess, I'd think it was worth a shit ton of money. Probably a drop in the ocean for him, like so many other things around here.

"How long would that take?"

"That depends if you want to scramble everything or delete it altogether. A nasty virus might take me a week or two. Anything more than that will take a lot longer. And it would need a delivery system."

"What sort of delivery system?" He seemed to like the idea.

"Anything from a USB drive, to something that would connect to his systems by Bluetooth. A USB would be faster, but more dangerous because it would have to be done in person. So would Bluetooth, but you wouldn't have to touch anything. Whoever would deliver it would still have to go there in person."

I felt like a spy planning to gain information from some foreign government, not a mobster trying to bring down the enemy. I remembered what Mum said about being morally grey, but as far as I was concerned, this was justice. If we messed with his systems, no one had to die. It seemed like the perfect compromise to me.

Unless he figured out who did it. In which case, we might be slightly fucked. I trusted the guys could do this in a way that wouldn't come back on us. There was probably a long list of assholes they could blame it on.

Mannix nodded slowly. "How good are you at disabling security systems?" The question was accompanied with another knowing look.

"I wasn't going to sit back and let you lock me in here against my will." I raised my chin. I wasn't going to apologise, but I wondered how he knew I'd fiddled with the code on the gate.

"Lucky guess," he said as though he read my mind. "It's exactly the thing I'd expect my girl to do. Exactly what I would do if I was you." He brushed his lips over mine.

"For what it's worth, it wasn't easy. It took me days just to get into the gate's system, much less mess around with it. If I can get around that, I can get around whatever security Bell has on his house. It would also take time and I'd have to know what he has in place first."

"If I can get you that information, can you get us in?"

"In theory," I said slowly. "It would be a lot riskier than infecting his systems with a virus. I could make it so it plays an obnoxious song whenever anyone tries to boot up a computer." That wouldn't do much damage to anything but his sanity. Unless he liked the song, in which case it would backfire.

Mannix chuckled. "As tempting as that is, that's going to do a short-term amount of damage. Someone like him will have all his shit backed up in seventeen different places. If we're really going to hit him, we need to take out as much as we can. Even if doing it is as risky as hell. What's life without a little risk?"

"Boring." I hadn't seen Ice arrive, but now he was crouched down beside us. Like Mannix, he only wore shorts and a sheen of sweat.

Ares stood right behind him, looking like a blond god.

"Who's boring?" Ares curled his lip in my direction, like they must be talking about me. His attitude towards me had thawed somewhat in the last week or so, but he was still an abrasive asshole.

Still, I couldn't stop thinking about his hands all over my breasts.

I knew he wanted more, but I wouldn't push him.

"Life without risk," Ice said without looking over his shoulder. "What are we risking and when do we leave?" He didn't even know what it was and he was all in.

I admired that about him. That and the way his damp hair coiled around his ears.

"We're risking dying, and not for a few weeks." Mannix raised his face and looked up at both guys. In a handful of words, he explained what we'd talked about.

"I'm in." Ice stood and did a perfect swan dive into the water.

"Sounds like fun." Ares followed him a moment later, so close he almost hit Ice as he resurfaced.

Rather than being mad, Ice laughed. "You're going to have to try harder than that if you're going to sink the Iceman."

"More like Ice*berg*," Ares said. "Always in the way when you're trying to steer your ship around."

Ice frowned at him for a moment. "Is that a euphemism for jerking yourself off? Because it sounds like one."

One of Ares's eyebrows jerked upward. "That sounds accurate, because my cock is the size of the Titanic."

I waited for a beat or two, but none of the guys took the bait so I decided to.

"You realise the Titanic is really small in comparison to modern cruise ships, right?"

He flipped me off. "I meant the Titanic compared to her contemporaries."

"Sure you did." Ice drew out the first word in teasing disbelief. "Also the Titanic is a wreck at the bottom of the ocean, in case you've forgotten."

Ares rolled his eyes and shook his head. "Bro, you're missing the point. The point is—"

"I know what the point is," Ice said. "Your dick is big and fancy. And likes being wet."

"And should probably stay away from Ice," Ares added with a grunt. He started to paddle across to the other side of the pool.

Ice frowned at his back. "Ouch. Lucky I'm the hot kind of ice, not the cold kind."

"Yes, you are," I said to him.

"Definitely," Mannix agreed.

They both locked eyes on each other.

My stomach did a couple of cartwheels and a backsault. Were they about to kiss? My heart raced like crazy at the thought of it.

"Tell us what you want," Mannix whispered, without taking his eyes off Ice.

Was it just that easy?

My tongue darted over my lips.

I started to say, 'Only if you want to,' but stopped myself. They wanted me to be honest about what I wanted, so that's what I'd give them.

"I want you to kiss each other." Blood pumped so loud in my ears I hardly heard myself speak, but I knew the words came out and were audible, because Mannix put his hands on Ice's shoulders and drew him closer until their chests met.

The first kiss was just a brushing of lips, but soon became deeper, more passionate.

The wet smacking of their mouths was almost enough to make me come on the spot.

And then they were drawing apart, their eyes still on each other.

"I've been wanting to do that for a long time," Ice said softly.

"Me too." Mannix looked at Ice like he hadn't seen him before. Not in this light anyway.

"Did you like that, Princess?" Mannix turned his head slightly to look at me.

I swallowed hard. "I liked that a lot. It was hot, and you two together is… It looks so right."

"It's as right as you with either of us, or both of us." Ice slipped an arm around me and pulled me closer to both of them. "Now if we can just convince Ares."

"Ares will come around in his own time," Mannix said.

We all turned to look over to where Ares swam laps of the pool.

As far as I could tell, they'd all done at least an hour or two of exercise in the gym, and now they were out here doing more. They were nothing if not dedicated to keeping their bodies looking fucking amazing.

I was one hundred percent here for it. That was the reason I was in the pool myself. To exercise and keep fit.

If Ares noticed us watching, he gave no sign. He powered on through the water, arm over arm, over arm. He could have contended with any Olympic swimmer, if he wanted to. I didn't blame him if he didn't. I understood the level of dedication it took to get to a high level of an athlete's chosen sport. I'd opted to focus on my studies and keep gymnastics as a hobby, and I didn't regret that. Even if I was good enough, I wasn't dedicated enough to make it to the top. I preferred to be the top in cybersecurity, and stick to climbing, swinging and tumbling for what spare time I had.

I grabbed Mannix's wrist and looked at his watch.

"I should hop out. I have to interview coaches in an hour." I wished Charlie hadn't turned out to be such a dickhead, because this process was a pain in my ass. What did I know about hiring staff? All I knew was that I wanted someone who wasn't going to try to kill me, or handcuff me to a chair, or hand me over to someone who would kill me, or…

Yeah, it was a long list.

"We're coming with you," Mannix said.

Ice nodded his agreement.

"Maybe I should hire Nicola to run the place while I coach," I said with a sigh. I headed for the ladder to haul myself up out of the water. "How did you get her to sell the place anyway?"

Mannix grinned. "We knew a few things about her she didn't want other people to know about." He was smug as hell.

Whatever it was, it must have been big. She was attached to the place. Did I want to know what she did? As long as it had nothing to do with the children, then probably not. Honestly, if it had anything to do with the children, she'd be dead right now.

I grabbed up my towel. It dangled from my fingers. "You bribed her?"

"I prefer to think of it as gentle persuasion," he said. "Bribery is such an ugly word."

"Since when did you care about words being ugly?" Ice asked him.

"Never," Mannix admitted. "But there's a first time for everything." He gave Ice a glance and I knew he was thinking about their kiss.

"As long as the first isn't the only time," I said.

Ice grinned. "Not a chance. That was the first time of many."

CHAPTER 16
ICE

"That's the last of them." Mannix nodded as the fifth potential gymnastics coach headed towards Kennedy's office. Most of them were older students of the gym, or those like Kennedy who used it recreationally. One or two of them were from other places, recently moved to Dusk Bay.

Very recently, judging by the look the fourth one gave us as she stepped towards the door. For some reason, her eyes were wide, nervous.

I couldn't resist sticking my face out towards her and saying, "Boo."

She let out a squeak and scurried out the door.

I chuckled. "I've still got it." I might have flexed.

"Yes, you do." Mannix watched the door until it closed. He had his best, 'don't fuck with me,' expression on his face. He'd walked in the door with it and it hadn't left since.

Personally, I liked it, but for some reason it seemed to intimidate everyone who walked through the door. If they couldn't deal with it now, then they wouldn't stay working here for long.

I leaned back against the wall and crossed my legs at my ankles. "You already know who she should hire, don't you?"

The big question here was, would he give Kennedy a choice? She wanted to run this place her way, and I respected that, but we needed to trust whoever she had working for her. She didn't need another Charlie.

I was still sulking because Mannix wouldn't let me take him down to my workroom. Kennedy didn't need him anymore and he *had* touched her. In my book, that made him a prime candidate for a bit of fun and maybe some experimentation. There was always something to learn when it came to inflicting pain.

"We can still use him," Mannix had said in his stubborn-as-fuck tone. There was no moving him when he was in that frame of mind.

"Use him for what?" Ares asked.

The only reply Mannix would give was to say, "I have a few things in mind. Ice can have him when I'm finished."

I held out my pinky finger. "Promise?"

Mannix gave me a funny look but hooked my pinky finger with his. "If there's anything left of him, I promise you can have it."

I pumped the air with my fist. "Yes."

In retrospect I shouldn't have gotten so excited, because that was days ago and Charlie was still running around in one piece. And so, the sulking continued.

"Two of them have parents who work for Ric DiMarco," Mannix said. "Of those two, one also drives a delivery van. The other works in a restaurant making pizza. It's a no-brainer."

"Absolutely." I nodded so vigorously I had to check my hair to make sure the bun hadn't come loose. "Pizza maker for the win."

Mannix snorted. "I can see where that would be useful, but a delivery van can go places others can't."

He had a point, but I still liked the idea of having a skilled pizza maker around.

Priorities.

"You know, I don't think Kennedy is taking into consideration her employee's future contribution to the family business," I said. "She might disagree with your assessment."

The idea was to pick a gymnastics coach, not a lackey for Mannix, Leo or Ric. Wasn't it?

"Then we'll have to persuade her," Mannix said reasonably.

"Why do I have the feeling my workroom is going to get really busy, very soon?" I would absolutely not put it past Mannix to dispose of the other candidates just to get his way.

"Because Kennedy's safety is important. Nothing and no one is going to get in the way of that."

"Including Kennedy?" I asked. "Our girl might disagree with that." I knew she knew how important her safety was. I saw that in the way she quickly and easily slipped into the role when Nixon was chained to the ceiling. The way she embraced her darkness was one of the hottest things I've ever seen. Followed closely by watching her fuck Mannix and Ares while I tortured the man.

I saw the darkness in her the first time we met, but now she was coming to see it. I loved every minute of it.

"Let me worry about that." Mannix was silent for a minute or two before he broke it by saying, "About that kiss."

I hadn't expected him to bring it up, but now he did, I was slightly worried.

"You don't regret it, do you?" I hadn't had to deal with rejection very often. I wasn't good at it. People tended to get hurt while I worked through my frustration. I was okay with that, but they weren't.

"No." His reply wasn't quick, but it was firm. "Just making sure you don't."

I'd never seen uncertainty on his face, and it was only a flash, but it was there.

Exploiting vulnerabilities was one of my superpowers, but I wouldn't do it with Mannix. Or anyone I cared about. The feeling it gave me was conflicting. I wasn't used to it from him and it threw me off a little bit. If anything, it made me like him even more.

Who knew there was an actual person with feelings under his rock hard façade?

"I have absolutely no regrets." I pushed myself up off the wall and stepped over to give him an awkward bro hug. I'd kissed him and I'd had his cock down my throat, but I wasn't used to actual affection with another guy. Hugging, snuggling, that was out of my wheelhouse, but I was willing to learn.

"Actually, I have one," I said. I looked for the flicker of uncertainty again, but it wasn't there. His stoic-as-fuck mask was back in place. In case there was some misery, I decided to put him out of it.

"I wish we did it sooner, and I hope we can do more of it."

His brief nod was the only sign of his relief. He put a hand on the back of my head and spoke in a whisper.

"You should know that, as far as I'm concerned, you're mine, as much as Kennedy is. If anyone touches either of you, unless it's Ares, I'll rip off their faces and make them eat it."

I whispered back. "That is so fucking hot. Also, I'd like to see that. How would you keep them alive long enough for them to eat their own face?"

He sounded like he almost choked on a laugh. "That's your department, I just make the threats."

I smiled. "Got it." Of course now my mind was in a whirl, thinking how to do just that for him. With any luck, I could try it on Charlie soon.

"If anyone touches you or Kennedy, unless it's Ares, I get to use my chair." I kept my chair for extra special occasions. As fun as it was to chain people to the ceiling, the chair was more personal. It let me get down to their level. Also, with their feet restrained, I got to do all sorts of interesting things to their toes.

They were fascinating thing, toes. Sensitive, often ticklish, and beautifully protected by nails. Until they weren't.

I could spend days playing with people's feet and never get tired of it.

"What happens if anyone touches Ares?" I jerked my head towards the new gym, where he was currently overlooking the renovation. He seemed to have taken it on as his own personal project. No one seemed to mind, so we left him to it.

"He punches them out," Mannix said. "Failing that, I'm sure we can think of some suitable punishment for them."

"Maybe we could set up that workroom out in the Simpson desert like we talked about," I said. I was curious to see how people would cope when being restrained and tortured out in the desert, under the relentless Australian sun. I suspected it would suck really hard. For them. And for me, because I hated extreme heat like that. Still, it would be worth it.

"We could buy an island and you could use the beach for that," Mannix said distractedly.

I followed his gaze and watched the fifth interviewee leave Kennedy's office and head for the door.

He gave us an uneasy look before he hurried out.

"I don't like the idea of any men working here," I remarked.

"There's going to be men working next door during and after the renovation," Mannix pointed out. "Although there are several women tradies in there now."

"We could make it a women-only gym." That would circumvent any drama with other men being near Kennedy.

"Then we couldn't use it." Still, Mannix looked like he was considering the idea.

"Then we make it women and us only." That was a simple enough solution as far as I was concerned.

"Let's see how we go when it's finished."

"Is it too late to change and make it a ballet studio instead? There would be fewer men there then." I'd still use it, because I quite enjoyed ballet when I was a kid. I never cared that some people thought it was a girly thing to do. It was hard work and it was fun, and I enjoyed being one of only two boys amongst all those girls.

"Or a beauty salon." I frowned. "Never mind. Guys would go there for their back, crack and sack wax. That would be much worse."

"Yeah, much," Mannix agreed. "That's something Kennedy doesn't need to see or think about."

"What do I not need to see or think about?" Kennedy stepped out of her office in time to hear his last comment.

"Other men's balls," I said lightly. "We were talking about what would happen if other guys were around here."

She gave me a funny look, like she couldn't quite put the presence of other guys, and her seeing their balls, together.

Fair enough, out of context it probably seemed like a strange thing to be talking about. On the other hand, we were us and strange was what we did. Okay, it was what *I* did, but the other guys went along with it most of the time.

Before she could figure it out, Mannix spoke.

"You're hiring the second one." He didn't even try to phrase it as a question. It was a statement he expected to be a fact. There wasn't even a millimetre of leeway or indecision. His face was somehow even more stony than usual.

Predictably, Kennedy looked annoyed.

"Am I?" She managed to keep her tone light, but it came with an audible bristle. "I didn't realise you interviewed them all before they got here."

Mannix gave her a look past his eyebrows. One slightly tinged with disbelief.

"We thoroughly vetted them long before they walked through the door. If they hadn't passed that, none of them would be here. The second one is the most suitable." He wasn't budging.

Neither was she. "I haven't made my mind up yet. When I do I'll—"

He caught her wrist and pulled her until they were chest to chest. "You'll hire the second one," he said again. "Otherwise the other four won't be around to be options."

"Are you threatening me?" She looked up at him, her gaze unwavering.

His eyebrows dropped. "No. I'm threatening *them*. The second one, Greta Ferguson, is qualified, experienced and has a job which brings references. All of those references back up the choice. The only reason she wasn't working here already, was because her parents' interests clashed with Nicola's."

"She was nice," Kennedy conceded. "I was leaning towards her anyway."

Mannix smiled. "Good." He loosened his grip on her wrist and tugged her in for a long, slow kiss. "You can tell her this afternoon."

No one was as smug as Mannix when he got his way, not even Ares.

Kennedy, on the other hand, looked slightly less impressed. I had no doubt she would hire Greta, but only because she wanted to. Pleasing Mannix was an added bonus.

I think the only one who didn't realise that was him.

CHAPTER 17

KENNEDY

"How's the virus going?"

Of all the people to take an interest, I was surprised it was Ares.

All the guys had a vested interest, but he was the one to ask.

Specifically, I was surprised he chose to talk to me. He barely said two words to me since that day down in the workroom. If I thought he was distant before, then he was even more so now. He didn't even bother to smirk or curl his lip at me. In fact, he seemed to be trying hard to avoid me. That was difficult when we were all living under the same roof, but he managed it most of the time.

When he actually asked me a question, it took a couple of moments before I could answer.

"It's almost ready," I replied. "With everything that's going on, and trying to keep up with my studies, I haven't had as much time as I'd hoped, but it's nearly there."

Now that Greta had settled into her new second job—she was going to keep driving her courier van as well—things started to calm down somewhat.

He stepped further into the study and looked over my shoulder, at the screen.

"Looks like a cat walked on a keyboard."

I think he meant it as an insult, but I laughed. "It does, doesn't it? If I asked my computer to read it out loud, it wouldn't know what to make of it. But if I fed it into another computer, it would screw it up."

"That's the idea, isn't it?" He pulled over another chair and straddled it backwards, his arms resting on the back of the chair.

"Basically, but at this point they could clean it up. If it could get past their security systems. There's a way to go before it'll do what we want it to do."

"Sounds like fucking with people's heads is easier than fucking with their computers." His eyes went from the screen to me.

"Probably. Modern computer systems are designed so people can't get past them with things like this. Human brains are both more complex and more simple."

"That's true," he agreed. "It's easy to mess with people and scare them, but wiping all the information that's in there..." He tapped the side of his head with the tip of his finger.

"That's a virtual impossibility. Especially when it comes to forgetting things we want to forget. That stuff is harder to dislodge than most things."

"Are you speaking from experience?" I asked gently. If he wanted to open up to me, I'd give him the chance to do that.

For a moment, I thought he might actually tell me, but then his expression shut right down, tighter than ever.

"We all have baggage. I bet you still remember that night in the forest after the masked ball. The way you felt when we appeared. Or did you stumble on us when we were already there?" He didn't give me a chance to answer.

"Do you think about the way Mannix sliced open Eric's throat? The way Ice stabbed him in the eye while I held him down so he couldn't run? Do Ice's words haunt your dreams, little mouse?"

In spite of myself, I shivered.

"I think about all of those things. Even knowing what I know now, it still gives me the creeps." It most likely always would.

I found my arms wrapped around myself. "Why are you asking about it?"

He smiled, clearly pleased he got to me the way he had.

"Just making sure you haven't forgotten what we're all capable of." He sat up and stared me down.

"I was there in the warehouse, remember?" I managed to keep my voice even. "I think you're saying that because you're scared."

He scoffed. "What do I have to be scared about, little mouse?"

I leaned towards him. "I think you want to fuck with my head because you're scared to fuck with my body. I think you're pissed off at yourself for touching me the other day. I think you're even more pissed off because you want to do it again. And again."

I moved closer. "And again."

His hand shot out and wrapped around my throat. His eyes were like chips of blue ice.

"Grinding against you one time doesn't mean I want to do it again. I got caught in the moment. All that blood, all that *pain*. It made my balls so heavy, my cock so hard. I needed release and you were there. That was it. Don't read more into it than there is."

I met his gaze. "Did you know choking is the new dozen roses?" His hand around my throat made me wet as hell. "Doing it just means you care."

His fingers tightened.

I had to suppress a moan. If he pulled me onto the top of the desk and fucked me, I'd be one hundred percent into it.

We both knew it.

He dropped his hand. "I wouldn't want you to think I care, when I don't." His tone was harsh, but rough with need.

I couldn't see past the back of the chair. I didn't need to. I knew his cock would be rock hard. I tried not to picture it, or imagine how it would feel if he slid it inside my body.

"Did you study delusion at uni? Because I know you don't hate me as much as you pretend to."

"Maybe I hate you more." He shifted uncomfortably in his seat. "I might be pretending to be nice once in a while to keep the peace."

If that was the case, he wasn't good at it. Or maybe he had different ideas of being nice than I did. Mine usually didn't involve sneering, smirking and generally being an asshole.

I cocked my head. "I don't think you hate me at all. I think maybe for some reason, you hate yourself, but I don't think you hate me. No more than you hate Mannix or Ice."

"Why would I hate myself? I'm hot, smart and awesome." He smirked.

I wasn't going to feed his already inflated ego by agreeing with him.

"I don't know," I admitted. "Maybe because you don't have the same power Mannix does, or his father does. Maybe because you don't get to slice people up the way Ice does. Maybe for some other reason. Were you not cuddled enough as a kid?"

His eyes flicked to the side and I knew I hit a nerve.

"You know, whatever you need, we're here for you," I said gently. "You don't always have to put up the tough guy act."

That brought his chin up. "Who says it's an act?"

"I haven't studied as much psychology as you have, but it's always an act," I said. "Underneath every exterior is a vulnerable person. Even yours. Even Mannix and Ice. Even me."

"It's not an act." His chin dipped slightly.

There was definitely a scared little boy under there somewhere. He'd lived so long in an environment where you don't show fear, in case someone used it against you. He'd suppressed it like the others had, but it was there.

What would it take to bring it out the rest of the way? And would he hate me if I saw it? Legitimately hate me, I mean.

I shrugged. "If you say so."

"I do say so. I'm starting to think I was right about you. You're a pain in the ass."

"Funny, I was thinking the same about you." He liked to think he was a big, bad, tough dude, and he was, but deep down there was a lot more to Ares Turner than he showed people.

He grunted. "I didn't hear you complaining about what I was doing to your ass the other day. In fact, you seemed to be enjoying yourself. Did you like the way I touched your tits? I know I left bruises on them."

I quickly glanced down and then back up again.

"I did like it," I said. "But the bruises have almost gone."

He glanced down too. "Shame. I must not have applied enough pressure. They should have lasted much longer than that."

I waited until he looked back up to speak again. "You'd like to leave more on them, wouldn't you? You get pleasure out of giving other people pain. Do you like getting it in return? Do you like being spanked, or do you want to be the one doing the spanking?"

The way his pupils contracted was all the answer I needed.

He leaned forward again. "If I spanked you, the bruises would last a lot longer. You'd be lucky if you could sit down for a month."

I leaned forward too, until our noses were almost close enough to brush against each other.

When I spoke, my voice was as rough as his was a couple of minutes earlier.

"Don't threaten me with a good time."

He looked straight into my eyes. His breath was on my lips.

I breathed it in. The taste it left on my tongue was warm, like cum, honey and coffee all mixed together.

"How wet are you?" he whispered.

"Drenched," I whispered back. "Dripping." If I wasn't careful, I was going to have a trickle of slick down the inside of my thighs. "How hard are you?"

"Like a fucking rock," he admitted. "You're going to be the death of me. You piss me off more than anyone I've ever met, but I also want to fuck you more than anyone else. But I'm not going to."

"You're not?" There wasn't more than a hair or two between our lips. One movement, one bump and we'd kiss.

"No. When I fuck you, it's going to be something you'll never forget. I'll paddle your ass until you scream and beg me to slam my cock into you. I'm going to give you more pleasure and pain than you ever imagined. When I'm done with you, you'll be nothing more than a puddle. You won't be able to walk for days. You're going to feel me for weeks."

I was already almost a puddle just from his words. These guys were going to be the absolute end of me. And I couldn't wait.

We sat like that for at least a few minutes more, inhaling and swallowing each other's breaths. When I thought he might give in and kiss me anyway, he sat up, away from me.

He gave me a look like he couldn't believe he'd said any of that, and he was angry with me for—I don't know what. Hearing it? Making him say it, although I didn't?

Whatever it was, I felt like we were right back at the start again. Or close enough to it anyway. Whatever walls he'd lowered slightly, he shoved back up into place. I could almost see him locking them and throwing away the key.

"You should hurry up with that virus." He was all businesslike now. It was almost as though the time between his first question and now didn't exist. Didn't happen at all. Like the only conversation we had was about the virus and the plan to go after Samuel Bell.

"I could if I wasn't being distracted," I retorted. If he was going to behave like nothing passed between us, then so would I.

"I'll get out of here then, little mouse," he said mockingly. He got up off the chair and started towards the door.

I turned back to my computer, but before he could leave I said, "You said *when* you fuck me, not *if.*"

He stopped in the doorway for a few beats, then stalked away.

CHAPTER 18

KENNEDY

"You're going to need this." Mannix held a dress bag over his arm as he stepped into the room and closed the door behind him.

We'd arrived in Sydney that morning, on the first flight out of Dusk Bay. Mannix only told us last night that we were coming at all. He'd hustled us on and off the plane and into a small hotel. It was the kind of place where none of the staff asked any questions, or paid much attention to people's comings and goings.

It was also the kind of place visitors shouldn't ask too many questions, because the carpet was stained, and so were the quilts covering both beds. I decided against peeling back the sheets to see what state they were in.

"When did you have time to organise this?" I slid the zipper aside far enough to reveal black silk. He'd only popped out of the room for about five minutes.

He shrugged one shoulder. "I organised it after I booked our flights. It should fit you." He nodded to the other guys and started to pull his own suit out of his suitcase.

Ice and Ares would wear the same suits they wore to Mum and Leo's wedding. Mannix wore a similar one, but in dark grey. Each of the guys wore a tie that matched their personalities. Mannix's was a couple of shades darker than his suit. Ares' was black. Ice's tie was brightly coloured, but mostly red.

"Try it on," Ice said.

I drew the zipper down all the way and pulled out the dress to slip it on. It fell to just above my knees. Spaghetti straps held the fitted bodice in place. The rest of the dress clung to my curves like a second skin.

"You look hot." Ice pulled up the zipper and nuzzled his face into my hair. "I'm starting to think you shouldn't go."

"She definitely shouldn't," Ares said with a grunt. "It's too big a risk to take someone who doesn't know what they're doing."

"Then you better not go, because I'm the one who knows how to activate the virus," I retorted.

"You could tell one of us." He matched my tone. "You're not the only one who can—"

"Enough," Mannix snapped. "We're all going. We only need to blend in long enough to do what needs to be done and then we get the fuck out of there. Samuel Bell should be busy playing the dutiful host, and most of the people won't know what we look like."

"It's the people who do know what we look like that I'm worried about," Ares said. "If anyone from Brutham is there—"

"We do the best we fucking can to avoid them." Mannix fixed him with a firm look. "This isn't our first rodeo. We all know what we need to do. We go in, do it and get out."

"Can we have a drink before we leave?" Ice asked.

Mannix's response was to shake his head. "We can get shitfaced afterwards."

Ice pumped the air with his fist. "Hell yeah."

"Wait until we have something to celebrate," Ares told him.

"I always have something to celebrate, I'm me." Ice grinned.

Ares gave him the side eye and a snort. "Whatever you say, bro."

Ice clapped him on the shoulder, hard enough to hurt judging by the expression on Ares' face.

"I do say," Ice said.

I tuned out their banter as I slipped my feet into a pair of heels. I twisted my hair into a neat bun and pinned it into place.

I felt sexy. Mannix couldn't have made a better choice. It seemed as though he knew me better than my mother did, or at least he had better taste.

I couldn't dismiss the possibility he saw the darkness in me and matched the dress to it. I hadn't exactly tried to hide it from him or the other guys. They got me like no one else ever had. For the first time in my life, I felt like I didn't have to hide.

"We could do rock, paper, scissors," Ice was saying when I tuned back in.

"What are you competing over?" I asked.

"Who's going to take that dress off you when this is finished," Ice said with a shit-eating grin.

Yeah, I should have guessed.

"Shouldn't we be going?" I picked up my phone and the USB, and raised my perfectly plucked eyebrows at the guys.

"I'd rather be coming, but let's get this done." Ice offered me his arm.

Mannix narrowed his eyes at him, but stepped out the door in front of us. Ares walked behind.

"That's not a limo," Ice remarked as we stepped out the front of the hotel toward a dark grey sedan.

"The idea is to blend in at old man Bell's party," Mannix said. "A limo would stand out like dogs' balls."

"Or mine." Ice grabbed his groin. "Mine stand out more than any dog I've ever seen."

"That's only because your cock is so small it makes your balls look big," Ares remarked.

"That sounds like jealousy talking to me," Ice told him.

Ares barked a laugh and slipped into the passenger seat beside the driver. He muttered something about Ice being delusional and pulled the door closed behind him.

Ice chuckled and gestured for me to sit in the middle between him and Mannix.

Mannix leaned forward and spoke to the driver, his voice too soft for me to hear. The driver nodded a couple of times and pulled the car away from the curb.

"It should only take us about ten minutes to get there, depending on traffic." Mannix sat back like a prince in his royal carriage. "Are you ready?"

I toyed with the USB stick, but nodded. "I think so. I mean, we've gone over this a hundred times, but there's still a lot that could go wrong. This—" I held up the stick, "should work perfectly."

I hoped.

It was everything else we could fuck up. So many variables we couldn't possibly account for.

"It'll be fine," Ice said. "Better than fine. It'll be *fun*. What could be better than inviting ourselves to a fancy party held by our enemy?" He sounded like he was ready to have the time of his life. Knowing Ice, that was exactly what he planned to do.

"Just about anything," I said. "If they catch us—"

"They won't catch us," Mannix said firmly. "We planned out every detail. Everything should go smoothly. And if it doesn't, we'll deal with it. Don't worry, we've got you. Your job is to get in, do what you need to do and get out. And look hot doing it."

He made it sound so easy I almost relaxed, but I kept turning the USB around and around in my hand.

Mannix caught my chin between his thumb and forefinger and turned my face towards him.

"Do you trust us?" He looked at me intently, searching for an honest response in my eyes.

"I trust you," I said softly. I did, but I was scared. It all seemed so easy when we were planning everything, but now, it was getting more and more real by the moment. Was it too late to turn back and go home? No one had to know we were ever there.

"Then trust that we know what we're doing. We'll be in and out in less than ten minutes, and no one will know we were there. When we're done, it'll take Samuel Bell a decade to fix what we've done. Reuben Brantley might even give us a medal." He grinned.

As far as I could tell, Reuben Brantley didn't give medals, but his opinion was clearly important to the guys. In their world—*our* world —the kind of power that might be bestowed on them by Brantley was everything. If we succeeded tonight, the impact would last for years.

If we failed, the four of us would end up dead, or worse. I didn't let myself think about what might happen. Whatever it was, it wouldn't be pretty for anyone.

"What does Leo think about this?" I hadn't seen him or Mum before we left.

Mannix's eyes flicked away from me, evasively. "He doesn't know. I spoke to Ric DiMarco about it. He supplied the car and the money for your dress. He has faith that we'll succeed."

I blinked at him a couple of times. "You went over your father's head?"

He placed a hand on my thigh, and slid it up under the hem of my dress.

"If we don't succeed, no one can blame my father. And if we do succeed, then he can't take the credit."

I suspected the latter was the point. Mannix wanted to own this operation. To use it to make a name for himself. I wasn't going to judge him for that. We all wanted to stand on our own two feet, independent of our parents.

This was exactly the kind of thing my mother warned me about when she suggested the guys were trouble. If she knew about this, she'd be worried at best and furious at worst.

Especially if she knew it was my idea.

Not the party, as such, but the virus. Given a chance, I might have thought of coming here tonight, while Bell was distracted with the festivities, instead of Mannix.

Maybe the guys' mothers should be warning them about me.

"Is Leo going to be pissed off at us?" I asked.

Regardless of Mannix's reasons for doing things the way he did, I didn't want my stepfather angry with me. That may lead to friction between him and Mum. I didn't want to be the cause of any problems between them. Although, at this point, my mother would take Leo's side over mine. While that thought should sting, I'd take the guy's side over hers in a bunch of things, including me staying in Dusk Bay and not fleeing somewhere that may or may not be safer.

"Only if we fail," Mannix said. "Then he'll distance himself from us and all of this as quickly as he can."

I could totally see that. Leo would do whatever he had to do to cover his own ass.

I glanced out the window to see the lights of the city flash past. I hadn't realised how much I missed Sydney until now. Dusk Bay was a smaller city, without the huge glass-sided skyscrapers and historic buildings. Both were just as gritty and busy, but Dusk Bay didn't have the harbour. The bay wasn't anywhere near as magnificent or as big. The waterfront houses were similar in both places though. Large, opulent and expensive.

We pulled up under a tree, a dark car amidst the shadows. There wasn't even a streetlight to illuminate us here. Once the driver turned off the headlights, we blended into the night.

A shiver of apprehension trickled down my spine. It ratcheted up to anxiety as I followed Mannix out of the car. The full smells and sounds of the city hit me the moment my heels touch the ground. Salt air, exhaust fumes, traffic, music from the nearby party. It was an assault on my senses, spiking my nerves.

"Are you sure this is a good idea?" I said as Mannix closed the car door behind us. "A cyber attack from a distance would be—"

"Not as much fun." Ice slipped his hand into mine. "You said this should be more effective, and what could be better than a direct attack on Samuel Bell? Knowing someone was inside his house will freak him the fuck out." He grinned.

"Don't forget he wants you dead," Mannix said. "He's getting what he deserves."

Before I could think of another argument or say another word, Mannix led the way up the leafy street.

After another moment of hesitation, we followed behind him.

CHAPTER 19

KENNEDY

As planned, the party was in full swing when we stepped up to the house. Mannix flashed a fake invitation and a smile at the security guard on the gate. She didn't seem impressed by his smile, but she nodded at the invitation and waved us through.

"You can't please everyone," he muttered as we stepped away towards the house.

"You better not try, or Kennedy and I will remove your toenails, one by one," Ice told him.

"Or his fingernails," I agreed jokingly. Or maybe I wasn't joking.

The thought of Mannix with anyone else ignited a bonfire of jealousy inside me. If any of the guys touched another woman, I might scratch her eyes out. These guys were mine.

"As if I'd go there with anyone else," Mannix said. "I have everything I need already."

He nodded for us to be quiet, while we stepped around the curved driveway and through the wide open front doors.

The sound of music and voices came from somewhere at the back of the house.

"Pool area." Ares nodded in that direction. "It also has a harbour view. This place is worth a shit ton of money. It used to be worth more, but a house down the street disappeared into a sinkhole a couple of years ago. Fucked with property value for a while there." His tone didn't even hold a slight hint of sympathy. If anything, he sounded pleased.

"I remember that," I said. "They never could figure out why a sinkhole opened right there."

Ares shrugged. "Yeah, whatever. That's another thing on a long list of things I don't give a shit about. Although, the owner of that house was smokin' hot."

I gave him a look which he returned with an even gaze. We'd barely spoken since the conversation we shared. Sometimes he looked like he was ready to say something civil. Most of the time he seemed more pissed off than usual, on the verge of telling me to fuck off.

I shrugged it off each time. When he was ready to talk, we could talk. Until then, he could keep on acting like he didn't give a shit. We both knew he did.

"The office should be over here." Mannix nodded toward the east and skirted around a handful of partygoers. No one gave him, or any of us, a second glance.

"I'd kill for a drink," Ice said loudly. "Do you think they have decent beer here?"

"Haven't you had enough?" Ares asked. Our cover story was that we came from another party, which was why we arrived late. People were more likely to avoid us if they thought we were already drunk.

In theory anyway.

"No way." Ice exaggeratedly waved his arm in the air. "I'm just getting started."

Mannix gave them both a look and led us over to a tall, wooden door. A keypad was set into the wall beside it.

He nodded to me and stepped to one side.

I turned on my phone and tapped in the command to disable the lock. It was connected to the house's Wi-Fi system. A few keystrokes later and I'd hacked into that to make it less secure. It was a simple matter to take control of the system after that. I could unlock almost anything in the house, and even send Samuel Bell on a wild goose chase with the GPS in his car. Lucky for him, we weren't here for any of those things.

Not today anyway.

The keypad flashed green and Mannix opened the door. He waved us inside and closed it behind him.

"That was easy." Ice smiled.

"Don't say shit like that." Ares scowled at him. "That's when things start to turn to crap."

We waited, but no one came running.

"Let's get this done." Mannix pointed in the direction of the computer sitting on the wide, timber desk.

The desk alone must have been worth a few thousand dollars. The art on the walls which I looked at with the light on my phone, would have been worth a few million. It was a shame to have them locked away in here where no one but Samuel Bell could enjoy them.

People like him didn't think it was a shame. He probably got a kick out of seeing things no one else could.

I booted up the computer and slid the USB into the slot on the side. Thank fuck Bell still had the kind of computer that took a USB. Otherwise I would have had to deliver the whole virus via Wi-Fi and that would have taken longer.

Who knew when he might get the sudden urge to go into his office to do something? Having to wait for the USB was going to be excruciating enough. Wi-Fi would take at least twice as long, depending on how good the signal was.

This whole operation was nuts as fuck as it was.

I asked myself again why I was here, but the answer was the same every time. Frank Nixon would have strangled me because Samuel Bell wanted him to. That was a good enough reason for this as far as I was concerned.

I tapped the keyboard and got the code rolling into the system, then leaned against the desk to wait, my hip pressed to the expensive wood.

"How long will this take?" Mannix asked. He looked agitated now. Even more than I felt. We'd all breathe easier when we weren't here in this house anymore.

"Approximately five and a half minutes." I glanced at the screen on my phone. I had tried to get it down to closer to three minutes, but it was what it was. If it did what we wanted it to do, it would take the time it took. In the long run, it would be worth it.

I fucking hoped.

"Perfect." He placed his hands around my waist and lifted me onto an empty part of the desk.

"What are you doing?" I said with a nervous laugh.

"I'm going to see which will finish first, your program or you." He grinned and shoved the hem of my skirt up my thighs. In the light from the computer screen, he pushed aside my panties and started to run his fingers over my pussy.

"I don't know if this is the time or place—" My breath gave me away by hitching as the pad of his thumb ghosted over my clit.

Or I could just roll with it, because he had me going like crazy, and the idea of being fucked on Samuel Bell's desk was insanely, intoxicatingly hot. The man tried to kill me, he deserved to have his desk messed up.

"Why didn't I think of that?" Ice grumbled.

"Because I'm the brains of the operation." Mannix grinned at him.

"Sure, let's go with that." Undeterred, Ice peeled down the front of my dress and leaned in to trace his tongue around my nipple.

Heat and fire replaced anxiety, which coursed through my body like a sudden inferno. Figures I'd be turned on here. Anyone could walk in at any moment and find us. We could be dead in the next sixty seconds, but I was as aroused as fuck.

Death, danger and these guys were becoming my aphrodisiac.

I glanced over to see Ares, a dark shape against the door. He seemed to be watching silently. In that case, we'd give him a show.

Mannix pulled me so my ass was on the edge of the desk, then laid me back. Ice moved around to the side of the desk, licking and sucking like I hadn't moved.

Mannix finger fucked me hard, determined, relentless. His fingers sank in and out of my slick heat, the heel of his hand rubbing up and down my clit.

Between them and the excitement of the moment, I felt like I might go absolutely crazy.

Approximately two and a half minutes later, I tipped over the edge to oblivion. I bit my lip hard to keep from screaming out. The last thing we needed was me to give us away by coming too loudly.

Mannix undid his suit trousers and freed his erection before gripping my hips and pulling my legs up around his waist.

"Bro, do we have time—" Ares started.

Mannix interrupted him by slamming his cock deep into my body, all the way to the hilt. He fucked me the same way he finger fucked me, hard, fast and relentless.

I bit back a cry at the sudden fullness and violence of his body meeting mine.

Ice covered the rest of the cry with his mouth, kissing me deeply while his hands explored my bare breast.

Mannix took about as long as I did before he stilled and came, lips pressed together to keep himself quiet. He grunted, long and low, panted then grunted again.

"Fuck," he whispered. "You're such a fucking good girl." He slid out of me slowly and tugged my panties back into place. He helped me to sit back up and fix my dress. "How long have we got?"

I blinked to clear my head and looked at my phone screen. "About twenty seconds."

He chuckled. "Perfect." He did up his pants and tucked his shirt back into place.

I watched the code roll by and counted the time down in my head. It actually took eighteen and a half seconds, but close enough.

"It's done." I tugged the USB out of the side of the computer and turned the computer off. "The next time someone turns it on, the virus will spread and fry the system. Hopefully, by then, we'll be long gone."

With the party on tonight, it seemed like a reasonable guess that Samuel Bell wouldn't be back in his office until tomorrow, if not Monday morning. By then we'd be comfortably back in Dusk Bay.

Hopefully.

Mannix placed a hand on either side of my face and kissed me hard. "You're incredible."

"Hell yeah I am," I said jokingly. "Let's get out of here." My pussy was throbbing from the way he fucked me, but I could still walk. Or run if I had to.

"Good idea," Ares said. "It might be the first one I've heard come out of your mouth." After a moment he had to concede a little more. "And the virus. But we'll see how well that works." Yeah, he wasn't good at conceding.

"It'll be amazing," I assured him. I stayed back with Mannix and Ice while Ares eased the door open.

We stood in the darkness and watched and listened. After a moment or two, we heard voices approaching.

Two men walked past, talking low to each other. If they noticed the open door, they gave no sign. They kept walking until they disappeared in the direction of the party.

"Looks clear to me," Ares said.

He led the way out the door and back the way we came, towards the front of the house.

Like on the way in, the front doors to the house were open and no one was around. The closest voices were several metres away at most. Figures moved around the garden, wavy ghosts as the party lights turned them into twisting and turning shapes. The lights strobed in time to the music, corrupting the forms even further.

Reasoning that if we couldn't see them clearly, they couldn't see us either, we hurried across the front lawn and into the darkness of the trees beside the driveway.

We were almost to the gate when a voice said, "What the fuck are you doing here?"

CHAPTER 20

ICE

I managed to keep my cool and contain my surprise. Without even trying to hide it, I put myself between them and Kennedy.

Mannix and Ares both did the same. A wall of awesomeness between her and them.

"The question is, what are you doing here?" I drawled. In the glow of the streetlight, I recognised the Brantley twins. Identical, I could never work out which of the fuckers was which. I knew the woman they were with though.

Interesting.

"I believe we asked first, didn't we Parker?" He must have been Hunter. He looked over at his twin, who had put himself between us and their woman. Judging by the fact they both wore jeans and t-shirts, they weren't here for the party.

"Yeah, we did," Parker agreed. "Since when did people like you get invited here?"

I didn't know if I should take offence at that or not, but I decided to. Or at least, pretend to.

"People like us? What do you mean by that, exactly?"

"People who aren't on the side of Samuel Bell," Parker said slowly, as though he was talking to a kid.

"Which brings us back to why the fuck are you here?" Mannix asked. He dropped his head to the side and looked around Parker. "Are the evil twins trying to kidnap Chloe Bell?"

"I'm Lila, you idiot." She stepped out from behind Parker. "I look nothing like my sister."

"You're also twins," I pointed out.

She rolled her eyes at him. "No shit, fuckwit, but we're not identical."

I leaned towards her, not bothering to be offended by her calling me names. "You look the same in the dark."

Hunter and Parker did identical twin bristles until Lila snorted.

"As if I'd be in the dark with someone like you."

I smiled. "Right back at you." I wouldn't turn my back on a woman like her. Especially one who clearly came with a sharpened set of claws.

"You still haven't answered the question," Mannix said. "What are the Brantley twins doing with one of the Bell sisters?"

"Would you believe we're trying to build bridges?" Hunter asked. He glanced at Lila and Parker. "We don't believe the Brantleys and the Bells have to keep being enemies. If we can figure out a way to—"

"So you're fucking?" Ares asked. "Let me guess, if your brother," he gestured at the twins, "and your father," then at Lila, "found out about this, they'd be pissed."

All three of them looked cagey as hell.

"That looks like a yes to me," I remarked.

Hunter leaned to the side to look around me. "Are you going to introduce us to your friend?" His brow creased like he was trying to decide if he knew her or not, but he clearly didn't.

I took Kennedy's hand and tugged her gently so she was beside me, but kept an arm around her.

"This is Kennedy Knight. She's Helen Knight-Cassani's daughter."

"Leo's stepdaughter?" Lila looked Kennedy up and down.

Kennedy looked back at her with open suspicion. "She's a Bell?" she asked me.

I could see the cogs and wheels turning in her brain, thinking about the implication of one of the Bell family seeing us out here.

"Imagine that," Lila sneered. "A Bell outside my own home."

"In the company of two of your father's mortal enemies," Mannix said. "What would he think if he knew?"

"More to the point, what would he *do* if he knew?" I asked.

"The same thing he'd do to you if he knew you were here," Hunter said. "So I propose a deal. You don't say anything about us being here and we won't tell him we saw you."

"If you agree that you don't tell *anyone* you saw us here, we have a deal." Mannix held his hand out to Hunter.

Of course, it would be Mannix who picked up on that little loophole.

Hunter knew it too, I saw it on his face. He hesitated for half a second, then took Mannix's hand and shook it.

"I agree it would be mutually beneficial if no one knew any of us was here. None of us will say a word to anyone."

I wondered if Lila would agree if she knew what she was agreeing to. Once she realised she couldn't access social media via her family's Wi-Fi, she might regret going along with this. Then again, she was a Bell. She'd probably renege on it the first chance she got. Whatever, as long as we were a long way from here when that happened.

"You really believe there can be peace between the two families?" Kennedy asked, her expression tentative.

I understood her reason for asking. Samuel Bell would be a lot less likely to want her, or any of us, dead if we were one big happy family.

"We know we're not giving Lila up," Parker said. "Whatever it takes to live our lives together, we'll do it. Even if we have to disappear."

Poor bastard, they were more than likely to disappear if Samuel Bell found out they were fucking his daughter. That shit would end up worse than Romeo and Juliet.

I put that into the, 'not my problem,' basket and shoved it out of my mind. No doubt they'd eventually realise they had no chance of making it work and they'd all get on with their lives.

Ares muttered something about guys thinking with their cocks. He shook his head and spoke again, this time loud enough for all of us to hear. "We should get the fuck out of here. We've had enough of this party."

"Yeah, let's go," Mannix said. He jerked his head roughly in the direction of the car.

"You didn't tell us why you were here," Parker said before we could take more than a couple of steps.

"We didn't, did we?" I asked. I looked at him contemplatively for a moment, before I shrugged and followed the others into the darkness. I glanced back over my shoulder, but the twins and Lila didn't follow.

"They're not supposed to be together?" Kennedy asked softly.

"Not even a little bit," I agreed. "They must have snuck over, hoping no one would notice because they're too busy with her old man's party." I had to give them some credit. They had the balls to do something like that.

"Lila and her sister Chloe are in their first year at Brutham," Mannix said. "The twins are in their second year. We helped the twins get through the trials last year. It never hurts to have a Brantley owe you a favour or two."

Kennedy glanced back. "They're Zeke Brantley's brothers?"

I'd forgotten she was a big fan of Wolf Venom. "Yes, they are. There doesn't seem to be much love lost between them though. I wouldn't ask the twins to get you his autograph. They might do it, but they'd want something in return. Trust me, you don't want to owe the evil twins any favours."

"Evil twins?" she echoed. "They don't seem so bad. They seemed interested in making peace between the two groups of mobsters."

"They're interested in taking care of their own hide," Mannix said scathingly. "They work for their brother, Reuben, and as far as I can tell, there's nothing they won't do for him. Including kill you if he decides he wants you dead. They wouldn't even blink."

"Kennedy isn't going to give Reuben a reason to want her dead," I said firmly. "Once word gets out about the virus, he'll be impressed. He might even wish he'd thought of it sooner."

Things like this usually weren't Reuben's method. If he thought he could get them close enough to Samuel Bell, he'd send an assassin instead. Hell, he probably had already. On a night like this, it would be exactly what everyone was expecting. They wouldn't have been looking out for people to sneak in and fuck up their computer.

"That's what I'm hoping," Mannix said. "The four of us are going to get noticed. We'll get the appreciation we deserve. And with it, more responsibility."

"Do you think I could get a bigger workshop?" My vision blurred as I imagined my ideal space. It would be three or four times the size of what I have now. Enough space to work with several different people. I might even bring in an apprentice. Maybe Kennedy. I had a feeling she'd get a kick out of it way more than she realised.

Just thinking about her using the pliers on Frank Nixon made my cock hard. Thinking about Kennedy doing pretty much anything made my cock turn to stone. I would have liked more time in Bell's office, so I could fuck her mouth. Oh well, there'd be time for that later.

"I don't see why not," Mannix said.

I fist pumped the air. "Hell yeah. I'm going to need a bath. A big one."

"Feeling dirty?" Ares asked.

I frowned at him and stepped carefully around a bike some kid left out the front of their house. They'd be lucky if it was still there in the morning and not stolen.

"Not for me," I said once I figured out what he was getting at. "I'd put acid in it and then feet or hands. While they're attached to the person—"

"All right, all right, I get it," Ares said hastily. As if he wouldn't be there to watch and enjoy it along with the rest of us.

Kennedy looked up at me. "Acid? That sounds…"

"Exciting?" I suggested. "Arousing? Hot as fuck? Fun?"

She exhaled half a breath. "Something like that, yeah." She let out the other half of her breath with the last word.

I squeezed her hand. "I knew you were the woman for me. Most of the girls I know would be grossed out. Or at least find it weird."

"I'm not most girls," she said.

I remembered the way she let Mannix fuck her on Samuel Bell's desk not even half an hour ago and grinned. "You certainly aren't."

"None of you are like most guys either," she said.

"Don't you fucking forget it," Ares growled.

"As if you'd let me," she retorted. "You in particular are very good at reminding me every chance you get."

"Ares only does it to remind himself. He has a fragile ego." I grinned as he flipped me off.

"Fragile ego, my ass," Kennedy said.

Of course, that was the perfect excuse to squeeze her beautiful ass. Not that I needed one, but I took it anyway. Her butt was perfectly round and firm. Exactly what you'd expect from a gymnast. I could happily keep my hand there forever, or slip it down her crack to toy with her rear hole. I wanted to lube her up and fuck her there. My balls ached at the thought of it. I was the first to fuck her pussy and her mouth, so why not her ass too? If that was greedy, I didn't care. When it came to her, I wanted all her firsts and her lasts, and as much in between as I could get my hand, mouth and cock on or into.

As I squeezed her tender flesh, I noticed Mannix looking back over his shoulder at Bell's house.

"You good?" I asked. I resisted the urge to look back too. Nothing said we were up to bad shit like glancing over our shoulders every few seconds. We were supposed to be playing it cool, so if anyone went past, they didn't pay us any attention.

His expression was a rare display of uncertainty. "I don't know. I don't trust Lila Bell and everything else seemed way too easy."

"It wasn't easy, it was executed exactly as planned," Ares said. "By you, in case you forgot. Now who has the fragile ego?"

"Still you," Mannix said easily. "My instincts tell me—"

The front of the Bell house lit up brighter than a Christmas tree.

"Fuck."

CHAPTER 21

KENNEDY

Someone shouted, "Over there!"

That was immediately followed by a flood of people pouring out the front gates. Were those guns in their hands?

I decided not to stick around and find out. I kicked off my heels and ran, the guys all around me.

Those were definitely gunshots that slammed into the grass and sidewalk around us.

How the hell they missed us, I had no idea. I very much doubted those were intended to be warning shots. Whether they knew who we were or what we did, they were aiming with intent. Whether that intent was to kill or to injure so they could catch us, I had no idea about that either.

Frankly, I didn't want to find out. I didn't like either of those options.

"Come on. We're out of range, but not for long." Mannix waved us all forward, his expression steely calm. Reassuringly so.

"Especially if they have a rocket launcher," Ice said.

Without glancing over at him I said, "Is that likely?"

"Actually, yes. Bell has an arsenal of all sorts of shit. It's unlikely he or any of his people could get it out and operational this quickly though."

"That's good to know." It was. I suspected a rocket launcher would give us a very unfair disadvantage. Not to mention make a mess out of the streets of Sydney.

"Come on, Princess." Mannix grabbed my hand. We weaved back and forth as we ran to the car and around to the other side of it.

"Get in," he urged. He yanked the back door open and gave me a shove. At the same time, he reached into the foot well and grabbed out three guns. He tossed two to Ares and Ice.

I scrambled inside and stayed down low, while the guys positioned themselves at the front and back of the car. The driver joined Ares near the back, his own gun in his hand.

"Stay down out of sight," Mannix ordered, waving at me to duck down as small as I could. "Don't freak out. We've got you. I promise." He left the door open but moved away.

I hated not being able to see anything, but I hated the idea of being shot even more, so I did what I was told. As for not freaking out, I couldn't make any guarantees.

There was a very real and painful possibility we might all die right here on the streets of one of the most affluent parts of Sydney. What would the news have to say about us?

Oh, right. Nothing. The Bell family or the Brantleys, or even Leo, would pay a shit load of money to cover the whole thing up. By the time they were done, the people living on the street would believe they imagined the entire thing. Or they'd be paid well enough to forget.

Something hit the side of the car and pinged. Bullets, I winced. Each one made a dent that cracked the plastic interior without passing all the way through.

Yet.

I looked up through the window as Ares took aim. His long fingers twitched as he pulled the trigger. His face was a study in concentration and determination. If this wasn't so scary, it would be hot.

Okay, who was I kidding? It was definitely hot. He knew what to do with that gun and he wouldn't hesitate to kill any of the people coming after us. None of the guys would hesitate. Hell, for all I knew this wasn't their first shootout. Maybe not even their thirteenth. They might be a regular occurrence in the life of Mannix, Ice and Ares. If I was ever going to reconsider my life choices, it would be right now.

It's a bit late for that, I told myself. I was curled up in the footwell of the car that was being shot at. And it was basically my fault, because I was the one who came up with the idea of putting a virus on Bell's computer in the first place.

Had they found it already? Or had Lila Bell and the Brantley twins betrayed us? If I died without knowing the answer to that, I'd be pissed off.

I shifted around to get comfortable. My hand brushed past something hard and cold. I felt around until I curled my fingers around the cool steel.

Another gun.

I'd never used one, but how difficult could it be? I hated the idea of being vulnerable and I didn't want to be a sitting duck or a damsel in distress.

I wanted to be one of them, by their side no matter what. I wasn't just a nerd girl who did gymnastics in her spare time. I was a badass nerd girl who belonged to these three beautiful guys. None of us were going down without a fight.

Unless you're talking about the good kind of going down, which right now I wasn't. That could come later. And so would we.

Yeah, nerves were jumbling my thoughts, but I snatched up the gun and slipped back out of the car.

The road was rough under my feet, cracked and broken, even in this part of the city. Part of me regretted kicking off my heels, but I couldn't have run as fast in them anyway.

I'd suffer the discomfort for a little while. It was better than being dead.

"Beautiful Kennedy, what are you doing?" Ice asked without so much as looking at me.

"I thought I'd help." I moved over beside him, my head and body low, and looked out over the street. At least a dozen people were headed our way, each moving slowly and carefully. They had us outnumbered, but we had a car to hide behind. Surely that meant we were in a good place. Right?

Yeah okay, I'm not that naïve, but it was a better barricade than none. Wishing for an armoured tank right now wouldn't make one appear.

"Give me that." Ice grabbed the gun out of my hand.

Before I could protest he said, "The safety is still on." He clicked something and handed the gun back. "Remember to aim it at the bad guys. That's anyone who isn't us."

"Thanks." That would have made me look silly. Aiming and firing and having nothing come out the other end. That would be almost as useful as bringing a knife to a gunfight.

His teeth flashed white in the darkness. "Any time." He turned and aimed. His shot was quickly followed by a grunt and a thud of someone hitting the ground.

"Shooting people is so impersonal," he complained. "Really not my style at all." He aimed and struck his target again. "At least they could give me a scream of pain or something. Anything."

I suspected he'd happily shoot them all in the knees and take them back to his workshop for a few days.

He ducked down as a bullet passed low over our heads, narrowly missing both of us.

"Now it's personal," he said.

"It wasn't personal before?" I asked.

"Not as much as it is now." He flashed me a smile and got off another shot. A male voice cried out in pain as the bullet took him in the wrist. The next took him in the chest.

"Better them than us," Mannix said. He took out two in quick succession, then dropped down lower.

As far as I could tell, they were coming slower now, and were down to about six or seven. The guys and the driver had killed or maimed at least five potential attackers.

Yeah, this definitely wasn't their first shootout. They knew exactly what they were doing. Did they learn this as boys or at university?

Finally, a university that taught practical skills. Of course, shooting people was only a practical skill in certain occupations and lifestyles, like ours. It probably shouldn't go mainstream.

A bullet, or three, slammed into the window on the opposite side of the car, cracking but not shattering it. Another couple of shots took out the tyres on the other side.

"Well, that sucks," Ice said. "We'll have to find another car so we can get out of here." He didn't sound too concerned.

He leaned in and whispered in my ear. "Over to the left, there's a tree. The man crouched beside it thinks we don't know he's there. I'm going to draw him out. If you aim low, you can't miss him."

That was a hell of an assumption, but I nodded.

"I can try."

"You've got this." He gave me a quick kiss that was full of the promise of a lot more.

We just had to survive this first. No pressure.

Ice took a few steps to the side and spoke loudly. "I think that's the—"

The man beside the tree rose, gun in hand. All of his attention was on Ice. That was his last mistake.

I took aim and squeezed the trigger. The recoil almost made me squeal in surprise, but the bullet caught the man in the right side of his chest. It was enough to give Ice time to shoot him in the left side of his chest, killing him.

The man staggered a few steps before he fell heavily to the ground and lay very still. The street lights shone off a puddle of blood that snaked out beside him and slowly grew.

Ice stepped back over to me and offered me a high five. "What a team."

I slapped his hand half heartedly and leaned against the car for a moment to catch my breath. The moment I picked up the gun I knew there was a possibility I would kill someone, or take part in killing someone, but doing it… That was another thing.

I wasn't sure if I'd get used to it, or even if I wanted to, but I couldn't let it get to me right now. If I let myself be distracted for too long, that could be exactly what they needed to end me.

"You did good, Firecracker," Ares said. He didn't look at me so he couldn't see my surprise, but he nodded, so he must have known I glanced at him. His expression gave away nothing, but for once he wasn't sneering. His focus hadn't dropped for a moment. Eyes as intense as ever, he watched the street for movement, the gun moving as he tried to pin down a target.

"Thanks," I muttered. I pulled myself together and stood back up again. I could do this. I had to. It was them or us and I was damned if it was going to be us. I was going to protect my guys the way they protected me.

Us against the rest of the world.

"Let's finish this," Mannix said. He moved to the side, almost out from behind the car, gun held in both hands. He aimed but missed. I couldn't even see what he was aiming at.

Another shot hit the side of the car, near the fuel tank.

"Someone thinks this is a movie," Ice said derisively. "The fuel tank isn't going to explode unless— Fuck." He grabbed my hand and yanked me down the street.

The pavement bit into my feet, but I glanced back to see a shadow flick open a cigarette lighter and throw it in the direction of the car.

At first, nothing happened. Then the first trickle from the ruptured fuel tank touched the road and dribbled towards the lighter. The moment they met, the liquid caught fire. It flashed and burnt high enough to reach the fuel tank.

It ignited the fuel around the outside of it, then the fuel inside the car.

Ice shoved me down onto the pavement and threw his body over mine as the car exploded.

CHAPTER 22

KENNEDY

My face hit the road. I grunted in pain as I grazed my cheek and the side of my chin.

I screwed my eyes shut and threw my arms over my head. A rush of heat poured over us, accompanied by shards of metal and glass. Bits of car rained down on us.

My ears rang from the sound of the explosion, but somewhere in the back of my mind I acknowledged the fact that I was somehow still alive.

Ice's breath in my ear confirmed he was too.

What about Mannix and Ares?

My heart raced. I was sweating profusely. All I could do was lie still and wait.

It would suck to make it this far only to stand up too soon and get hit by a flying engine. Okay, a smaller car part was much more likely, but that would suck just as hard.

"Beautiful?" Ice murmured. "You okay?"

"Yeah. You?" My eyes felt glued shut, but I managed to force them open. The road looked like a war zone. Bits of car were scattered everywhere. The road where it sat was singed black. Most of the cars around it were smashed up. Shattered windscreens, blasted paint, deep dents.

Fuck.

"Kinda." He peeled himself up off me and looked around, dazed. "We need to get out of here."

"You're hurt." His suit jacket and shirt were in shreds. Where the fabric was torn, he was bleeding.

He glanced down and grinned. "I'm going to have some epic fucking scars. But we really need to get out of here, or we won't live to see them."

Who else but him would be impressed by being injured?

He pushed himself to his feet and gripped my arm to pull me to mine.

My ears still rang, making balancing a challenge.

"Ares and Mannix…"

"They'll find us." He slid his hand down my arm to lace his fingers in mine and pull me away from the wreckage.

At some point, I'd lost the gun, but I still had my phone and the USB stick in my hand. I would have preferred the gun right now.

We staggered a few metres until we reached the grass. It wasn't until we hit the softer surface that I realised how sore my feet were. They were bleeding too.

I paused and leaned against Ice long enough to tug a piece of metal out of my ankle. I winced as it slid free and reminded myself to get a tetanus shot when I got the chance.

I glanced back over my shoulder to see upright shadows moving towards the site of the explosion. Fuel on the road still burned, the smoke made the shapes dance and writhe like ghosts. They must have stood back when the car blew up, but now they were searching for us again.

I saw no sign of Mannix or Ares.

We retreated into the shadow of a few trees and stopped to catch our breath. Sirens wailed in the distance. They quickly drew closer.

"We need to be away from here before the cops come," Ice said. "They'll have too many questions we don't want to answer."

"Are you sure?" I searched for his eyes in the darkness. "We're the innocent victims in a case of attempted murder."

He laughed softly. "Victims, yes. Innocent, not so much. It's better if they don't know we were here. They'll call it an accident and move on. That's what we need to do." He tugged my hand and we slipped further away.

"Right now, Samuel Bell won't be sure who we are, or who fucked with his computer. If the police detain us, then he'll know. And we can't be sure if any of them are on his payroll."

"I hadn't thought of that," I admitted. He was right. All of that would be bad.

"Lucky you have the Iceman around." He flashed me a brief smile, one that spoke of the pain he was in.

"Do you need to rest for a minute?" I asked. It was too dark to get a real idea of how badly injured he was, but it must be pretty bad if he was showing any sign of it. If he let it get past his laid-back exterior.

"Nah, I'm fine." He sounded dismissive, but not entirely convincing. "If we weren't in a hurry, I'd pin you to a tree and fuck you silly."

I suspected he thought about doing that anyway, but the sirens were closer now, and the voices behind us louder and more insistent.

"They can't be far. Spread out and look."

"I guess they didn't find Mannix or Ares yet," Ice remarked. He was walking faster now, all but dragging me with him.

I had to trot to keep up, which hurt the hell out of my feet. I pushed the pain aside as best I could and kept going. The thought of being caught by Bell, or sidetracked by the cops, was a good incentive to keep putting one foot in front of the other. The further and faster we went, the harder it became to ignore it.

After a while, it swamped my thoughts. All I knew was pain and moving forward, step by step. I couldn't even say how fast I was going or where we were. Pain encompassed everything.

Tears blurred my vision and trickled down my cheeks, but I didn't slow.

Not until Ice came to a sudden stop.

"Long time no see," one of the twins drawled.

I blinked to clear my eyes. I thought it might have been Hunter, but I wasn't sure until he spoke again.

"Parker was just saying he wondered if you were inside the car when it blew up. I guess not."

"We're not that easy to kill," Ice bragged.

Parker turned on the light on his watch and waved it up and down at us quickly before turning it off.

"Maybe not, but you look like shit. And it sounds like we should vacate the area pretty fucking quickly."

"That's what we were trying to do, bro," Ice told him.

"Lucky you bumped into us then," Hunter said. "Come on, we'll give you a hand." He slipped an arm around me. We made it a few steps before he realised I wasn't keeping up.

"My feet," I whispered. I didn't want to make a fuss, but I also didn't want to slow us down. I'd feel like crap if we all got caught because of me.

"Piece of cake," he said cheerfully. He leaned down and placed his arm under my knees, the other under my arm and swept me up.

"The fuck?" Ice growled.

"Chillax, dude," Hunter said. "Your girl is hurt and you're in no shape to carry her. Parker and I can always leave you here if you prefer."

"No," I said quickly. "It's okay. Hunter is helping me, nothing else."

Ice groused under his breath, but trudged behind us. Hopefully he wasn't thinking of chaining them in his workroom and doing things to the twins because one of them dared to touch me.

Under any other scenario it was okay, but in this case, without Hunter's help, I'd be fucked. I wondered why the guys called them the evil twins. They seemed nice enough to me.

I leaned my head against Hunter's chest and tried to keep my eyes open. He was at least as hard as the other guys, although he was younger than me. Not by much, but by enough. Even if they didn't have a girlfriend, I wasn't even slightly interested in either twin. They were attractive, and ripped, but they weren't my guys.

Besides, I had my hands full with three. I didn't need five boyfriends.

"So you managed to piss off old man Bell, huh?" Hunter asked.

"I guess so," I said noncommittally. "I get the impression that isn't difficult to do."

"Not even a little bit difficult," he agreed. "He's even more high strung then our brother, Reuben. Samuel Bell kills people if they look at him the wrong way. Reuben just puts them on his shit list and makes their life hell. If he can be bothered with them. Mostly, doing that is a waste of money and resources. I guess that's why Bell kills people. It's cheaper."

I hadn't expected to get a crash course in mobster economics 101, but he had a point. Killing people was probably a lot cheaper than what Ice did to them in his workroom. I knew if I suggested that, he'd reply that it wasn't as much fun.

Sometimes saving money wasn't everything.

"What did you do to piss him off?" Parker asked.

"You don't want to know," Ice told him. "If only because someone is going to ask sooner or later and you won't have to lie if you don't know."

"What makes you think we have a problem with lying?" Hunter glanced over to Ice.

"Absolutely nothing," Ice said. "In this case you're better off not knowing and I'm not going to tell you anyway, so this conversation is basically moot."

Hunter shrugged, making me rise and fall in his arms. "Suit yourself."

After a moment he spoke again. "You weren't sent to assassinate Bell, were you? Because if you were, you are the least stealthy assassins we've ever seen. Right Parker?"

"Exactly," Parker agreed. "Hunter and I are stealthier than you."

"Wait a minute, Park." Hunter looked over at him. "Are you suggesting we're not stealthy?"

"I mean, we could be if we wanted to, but we're usually not called on to sneak around."

"That's true," Hunter conceded. "But when we sneak, no one sees us coming. Like that time with Penn, Wolf Venom's keyboardist."

Parker grinned. "Yeah, that was awesome. He had no idea until we... We shouldn't tell you about that. If you're not going to share, then neither will we."

"I don't think I want to know," I admitted. The band's keyboard player had a reputation for being an asshole, but he was a gifted musician. I was content only knowing him for his music and not anything that went on behind the scenes. If they wanted to tell me a few stories about Zeke, then I'd listen.

It dawned on me I was being carried by the brother of none other than Zeke Brantley, my favourite singer in the whole wide world. Holy shit. This might be the closest I ever got to him, and I wouldn't be able to tell anyone about it.

Figured.

"You probably don't, but it was awesome. Trust me on that." Hunter smiled down at me. He was the kind of guy who was too good-looking for his own good or anyone else's. I bet he got away with all sorts of shit he shouldn't. That might be why the guys called them the evil twins, because they did things just because they could. If that made them evil, then what were we? Killing people wasn't exactly something nice people did, was it?

The sirens were almost deafening now. Everyone within a five or six block radius would hear them.

We ducked in behind a fence as flashing lights came screaming around the corner. Two police cars and an ambulance, followed by a fire truck flew past us toward the scene of the explosion.

People started to step out of their homes, bolder now the authorities were here.

We stayed crouched down for several minutes, or approximately three million rapid heartbeats.

"I don't think they saw us," Parker said. "If anyone was coming after you, they would have scattered by now."

I would have been relieved if I knew where Mannix and Ares were. They were okay, they had to be. If they weren't... My heart wrenched at the idea.

"Okay, let's keep going," Hunter said.

We were about to step out of the darkest shadows when we were all illuminated by the light of a phone.

"There you are," Lila Bell said lightly. "Good work. Daddy will be pleased."

CHAPTER 23

KENNEDY

Shit.

For half a second, I thought she was joking. That she'd help the twins to help us get away. She was dating them after all, wasn't she? Did that mean she wanted the same peace they did?

A glance at Hunter's face showed he thought the same thing. Then the cogs and wheels in his mind turned. I saw that too.

Along with the exact moment Ice and I were fucked.

"We figured you'd be around here somewhere," Hunter said lightly. "Parker was just saying you couldn't be far away. Weren't you Parker?"

"Yeah." Parker cottoned on to what Hunter was saying. "We were trying to find you while staying out of sight, in case your dad's men mistook us for these two." He jerked his thumb towards Ice and I. "We found them lurking back there and figured we'd bring them to you."

My whole body stiffened. Fucking motherfucker. So much for helping us. I should have known they couldn't be trusted. What part of 'evil twins' did I forget to pay attention to? Just because they seemed nice, didn't mean they were.

And now we were screwed.

"Where are the other two?" Lila fixed one then the other with a firm look. If it wasn't obvious before who was in charge here, it was now.

Not the twins. She couldn't have been more than eighteen, but she clearly had them pussy whipped.

"We haven't seen them," Hunter said. "We can take these two to your father then go out looking again." He made it sound like he was going out for ice cream, or more alcohol when the party was at risk of running out. Not looking for my guys to hand them over to their enemy.

Now I wondered what they did to Wolf Venom's keyboard player, because they seemed to be lacking a conscience. If they'd hand over their allies to their enemies, they were shitheads to say the least.

The look Ice gave them lived up to his name. For once, he wasn't smiling. He was mentally cutting small strips of skin from each twin. Or tearing off their toenails before breaking every bone in their body. He was listening to them scream and beg for mercy or death. He was watching them dangle from the ceiling by their wrists, their feet centimetres from the floor, hungry and without water for days. Or with just enough water to keep them alive while he worked on them a bit more.

I was glad he had something to console himself with, because all I had was my anger. Of that, I had plenty. I would have cheerfully used the pliers on either of the twins. I could start with the balls and go from there. Okay, thinking violent thoughts was helpful to a limited extent. The realisation I couldn't do anything to them increased my anger.

"Put me down," I hissed.

Hunter looked down at me and cocked his head. "I don't think so. I think if I do that, you'll try to run. You'll only end up hurting yourself if you do that." His tone was perfectly reasonable and conversational, and accompanied by an expression that was borderline giving a shit. Or would be if I bought even a little bit of it.

"Now you care," I said sarcastically. The asshole and his asshole brother threw us under the bus, right at his precious, fucking girl-friend. What a pair of suck-ups.

Ares would have made some snide remark about Lila having a gold plated pussy, or one that contracts back to virgin tightness after she's fucked. Something that would make them hand us over to her and her father. Maybe they were fucking Samuel Bell too.

Whatever, I didn't give a shit if they both sucked him off every night. Or each other for that matter.

Okay, I didn't think about that too deeply, because that was way hotter than it should have been. The very last thing I needed, or wanted, was to be turned on by these asshole twins.

"Of course I care," Hunter said. "We've been looking for a peace offering for a while now, and you two are perfect. Bell will be happy, and Reuben, he'll pretend he never heard of any of you."

He turned to Ice and said, "What is it they call you three? The Devils of Dusk Bay? Personally, I've always thought that was an over-exaggeration, but either way, it's a point in our favour. Leo might even be happy to be rid of you."

Leo might start pulling off heads if anything happened to his son. As for the rest of us, I wasn't convinced he'd give a shit. At least my mother would miss me. And the kids at the gym.

"Who calls us that?" Ice asked. "Because that's a cooler nickname than the evil fucking twins."

His gaze slid off Hunter, over to Lila. "What do they call you and your sister? The other evil twins? I know, the twisted, no, *wicked* sisters. That has a ring to it, don't you think?"

I didn't see she had a gun in her hand until she raised it.

"I think I'm the one calling the shots." Her tone was colder than Antarctica. "Take them inside. We'll try to bypass the circus the idiot neighbours called in."

She made a face like she'd just swallowed a glass of lemon juice. Evidently dead people and an explosion was an inconvenience to someone like her. Heaven forbid she got a bit of someone's brain on the bottom of her shoe. I wouldn't mind having her brain on the bottom of my shoe. If I was wearing shoes.

"Let me guess, you're the evil twin out of you and your sister," I said. I tried not to flinch when she turned the gun on me.

She gave me a look like I shouldn't goad her, but said, "I'd kill you now and get it over with, but I know who you are and what you did. You're the only one who can undo it."

That was assuming a lot, but I had the sense to keep my mouth shut. Even if I couldn't undo the virus, it might be the only thing keeping me alive right now. As long as they thought I could do it, I might stand half a chance of finding a way out. It wasn't much of a life ring, but I'd cling to it for as long as I could.

"For the record, if you kill him, I won't help you." I nodded toward Ice. "That goes for if you maim or injure him in any way." Just in case they thought there was a loophole in there somewhere.

She looked as though she might kill him anyway, but then she nodded and waved for the twins to walk ahead of her.

Did she not trust them to walk behind her? I wasn't sure I could blame her if she didn't. I didn't trust them as far as I could spit.

I hated the fact Hunter had to carry me, but I was grateful for two things. Firstly, that I wasn't draped over his shoulder like a sack of potatoes. And secondly, that it let my feet rest and gave me time to think. I needed to keep my eye out for Mannix and Ares, and an opportunity to escape. I managed to get myself out of Leo's fortress, I could get myself away from Bell's. Ice and I would find a way.

We skirted around the police who started to set up a perimeter around the wreckage. The firetruck was still there, but the fire was out. The road was now covered in foam.

In front of the ambulance, several bodies were laid out, all of their faces covered. A couple of police officers carried another one over and set it beside the others. I recognised the driver of the car who brought us here only an hour or two ago.

If he hadn't made it, then…

My breath caught in my throat, but I couldn't let myself think about the possibilities the guys didn't survive. They did. They *had* to. They were out there somewhere, hiding or looking for me. They might be injured, but they weren't dead. I wouldn't allow them to be dead. I didn't give a fuck if it didn't work that way. They were alive because I said they were.

That was what I told myself anyway, over and over. Whatever it took to hang onto my sanity.

I glanced up at Hunter, but his eyes looked straight ahead. What the fuck was his agenda, really? He claimed he wanted peace between the families and maybe this would achieve it. And maybe it wouldn't.

There was a distinct possibility that all he was doing was taking us to our deaths. Wasn't he supposed to be an ally?

I considered the possibility he was playing Lila Bell, but I doubted it. Both twins seemed to genuinely care about her. Why, I had no idea. Maybe because love was blind, hearing-impaired and not entirely sane. I only had to look at my relationship with the guys to realise that.

Wait a minute. Had the word love snuck into my brain?

Yeah. Yes it had. I cared about them, but until now I hadn't thought any further than that. It made sense though. None of us had any intention of letting the others go. What else would that be but love? A twisted, crazy kind of love, but still love.

He must have realised I was looking at him, because Hunter glanced down at me and smiled.

Ares would have been proud of the glare I gave him in return. I even managed to curl my lip. Go me.

Hunter smirked. Of course he would, he was holding all the cards.

"I know you haven't been around Mannix and the other guys for that long," he said slowly. "Long enough that they've managed to suck you into some crazy shit. But not long enough that you can't get yourself out of it if you want to."

"How would I do that?" I asked as if I was actually interested.

"I'm sure you'll think of something," he said. He glanced back at Lila, a hint of uncertainty on his face. It occurred to me maybe he had no idea why her father was after us, and what I could fix for him.

Hunter was clutching at straws, but while he was doing that he gave me an idea. Was it a good idea? I didn't have a clue. It might be. It might backfire in my face.

"Right," I said softly. I closed my eyes and tried to ignore the fact we were walking toward the gate leading into Bell's house. I considered shouting out to the police for help, but I bit my lip instead.

As Ice said, they would have a lot of questions and I didn't have all the answers. Added to that, the street was full of innocent people now, and Lila had a gun. There was no doubt in my mind she'd use it on someone to punish me for crying out. She seemed like the sadistic kind. Much more so than Ice. He tortured people for fun, but they weren't innocent people. That was an important distinction.

Ice walked beside us with a stiff back. Every so often he'd glare at one twin or the other, all over his shoulder, but mostly his eyes were on or around me like a bodyguard. He would have preferred to be the one carrying me, I saw that in his body language, along with the fact he was still in pain.

We stepped through the gate and my heart sank further. We were caught in the spider's web and I had no idea if we would ever get out again.

CHAPTER 24
KENNEDY

Security guards fell in around us when we passed through the gate. Lila didn't even have to say a word. We went from a gun on us to several.

What felt like a death march, we went up the brightly illuminated driveway and back into the house.

"This is nice," Ice said as though we never stepped foot in the place. "It could use a little more red."

No one answered him. I gave him a glance to suggest he not provoke anyone, but Ice was going to be Ice. He almost seemed to be enjoying himself. No one said he was completely sane.

We were taken to the office. It felt like days ago Mannix fucked me on the desk which Samuel Bell now sat behind. It had to be him, because no one else would dare to sit there. The resemblance to Lila was obvious. They both had dark hair and eyes that seemed to see right through me. He looked as though he could eviscerate my soul with a glance.

I managed to hold his gaze without wavering. I wasn't going to show any sign of fear or weakness. The moment I did, he'd exploit it. Still, it was difficult to avoid being intimidated. He was clearly used to getting exactly what he wanted when he wanted. He reminded me of Mannix, Ares and Leo. Ruthless, determined and powerful.

Right now, he held all the cards.

He turned his gaze to the evil twins and his frown noticeably increased in depth.

"Hunter and Parker helped us catch these two," Lila said quickly. For the first time, she seemed slightly rattled. Only slightly. Her chin was still raised, defiant. "She's the one who put the virus in the computer."

"Are you certain of that?" Samuel Bell spoke for the first time. His voice was deep, gravelly.

Now Lila seemed uncertain. "Do you know who she is—"

"I know precisely who she is." His voice was low, but she stopped speaking the moment he started. "Kennedy Knight. Stepdaughter of Leo Cassani. Computer science major. Gymnastics coach and owner of her own gym." He nodded for Hunter to put me down.

Thankfully the flooring under my feet was carpet, and I managed to contain a wince.

"Then you know I'm harmless," I said. "I was in the wrong place at the wrong time. If you don't mind, we'll get out of your hair." I gestured to Ice.

Bell ignored me and turned to Ice. "Isaac Miller. You have an interesting reputation yourself."

Ice grinned. "Thanks. I try. It would suck if anyone thought I was boring."

That was something no one could ever accuse him of being.

Bell looked unamused. He turned back to me. "If I hadn't needed a file tonight, that virus might have gone unnoticed." He looked at his screen and nodded. "I can see it at work. Deleting my files and corrupting my system. Can it be undone?"

I considered how to answer that. In the end I decided on honesty.

"Yes. And also no. I can stop it from making things worse, or deleting anything else. It may be possible to recover some, even most of the deleted files, but it would take time. And someone who knew what they were doing."

"You," he stated.

I shrugged. "I know how the virus works. I could disable it faster than anyone else." I was banking on him believing me. Other people might be able to fix it faster, but unless they were on the premises, it would take precious time to get them here. I was his best bet. If I was inclined to help him.

He nodded. "Do it." He looked past Lila to one of his security guards. "Take Mr. Miller downstairs. See to his injuries, but restrain him."

He returned his dark gaze to me. "You understand what happens to him is up to you. One toe out of line and he'll lose one of his feet. Try to screw me over and he'll be missing other, vital body parts. He'll wish he was dead."

Any normal person would be scared at being threatened like that, but not Ice. He was actually grinning. Only he would be excited at the prospect of being tortured and mutilated. I was almost certain he wasn't putting on an act so I'd feel less pressured and scared. He was still smiling as he was led from the room.

"I understand," I said evenly. "I'm going to need access to your computer."

Bell stood and gestured for me to sit in his chair.

I grimaced at the warmth as I sat, but leaned forward and focused my attention on the screen. The virus worked faster than I anticipated. If I had to guess, I'd say at least thirty percent of his files were toast.

"Yeah, this might take longer than I thought."

Bell placed his palms on the desk and leaned over towards me. "For every hour, Mr Miller loses a toe. When he has no more, we'll start on his fingers."

I looked up at him. He wasn't going to let us walk out of here alive. I knew that with absolute certainty. Hunter was right when he said Mannix's family, and the Brantleys, would pretend we didn't exist. We'd be lucky if we had something as fancy as a shallow grave.

"I've stopped the virus from doing more damage, but the time it takes to undo what it's done is what is going to take," I said, reasonably. "Threats aren't going to make it any quicker. I'm not even sure if I *can* undo it."

"Find out," he snapped. He straightened up and paced across the room, past his daughter and the twins.

I gave Hunter and Parker a dirty look. Neither asshole had the grace to look regretful or even embarrassed. If anything, all they looked was nervous. Of course, they were in the spider's web as deeply as I was.

"If Ice runs out of toes, you can always take theirs." I nodded towards them and gave them both a look of pure venom.

Lila cut me a matching look. I think she would have shot me then and there if she was allowed to. The feeling was mutual.

I smiled sarcastically at her, then turned my gaze back to the screen. She was the bitch who made this bed, she could lie in it with them. I wouldn't lose any sleep over either of the twins being tortured. In fact, the thought cheered me up.

I pinched the bridge of my nose and skimmed through a bunch of files and directories. There were a lot of them left, which contributed to the computer being slow. Or at least, slower than it could have been. If it was anyone but Bell, I'd offer to help expand its memory.

"We are just going back out to find the other two who were with her and her boyfriend," Lila said. She stepped toward the door clearly expecting to be stopped, but wanting to be gone from there as quickly as possible.

"Mannix and Ares," Parker supplied helpfully. "Leo's son and one of his friends."

I made a note that, if I survived this, I'd hack the twins' bank accounts and send all their money to a worthy cause. Maybe a charity for homeless people.

In spite of the guys' warning not to hack into Brutham Academy systems, I was tempted to do that too. I could give them both a failing grade and get them kicked out.

People often underestimated how much power a vengeful nerd actually had. Especially one who was good with computers. The things I could fuck with… It was a long and ugly list. Or beautiful, depending on your perspective.

"I'll send some people after them," Bell said. "You go upstairs to your room. You two, get out of my house. If I see you back here, you can join Mr. Miller downstairs. If you so much as think about my daughter again, you'll regret the day were born."

When I looked back up, the room was empty except for me, Bell and one of his men who still had a gun held in his hand.

"You know they're not going to stop seeing each other, don't you? Teenage rebellion and all that." I shrugged one shoulder. I wasn't trying to provoke him, not really. If it gave the incentive for some sort of vendetta against the twins, then I was all for fuelling that fire. I hadn't realised I had such a capacity for holding a grudge, but apparently I did. It was always good to learn these things about yourself.

Oh, he knew all right. Even though his face was as composed as ever, it was right there in his eyes. Along with the knowledge if he had the twins killed, his daughter would never speak to him again. I got that, I wouldn't speak to my mother if she had the guys killed. Although, my guys were worth a thousand of the twins.

"Can you fix it?" he snapped. His patience was becoming threadbare, but it still wouldn't get this done any faster.

I looked back down and let my fingers race across the keyboard. "I've recovered about ten percent of your files." Surprisingly, none of it seemed to be porn.

"I should be able to recover another ten to fifteen percent, but at least five to ten percent is gone permanently."

He growled under his breath. "Can you tell what's gone?"

"Only the empty directory names of one or two," I admitted. "One titled *Hammer* is empty. Another one just called *four-five-sevenx*, is also gone. Otherwise it's just... Gone."

It could have been anything from his plan for world domination, to photos of his precious daughters. Hell, for all I knew it was a menu from his favourite restaurant. The only way to tell was if he looked for himself and remembered what he had and where he had it.

He looked pissed. More so than he already had. "Recover what you can."

My heart raced and a feeling of dread settled over me. I was sitting in the eye of the storm and whatever was coming was going to be a shit load worse than this. If I was lucky, I'd be dead in a couple of hours. If I wasn't lucky, I would wish I was dead in a couple of hours.

My hands hovered over the keys. If I was dead anyway, then shouldn't I do what I came here to do? If I didn't, then what was the point of all of this? Mannix and Ares were probably long gone by now. This way, they'd have something to show for coming here in the first place. That might be enough to make up for losing Ice and me.

My palms were sweaty and my fingers trembled. I considered negotiating but knew there was no way we'd get any concessions from Samuel Bell. Even if I threatened him, he wasn't going to let Ice leave.

Nothing and no one was going to save us.

I looked up to see Bell watching me. His otherwise smooth brow was crinkled with a tiny frown. I've never seen someone so in control of his own emotions. His control was tight, but not flawless. Not robotic. He was a guitar string drawn tight. With the right pressure he'd snap. It wouldn't be a violent snap. More like a softly spoken order to kill me. But still a snap.

His chin lifted a fraction in warning. He knew exactly what I was thinking and we both knew what would happen if I ignored that warning.

My eyes still on his, I pressed the button to reactivate the virus and double its speed.

CHAPTER 25

KENNEDY

The room was pitch black. Completely devoid of light and sound.

The ground was hard and the walls were dry. That was the only thing I could tell about the space. That and if I walked five steps from any corner, I'd graze my knuckles on the opposite corner. There was no water. No food. No bedding.

Nothing. After I reactivated the virus, I thought he'd kill me immediately.

Instead, he'd nodded to his minion, who took me at gunpoint down a set of stairs at the back of the house. He'd unbolted the door and waved me inside.

I slumped down to the floor as tears trickled down my cheek.

I waited for my eyes to adjust to the darkness, but they never did. I listened for a sound, any sound, but it didn't come. The silence made my ears ring.

How long would it take before that drove me completely crazy?

That was exactly the point of a room like this. I remembered seeing one when Mum took me to Port Arthur in Tasmania. They sadistically used sensory deprivation rooms to punish inmates and drive them insane. Figures Bell would have one. It might be an understatement to suggest I was regretting my life choices right now. If I hadn't reactivated the virus, he might have killed me by now or at least put me in a room with some light.

Did Ice's workroom have a place like this? If it didn't now, it would if we got out of here and I told him about it. Off the top of my head, I could think of four people I'd put in it.

I sighed and sat back against the wall. Maybe I deserved to be in here, alone in the dark. I learnt a lot about myself since moving to Dusk Bay, and most of it wasn't very nice. I had a darker, more twisted soul than I ever would have suspected. A sadistic side that held onto a grudge with an iron grip.

Formerly innocent, naïve Kennedy Knight was not a nice person.

And I was going to die here.

In the dark.

Without a sound.

Alone.

TRAP

DARK MASQUE BOOK 3

CHAPTER 1

KENNEDY

The darkness was unrelenting.

Eyes open.

Eyes closed.

It made no difference. There was nothing here but me and the endless ringing in my ears.

I found a bucket in the corner I could use for a toilet, but what I really needed was a drink of water. Food too, but mostly water.

After a few hours, I started to talk to myself. Softly at first, just to hear a sound. Then I sang for a while before my throat got too dry and I had to stop.

I began to wish I was chained to the ceiling in Ice's workshop, having him peel off layers of skin. He gave his victims water, and a break from the torture.

This… This was unrelenting. I had no idea if it was days or hours. Time had no meaning here.

If there was a positive side, it was that I had a lot of time to think. I had no shortage of thoughts and questions that had no answers. They started with— was Ice in a room like this? Was he still alive? Was he being tortured like he tortured Frank Nixon and fuck knows how many others?

Those thoughts lead to wondering where Mannix and Ares were. We became separated when Bell's men blew up our car. Ice threw himself over me to keep me safe. I had no idea where the other guys went or if they were still alive. They might be dead, or they might be in the room next door.

I thought about shouting for them, but they wouldn't hear me. The whole point of this room was that *no one* could hear me, and I couldn't hear them. I could shout myself hoarse and it wouldn't get me anywhere. Nowhere other than thirstier than I already was. My mouth was so dry, I felt like I'd swallowed a desert.

The other thought I kept coming back to was regret. If I hadn't reactivated the virus on Bell's computer, I'd be dead right now. The only reason I was still alive and in here was because I pissed him off. I'd be dead soon enough. He wanted to make me suffer first.

Congratulations, I thought, *mission accomplished*. This was the most fucked up piece of misery I'd ever had the misfortune to experience.

For the first couple of hours, I was in denial that I was stuck here for any length of time. Then came anger.

Honestly, if anyone opened the door, I'd be happy to move on to the bargaining stage. I wasn't sure if there was anything I wouldn't do to get the hell out of here.

The door remained firmly closed.

I began to fixate on how they made a door that had absolutely no gaps. Maybe it had gaps, but the corridor outside was too dark to show them. The corridor might be a similar bottomless pit of sensory deprivation. I barely remember being brought down it.

Great, now my memory was fucked up. Was I concussed after the explosion? I felt around my head, but found no lumps or bumps or blood.

I curled up in a corner and tried to sleep. Why a corner, I don't know. I guess it felt safer than sleeping in the middle of the room. There was some logic behind it, but where I slept was unlikely to make any difference if someone came for me.

Whatever, it made me feel better for a minute or two.

I got a non-zero amount of sleep, but hell if I know how long it was. When I awoke, I was surprised I was still alive.

I was disappointed too. Disappointed to wake up still here. Disappointed to wake up at all.

Fuck my life.

If I could do it all over, would I do it the same way?

I had no answer for that question. Bell tried to have me killed. Having his computer systems scrambled and screwed up was small in comparison to that.

On the other hand, I could have let the grudge go and moved on with my life, knowing he'd come after me again at some point. It wasn't even about me at the time. Samuel Bell wanted to get at my stepfather, Leo Cassani. He decided to go via me. Kennedy Knight, computer science student and owner of a gymnastics studio.

I was nothing in the scheme of things, but he came after me anyway.

And me, well, apparently I hold a grudge.

Since I was never walking back out of Bell's house alive, I'd decided I might as well take his systems down with me.

I could have restored most of what the virus impacted. All he'd needed to do was assure me I'd leave in one piece. And Ice along with me. A promise not to try again later to kill me wouldn't go astray either.

Would I have believed him if he gave me such an assurance? Probably not, but I might not have ended up here. At best, I would have spent the rest of my days looking over my shoulder, just in case.

Yeah, that didn't sound like much of a life to me, either. It would have been a fuck ton better than this.

I breathed a mouthful of dry air into my parched throat. I should try to do some stretching exercises to keep myself limber and sane, but I also needed to save my strength and what little moisture I had left.

Sanity wouldn't be any use to me if I was dead.

I pushed myself to my feet and decided on some gentle stretching.

Curious, I raised a hand above me. I couldn't touch the ceiling. One mistake whoever built this room made, thank fuck, was the ceiling height.

If they wanted to torture someone even more than depriving them of sight and sound, they'd make the ceiling too low to stand, and the walls too close together to lie down.

Ice would get a laugh out of that thought. He got a laugh out of a lot of strange and twisted things. Mannix said he was fucked in the head. Maybe he was. I thought he was just a bit different, that was all. Just a bit weird. There was nothing wrong with being weird.

Shit. My thoughts were getting more scattered and random.

I raised my hands in front of me and walked the handful of steps to the opposite wall.

I grazed my hands on the stone and wondered what it would take to smash my way out.

Since this room was underground, it was unlikely there'd be anywhere to go. Since I had nothing to smash it with, this whole line of thought was moot. I had a moment of cheer imagining bringing the whole house down on top of me and everyone in it.

Sadistic? Maybe.

Satisfying as hell? Definitely.

I turned around and walked a few steps back the other way until I reached the door.

I ran my fingers up and down in case there was a weakness I hadn't felt before. If there was, I didn't find it now either. There wasn't even a knob or a handle, or a keyhole to pick through.

Nothing but a solid, metal door, probably as thick as my arm. I rapped my knuckles on it in a mixture of curiosity, frustration and the need to hear some sound.

It wasn't hollow and didn't even give slightly. Whoever put this door here meant for it to stay for a long, long time.

"Sadistic asshole," I muttered. Who put a torture chamber in a multimillion dollar harbourfront mansion?

Yeah, there could be a lot more of them than anyone knows about. I remembered one of the guys telling me how a house down the street sank into a sinkhole a while ago. Maybe it wasn't a sinkhole, or a random occurrence. Maybe it was a room like this, collapsing in on itself. How long had it been there? It might predate the house. If another, similar room collapsed, then so could this.

I waited, but nothing happened. Not even a rumble of the earth shifting, or the walls caving in.

I wanted to pound on the door and insist they let me out, or at least feed me and give me something to drink. That would be a waste of time and strength. If the door was as thick as it seemed, no one was going to hear me. I could scream at the top of my lungs and no one would ever know. There might be someone a metre or two away from me doing just that.

If the space was bigger, it would be the perfect place for a loud party. We could turn the music up full volume and not bother the neighbours.

There my thoughts went again, being scattered and random. How long would it be before I started to giggle to myself or something like that?

What is it they say? No one knows how to shred a human better than another human. People spent thousands of years perfecting torture methods and ways of fucking with each other. Hell, I learnt about a few of them at uni when I studied psychology. Ares probably knew a bunch more. Ice too.

I leaned my forehead on the cool of the door, and tried not to let tears get the better of me. If I had the tears to cry, I didn't have them to spare.

Focus on being angry, I told myself. *Crying won't get you anywhere.* I could hold anger as well as I held a grudge, but if I cried, then Samuel Bell won. If I slammed my fists into the door over and over until they were a bloody mess, he won.

Guess what happened if I completely lost my mind, or died in the corner of dehydration.

Yeah, he won.

Fuck that.

I lifted my head and placed my palms on the door. Under my fingertips were barely noticeable dents in the metal. I felt around them and decided they were indentations from fists. I bet if I felt down lower, I'd find indentations from feet, or shoes.

"You don't get to win, asshole," I said to the darkness. I didn't shout. My voice was barely above a whisper, but the words sounded loud in my ears. Hoarse and forced.

"You don't get to win," I said again. "I might die here, but I'm not giving up until the last breath leaves my body. I'm not going to cry or go insane. I'm not going to try to break down the door or the walls. I'm going to conserve as much of my strength as possible. At some point, someone is going to come and check on me, and I'll still be alive. You know how I know that? Because there's no bones down here. You don't shove people in here and let them die. There's no smell of death, no hint that anyone has ever actually died in here."

I might be clutching at straws. A hundred people could have died in here and Bell's people were that good at cleaning up.

I pushed the thought away. I liked my theory better. It was much better for my mental health to think people got out of here in one piece.

Any moment, someone would come and open the door. They might even apologise for keeping me down here for so long. They misunderstood. They were supposed to take me to some fancy guest room while I thought about what I did. They'd bring me a tray of bacon, eggs and toast, along with a soup cup-sized coffee.

I leaned my head back against the door and exhaled. I was losing it. He might just win after all.

The door still stayed firmly closed.

CHAPTER 2

KENNEDY

Click.

Something jolted me awake.

I shot up. What the—

I pressed my back and the palms of my hands against the wall. Blinked, in case I was hallucinating.

The difference was subtle, but the darkness wasn't absolute anymore. It took me a moment to realise the door was opening. The corridor outside was dimly lit, but the difference was almost night and day.

I pushed myself up the wall and stood pressed against it.

"Who's there?"

The response was an almost blinding light right in my eyes.

I threw my hand up in front of my face and winced.

"My father wants to see you." Female voice, about my age.

She lowered the phone.

I lowered my hand.

She wasn't Lila. It wasn't difficult to guess who she was.

Chloe Bell shared the same sharp edge and cold eyes as her sister and father.

She wasn't identical to her twin sister, but the resemblance was strong. They both had dark hair and heart shaped faces. Chloe's lips were fuller, and she was slightly taller.

"Unless you want to stay here, I suggest you come with me." She had no gun that I could see, but her tone suggested she expected me to obey.

I would, because pretty much anything would be better than being locked down here.

My eyes on her, watching for any movement, any sign she might come at me, I stepped through the door and into the corridor.

"You stink." She wrinkled her nose.

"Someone forgot to install a shower in there," I said dryly.

She looked at me for a moment, then laughed. "Yeah, I guess they did. I think that shithole predates plumbing." She didn't seem to approve of her father locking people in there.

What do you know? We had that in common.

"Where's Ice?" She seemed more reasonable than her sister, but that might be a good cop, bad cop act. A ruse to get me to trust her. The joke was on her if she thought that would happen. I wasn't that naive anymore.

"If I had to guess, Dad is keeping him locked away somewhere to ensure your behaviour." She shrugged one shoulder and tapped on the door at the end of the corridor.

The door was opened from the other side. She stepped through and gestured for me to do the same.

I eyed the guard as I walked past, but she looked back at me, unblinking.

"Why does he care if I behave?" I asked. "Isn't he going to kill me?"

"If he wanted you dead, you'd be dead," she said bluntly. After a moment she spoke again. "I don't know what he wants you for."

If it was worse than death or sensory deprivation, then it would probably suck. Or he thought I would.

I wasn't sure what I'd do if that was what he expected in return for letting me live. Becoming a sex slave for someone like him wasn't on my list of career choices. Would I have a choice? The alternative might not be death, it might be going back to that room.

I wasn't prepared for the surge of fear and desperation at the thought of that. I couldn't go back there. I'd rather be covered in honey and tied to an anthill than go back there.

I was about to ask for a drink of water when I realised she was leading me into a huge, opulent kitchen. It was a study in white, veined marble, and rich, hardwood floors. Past the kitchen was a sitting area with a stunning view of the harbour. The view alone was worth millions.

She reached into an upper cabinet and pulled out a glass. She handed it to me and stood back.

"No doubt you're thirsty." She waved towards the gooseneck tap that arched over a massive farmhouse style sink. She watched me carefully, clearly mindful that I could break the glass and use it as a weapon.

Instead, I stepped over to the sink and filled the glass to the top. I gulped it down and refilled the glass. I drank the second one more slowly. If I drank too fast, I'd throw it all back up. That would be a waste of precious moisture.

It tasted better than chocolate.

After a third glass of water, I set the empty glass on the benchtop beside the sink and nodded my thanks.

"Is this something you have to do often?" It was much easier to talk now with a lubricated throat.

"Not now that I'm usually away at school," she said. She glanced at her phone. "I'll take you to my father's study, then I have to catch the train back to Brutham."

I remembered what the guys said about Brutham Academy. How the third and fourth year students got to hunt the first years, and how a lot of the first years didn't make it out alive. They said the twins, Hunter and Parker, would help Lila. I wondered who would help Chloe. In spite of her last name, she seemed nicer than any Bell I met so far.

"I don't suppose there's any chance I could go with you instead of going to his study?" I asked hopefully. "I quite enjoy train travel." Especially if I ended up a long way from here.

Her regret almost seemed sincere, but it was as firm as the locked door was. "You wouldn't get past the front door."

I sighed. "I had a feeling you'd say something like that." We passed a few guards on the way. They all watched both of us like hawks, especially me. I thought about making a run for it, but I'd be lucky to make it more than five or six steps.

She nodded and led me back toward the office where all of this started in the first place. She knocked on the door and waited a moment before she opened it and went inside.

Regretting my life choices, I followed.

Samuel Bell was behind his desk, unpacking what looked like a brand-new computer. State-of-the-art, top-of-the-line, memory for days. I couldn't help being a little envious. I had a decent laptop, but it was nothing compared to this. Of course, the right person could build a better computer, but it was impressive nonetheless.

He paused in his unboxing and scowled at me. His gaze slipped from me to Chloe and he nodded.

Without another word, she slipped back out the door and closed it behind her.

He went back to unpacking while I stood near the door waiting, and watching. The message was clear. When he was ready, he'd speak to me. Fine, whatever. There was sunshine coming through the window behind him. I could stand here for as long as it took, enjoying the fact it wasn't darkness.

Finally, he looked back up. "As you see, I needed a new computer. The other one was…compromised."

Yeah, that was a nice way of saying it was fucked.

He continued. "Fortunately, it wasn't connected to my wider network. Just a smaller one within the house. Replacing all my files will take some time, but no more than three or four hours. What you did, it caused a minor inconvenience."

Well that sucked. I was locked in that room for how long, over a minor inconvenience? He was a vindictive asshole, wasn't he?

"However," he pulled a keyboard out of its packaging, "I needed a new computer anyway. This gave me the excuse to get around to buying one."

So I did him a favour. What did I get in return for that? A medal? My own private island? My freedom?

"I'm impressed with your computer skills. None of the people I currently have working for me could have done what you did as quickly as you did. None of them would have had the balls to sneak into my office during a party to do it either."

How did I respond to that?

"I like a challenge." I wasn't sure if that was the right response, but that was what came out of my mouth.

"So it would seem." He tossed the packaging aside and placed the keyboard in front of the screen.

I stared at him. Was that all he could say?

"Am I here to set that up for you?" I nodded toward the computer. "Because you didn't need to lock me away for that."

He chuckled. "It's good to see a stay in the basement didn't break you. I didn't think it would. No one who did what you and those three boys did would break that easily."

"I'll be sure to add that to my badass card application form," I said sarcastically. I should have the required amount of points by now, right?

He surprised me by saying, "I want you to work for me." Before I could respond, he raised a hand. "We both know that's not going to happen. Leo Cassani would never allow his stepdaughter to work for the enemy. Neither would his son. I hear they keep you on a short leash."

I couldn't keep the annoyance of my face. "I'm not on a—" I cut myself off. He was trying to get a rise out of me and it wouldn't work. "What do you *really* want?"

He stepped around to the other side of his desk and leaned against it, his arms crossed. He gazed at me with dark brown eyes that seemed to bore right into my soul.

Up close, I saw he hadn't shaved for a couple of days. Dressed in a dark suit, perfectly tailored, an expensive watch and shoes I could have seen my reflection in, he looked like a rich mobster.

I reminded myself that he was exactly what he was, and returned his gaze.

"You're not scared of me." It was a statement, not a question.

I was terrified, but trying not to show it. It was nice to know I succeeded in something at least. I failed in messing up his computer system, and apparently he wasn't bothered that he tried to kill me.

I resisted the urge to lick my lips. "Should I be? The worst you can do is kill me." Or put me back in the basement.

His lips twisted up in a smile that gave me the shivers. "You should be very scared of me." His voice was low, almost pleasant except the knot of threat tied around it.

"There's nothing I can't do to you or *with* you. No one to help you. No one to stop me. And when I'm done with you, I could make you disappear so thoroughly no one will know you ever existed."

His words sent a pulse of fear right through me. He was right, he could do all of that and more.

"But you're not going to," I said slowly. This wasn't about sex or torture, there was something else going on here. I didn't have the foggiest idea what it was. I wasn't sure I wanted to know. The only thing I was sure of, he wouldn't give me a choice.

"I'm not?" He seemed amused.

"No, you're not. Because you need me for something." A man like him would have women falling over themselves to sleep with him, and enough money to pay his minions to do whatever he wanted. No, there was something else going on here. He needed something from me no one else could give.

"Smart girl," he said approvingly. "As it happens, I do need something."

CHAPTER 3

KENNEDY

"Hey," I greeted Ice more cheerfully than I felt.

Too many thoughts battled with each other in my brain. Could I do what Bell wanted me to do? Did I want to? The implications of everything he said to me hadn't even started to sink in. How long would it take until they did?

Those were questions and answers for another day. Right now I wanted to get out of here. Preferably before Bell changed his mind. A man like him could and would do exactly that, just because he was able to. He'd find a way to get what he wanted done with or without my help.

"Finally. I was getting bored." Ice was chained to the wall with his hands above his head. The chain was so short, the bolt so high up, he stood on his toes.

"That looks painful." How was he not screaming? I wanted to scream just looking at him.

He glanced down. "Yeah, it's a bit tedious. As torture methods go, it's simple but effective. Not as effective as the boredom. A guy like me needs mental stimulation."

"They could have put on the TV and put on something you hate," I pointed out. I didn't know what that was. I wasn't in a position to trash talk anyone's TV choices, since I watched a lot of different things. Some things were better than others.

"Like cricket?" He grimaced. "Yeah, that would have been much worse. How are things with you? It's good to see you're still alive and hot as ever." He looked me up and down.

Leave it to Ice to flirt with me while hanging from the ceiling.

"I could use a shower, but I'm here to get you out of here. We should hurry, I think that guard overheard what you said about cricket." We might both end up chained to the ceiling with the sport on some big-screen we couldn't ignore.

That would still be better than the basement.

"We get to go home?" He cocked his head at me in question. Then his eyes turned to steel. "What did you have to do to get us out of here? If he touched you—"

"He didn't," I said quickly. "We didn't do as much damage as we hoped to do, so he's letting us go." That was the truth, but not all of it. I'd tell him everything later, when we were out of here. I couldn't guarantee what might happen otherwise.

I stepped aside as a guard with a key unlocked Ice's chains.

The guard also stepped aside, letting Ice fall hard to the concrete floor on his knees.

He grunted in pain. "I might have overestimated how much weight my feet could take after standing on tiptoe for hours." He rubbed his wrists and managed to clamber to his feet before I could move to help him.

"Are you okay?" I couldn't carry him, and I doubted Bell would offer any help. I could really use Mannix and Ares right now. I wished I knew what happened to them. If they were dead…

I couldn't let myself think that. I had to focus on getting Ice and me out of here.

"It takes more than a little chain to slow down the Iceman." He smiled, but it was forced. His feet and wrists clearly hurt more than he was willing to show. He was as stubborn as me. And, for now, as alive.

In spite of that, he let me put an arm around him before we walked out the corridor.

All this time, he was in the room next to me. He'd had light from the bulb in the ceiling. And water, judging by a jug on the table in the corner.

Evidently Bell liked some variety in his torture. Fair enough, so did Ice.

The first few minutes were slow going, especially the slog up the steps into the back of the house. Ice tried not to let on that he was in pain, but I saw it in his eyes and in the way he gingerly stepped from tread to tread.

"Lucky they're not too inventive here," he whispered. "I would have broken my toes and *then* strung me up like that."

"I don't think you should give them any ideas," I whispered back. "They might do that next time."

"Let's hope there isn't next time." He fell silent then, focusing on his breathing and putting one foot in front of the other.

The guards led us out the door and around to the gate. Neither of them looked impressed having to open it and usher us out. They both kept their hands near guns on their hips, their eyes on us.

They clearly wondered why the hell Bell was letting us go.

I could imagine the speculation in their minds. Mostly involving me bent over or on my knees. If only they knew the real reason. Everyone would know soon enough.

I flashed them both a smile as we stepped out onto the street. My heart was racing. Palms coated with sweat. I waited, but neither guard drew their weapon.

They stepped back through the gate and closed it behind them.

"How about that," Ice said. "They're actually letting us go. I thought they were going to shoot us and leave us on the street as a warning to anyone going past." He turned around and looked up at the fence. "Those spikes would be perfect for the heads of their enemies to languish on."

"That might have been acceptable practice back in the dark ages, but it wouldn't go unnoticed in the middle of Sydney," I said wryly.

Although, it was unlikely anyone walking past would think they were real. They'd assume they were something to do with Halloween or April Fools' Day, or whatever. They'd probably take photos and talk about how realistic they looked and how they rotted realistically as the days passed. The fucking videos would probably go viral.

"That's true." Ice almost seemed sad about the fact. "We could do it in Dusk Bay. Leo's house is remote enough to have a couple of heads on the gate for a few days." He actually seemed to consider the idea.

"I don't think Leo would appreciate having heads on his fence. I know my mother wouldn't like the idea." At least, I didn't *think* she would. Who even knew at this point? Right now I wasn't sure if the sky was actually blue. If I had a rug under my feet, it was gone now.

Ice pouted playfully but quickly seemed to forget about the idea. "They've cleaned up where the car exploded." He nodded in that direction.

I followed his gaze. Whoever cleaned up did an amazing job. There was almost no sign of any fire or explosion. There was a faint singe mark on the road, but no shattered glass, nothing. There weren't even any bloodstains on the road. No indication the authorities were here. It was as though the whole thing hadn't happened at all.

If I wasn't there, trying not to be blown up or shot, I wouldn't have believed it. We stood on just another quiet street in an affluent part of Sydney.

"We need to find out what happened to Mannix and Ares," I said. "Do you think they…"

"Found somewhere safe to stash themselves until this blew over? Definitely." He nodded. "In fact, I know exactly where they would have gone." He ran a hand over the back of his head and straightened his messy bun.

"Need a lift?" I didn't even see one of the twins until they stepped out of the dark SUV parked a few cars down. "Hunter and I are waiting for Lila, but if it's the place I'm thinking of, it's not far."

I hadn't noticed before that Parker had a slightly crooked nose. From the look of it, someone broke it for him. Whoever they were, they were my hero. I'd happily give Hunter a matching nose with a baseball bat. Or a chair. Or a brick. I wasn't fussy.

"Why the fuck should we go anywhere with you?" I said at the same time as Ice said, "Sure."

We exchanged looks.

"You trust them?" I asked, unable to believe he'd consider getting in a car with those assholes.

"Fuck no, but right now we need a ride, and they're offering. Unless you feel like an hour walk, then they're our best bet. Besides, they wouldn't betray us twice, unless they really hate living. Because the minute Bell finds out they're out here waiting for his daughter who they're not supposed to be anywhere near, he's going to kill them." Ice gave them a pointed look and opened his mouth like he might shout loud enough for Bell to hear.

"Your boyfriend makes a compelling case," Parker said quickly. "Hop in."

Without waiting for a response, he slipped back into the car and closed the door behind him.

No wonder I hadn't noticed them before, the windows were heavily tinted. I guess it's something you do if you're lurking around outside your girlfriend's house when her father potentially wants you dead.

I couldn't decide if they were that dumb or had balls for sticking around where they clearly weren't wanted. A combination of the two, perhaps. Love made people do some pretty strange things, including lurking and risking death.

"This is crazy." I stepped over to the back of the car, but stopped with my hand on the handle.

"You say that like crazy is a bad thing." Ice grinned. He put his hand over mine and opened the car door. As if to prove it was safe, he climbed inside first.

I sighed, shook my head and followed him in. He was right, an hour walk would suck, especially with no shoes. Who else could the twins betray us to now anyway? Bell let us go, there was no point taking us back.

At least, I fucking hoped not.

"Hey," Hunter greeted as the door clunked closed behind me. "Good to see you alive and kicking. I thought you guys were toast."

"Fuck off," I told him. Yeah, he did have a perfectly straight nose. On one hand, it was a good way to tell them apart. On the other, it would be fun to see him suffer.

Hunter clicked his tongue. "Don't be like that. We didn't have a choice, but we're genuinely glad you're not dead. We are on the same side, after all."

I sat forward. "The only side you two are on is your own. If it benefited you, you'd kill us or drop us off with...someone."

"Of course we would," Hunter agreed. "But right now, what benefits us is you two being alive. If you weren't, we'd have had to explain to Reuben what happened. And then we'd have to tell him where we were and why. And then we'd have to face him being angry. Trust me, you don't want to see Reuben angry. He's not very nice when he's not angry. When he is..."

I leaned my arms on the back of the seat in front of me. "Am I supposed to give a shit if your brother is angry with you? Because I have news for you, I don't." Maybe it was Reuben who broke Parker's nose. Or someone who worked for him. If that was the case, maybe Reuben wasn't so bad.

"Why did Bell let you go?" Parker asked. "Let me guess, one of you can do something for him that no one else can do." The question hung in the air, so heavy it was difficult to breathe.

My only answer was to sit back and click my seatbelt into place.

In the corner of my eye, Ice watched me speculatively. I knew he knew Parker was right, but he wasn't going to ask about it in front of them. I sure as hell wasn't going to talk about it in front of them.

I didn't want to keep secrets from him, but I had no idea what he or the other guys would think when I told them.

CHAPTER 4

ARES

"This is bullshit." I paced back and forth, stopping every so often to peer out between the curtains. "We should have stayed."

I scowled over at Mannix, who was no way as fucking calm as he was trying to pretend he was. That was bullshit too. No one bought his façade. He might as well have spent the last twenty-four hours stalking back across the room the way I was. We could have taken turns. There wasn't enough room for two caged lions to flex their muscles and anger.

"I made the right call," he said in that tone he learned from his father. The one that says, 'Don't question me. Don't fuck with me or I'll fuck back.' The one I wasn't in the mood to listen to.

"Yeah? How long are we going to wait and hope they turn up? Another hour? A week? They could be fucking dead for all we know."

The words stung my throat as I said them. I couldn't even speak their names. They should be here with us. Ice and Kennedy. They were ours. Mine. If they were dead, I was going to start a war, even if it was me alone against everyone else.

But I wouldn't be alone. Mannix would be beside me, trying to call the shots. Trying to be a general. He was a bossy prick, but he was usually right.

That was the hardest fucking part of all of this. When the car exploded, we went one way and Kennedy and Ice went the other. I tried to follow, but a handful of Bell's minions cut us off. We barely managed to evade them. We quietly killed a couple but then we had to hide.

The next thing we knew, the place was swarming with cops and we were forced to slip away.

Mannix insisted we come here to one of his family's safe houses and wait for Ice and Kennedy to show up.

And so, we waited, catching an hour or two of sleep here and there. I wanted to go back and look for them, but Mannix was insistent.

"They're not dead." He barely even blinked. His face was carved from stone. When he spoke, his mouth barely moved. His eyes were locked on the gap in the curtains. His hands were curled around the arms of the chair he'd sat in for the last three or four hours.

"You can't know that—"

"They're not dead," he said again. "I'd know if they were." His gaze flicked over to me and, for the first time, he seemed uncertain. Not whether they were alive or not, because he clearly believed that deep in his soul. He was uncertain about what he'd do if he was wrong.

"I don't want to lose them either," I muttered, my chin close to my chest. I wasn't good at this sharing emotions stuff.

Neither was Mannix. He'd claimed both of them as his. That was about as close to saying, 'I love you,' as I'd ever seen from him.

I hadn't even done that much. Kennedy was mine, but so far I'd resisted telling her that. When I saw her next I'd let her know she belonged to me, the same as she belonged to Mannix and Ice.

I'd claim every centimetre of her. Bury my cock so deep inside her I might get lost and never find a way out. By the time I was done, she'd understand that she was my territory.

Mine and Mannix's and Ice's. If any other man ever touched her, I'd break their neck.

The side of Mannix's mouth twitched. "Told you you didn't hate her. You're a stubborn prick."

I flipped him off. "I never hated her, I just do shit in my own time." The moment I saw her, I wanted to tear her clothes off, tie her to my bed and fuck her brains out. If she was any other woman, I would have.

When we met, she seemed so innocent, so sweet, so fragile. Goes to show first impressions aren't always right, because she's fucking none of those things. Especially fragile. If anyone suggested she was stronger than me, I'd rip off their nuts and shove them up their ass, but she was.

"We need to go back to Bell's shithole." The mansion itself was nice enough. Nicer than any place I lived as a kid by a long way, but anywhere Samuel Bell, his asshole family and his asshole minions tainted everywhere they went.

We shouldn't have planted a virus in there. We should have planted a bomb. We could have taken out a bunch of them in one shot. I bet Reuben fucking Brantley would be impressed if we took out his biggest rival.

Unfortunately, anything that big wouldn't go unnoticed by the cops. Even if Brantley paid them off, they'd have to find a scapegoat and we'd be the ones thrown right under the bus.

Fuck that.

"If they're inside, we can't help them." His stony expression was back. "If they're dead, we can't help them. We can only assume they got away and will make their way here. Ice knows to come here. He'll find a way." He didn't want me to keep arguing, but I wasn't done.

I wouldn't be done until I saw them both with my own eyes.

"And if he and Kennedy got separated?" I asked. "She won't know to come here." We should have fucking told her, but we were so convinced we knew exactly what we were doing. That we'd all get out in one piece. We got cocky.

If I wanted to be an asshole, I'd suggest it was Mannix who got cocky. He was the one leading us. He was calling the shots. I could lay all the blame on him and have an excuse to punch his lights out.

But either Ice or I could have told Kennedy about this place and Mannix would have agreed that she needed to know. Hell, he would have shown her on a map on her phone and made sure she knew exactly how to get here.

If she didn't know where to go, it was the fault of all of us. If she was lost or dead, I was as much to blame as anyone.

Fuck.

Mannix pressed his lips together so hard they turned white. "If she doesn't come here, she'll go back to Dusk Bay. Or she'll contact her mother, who'll let us know. She's resourceful, and smart." He shot me a challenging look, as though I'd deny his statement.

I wouldn't. He was right on both counts. Kennedy was the smartest person I ever met.

And she had the best tits. All I wanted to do right now was run my tongue all the way over them and bite her nipples until she screamed. And then go on biting them.

"How long are we going to wait?" I asked again.

We couldn't sit here forever in the hope they turned up or we got a phone call telling us where they were. Sooner or later we have to go home to Dusk Bay and face Mannix's family. They'd want to know if we succeeded in our mission. No doubt they'd want every minute detail of it.

They had plenty of information on Samuel Bell's place, but if there was a chance we saw something no one knew about before, they'd want to know about it. Fuck only knows if we had. It wasn't like the higher ups in the organisation told guys like us much of anything. We were the worker ants, expected to do what we were told and not ask too many questions. At the same time, we were expected to risk our lives at the drop of a hat, because right now, we were expendable.

At least, unless Kennedy's virus worked the way it was supposed to. We'd be a lot less expendable with something like that on our resumés.

Before Mannix could answer, I said, "Don't say as long as it takes. Not unless you know exactly how long that will be." I didn't need any half assed promises, or vague responses. That wasn't who I was. That wasn't who Mannix was either. We got shit done.

Not today. Today we sat in a small room in Sydney, maybe ten or so kilometres from Bell's place, breath held like we might run out of oxygen at any minute.

He tipped his chin back, his gaze grazing the ceiling. "I know we can't stay here forever." He exhaled out his nose in frustration. "We'll stay until morning. If they don't turn up, we'll go back home." Every word seemed to cause him physical pain.

I knew he wanted to tear off heads as much as I did. I also knew what the repercussions would be for him if he did. He was supposed to take over from his father someday. If he went off half-cocked, that would never happen. And because he was Mannix, he'd never go off half cocked. He'd go off full-cocked and burn the world down to find Kennedy and Ice. He'd make people pay for anything they did to them.

And me, I'd be right beside him every step of the journey. Between us, we'd leave the world in ashes and have no regrets doing it.

I nodded. That was the best I was going to get. There was no point in pushing him further.

"Get some rest," he said. "Pacing around like that isn't gonna help anyone."

"It's helping me," I snapped. In spite of that, I perched myself on the edge of one of the beds and flopped back. If I counted the stains on the ceiling, that would pass a minute or two. I could spend another couple of minutes speculating on what exactly the stains were, but I didn't particularly want to know. Probably blood and cum. How it got there was anyone's guess. I didn't give a shit.

Ice, on the other hand, he'd be fascinated. And impressed if any guy managed to cum all the way up there. The guy was fascinated with all sorts of weird crap like that. Things no one else would notice, much less care about. He was like a kid, endlessly looking at the world around him and trying to dissect it, either literally or figuratively. Usually literally. I've never met anyone who liked to slice things up as much as he did.

In some ways, the four of us couldn't be any different, and in others we were so alike it was scary. We were all stubborn, ruthless and held grudges. And we all liked it when Kennedy orgasmed.

"You're right," Mannix said softly. "This is bullshit. We should all be home by now."

I turned my face to look at him. That was the first time I'd ever heard him admit someone else was right. He was in no way admitting he was wrong. He was just agreeing with my assessment of the present situation.

"We'll get there," I told him. "They'll turn up any minute now and we can all get the fuck out of here."

"Yeah." He sagged slightly in the chair, his gaze now on the stained carpet on the floor. "We have to, because I won't lose either of them. I can't."

I turned my face away from his vulnerability. He wouldn't want me to see it. If anyone asked later, I'd swear on anything you put in front of me, that he was stone cold, rock hard the entire time, just like me. Neither of us faltered. Neither of us fell apart.

My eyes once again found the gap in the curtain. I watched the fading daylight. In another hour, it would be dark and we'd have to go in search of food. In the meantime, we waited.

CHAPTER 5

KENNEDY

"This is the place." Hunter pulled the car up outside a small block of rundown apartments.

I eyed them doubtfully. I wouldn't put it past the twins to take us somewhere random and leave us here for shits and giggles.

I glanced over at Ice as he nodded.

"This is right." He saw me looking at him and smiled reassuringly.

"Did you think we'd drop you off at the wrong place?" Parker asked. He actually looked offended.

I actually didn't give a shit. "That was exactly what I thought." I undid my seatbelt and opened the door. Thankfully, the door *did* open. For half a second there, I was worried we'd be stuck in here.

Yeah, where these two were concerned, I had some small trust issues. Not to mention the desire to punch Hunter in the face hadn't diminished much in the drive over. I decided it wasn't worth hurting my hand for, but I wouldn't rule out hurting him at a later date. Or his brother.

"Ouch." Parker looked over the seat at me and pouted, but he didn't look too concerned. If he did, that was too fucking bad. He gave me a long, curious look.

I knew he wanted to insist I tell him what Bell told me. He also knew I wasn't going to tell him jack shit. Even if they hadn't gone along with Lila and handed us over to Bell, I wouldn't have. Honestly, I hadn't even gotten my head around it yet.

I gave Parker a sarcastic smile and stepped out of the car.

Ice climbed out behind me and closed the door. He did that guy thing of tapping the roof of the car to let them know they could drive away, as if the closing of the door wasn't a dead giveaway.

Both twins gave us a cheerful wave before the SUV peeled away from the curb and disappeared into the traffic.

"I'm guessing those two have a short life expectancy," I said dryly.

Ice took my hand and chuckled. "They're useful in their own way. They got us here after all."

"It's also their fault we got caught in the first place," I pointed out. "They didn't have to let Lila boss them around."

He grinned and didn't say anything.

I frowned at him. "Are you suggesting I'm allowed to boss you around?"

He stopped and pressed his lips over mine in a kiss so soft it made my heart flutter. "Any time, Beautiful."

"I'll remember that," I assured him. I briefly wondered if the other two would let me do the same. In the same thought I reminded myself they had to be alive first.

I tipped back my head and looked up at the apartment building. "If they're anywhere, they'll be here?"

"Here or not too far away," he agreed. He didn't say it, but I knew he was thinking the same thing I was. On tender feet, he led me to the elevator and pressed the button for the sixth floor.

The doors slid open to reveal a small, well-used elevator car.

"Imagine how many people have fucked in here." He traced a finger down my cheek as the door closed.

A shiver travelled down my body and to my core.

"I'm guessing a few." My voice sounded choked to my own ears. "Is there a name for that, like the mile high club?"

A frown flitted across his brow. "I have no idea. I'll have to look it up the next time I get my hands on a phone or a computer." He slipped his hand around the back of my head and brought my face to his in a deep, wet kiss. He slipped his other hand up the front of my dress and tugged it down, along with the cup of my bra.

The elevator could stop at another floor at any time, and the door could open, but rather than deterring me, the idea made me more excited.

I reached down to undo his jeans and slid them down just far enough for me to wrap my fingers around his cock.

He grunted and pushed himself into my hands a couple of times.

He pushed up my dress and shoved them and my panties down, before slipping his fingers between my legs and over my pussy. He found my clit and started to work me with quick, deliberate strokes. He had me panting in moments.

"You're so wonderfully wet already." He tugged my dress up further before he turned me around and bent me over.

He placed his hand between us and guided his cock before slipping it deep into my pussy.

I groaned at a being filled so suddenly and deeply.

"I can't get over how incredible you feel every time," he said breathlessly. He paused for a couple of breaths, then started to pound into me, over and over.

I pressed my palms against the wall to steady myself. The vibrations from the moving elevator passed all the way through my body, adding to the sensations and pushing me closer and closer to the edge.

Light flashed under the doors with each floor we passed.

Second.

I reached down to rub my own sensitive, aching nub. I was so close now.

Third.

Ice thrust harder and harder. "God… Beautiful… Come with me."

Fourth.

I groaned and came hard, clenching his cock and making my fingers damp.

"Holy shit." He stilled and came too, spilling himself inside me while he grunted and ground himself against me.

Fifth.

He slid out and we hastily fastened our clothes and smoothed them back down into place.

Sixth.

I was straightening my hem when the doors slid open.

"Here we are." He managed to sound like he wasn't panting or out of breath. His cheeks weren't even flushed.

Mine were, I could feel them.

I took a moment to compose myself before I stepped out of the elevator behind him.

We were in another corridor, this one lit by windows which looked like they hadn't been washed in my lifetime.

It was better than total darkness.

I looked at a sign on the wall. "Which number apartment?"

"Nine." He grinned.

I rolled my eyes. "Whose idea was that?"

"Just a lucky coincidence." He shrugged.

I turned to the right and followed the corridor that led to apartment six-nine.

"Who knows about this place?" Just because Bell let us go didn't mean there wasn't someone waiting to ambush us or fuck knows what else. The fact the evil twins knew made me beyond uneasy.

Ice rubbed the back of his neck. "A handful of us. There are places like this all over the country. Some we know about, many we don't. If we all knew about all of them, they'd be at risk. As for this one, we have to take the chance, or we head home to Dusk Bay." He cocked his head at me questioningly.

I looked from him to the door and back again.

"If anyone is lying in wait for us, they would have seen us arrive," I reasoned.

"If they had cameras in the elevator, they would have seen us come too," he said with a smile.

I made a face at him, then raised my hand to knock on the door.

"Wait, is there a secret knock or something?" For all I knew, I had to knock six times and then nine so they'd know it was us.

"There should be, shouldn't there?" He let his hand drop and slap against his thigh.

"Go ahead and knock." He stepped up next to the door and positioned himself between me and any trouble if trouble opened the door.

I knocked.

We waited.

I knocked again.

The lock clicked and the door opened enough to show it was fastened to the frame with a chain. One that looked more sturdy than the rest of the building.

"Shit."

The door closed and the chain was pulled aside before it opened again. Mannix reached out and grabbed my arm to tug me into the room.

I found myself surrounded by guys and embracing arms. Everyone tried talking at once and you can imagine how well that went.

After a minute or so, Mannix barked, "Everyone, shut the fuck up." He kicked the door shut and waved Ice and me over to the bed.

I sat in the middle. Ice sat on one side, Ares on the other.

Mannix pulled over a chair and flopped down on it. He stared at me and Ice like he couldn't believe we were there in front of him.

Honestly, I felt the same way about him and Ares.

"It's about time you got here," Ares said with a grunt. "Mannix wanted to leave without you. Another hour and we would have left for the airport."

Mannix scowled at him but didn't answer. Instead he took my hands and asked what happened to us.

In as few words as I could use, I described the room, and the way our plan didn't work the way we hoped.

Ice then did the same.

When he was done, I looked down at the floor. "He let us go because there's something he needs me to do, but I can't tell you until we get back to Dusk Bay. I can only ask you to trust me and hope you don't hate me."

"We could never hate you," Mannix said. "I can insist you tell me and you'll have no choice."

"Don't insist." I looked at him with pleading eyes. This was difficult enough without him going all mafia boss on me. He might say they couldn't hate me, but if they knew what this was about, they might change their minds.

He looked conflicted, but he nodded.

"Fine, but I want to be in on it when you can talk about it." He gave me that look like he expected to be obeyed, no matter what. It was kinda hot, even though he must know it wasn't necessarily that simple.

I quickly realised he did know, he just didn't care. Whatever was going on, he'd be privy to it, or heads would roll. I wondered if anyone ever told him no and got away with it for very long. It was hot, and it was scary.

"I'll make sure you're there," I said finally. "All of you. You deserve to hear it after everything we've been through." I hated to leave them out of the loop, but the loop might wrap around my neck like a noose soon enough.

Mannix's expression softened. "Ares and I didn't go through much compared to you two. That was fucked up and I'll make sure Bell pays for it."

"Can we build a sensory deprivation room?" Ice asked suddenly.

Mannix didn't even hesitate to respond. "Yes. Yes we can. I can think of the perfect first visitor when it's done."

"Me too," I said dryly. "Hunter and Parker Brantley."

"Them too," Ares agreed. "Better make a few of these rooms. We're going to need them."

I couldn't contain a shudder at the idea of going anywhere near another place like that.

Hopefully the guys didn't expect me to check out the handiwork when it was built. I was going to have nightmares about it for a while. I might have to see if I could find a night light in one of the shops in the airport before we flew out. Just a soft one. I didn't think I'd be able to sleep in the dark. Not tonight.

Fuck knows when.

Mannix called for a car to come and pick us up, while Ares dug out some food from the small fridge and made Ice and I sandwiches.

While I ate, I was only too aware of three sets of eyes on me, all wondering what Bell wanted of me.

If they knew, they might cut my throat and leave me here for someone else to find.

CHAPTER 6

KENNEDY

I'd been confined behind the iron gates of Leo's house before. When they closed behind me this time, there was something eerily final. Like the clang as the two sides met and locked meant I'd never leave.

"You okay?" Ice's hand rested on my thigh. He hadn't left my side since we found the other guys.

Ares and Mannix hadn't gone too far either, but neither had much to say.

Ares, in particular, hadn't said more than a word or two. He kept looking at me with an unreadable expression that could indicate anything from him being happy to see me, to him wishing I was dead.

Our relationship was complicated to say the least.

"Yeah, kind of," I said. As okay as a person could be when she felt like she was being taken to her execution.

Part of me hoped Leo and Mum were home, so I could get this over with. The rest of me wished they'd gone on an extended vacation around the world so I could put this off indefinitely. A year or two should do it.

"Whatever it is, it's not gonna change how we feel about you," he said softly.

Ares, who sat on the other side of him, looked around him at us both. "Don't count on it. That depends what she has to say or do. If it's nothing too bad, she would have told us by now."

As usual, his accusing words pissed me off.

"That's assuming a lot," I said coolly. "If I could tell you, I would have."

"It's easy to say that when you have no intention of telling us." He smirked.

"You're not going to pressure it out of me." The look I gave him was supposed to be stone cold, but I suspected it came off looking mildly irritated. He knew exactly how to get under my skin. Asshole.

"Enough," Mannix snapped. He looked over the front passenger seat at us and jerked his head towards the driver. The message was clear. Don't argue in front of someone else.

Our business was our business and not for anyone else to overhear.

Ares slumped back in his seat and crossed his arms, but he gave me a last look like this conversation wasn't over.

I sighed. As far as I was concerned, it was more than over. Until we got back into the house.

"Whatever it is, we'll deal with it," Ice whispered. "Like we deal with everything else."

"By killing people?" I was only half joking.

"If we have to," he said. "Whatever it takes, we've got you. Right, Ares?" He turned his face and gave the other guy a look.

"If you say so," Ares grunted.

The driver pulled the car into the garage. The door rolled shut behind us.

The clang of metal hitting concrete was louder and more final than the gates.

A layer of sweat on my palms, I pushed open the car door and got out.

Ice scrambled after me. Mannix stepped out of the front passenger seat and put a possessive hand on my lower back. With Ares trailing behind, they led me inside.

"There you are!" Mum's voice bordered on shrill the moment we stepped into the enormous kitchen. "I was starting to worry."

The next thing I knew, she had her arms around me, hugging me and kissing my cheek.

"I'm fine," I protested. I hugged her back for a minute before untangling myself from her. "Is Leo here?"

She leaned back, her brow creased. "Yes, he's in his office. Why? Do you need to—"

"I'll get him," Mannix said. He looked at me like he'd prefer not to let me out of his sight, but trotted off, his back stiff.

Mum led me over to the couch and sat me down. "What is this about? Are you sure you're all right?"

Before I could answer, Ice said, "I'll make some coffee."

"Good idea." I could use a cup or two. Didn't prisoners on death row get a last request? This was mine.

Wait, should I have asked for a bottle of vodka instead? Oh well, it was too late for that.

I caught Ares's eye as the blond god leaned against the wall, arms crossed, one foot pressed against the wall behind him. He wore the same expression he had since we were at the apartment. Guarded, watching. He reminded me of a lion biding his time while he waited for an opportunity to leap on his prey. Or a hunter who set a trap and sat back until it was set off.

And me, I felt like a little mouse who was too enticed by the cheese. Any moment now, the trap would snap and I'd be caught in that snare forever. Unable to run or fight or flee.

His eyes lingered on me, but he looked away at the sound of approaching footsteps.

I followed the sound as Leo and Mannix stepped into the room.

Judging by the look on Leo's face, Mannix had filled him in briefly. He clearly still had questions and was expecting answers. Did they realise how alike they were? Neither of them were good at taking no for an answer. Come to think of it, none of us were.

Leo got straight to the point.

"I hear things didn't go to plan."

Ares snorted.

"Things went sideways," Mannix said. "But we got in and out alive."

"Thank goodness you did," Mum said. She put an arm around my shoulders and squeezed.

Leo looked less impressed. He would have preferred if we'd succeeded.

Me too.

I half-listened as Mannix filled him in, going into detail every step of the way. More detail than I would have thought to give. Honestly, more detail than I'd noticed. From the exact time we stepped foot in Bell's mansion, to how long it took us to get to his office.

Mannix described the layout of the office, down to the clock on the wall. He didn't mention fucking me on the desk, but he left out nothing else. Either he had a photographic memory or he paid more attention than I did.

Leo listened carefully, asking questions here and there, but mostly absorbing what his son said, taking mental notes. Probably planning something else against Bell based on what we found there. That was inevitable.

Mannix finished with him and Ares getting separated from me and Ice.

Ice took over from there, describing how we met up with the twins and then Lila Bell. How she'd assumed Hunter and Parker apprehended us for her and, at gunpoint, took us back to her father.

Leo looked furious. If the Brantley twins were in front of him, he'd probably bang their heads together until they were a bloodied mess.

I'd be inclined to help him.

My coffee was almost cold before I remembered it was in my hand. I drank it anyway. Why waste perfectly good coffee?

Ice mentioned himself being chained to the ceiling for a while, but made it sound like it was nothing too terrible. Apart from being bored, the experience didn't seem to have had a lasting impact.

I wished I was half as tough as he was. Or half as crazy. Whatever it was he had going on, I wanted some of it. Especially right now.

My heart galloped in my chest like it was trying to escape the rest of me.

Get out while you can. I was surprised no one could hear it. It pounded so hard it hurt.

All eyes turned to me while I described the basement room. The one good thing about it was that there wasn't much to describe. Metal door, stone walls, darkness, soundproof.

I was done in a sentence or two.

That was the easy part behind me though.

I told them about Chloe opening the door and letting me out. I told them she seemed a lot more sympathetic than Lila had. 'Seemed,' being the key word here.

No one in the room seemed inclined to cut her any slack. After all, she was a Bell. That made her just as suspect as Lila.

I considered pointing out that they supported Reuben and Caleb Brantley, in spite of Hunter and Parker being a pair of pricks. Since that wouldn't go down as well, I decided not to bother.

I described the steps up to the main house, trying to be as detailed as Mannix, but they were steps. Tread, riser, tread, riser. Concrete. A crack here or there. There wasn't much to tell.

I closed my eyes and thought back before describing the walk from the basement steps to Bell's office.

"There were more guards around than there were when we went in," I said slowly.

Ice grinned. "We must have given them a scare."

"We rarely send anyone directly into places like that," Leo said. "They don't usually end well." His eyebrows dropped. He seemed to be thinking of something in particular. This was far from his first rodeo. How many people had he sent to their death?

If I had to guess, I'd say a non-zero number. Maybe so many another four wouldn't have mattered, even if one was his son.

Mannix gave him a dark look.

Leo hadn't hesitated to send his younger son straight into the lion's den.

Although, Mannix insisted on going. He knew the risks when he led us in there. He calculated those versus the reward and decided it was worth it.

We all had. We knew there was a chance we wouldn't walk out of there. Maybe it was rash, but we all went in with our eyes open. If we had it to do over again, would we?

Probably, but next time we'd succeed.

"Luckily, this did end well," Mum said. "I don't know what I'd do if anything bad happened to my baby girl." She then proceeded to give every guy in the room look like it was one hundred percent their fault I was in danger at all.

I pressed my mouth into a line. I was as much to blame as they were, but she had to wear some of it herself. She dragged me into this life to begin with.

"We wouldn't have let anything happen to Kennedy," Mannix growled.

I looked down at the floor.

"Definitely not," Ice agreed.

"Cut to the chase," Ares snapped.

All eyes turned to him, including mine.

"Kennedy has something to say." He nodded to me. "Spit it the fuck out."

Now everyone was looking at me instead.

Ugh.

"What is it?" Mum asked. Her brow was creased with maternal worry.

She cared, I knew she did, but part of me was so angry with her I wanted to hurl the last couple of mouthfuls of my coffee in her face.

"Samuel Bell let me go," I said just loud enough for everyone in the room to hear. "He let Ice and I go because he wanted me to give you a message."

I looked directly at my mother.

She looked confused, then her face paled. "You don't have to—"

"Yes, I do." I exhaled out my nose and looked around at everyone. These were the last moments these words went unsaid, and I wanted to make them last. Once they were gone, they were gone forever.

"Samuel Bell said he knows he's my father."

CHAPTER 7
KENNEDY

The silence was like a void after a thunder crack.

My mother sat stunned. Her face was white with a little green.

The only sound in the room was the tick of the clock on the wall. It counted down the seconds. A minute. Two minutes.

Finally the silence was broken by Ares's low exclamation.

"What the fuck?"

I looked over at him, expecting to see hatred in his eyes. I saw surprise. No doubt when it sank in…

Leo sounded dazed. "Helen?"

Trembling, she turned to him.

"It was… It was…" she stammered.

He seemed to rally, pulling himself together in the face of my words.

"It was what?" he said carefully.

"It was a long time ago." Her eyes were wide. She was scrambling for the words and maybe something to cling onto.

"Did he rape you?" Leo's question was direct, his face tinged with pink. He obviously hadn't decided how to respond. Her answer would guide him.

"No," she said quickly. Then more softly and slowly, "No. It was at Brutham. We had a…connection."

Ares snorted. "Obviously."

She ignored him.

"I think we both knew it couldn't go anywhere but we gave in to temptation. Then we both graduated and went our separate ways. A couple of months later, I realised I was pregnant. I never told him. I put him out of my mind and moved on."

"So it's true?" I whispered. Until then, I wasn't sure. In the back of my mind, I expected her to deny it. To laugh at the absurdity of the suggestion. To tell me it was just a mindfuck from Bell. The truth knocked the breath out of my lungs for a while.

Somehow, I managed to put together coherent thoughts and words. And an accusing tone to match.

"You told me my father left because he wanted to be with someone else." All my life I thought maybe I did something wrong. Something so horrible it made him leave. I'd wondered if there was something I could have said or done that might have made him stay. Maybe if I was better behaved. Cried less. *Something.*

Now I knew why I didn't remember him. Before yesterday, we'd never met.

Mum sighed. "It was complicated. Then, when I started to work for the Brantleys, it became more complicated. It was better if no one knew. I didn't mean to deceive anyone. I thought it was for the best."

"But he knew," Leo said coldly. "He did the maths and he knew. You were never married?"

"Not to him, no," Mum said quickly. "Even if I told him…" She shook her head. "His family had plans for him. He was always going to marry Penelope. Chloe and Lila's mother."

"Would you have married him if you could?" I asked. How different would my life be if she had? Would I be a coldhearted minion like his daughter Lila? My *sister* Lila.

I hadn't let myself think about that yet. I had two younger sisters. One happy to lock me up, the other happy to let me out. Or at least, happy to follow orders.

Figured my family would be as dysfunctional as fuck.

"I don't know," Mum admitted. "It doesn't matter now; that's the past. It's done."

"It matters because if you were married when Kennedy was born, she would have been the legitimate heir to the Bell family and everything that goes with that," Leo said.

His eyes settled on me.

I knew what he was getting at. If that happened, we'd be mortal enemies. In theory.

"Including two ambitious younger sisters who are prepared to tear each other apart to be heads of the family, much less you," Mannix said.

If I thought Ares was unreadable, he was nothing to Mannix's expression right now. I had literally no idea what was going through his head.

It was absolutely terrifying.

"I, for one, don't care," Ice said lightly, sweetly. He came to sit down on the other side of me and put his arm over my shoulders.

"Firstly, Kennedy is still Kennedy, regardless of who her sperm donor was. Secondly, if she wants to start going by Knight-Bell, I'm all for it. It sounds badass. Like, don't ask for whom the night bell tolls, for it tolls for thee." He grinned.

I shook my head at him.

"I think my life expectancy might be reduced somewhat if I go by Bell."

If the expression on Leo's face was any indication, the jury was still out on my life expectancy as it was. If he wasn't impressed by Chloe being nice to me, then he'd be unmoved by our existing relationship being a more or less positive one.

My relationships with the guys in particular. Leo could just as easily withdraw his blessing.

"I don't care either," Mannix declared finally. "Kennedy is ours regardless of who her father might be." He shot Mum a look, clearly laying every drop of blame firmly in her lap.

"Bell has no claim on her, especially if he knew she existed all this time and didn't bother to say so. That includes his spawn. If they think otherwise, they'll have to go through us."

Ice jerked his thumb towards Mannix. "What he said."

Ares grunted something that might have been an agreement.

I managed a faint smile for all of them, but my eyes still found Leo's. At the end of the day, if he wanted me gone, I'd have to leave or it would start a war between him and the guys.

Or he'd have me killed. Would he ask the guys to do it? Would they if he did? No, they wouldn't. A war might be a walk in the park compared to how it might all go.

Leo looked back at me, his gaze unwavering. "You had no idea?"

"None." It was an effort not to flinch, but I managed.

"I didn't—" Mum started.

He cut her off. "I want to hear it from Kennedy." He gave her a glance that clearly said he'd deal with her later. It seemed the honeymoon was over.

I was sorry for that but I'd had no choice but to drop this grenade in the middle of everything. Besides, I wanted the answers myself. Even if they came with a lot more questions.

"I didn't have a clue until he told me," I said. "Even then, I didn't believe it until Mum confirmed it. I mean…he put me in that basement room. That's not exactly the thing a loving father does to his daughter."

I was struggling to get my mind around any of this. When had every aspect of my life become so complicated? Oh, right, before I was born. All of this would have come out sooner or later. That fact simplified nothing, did nothing to make me feel better about everything. What other truth bombs would land before this was done?

"Not a *loving* father, no," Leo agreed. "I wouldn't put anything past Samuel Bell. His daughters knew exactly where to find that room, didn't they?"

My lips dropped apart and I nodded.

Fuck, what kind of monster was he? Torturing a stranger, especially someone who did wrong by you, was one thing. Locking your own child in a place like that—that was horrible.

"The father of the year award *doesn't* go to Samuel Bell," Ice said.

"No, it doesn't," Mannix agreed. He looked at Leo, clearly wondering if he'd qualify. Leo's response to me would be the answer to that.

Leo all but ignored him. "Bell also sent that man after you."

I stared. "Frank Nixon. He wanted to strike out at you."

"Or me," Mum said softly. "It might have been retribution for not telling him about Kennedy."

"It was Bell being an asshole," Mannix said. "He doesn't need a reason. He could come after any one of us, or all of us, because he feels like it. One day it might be about retribution, the next day it might be because he ran out of toilet paper."

"That would be a bummer," Ice said, his expression deadpan.

Ares snorted again. That seemed to be the only method of communication he was capable of right now.

That was relatable. I was having a hard time putting words or thoughts together too.

"What…happens now?" I asked tentatively.

"Nothing happens now," Mannix said without hesitation. "You go on being you. Nothing has to change."

As if he hadn't spoken, Leo said, "Did Bell give you any indication if his daughters knew?"

I frowned and went over everything he said, and everything they said, in my mind.

"He didn't," I said eventually, "but that doesn't necessarily mean they don't. Either Lila knew or she hated me on sight. Either Chloe knew or she felt sorry for me. They didn't give away much. Certainly no more than that."

I pinched the bridge of my nose. "If I had to guess, I'd say they don't know. I'm not basing that on anything in particular though, they just didn't seem very…sisterly."

"I'd operate under the assumption that if they didn't know before, he's told them," Leo said. "And even though you're not the legitimate heir, they may not see it that way."

I pinched a little harder. "Wonderful, I made enemies just by existing."

"Welcome to my world," Mannix said dryly. "All the more reason we're going to stick together. Right, Dad?"

Leo regarded his son for approximately an hour or two.

Okay, it wasn't more than a couple of minutes. He had a way of keeping people on the edge until he was good and ready to pull them in or push them off.

"Kennedy is still my stepdaughter, and I'll do everything in my power to keep her safe as the rest of us. However—" he raised an eyebrow at me, "—if I see any indication that you're working against us, I won't hesitate."

He didn't need to elaborate, we knew what he meant. He'd kill me and not blink. Not regret it.

"I have no intention of working against any of you," I assured him. "All I want right now is to finish my degree, run my gym and eventually my own cyber security business."

"I strongly advise keeping your head down for a while," Leo said. "This may blow over and it may not. You might have to get used to being inside the fence for quite some time. And if you go outside, you're not going alone."

"No, she's not," Mannix agreed. "Kennedy will have someone with her at all times."

I sighed. "Please tell me you'll let me go to the toilet alone."

"At all times," he repeated. "From now on, there's only four people I trust. That doesn't include any of the staff." He didn't add that my mother wasn't included, that was obvious.

She kept something important from us all this time, that made her suspicious at best.

I wasn't sure I could trust her anymore. If she lied about my father, what else did she lie about? If it wasn't for the obvious resemblance and the red hair, I'd wonder if she was actually my mother.

"I really think you should consider calling yourself Kennedy Knight-Bell," Ice said.

Obviously he wanted to break up a tense moment. It worked to some extent. I managed half a chuckle and the mood lightened slightly.

I swatted him on the arm. "Not a chance." If my younger sisters didn't know about me before, they would if I went around calling myself that. It occurred to me that if somehow Lila married one of the Brantley twins, I'd be related to those assholes too.

Ugh, this kept getting better.

Of course, I'd also be related to Zeke Brantley, but at this point I didn't think that would be worth it. I'd need front row tickets to Wolf

Venom concerts for life, even to make it slightly better. Not to mention a lifetime of backstage passes and tour merch.

"If it's okay, I'd like a long soak in the bath, and then some sleep." I tried to stifle a yawn but failed. The last couple of days were exhausting and I was over them.

"Of course," Mum said. "You must be tired after everything you've been through and done. We're so impressed with you."

I could only manage a watery smile for her. At some point I'd forgive her, but not right now. Right now, I had a bunch of stuff to figure out and come to terms with.

"Kennedy." It was the first word Ares said since we were in the car. "I want to talk."

He'd given me no indication of his thoughts on my paternity. I had a feeling I was about to get every detail and I may not want to hear what he had to say.

CHAPTER 8

ARES

I ignored the looks from everyone else and took her up to my room.

I grabbed her arm in a grip that was intended to be bruising, and pushed her inside before I locked the door behind us.

I shoved her over to my bed and down on her ass before I stepped away. I paced a few steps, then turned around to face her.

She looked at me with a combination of fear and defiance. Mostly defiance. Good, that was exactly what I wanted from her. She was no damsel in distress. I wanted her to stand up to me, but I also needed her to know exactly how I was feeling.

"Ares—"

"Shut up," I snapped. I curled my hands into fists. "This is fucked up. Everything about this is fucked up." I slammed a fist against my thigh. Revelled in the shooting pain. It wasn't enough.

"You think I don't—" she started again.

"I said shut up," I growled. "Shut up and listen."

She glared at me, but sat back and rested her hands in her lap.

I exhaled and closed my eyes for a moment. "I grew up with *nothing*. We were lucky to get more than a meal a day. Everything was secondhand at best. I went to school in a uniform that should have been thrown out years ago. Too big, too small, whatever. Nothing ever fit right. Every item of clothing I got had some other kid's name on the label. If I was lucky, I'd find a jumper in the lost and found. If I wasn't lucky, I was cold."

I opened my eyes but didn't look at her. The last thing I wanted to see on her face was pity. It was a shitty past but that was what it was, the past. As far as I was concerned, I'd say this, then never talk about it again.

"Then I met Mannix and Ice. He went by Isaac then, until one of our teachers kept pronouncing it Ice-aac, instead of Ize-aac. We started calling him that too. At some point, it changed to Ice."

I closed my eyes and shook my head at the memory. Life seemed a lot simpler back then. Even when my family had nothing.

I looked at her now to see a faint smile on her lips. Fuck, she was gorgeous. The red hair and freckles really did it for me.

"The three of us were inseparable from the moment we met," I said. "I don't remember when, but at some point I became aware of what Mannix's family was all about. That included money and power. Two things my family had none of. Two things I wanted desperately. And all I had to do to get it was hate the Bell family."

I glanced down at the floor. The carpet was clean. So clean. Anywhere I lived as a kid, it was always covered in stains. Fuck only knew what from, but there were plenty of them. Never here though. If anything was dropped on the carpet, it was cleaned. If it didn't come out, Leo would probably have it ripped out and replaced. Fucking rich people.

"If I tried to think back to a time when I didn't hate Samuel Bell and his family, his whole organisation, I wouldn't find one. It's deeply ingrained. It's part of who I am."

I looked back up at her. Her expression was wary now.

Yeah, I'd be wary of me too.

"And here you fucking are." I waved a fisted hand in her direction. "You're one of them. Samuel Bell's fucking daughter. His blood runs in your veins, and I fucking hate it. I *hate* it."

I stalked over to her, shoved her onto her back and straddled her thighs.

"No part of you should be his," I growled. "Every part of you is *mine*." I wanted to tear her apart, pull out any bit of her that was from him and put her back together again. Cleansed of any traces of taint.

I wrapped my fingers around her throat and squeezed. "Every part."

The defiance hadn't left her eyes. It made my cock rock hard. She tilted her chin back and met my gaze, unwavering.

That made me angrier than ever.

I grabbed the front of her shirt and ripped it apart, the two pieces falling away from her body. I tossed them aside and tugged the straps of her bra off her shoulders. I pulled it until it was down around her waist, exposing her beautiful, milky breasts.

With no mercy whatsoever, I drew one of her nipples between my teeth and bit hard enough to make her cry out. The sound was like music. Better than music. It was desperate, erotic sin.

I bit the other one even harder, then bit all around her breasts. Not enough to draw blood, but enough to leave bruises and marks. My marks, to show everyone she was mine.

I climbed off her, sat beside her while I undid her shorts and yanked them down her legs. She wore little black lace panties that made the most satisfying sound when I ripped them off her body. I tossed them over my shoulder, then slammed her onto her stomach to unhook her bra.

I grabbed her wrists and all but dragged her up my bed, where I kept straps attached to the headboard. I looked her in the eyes as I bound first one wrist, then the other. Nice and tight.

I leaned in to whisper in her ear. "The safe word is koala." I was full of fury, but not blinded enough to be unaware that she may need to put limits to what I was about to do. I was an asshole, not an abuser.

She nodded but didn't make a sound.

I reached into a drawer and pulled out a paddle. Not the gentle, padded kind with velvet or whatever shit people used. The panel itself was hard leather, the handle smooth, well worn wood.

Channelling every drop of hatred for the blood that violated her veins, I brought the paddle hard down on her ass.

She cried out in pain and surprise, but didn't say a word. Didn't ask me to stop.

I waited a moment, watching as her cheek turned a beautiful shade of red.

I smiled to myself. She was a work of art. A beautiful sculpture under my hands. Mine to shape and shade however I wanted.

I wanted, needed more.

I brought the paddle down again and again on her tender flesh. Her ass turned redder and redder. Every ounce of fury went into every spank, as though I could beat the Bell out of her.

Over and over until I lost count. My breath came out in pants. My cock was so hard I thought it might burst.

Finally, when I was almost out of steam, she patted the mattress beside her and in a muffled voice, said, "Koala."

I immediately threw the paddle onto the floor and rolled her over onto her back. Tears poured down her cheeks, but she hadn't lost even a drop of defiance.

I wiped the tears off her chin with my thumb and asked, "Who do you belong to?"

"Mannix, and Ice, and you," she said softly.

"Hell yeah you do." I pressed a hand down between her thighs and over her drenched pussy. "You're so wet. You liked getting spanked, didn't you?"

"Yeah, I did." She cleared her throat. Composed herself and lifted her chin. "But now I want you to fuck me."

She gave me a challenging look, reminding me of our conversation a few weeks ago. The one where she pointed out that I said *when* I fuck her, not *if*. I'd also told her I'd give her pain. I'd done that.

I thought about taunting her. leaving without fucking her, just so she couldn't be right. But my cock was so hard, I was surprised it hadn't broken my zipper to escape.

"You do, huh?" I wasn't going to torture myself, but wasn't going to make it that easy for her either. "What does a good girl say when she wants to be fucked?"

"Shut the fuck up and give me that dick like a good boy?" she teased.

I snorted a laugh, but pulled off my jeans and boxers and straddled her again.

"If you think I'm a good boy, you don't know me well enough." I gripped the hem of my T-shirt with one hand and pulled it off my head. "Because I'm very, very bad."

I pried apart her knees with my thighs, smiling at her wince of pain. She was going to feel that spanking for days. Now I was going to fuck her hard enough for her to feel me inside her for even longer.

Her arms still restrained above her head, she had no choice but to lie there while I positioned my cock and slipped my tip inside her body. Then a little more.

"Fucking hell," I murmured. I was bigger than the other guys and she was nice and tight. I stopped halfway in to let her get used to me. Her muscles squeezed me like a clamp. A hot, wet clamp.

She moaned, her eyes wide. "You're so big. Holy…"

"You can take me." Whether she liked it or not.

I pushed myself in further. Her muscles resisted, but I kept pressing and pressing until I was all the way inside her gorgeous body.

"There we go, good girl. You were made for my cock."

She seemed to be beyond words and right now. So was I.

I rested inside her for a minute or so, then started to thrust. Slowly at first, then increasing in speed until I was pounding in as hard as I could.

I reached in under her knees and lifted her legs over my shoulders so I could slam in deeper. With every stroke, my tip hit her inner wall.

"Oh my…" Her upper body twisted and writhed against the restraints. Her nipples looked as hard as my cock. Her breathing was ragged. She was close to coming.

I managed to muster the words to say, "Tell me what you want."

She moaned. "I want to come. I need to."

"Is that all you want?" I slowed my thrusts to even, deliberate strokes.

"I want you to come too," she said, her face screwed up in concentration. "I want you to come inside me."

"What else?" I pressed.

She panted. "I want you to fill me with your cum. Please…"

"Come for me," I told her. "I want your pussy to come around my cock. And then I'll fill you up, so full you'll overflow."

Her back arched and she screamed as she came hard, her beautiful muscles contracting around my erection, stealing the last of my self control and making me come just as hard. My stomach tensed, then my balls, before I exploded inside her. Filling her as I promised I would.

She milked me for every drop. By the time I sagged across her, I was dry on the inside, but coated with sweat on the outside.

It took me a couple of minutes to catch my breath. Gently, I lowered her legs back down to the mattress and untied her hands. I put my arms around her and drew her to me, my body slick against hers.

"You're mine," I whispered. "No one is going to take you away from me. You belong to me. I love you."

Her body stiffened and for a moment I thought she'd laugh, or say something sarcastic. Finally, mercifully, she relaxed.

"I love you too. Even though you're literally a pain in my ass."

I chuckled against her hair. "You enjoyed every minute of it."

She exhaled at the same time as she spoke. "Yeah, I did. Let's do it again once my skin has healed."

I had every intention of doing just that, but she'd need a while to recover from my anger. Anger which was dissipated now, thanks to her. I couldn't remember a time in my life when I felt as peaceful as I did right now. I could have lain here forever with her in my arms. But then, what kind of boyfriend would I be?

"I'll draw you a bath and pick you out some bath bombs." I couldn't spank her and not take care of her afterward. After all, it would help her to heal more quickly so we could do it again.

No way it had anything to do with me being nice. Not for a second.

CHAPTER 9
KENNEDY

I winced as I slipped onto a stool.

Should I be horrified Ares took his anger out on me? Maybe, but I'd found his fury arousing. It was another piece of the puzzle that continued to prove I wasn't as normal as I thought I was.

Or maybe this was normal and people didn't talk about it.

Whatever, this was *my* normal.

Think whatever you like, I was grateful to Ares. In some way, I felt I'd violated this place by being here, given who my father was. Ares gave me my punishment. Now I was cleansed. The self-loathing that tried to creep up on me, was gone.

Replaced with pain every time I sat down.

I wouldn't be forgetting last night anytime soon.

My mother walked into the kitchen in time to see the expression on my face.

"Are you all right, sweetheart?" she asked.

She was my mother, of course she was concerned about me.

Today, that concern irritated me.

I picked up my spoon and dug it into my rice bubbles with a vengeance.

"I'm fine," I said coolly.

She sighed and placed her hands palms down in front of me. "You have every right to be confused about everything."

I swear I tried to keep my eyes from rolling, but they acted without my consent.

"I'm not confused, Mum. All my life you lied to me about who my father was. You kept on lying when you brought me here, right to his enemy. Right to where I could get stalked and attacked. And because that wasn't enough, you let me go there, knowing my own father might kill me."

Yeah, I wasn't confused, I was pissed the fuck off.

"I don't think of him that way," she argued. Like somehow that would make everything better.

"Neither does he, apparently." I left my spoon in my cereal and leaned my elbows on the bench. "He didn't exactly welcome me with open arms and fatherly love."

"He didn't kill you," she pointed out. "He would have if he hadn't known who you were."

"Is that supposed to make me feel better? Daddy's way of showing me love is not killing me? That's at least a thousand kinds of fucked up."

"Watch your language," she snapped. "You have to appreciate the position I was in."

As far as I was concerned, I didn't have to appreciate anything, but I pressed my lips together and listened to what she had to say.

"I was barely older than you and pregnant by a guy I could never be with. I cared about him, even though I knew what he was like. Sam was very much like your three boys are right now. Arrogant, possessive, controlling. Why do you think I warned you about them?"

Without waiting for a response she continued, "I don't want you to end up in the same position I did. Pregnant and alone. If you think for a second those boys will stick around if you—"

I couldn't hear any more without interrupting. "First of all, I'm not going to get pregnant. Secondly, none of them would abandon me if I did. Just because things didn't work out for you doesn't mean they won't work out for me." It didn't mean they would either, but the guys would never turn their backs on their child. Their pride wouldn't let them, even if their possessive natures would.

She looked at me like she thought I was a naïve child.

She sighed. "I don't want to argue with you, Kennedy. I made a mistake and I've done everything in my power to make up for it."

She scratched her perfectly shaped eyebrow. "I figured sooner or later he'd realise there was a chance you were his. I thought once he knew that, he'd take you away from me. So I got in as deep as I could with the people who wouldn't let that happen. In the process, I fell in love with Leo. I knew if you were here, with us, you'd be safe from him. I didn't count on all the other things that happened, and for that I'm sorry, but when you're a parent, all you can do is your best and hope you don't mess it up."

"So I was a mistake?" I asked softly. Of all the things she said, that was one thing my brain decided to fixate on.

Her mouth moved as she scrambled to find the right answer to make me feel better.

"Getting pregnant was a mistake, but having you was the best thing I ever did. Keeping you away from Samuel Bell was the second best thing."

"Did you ever think that if you told him, he'd want to be with you?" Surely that crossed her mind?

She lowered her elbow to the bench and rested her head on her hand. "I thought about it, of course I did, but I knew it wasn't possible. And, to be honest, I wasn't sure it was what I wanted. Like I said, he was ruthless and driven. We never would have lasted and he wouldn't let me leave with you. You were more important to me than any man. Than any other relationship I've ever had."

I couldn't resist asking the question. "Would you leave Leo if I needed you to?"

She didn't meet my eyes.

"I didn't think so." I picked up my spoon again. "I'll do my best not to put you in that position. I'm angry with you, but I know you two love each other and I support you, no matter what."

Unless Leo wanted me dead, in which case I withdrew any and all support, past, present and future.

"Is this where you ask me to support your choice, no matter what?" She straightened up and looked at me through knitted brows.

"I don't need your approval, but if you want to give it, then yeah." I shrugged one shoulder. "I'll take it."

"Why does it hurt you to sit?" she asked.

"You don't want to know," I shot back immediately. "But I can assure you everything was fully consensual."

She grimaced. "It better be, because no one does pissed off like a mother whose baby was hurt."

I resisted making a snide comment about her hurting me. At the end of the day, I got where she was coming from. If I'd had a fling with someone like Hunter or Parker Brantley, for example, and fell pregnant, I'd run and hide too. Not that I would sleep with either of them. Ewww.

Watching Bell get more and more powerful, and knowing there was even a slight possibility he'd take her child away, must have been terrifying.

No, it wasn't that surprising she accepted the safe harbour the Brantley family offered.

When I thought about it, it all made a whole bunch of sense. I just wished I knew sooner.

Or did I?

Would I have gone to Sydney knowing he was my father? Would I have snuck around his house, trying to stay away from him and his other daughters?

No, I would have tried to sneak a peek at at least one of them, to satisfy my curiosity about my roots. And, when Lila caught us, I might have blurted out the truth to try to save myself. I doubted she would have welcomed me with open arms. A bullet in the head seemed more likely.

The reality was, if everyone knew, I wouldn't have stepped foot in this house in the first place. I never would have met the guys. I never would have gone to Bell's. I would have stayed at uni and kept an eye out over my shoulder, in case he or one of the Brantley clan came after me. I would have spent the rest of my life making sure I never had my back to an open door, always nervous walking past a window.

Now everyone knew, but I had people around who wanted to keep me safe.

"I'm sorry you had to find out the way you did," she said, breaking through my thoughts. "If I suspected for a minute what would happen, I would have… I dunno. Stopped you from going? Told you myself? *Something*."

I swallowed a mouthful of rice bubbles. "It is what it is. There's no point beating yourself up about it."

"That's what I have you for," she said jokingly.

As if to prove her point, I poked her in the arm with the handle of my spoon.

"Ouch." She laughed and rubbed her arm.

"Something's been bothering me," I said slowly. "You said he wouldn't have let you leave with me."

"He was always very possessive of his possessions." She wrinkled her nose.

"He was quick enough to let me leave yesterday." I lightly tapped the back of the spoon against the rim of the bowl. "He didn't seem interested in a long, drawn out family reunion or anything like that."

Mum frowned.

"In fact, he seemed more interested in me delivering my message to you." I watched carefully as her frown deepened. "Maybe you don't know him as well as you thought you did. Or as well as you did back then." People change, and twenty-something years was a long time.

She shook her head. "No, it means something. He never does anything without some kind of intent. He let you come back here, knowing he could change that anytime he wants to."

Her expression made my blood run cold. It went colder still when her words sank in.

"You think he might come after me and try to…what? Bring me back into the fold?"

She shook her head. "I honestly have no idea what he might intend. From what I've seen over the years, he's unpredictable at best. Determined and as ruthless and arrogant as ever, at worst."

"And you question my taste in men," I muttered. She could be talking about any of the guys. In them, it was hot. In someone like Samuel Bell, it was terrifying.

She laughed humourlessly. "Being young and silly makes you do young, silly things. You may look back one day and wonder what you ever saw in those boys."

"Not a chance," I said. I wasn't letting them go. They weren't going to let me go. We were in this together, no matter what.

One side of her mouth drew back."You say that now—"

I cut her off. "I say that now and forever. I know you're not their biggest fan, but when you get to know them you'll realise how amazing they are." I hoped she had no intention of asking me to choose between them and her, because she may not win.

"I hope you're right," she said warily. "In the meantime, be careful and keep your eyes out for anything or anyone out of place. It may be that he's mellowed in his older age, or that he's put his other daughters first, but I wouldn't put anything past him. He has a long memory and holds a grudge."

Well, wasn't that fucking great?

"I should finish eating, I need to get to work." Assuming no one blew the place up in my absence.

CHAPTER 10

KENNEDY

Nothing in Dusk Bay looked out of place. As far as I could tell, nothing was blown up, nothing imploded. None of the buildings disappeared into a random sinkhole.

None of that helped put a dent in my unease. On the contrary, it grew the closer we got to the gym.

I was ready to put it down to a healthy dose of paranoia, until I looked over at Mannix.

He watched out the window with narrowed eyes, taking in everything, his lips pressed tight together. A day or two of stubble made him look older, sexier. An air of barely contained violence hung over him.

He was the alpha male, the apex predator ready to hunt, ready to kill. His prey— anyone who got in his way.

In his present mood, even I would step aside. He wouldn't hurt me, not deliberately, but he was dangerous, and anyone who forgot that, even for a moment, was a dumbass.

Or a corpse.

"What is it?" I asked softly.

He responded with a shake of his head so slight I would have missed it if I wasn't watching.

"I don't know. Something. Don't let your guard down. The minute we do, we're fucked." His fingers closed over the gun he kept at his hip, hidden by his shirt.

"I wasn't planning to. When do I get one of those?"

"You don't," he replied. "Having a gun makes you a target."

"What does having one make you?" I asked. Hadn't I already proved I was no shrinking violet? In spite of what Mum said about Bell potentially coming after me, I was determined to stand up for myself.

Naturally, the guys had other ideas, so here I was in the back of the SUV, being driven to work in the company of all three of them. None of them seemed inclined to let me out of their sight.

This couldn't be their lives until the end of time, could it? Guarding me twenty-four hours a day, seven days a week. I didn't mind the company, but they had their own lives to live. Sooner or later, they'd start to resent me. That would end us faster than anything Bell might do.

"It makes me someone who knows how to use one," Mannix said. "And when. Don't worry about it, we've got you."

That sounded very much like, 'Don't worry your pretty little head about it, us menfolk will take on all the bears while you traipse around the kitchen, barefoot and pregnant.'

I bristled.

"Maybe I want to have me too," I snapped. "Maybe I want to be able to protect you guys if I need to."

He gave me a look that said both, 'don't argue with me,' and that he was sceptical about being protected by a woman. Or by me, anyway.

"I think Kennedy is right," Ice said. "She did well with a gun in Sydney. I don't see any reason she shouldn't have one now. Although, it might be dangerous to do gymnastics when you're packing. You might do a backsault and shoot yourself in the foot."

"Lucky I'm not stupid enough to do something like that," I said dryly. What was it with the guys today? Were they being particularly sexist, or was I touchier than usual?

Possibly both. After what we went through, it made sense we were on edge, but I didn't like us taking it out on each other.

"Are you sure about that?" Ares asked. He looked around from the front passenger seat and smirked.

I flipped him off.

Even after saying, 'I love you,' to each other, he was still the same old Ares. Sarcastic, smug asshole. Exactly the way I liked him. I would have hated it if he changed or walked on eggshells around me. It seemed we were destined to be affectionately antagonistic towards each other. I was here for it.

"I wouldn't do anything that stupid," I said. "I'll leave doing dumb shit to you."

He narrowed his eyes at me. "Bitch."

I smiled. "Asshole."

"Red Riding Pussy." His eyes shone.

"Banana Head." If he was going to insult my hair colour, I'd insult his.

Ice laughed. "Banana Head. That's hilarious."

"Fuck off," Ares told him. "Bun Head."

Ice snorted, clearly not offended in the slightest. "I've been called worse than that."

"Is that a challenge?" Mannix asked.

"That depends, do you dare to accept it?" Ice asked. He glanced at Mannix in the rearview mirror.

"I dare," Mannix agreed. "But let me get back to you on that. We're almost at the gym. More focusing, less thinking up creative nicknames and insults. For the record, I think Banana Head is perfect." A smile tugged at the corners of his mouth but didn't quite come to fruition.

"You can fuck off too," Ares said, but he turned his attention back outside the SUV.

I met Mannix's gaze and grinned. Yes, it was dangerous to get distracted, but for a minute or two it was nice to forget about everything but insulting Ares. After all, the more I insulted him, the better the punishment he gave me for it. The thought made my pussy throb. Fortunately my t-shirt covered the bruises all over my breasts from his teeth. It would take time before those faded away.

In the meantime, I wore them like badges of honour.

Ice pulled the car up in front of the gym and put it in park.

Like everywhere else, nothing looked out of place, but the feeling of unease increased.

There was definitely something very fucking wrong here.

I stepped out of the car. The hair on my arms stood on end as though they too were at high alert.

The guys hurried to surround me.

I wanted to tell them to disperse and behave like normal human beings, but given the way my senses tingled, I might be better off with them around me. All three had their hands near their guns.

I pulled out the key and unlocked the door to the gym.

Pushed it open.

I saw him immediately.

"Fucking hell."

Charlie stood at an awkward angle, leaning heavily to the right. Around his neck, the silk which hung from the ceiling was wrapped tight. His eyes were open, staring at nothing. His hands were by his sides, as though someone held him down, or he hadn't tried to fight back.

He was definitely dead. For a while, by the look of him.

I put a hand over my mouth. "How long—" I looked over at Ice. If anyone was able to tell how long Charlie was dead, it would be him.

Looking completely undeterred at finding a dead body hanging in the gym, Ice walked over and placed a hand on Charlie's neck.

"The good news is he is very much dead," Ice said slowly. "Too long ago to try to revive him if we were inclined to do so."

"The bad news?" Mannix was stepping around the gym, looking for any more surprises.

"He's still slightly warm," Ice said. "If I had to guess, I'd say he died about an hour ago. Without a thermometer, I can't be certain, but close enough."

"What is he even doing here?" Ares narrowed his eyes as though Charlie was still some kind of threat. He turned those accusing, blue eyes on me. "Didn't you fire his ass?"

"I very much fired his ass," I agreed. "As to what he's doing here, your guess is as good as mine. Wild guess though, it's a message for me, from my dear father."

Asshole.

"What a shame." Ice sighed. "I was looking forward to getting my hands on him myself. I would have already, but we got busy with other things." He shot Mannix a frown for some reason.

"I'm sorry you missed out on your fun," I said sarcastically. "Is there any chance you can remove him from my silk?" I was going to have to have that pulled down and washed. Or better yet, burnt. I couldn't use it now. Or teach children to use an apparatus that was used to strangle someone.

"Sure." Ice unwound the polyester fabric from Charlie's throat and let him flop onto the mat like a heavy doll.

Charlie lay there looking roughly in my direction, eyes still open as though accusing me of having something to do with this.

"He brought it on himself." Ares stepped out from the back of the gym. "Somebody broke the lock in the back door to gain entry. My guess is Charlie. Somebody stumbled upon him and ended him."

He seemed satisfied with that conclusion. He certainly wasn't going to shed any tears over Charlie's death.

Neither was I, but it was as disturbing as hell. Of all the things I expected to find here today, a dead former employee wasn't one of them. Thank goodness it wasn't one of the kids. The thought made my stomach turn.

"It could have been Bell's people breaking in and bringing him with them?" I suggested.

"They would have picked the lock," Mannix said. "Or waited until you unlocked the place. Breaking and entering is too petty a crime for people like them and us. We only resort to it when we have to."

"Or we pay someone else to do it," Ice said. "But I tend to agree. More than one person found him here and killed him. Otherwise things would be in disarray and his skin would be bruised. He barely even has a hair out of place."

"Wonderful." I sat down on one of the padded boxes we used for vaulting and other things. "So Charlie broke in for what? Revenge? Money? To steal a few gym mats? And at least two more were trying to break in, but killed him instead?"

None of this made any sense. As far as I could tell, most of the people in Dusk Bay loved Charlie. He was very good at putting on a façade of being a nice guy. Everyone's best friend. The perfect gymnastics coach. Until he was handcuffing you to a chair and calling up the people you're running from to tell them where you are. Lucky for me that turned out okay.

Unlucky for him, it seemed.

I pinched my nose and sat thinking for a couple of minutes, trying to get my head around all of this. Trying, but failing.

Finally, I got up and walked over to the office. I peered through the window which separated the office from the rest of the gym. All I saw was darkness, apart from a light on the charger to indicate the computer was fully charged.

The door, worn from years of use, was closed. The white paint on its surface was faded, chipped and scratched here and there. Much of the surface was dotted with old pieces of sticky tape, some with scraps of paper still attached. At chest height, was a piece of A3 paper with a grid of all the classes, their times and the students' names. Several names were crossed out as children left, and a few more were added in blue pen underneath the printed lists.

I made a note to print out a new one. This one was looking messy. Maybe when the new term began.

I tried the handle. It was still locked. I pulled out the key, unlocked it and opened the door. It swung into the office with no effort or sound.

My gaze scanned the room and I frowned. "It doesn't look like anything was taken. Or even touched. Unless they locked up behind themselves."

"Step out of there," Mannix said, his body as stiff as his tone.

His anxiety was immediately contagious. I was already as on edge as fuck, but his urging made it worse.

"Why? What are you—"

He cut me off. "Princess, step out of the fucking office. *Now*."

I shrugged, but did as he ordered. "Fine, but I don't see—"

He kept his eyes on the office, but responded to me. "Let us see. You said it yourself, they might have locked up behind themselves."

My blood froze.

CHAPTER 11
KENNEDY

"You think someone planted a bomb in there?" I looked back through the office door and squinted, as though one might suddenly jump out at us and shout, "Boo." Or, you know, explode.

"I think it's possible." Mannix's gaze swept across all of us. He was obviously wondering if he should tell us to get out of the building while he searched.

"They might be waiting for us outside," Ares said, narrowed eyes looking toward the street.

Mannix nodded. "Stay there." Without further hesitation, he hurried into the office and closed the door behind him. Neither the glass nor the door would be much protection against a bomb, but that was Mannix. He'd always do what he could to protect the people he loved.

Ice pulled his phone out of his back pocket and tapped on the screen.

"What are you doing?" Ares eyed him doubtfully.

"I thought I'd put on some suspenseful music." Ice glanced up and grinned at him.

"How about you fucking don't?" Ares growled. He raised a hand like he was about to knock Ice's phone out of his hand.

Ice swivelled his upper body to keep the phone out of Ares's reach.

He tapped the screen and the theme song from the movie franchise *Jaws* sounded out of the phone's speaker.

"You're an idiot," Ares told him.

I flopped back onto the block I vacated a couple of minutes earlier and wondered why this was my life now. I was in my gym with one guy searching for a bomb, another guy playing crazy music, while another was pissed off and forth one was dead.

How had I even come to be in this place?

"Should we have left Charlie how he was and contacted the police?" I asked.

"I've already texted to have someone come clean him up," Ares said. He was watching Ice. The moment the other guy got close enough, he snatched his phone out of his hand and mashed his finger on the screen.

The music didn't stop playing.

"If you don't turn this fucking phone off, I'm going to shoot the shit out of it." He threw it at Ice's chest.

Ice caught it and pressed on the screen until the phone was silent. "Spoilsport. I could start humming."

"Only if you want me to shoot the shit out of you," Ares growled. He stalked over to the back door and stood waiting, presumably for the cleanup crew.

"I always thought his problem was that he needed to get laid," Ice said thoughtfully. "Evidently it runs much deeper than that."

"Fuck off," Ares called out. "Maybe the problem is that I have to put up with you."

Ice cocked his head like a puppy. "I guess that's possible, but I've never found myself that difficult to tolerate."

"You're very tolerable," I assured him. "Better than tolerable."

He moved over to sit beside me and draped his arm over my shoulders.

"This might not be the time to tell you, what with potentially being blown up or whatever, but in case we don't get another chance I thought you should know." He looked at me softly and smiled. "Kennedy Knight-Bell, I love you."

My heart skipped a handful of beats like a routine full of cartwheels.

"Isaac 'Iceman' Miller, I love you too. But if you call me Knight-Bell again, I might let Ares shoot you," I said sweetly.

He chuckled. "It's so hot when you're a badass. Which is most of the time. In fact, I'm so turned on right now, I'd happily fuck you over this box." He tapped his other hand on the padded surface beside him.

"Even with Charlie staring at us with dead eyes?" I jerked my head in his direction, but didn't look.

"Especially then," Ice agreed. "I've never been into necrophilia, but fucking in front of corpses has always had a particular place in my heart. Not as much as when they're still alive though."

He really was a couple of nuts short of the tree, but I adored him for it. Life was too short not to roll with it the way he did. Well, maybe not exactly the way he did, but with a positive approach to things.

We both turned and started to stand at the sound of voices from the back door. After a moment, I realised it was a couple of men in dark coveralls. The cleanup crew. Ares had let them in.

They hurried in, barely acknowledged my existence before they scooped up Charlie and hurried back out with him carried between them.

"What are they going to do with him?" I asked. "People are going to know he disappeared. As soon as they do that, they'll ask questions." I had no idea what to say if they asked me.

"They'll figure out something that will make it look like an accident," Ice said. "No one will be asking or answering any questions about him. His family will get closure, and no one will look twice in the direction of any of us. Which is fair enough, because we actually didn't do anything this time." He scratched the side of his head and shrugged.

"Yeah, I guess we didn't," I agreed. "When Mannix is done in the office, I can check the video feed and see if it caught anything."

We had the same doubtful expression on our faces. If whoever killed Charlie had the skills to pick a lock, they would have disabled the security cameras.

"Why didn't Charlie trip the security alarm?" I asked. I forgot it existed until now. I wasn't used to living my life with measures like that.

"It must have been disabled before he broke in," Ice said thoughtfully.

Thoughts tumbled around in my head and it took a moment to make them coherent.

"So…it's possible they were watching. Turned off the alarm, let him get into the place, then followed him and killed him?"

"Or turned it off, meaning to let themselves in, but he happened to turn up at the same time. Or he saw them and followed. He might have been trying to stop them." Ice turned his phone around in his hands.

That suggestion made my blood run cold again. Was there any possibility Charlie was trying to do the right thing? He might have been trying to protect the place to be nice or in the hope of getting his job back.

I might have considered hiring him again, but that was out of the question now. The animosity between us when we saw each other last would stand between us forever, no chance to make amends.

Would we have made up, given more time? That was moot, because we couldn't anyway.

"You said the people that killed him were unlikely to be the ones who broke the lock," I pointed out. "Unless they're trying to pin that on Charlie. We're never going to know are we? They would have turned off the cameras so no one could see what they did."

For some reason, that made me feel more violated than ever. It was bad enough that people were running around in my gym killing people, but they were covering their tracks and leaving us firmly in the dark.

Except for one thing. Samuel Bell was behind all of this. Perhaps not Charlie breaking in, but the rest of it. If Charlie had been trying to help, he was dead because of me. My hands might as well have been coated in his blood.

"Sometimes getting the answer doesn't matter," Ice said. "Either way, Charlie was somewhere he shouldn't have been and he's dead because of it. It's unlikely to be the end of whatever this is. Even if there isn't a bomb, there's a reason for everything. Shit like this doesn't go down at random."

"That's what I'm worried about." I watched the cleanup guys slip out the back door.

I caught a glimpse of them loading Charlie into a van parked on the street behind the gym. They hefted him in like a sack of potatoes and slammed the doors shut behind him. They climbed into the van and were gone like they were never here.

Like Charlie never existed at all.

I sighed. We had our disagreements, but he wasn't the worst person in the world. Not even the second worst.

"The kids are going to be devastated," I said softly. Just because he wasn't their coach anymore didn't mean they didn't adore him. People like him played a big part in kid's lives. Their first somersault. First handstand. First cartwheel. For many it was a chance to discover a sport they enjoyed. For others it was just a few hours of fun.

Either way, Charlie was the centre of a lot of it and now he was gone.

It wasn't that long ago I'd never seen a dead body. Now I'd seen more than I could count. I'd come close to becoming one myself. Was this my life now? Death everywhere? Would I get used to it at some point? Did I want to? Were the guys worth all of this?

"They'll get over it," Ice said. "After all, they still have you."

"Unless we get blown up." I pressed the palms of my hands to the block and levered myself higher to peer into the office. Every so often, Mannix's head bobbed up and down as he crouched and stood and crouched again.

"Unless that," Ice agreed. "I might go and see how Mannix is doing in there. Stay here." Before I could argue, he jumped off the box and strode over to the office.

Hating to sit idly by, I stood and walked over to the silk beside the one which was used to strangle Charlie. I gripped the fabric in two hands and started to climb.

When I was high enough, I drew up my legs and climbed higher, using a series of knots with my feet to push myself up. My ass hurt, but I pushed the pain aside and kept going.

I reached the ceiling and wound the silk around my wrist a couple of times. I wound my foot under the silk and stood on that foot with the other, locking me in place.

Satisfied I wouldn't fall, I swung a couple of times, until I was close enough to grab the other silk. I pulled myself over closer, tugging until I could reach the heavy clip on top of the silk. It was tight, but I managed to unscrew it and unclip the silk from the hook that fastened it to the ceiling.

I let it go. The silk fell to the floor in a flutter of tainted, polyester fabric.

I watched its passage until it landed in a puddle on the mats below. It looked beautiful and innocent, not like something that was used to murder a man in cold blood.

Was it really necessary to do something like that in a space like this? This was supposed to be where children came to have fun and learn new skills. Not where adult men came to die.

I let go with both hands and held the silk with my thighs as I plummeted towards the floor. A metre off, I stopped myself and grinned at the adrenaline rush. I lowered my palms to the mat and did a somersault, letting go of the silks at the last moment. I landed on my feet and dropped my hands to my sides.

"That was fucking hot," Ares declared. He looked impressed.

I smiled and gave him a curtsy. "The silks are my happy place."

"Me too," he agreed. "Silk sheets." His gaze slid up and down my body.

I laughed, but it died away when Mannix stepped out of the office, a grim expression on his face.

CHAPTER 12

KENNEDY

Mannix rubbed the back of his head. "I didn't find anything that looked like a bomb. It doesn't look like anything in there was touched." He glanced over his shoulder like he was sure he missed something, but knew he hadn't. He'd searched thoroughly. If there was anything to find, he would have found it.

Ice cocked his head at Mannix. "So, no bomb?"

"No bomb," Mannix agreed. "That doesn't rule out a virus on the computer. I wouldn't put it past them to use our tactic against us. But…" He frowned and shook his head. "If they were going to do that, they'd go after someone higher up than us. Attacking us like that they wouldn't achieve very much. Bell is an asshole, but petty revenge isn't usually his style."

"There's only one way to find out." I took a step towards the office, but Mannix grabbed my arm.

"It can wait." Something in his tone made me stop and look at him.

"You're going to need a new one of those." He nodded toward the silk that lay on the mat.

"Yeah, I'm going to have to order one." I wrinkled my nose.

"Yes, you are, because we're going to make that very one sticky."

He hooked his fingers into the front of my shorts and pulled me to him. Before I could protest, he had them undone. He shoved them and my panties down my thighs.

They fell to my feet, leaving the bottom half of me bare.

"I don't know if this is a good idea." I still stepped out of them. I knew that expression on his face all too well. He wasn't asking.

"It's not a good idea," he agreed. "It's a great idea. It's Sunday. No kids are coming. The only ones who are coming are us."

He nodded to the other guys. Between them, Ares and Ice pulled off my shirt and bra.

They lay me down on my back on the fallen silk. It smelled of sweat, cleaning detergent and last gasps.

Charlie dying tangled in the fabric was precisely the point. Mannix and the others were turned on knowing his body dangled there. Knowing he took his last breath amongst the folds of blue polyester.

That was both twisted as fuck and hot as hell at the same time.

I glanced toward the door. We'd left it unlocked.

A row of blocks stood between us and the large glass windows at the front of the gym. If anyone walked past, chances are they wouldn't see us. If they didn't try the door, then no one but us would ever know.

Mannix bent my knees and parted my thighs with his hands. He gave me an intense look before he lowered his mouth to my pussy and licked me from front to back.

I shivered. His touch was unusually feather light, but it drove me wild even faster than when he was rough and merciless. From the look in his eyes, he knew it too.

Ice sat beside me, his legs tucked underneath him. He looked at me like I was a sculpture, a work of art for him to appreciate.

He pulled out his phone and gave me a questioning look.

I hesitated, but eventually nodded. I trusted him not to share with anyone but Mannix and Ares. Of course he wouldn't. If anyone else saw me naked, Ice would poke their eyes out.

He smiled, held up his phone and took a couple of photos of me, Mannix's face between my legs.

"Something for later." He put his phone away, leaned forward and went to work on my nipples. Licking and sucking like they were the sweetest treat he ever had.

Ares undid his shorts and lay beside me, his cock in front of my face. He really was huge.

"You could put out someone's eye with that thing." I closed one of mine and looked at him appreciatively.

Ares chuckled. "Open up," he said. "I'm going to fuck your mouth."

I opened my mouth and he pressed the tip of his cock between my lips. He was so big, I wasn't sure how much I could take.

"Good girl. You can take more." He pushed in deeper, all the way to the back of my throat. "There you go, I knew you could take me." He grabbed my hand and placed it on his balls.

I massaged and sucked as Mannix nipped and teased my clit.

Pleasure curled through my body, starting at my core and expanding from there like a slow growing vine. It grew faster when he slipped his fingers inside me and fucked me with his hand and his tongue.

My orgasm exploded like a supernova, burning hot enough to incinerate me and everything around me. I took my mouth off Ares's cock long enough to breathe while I shattered.

My whole body was deliciously on fire. I arched my back and rocked against his face, coating his mouth and hand with my juices.

I shouted Mannix's name to the ceiling. And again when I came for a second time.

By the time I came down, my head was spinning, but my body throbbed for more.

Mannix raised his face and smiled. "I want you both to taste how she tastes when she comes."

He moved up beside me, stopping to kiss Ice before he reached me. His tongue swept over my lips, sliding inside and spreading my flavour.

Ice smacked his lips. "Delicious. If I could bottle the way you two taste together, I'd be rich. Okay, richer."

I wasn't sure anyone would buy something like that, but people bought all sorts of interesting things, so why not my juices?

I licked my lips. Not bad.

The taste of myself on my lips, I went back to spoiling Ares' cock.

"Did you bring what I told you to bring?" Mannix asked Ice as he started to shed his clothes.

I watched from the corner of my eye without stopping sucking and licking. Ares groaned in pleasure. I loved the sounds he made. They were pure magic. Pure, hot magic.

Ice frowned at him for a moment, then realised what Mannix was referring to. "Right." He patted his pockets. "Phone. Gun. Ahhh… Here we go. Lube." He pulled out a small tube and tossed it to Mannix.

Mannix caught it. "Strip."

Ice did so without hesitation.

"Fuck her." He nodded towards me.

"Gladly." Ice smiled at me.

I smiled back with my eyes, my mouth being busy and full of cock. I wanted him inside me right now. My pussy ached to be filled. I bent my knees and parted my thighs for him.

"Beautiful." Ice knelt between my knees and positioned his cock before he slid the entirety of his length deep inside me.

I sighed with pleasure at being filled. Nothing in the world felt quite like it.

"Lean forward," Mannix told Ice. He squeezed lube onto his fingers and moved around behind the other guy.

I watched Ice's expression as Mannix prepared his rear hole. I couldn't see, but I could imagine, and what I pictured was pretty fucking hot.

"Ready." It was a statement, not a question. Mannix gripped Ice's hips and moved his own hips forward.

Ice's eyes widened. Mannix was sliding inside him.

Holy shit.

The movement pushed Ice deeper inside me. I groaned around Ares' cock.

Mannix stopped to let Ice get used to him, then started to move, slow and careful.

All three guys pumped and ground in rhythm, deeper and harder into me, driving me closer and closer to the edge of blissful oblivion.

I took my mouth off Ares again and worked him with my hand while I came. This time was longer, but somehow softer than the other two. Floating on a cloud rather than being in the centre of a tornado. The bliss went on for days, gently pushing every other thought or feeling aside until that was all that existed.

When it drifted away, finally, I sighed.

"Fuck, that's always hot. Open back up."

Ares just managed to slip his cock back between my lips in time for his own orgasm. He thrust hard a couple of times, eyes scrunched closed in concentration and ecstasy.

He grunted and tangled his fingers in my hair. He tugged hard as his body stilled.

"Fuck yeah."

Hot cum squirted from his tip, flooding my mouth and down my throat. I sucked harder, wanting every drop from him. Every last bit.

Finally he sagged, panting out his nose, his face tinged pink. He slipped his cock out of my mouth and fixed his blue eyes on me.

"Swallow it." He watched me like he wasn't sure I'd do exactly as he ordered. As if I'd spit in his face, or on the silk.

I swallowed.

He smiled, satisfied, like he got the cream instead of me. "You're so fucking hot." He leaned down to kiss me, his tongue swiping over my lips and plunging inside.

He fucked my mouth with his tongue as Ice fucked my body.

As Mannix fucked his.

"Fuck, you feel so good," Mannix panted. "So tight."

Ice grunted something that could have been an agreement. "I'm going to come inside you, Beautiful."

"I was going to say that," Mannix said with a small laugh. Right before he came. His eyes half closed, mouth half open, the same blissed out expression Ares had on his face a couple of minutes earlier.

"Fucking hell, you're so…ahhh. Holy fuck…"

Ice followed a moment later, thrusting into me and moaning so loud I couldn't stop myself from coming for a fourth time.

This one was longer, but so powerful it rocked my entire body, down to the roots of my hair, my toenails, my fingertips.

We all flopped down, panting. Every bit as sticky as Mannix promised.

I was definitely going to need a new silk now, because this one was ruined.

CHAPTER 13

KENNEDY

"Shit."

Mannix's sudden exclamation made me pause, my finger on the button to open the gate.

"What is it?" I was feeling more relaxed after our group fuck, but the single word put me right back on edge.

"Open the gate and don't panic." He nodded towards my hand and waited until the gate was open wide enough to drive the SUV through. In other words, with half a hair between the car and the gates.

How he made it through every time, I didn't know. I would have scraped half the paint off if I tried.

"You realise the words most likely to make me panic are, 'don't panic,' right?" I asked.

A couple of dark cars were parked to the side of the driveway. They could suggest any number of things. Most of them one hundred percent not good.

Mannix didn't smile in response. He pulled the SUV into the garage and waved us all toward the door that led into the house.

All three guys wore the same, intense expression on their faces. They were definitely expecting something bad. Not so bad we turned tail and ran, but bad nonetheless.

I stopped in front of the door and raised my hands, positioning myself so no one could open it.

"Would someone please explain what's going on?" I lowered my hands to my hips and looked from one to the other. "I'm not going inside until I get some answers."

I narrowed my eyes at them, for added effect.

"Chances are my brother is here," Mannix said finally and reluctantly. Apparently my attempted intimidation worked. Go me. "With Daze, Ric and Hilton."

"Okay," I said slowly. "I'm guessing this isn't a family catch-up?"

Instead of answering, he put his hands on my shoulders and moved me aside. Keeping one hand on my shoulder, he steered me through the doorway.

We followed voices to the formal living room to the side of the house.

"Here they are." Mum greeted me as though we were supposed to be home hours ago. Her expression matched Mannix's.

Leo stood beside her, guarded, his body stiff.

Daisy Lasalle, or Daze as she was known, sat on the long white couch, Ric DiMarco on one side, Mannix's brother Gunnar on the other. Her third boyfriend, Hilton Blake, sat in an armchair beside her, legs crossed at his knees.

I glanced at her and smiled. She smiled back reassuringly, but both of our gazes soon slid to the other two men in the room.

If I wanted to ignore them, I couldn't have. Their presence made the air heavier, like a massive thundercloud, heavy with promise of destruction.

"This is Caleb Brantley," Leo said, his tone lighter than his expression.

Caleb regarded me with dark, dangerous eyes.

I could have guessed who he was just by looking at him. The resemblance between him, Hunter and Parker, and Zeke Brantley was obvious. He wore a perfectly tailored suit and dark tie. Everything about him screamed money and ruthless power.

"And Mack D'Antonio." Leo nodded to the other man. He was equally well dressed and dangerous looking. A handkerchief peeked out of his suit pocket, matching the piercing blue of his eyes. The kind that could eviscerate a soul with a glance.

"Hey." I tried to smile but the way everyone was looking at me made me want to pee myself.

Caleb looked me up and down like I was a slab of beef in the butcher shop and he wasn't sure he liked what he saw.

Mack seemed unimpressed. He carried the air that he'd pull out a gun and use it without a second thought. He'd be hot if he wasn't kinda scary at the same time.

"It's good to see you again." Daze put her coffee aside and stood to give me a hug. "Leo tells us you've had quite a surprise about your parentage. I wanted to come and see you. Everyone else came along out of curiosity. Don't worry about them, they won't bite you. I won't let them."

She gave *all* the men in the room a narrow-eyed look, including Leo and my guys.

"You don't have the authority here," Caleb said, his voice both soft and cold.

I could have gone skiing on his tone.

Daze didn't back down. "Maybe not, but I won't let a young woman be hurt just because of who her father is."

"If any harm comes to Ms Knight, it won't be because of that," Caleb said. "Her parentage is irrelevant. I'm more concerned with her behaviour."

My behaviour?

I would have moved over closer to my guys, but there was no need. They stepped around me like a wall of hot muscle.

"Kennedy has done nothing out of line." Mannix's tone was as cold as Caleb. "She risked her life to help try to take down Samuel Bell."

"Tried and failed," Caleb pointed out.

"But still tried." Mannix wasn't giving a centimetre.

"My daughter has done nothing wrong," Mum argued.

Caleb turned his cold, dark eyes to her. "Your failure to mention her paternity also makes you suspect."

She actually took a step back from him. It was the first time in my life I ever saw my mother truly scared.

Her tongue darted over her lips. "I was trying to protect my child. I wanted her to have a better, safer life than she would have had if he knew about her."

Caleb was perfectly illustrating why she wasn't forthcoming. If this was the reaction, maybe I was better off never knowing.

That cat was firmly out of the bag. How did Caleb know? I doubted I needed to look much past Leo. These were the kind of things a dutiful minion didn't keep from their boss. If I ended up under a bus, it was because he threw me there.

"I have no intention of having anything to do with him." I tilted my chin and met Caleb's eyes. Somehow I managed to sound like my knees weren't shaking. This man held my life in his hands. He could end it with a nod.

And then the guys would go to war with him. One they couldn't win. Caleb had the numbers on his side in this room alone. One look and all of our blood would stain the carpet.

Oh goodie.

"My loyalty is here." I didn't mean him specifically, but if that was how he interpreted it, then fine. It wouldn't hurt if he believed that. It was close enough to the truth. My guys were loyal to him and I was loyal to them. By extension, what I said was accurate.

I considered reminding Caleb his twin brothers' loyalty might be more suspect than mine, but decided that was a can of worms I was better off not touching, much less opening.

Caleb seemed angry enough as it was. He was the second oldest Brantley brother. I wondered if Reuben was scarier than him. If he was, I didn't want to meet him.

Caleb was more than enough.

And Mack. What was his role in all of this? There was a passing resemblance between him and Hilton, along with the same dark intensity. But then, all of the guys in the room had that.

It was like a testosterone factory in here. Or an alpha male convention.

Caleb stared me down.

I almost looked away.

Before I did, he said, "Be sure it is. Those three boys have given us enough trouble going off on their own. Don't let them drag you down with them." The message was obvious. Don't drag them down either.

I had no intention of that. Although, where could I possibly lead them that they wouldn't go on their own, or wouldn't be sent by someone like Caleb Brantley?

I reminded myself I was only starting to learn about this life. What little I knew was probably the tip of a big, dangerous iceberg, so to speak. One with possibilities I couldn't even imagine right now.

"My understanding was that the virus idea was Kennedy's," Ric said. "It seems she's well on her way to leading those three astray."

Gunnar grunted his agreement. "It's not like my brother needs much help, but if he was going to fuck up, it would be because of a pretty face."

"Pretty faces have a way of doing that," Hilton said. He turned a smile on Daze.

She smiled warmly back at him.

"A tight pussy is the root of all evil," Ric remarked.

Daze rolled her eyes playfully. "Men have been thinking with their cocks since the dawn of time. And blaming women for it."

Mack rolled his eyes.

"I don't think Mack agrees with you," Ric said.

"Men and women have both been thinking with their genitals since humans began," Mack said, his voice cold whiskey over ice. "That's never changed and it never will."

I hadn't noticed a network of scars down the side of his face until now. What would have caused those? They looked old, like he got them when he was my age. Were they from a reckless youth, or something more?

I wouldn't put it past anyone in this room to do dangerous things that resulted in scars, including myself.

"Why did the virus fail?" Caleb asked suddenly.

I turned my gaze back to him. "He anticipated something like that being sent at him at some point," I said. "I didn't, *couldn't*, account for that. There was no way to know how he had things set up."

"Unless you went there ahead of time," he said.

"Unless that," I agreed. "There was no way to do that though, or to know that we needed to."

"You should have anticipated." His gaze burned into my soul.

"Maybe, but I'm new to this." I wasn't backing down. He could point all the fingers he wanted, we did the best we could with the information we had.

I could blame the people who got that information in the first place, but that didn't seem productive. Also, since they worked for him, he was probably well aware of the shortcomings. If he'd come here looking for a scapegoat, he'd have to keep looking. I wasn't putting my hand up for that role.

He turned his eyes towards the guys. "You're not new to this. Not as new as she is."

Mannix shrugged. "We knew what we knew and we did the best we could with that. We gave Bell a fright and got out of there alive. And we took at least a dozen of his people down."

Surely that counted for something?

Caleb turned back to me. "Did he give you any indication he'd welcome interaction with you?"

I blinked in nervous surprise. "He didn't exactly send me an invitation to Christmas lunch, if that's what you mean. I haven't been inundated by twenty-one years of back-birthday and Christmas presents."

Yet.

"But he didn't tell you to stay away?" Caleb asked.

I glanced at the guys, then told him about Charlie.

Mum gasped in horror, but no one else seemed all that surprised or concerned.

"Unless it had something to do with you, then it's possible my fa— Bell had people kill Charlie in my gym," I concluded.

Caleb nodded slowly. "If that's the case, he'll contact you at some point. I want you to keep me posted."

"No," Mannix said.

All eyes turned to him. "If you're thinking of sending her as some kind of double agent, to work against Bell in his house, then no fucking way. I am not risking her like that." He gave Caleb a death stare.

Caleb responded with indifference. "If I send her, that's where she'll go. This isn't a debate or a democracy. If I give an order, you'll follow it. I don't give a shit if you like it or not."

He didn't even have to raise his voice, his tone insisted on obedience. Since the alternative was probably a horrible, painful death, no doubt he got it more often than not.

Mannix growled in the back of his throat, deep but soft. "If you send her—"

I grabbed his arm before he could do or say anything he'd regret. "He wouldn't send me if it wasn't safe, but I doubt Bell is going to contact me and extend an invitation. Don't argue over nothing."

I thought he was going to shake me off, but instead he exhaled loudly and took a step back. "Fine, but if anything happens to you because of him—"

"Nothing will happen to me. You're here to make sure of that. Whatever happens, I'll be fine. Okay?" I locked stern eyes on his stubborn ones.

He gave a short nod. "I need coffee. Let's get out of here."

I glanced at Caleb long enough to see him jerk his head towards the door, giving us permission to leave his presence.

I couldn't get out of there fast enough.

CHAPTER 14

KENNEDY

Mannix and Ares took turns pacing across the room.

Ice and I lay on Mannix's bed, thighs pressed together. His nose was buried in my hair. He slowly wound tendrils around his fingers. My eyes were half closed as I tried not to drift off to sleep.

"Can you believe that asshole?" Mannix growled. It was his turn to pace, while Ares leaned against the wall and watched him. "He actually suggested sending Kennedy back to Bell. As if we'd fucking let that happen."

"If he makes her go, we can't stop him." Ares didn't seem to like the words he was speaking any more than Mannix did.

"The hell we can't," Mannix snapped. He stalked over to the window and back again.

"What are you going to do? Go to war against the whole Brantley family? Bro, we're no use to anyone if we're dead." Ares' customary scowl was back in place.

"I'd rather be dead than let Kennedy go back there," Mannix said.

"If you're dead, he's going to send her back anyway," Ares pointed out.

Mannix rounded on him, but couldn't deny the truth of what he said.

"He might not be planning to do that," Ice said without lifting his face to look at them. He inhaled like he was breathing in the scent of me. As if I was some exotic perfume, or drug.

"I hope he's not," I said sleepily. If I ended up back in the basement room, I doubted anyone would let me go a second time. How long would it take to die down there? Not long once I gave up on the idea of ever getting out again.

I shuddered.

"You okay, Beautiful?" Ice asked. His eyes peered through a wall of my hair like he was looking through a hedge.

"Yeah, just remembering the basement."

To my surprise, Ares walked over and slumped down beside me. I hadn't seen him look worried before, but he did now.

"It's okay to be affected by shit like that. That kind of sensory and sleep deprivation is designed to fuck with people. It's literally one of the worst forms of torture known to humans."

Right, he studied psychology. If anyone knew about stuff like that, it was him.

I smiled faintly. "Is, 'shit like that,' the clinical term?"

"In my clinic it is." He cocked his head. "You want to talk about it?"

"You should," Ice said. "It'll make you feel better."

He was probably right, but I didn't know what to say.

I squeezed Ice's hand when he curled his fingers around mine.

"It was a whole bunch of nothing," I said finally. "It felt like I was stuck in a black hole, with nothing but my thoughts."

It wasn't one of those nice, relaxing sensory deprivation tanks people pay money to lie in for an hour or so. This was hour after hour in a cold, dark space.

"Places like that can cause hallucinations," Ares said. "The brain can do strange things when it has nothing else to do."

"Are you saying this is a hallucination?" I poked him on the arm with my fingernail. "You feel real."

"That's because I am real." He grabbed my hand and brought it to his mouth.

I thought he'd kiss it. Instead, he placed my pointer finger between his lips and sucked gently.

Fuck, that was hot.

"I might not be real," Ice said dreamily. "Sometimes I feel like I'm not. I might be real and I might not be here at all."

"You're not all here," Ares agreed.

"I've heard sanity is overrated anyway." Ice smiled.

"Who told you that?" I asked.

"Not me," Mannix said from the other side of the room. "We're all a little bit out of our minds here."

"Speak for yourself." Ares shot him a look.

"I was." Mannix shrugged. "If you're the only sane one around here, then the rest of us are fucked."

"There's nothing wrong with being fucked," Ice said. "In fact, it's one of my favourite things."

"Unless we're being fucked *over*." Mannix, who seemed to have forgotten for a moment how pissed off he was, resumed pacing. "Then it's not fucking okay."

"Would Caleb send me back to Bell if it wasn't for some specific purpose?" I asked.

"He might ask you to spy on Bell for the rest of your life," Ares said. He also looked pissed off again. "Which wouldn't be very long if you got caught. Or even if he suspected that's why you were there."

There was a big difference between proclaiming my loyalty to the Brantley family and being asked to do something like that. Especially for a long period of time.

"Do they know the twins are seeing Lila?" Bell was clearly not happy about it, but what would Caleb think?

"Either they don't know, or they sent the twins in to seduce her." Mannix shrugged indifferently. "I don't know and I'm not gonna ask. That shit is well above my pay grade."

I grimaced. "Is that something that happens often? Guys sent to seduce women? Or the other way around?" If they did that to me, I'd be gutted. Imagine falling for someone only to find out it was all an act. A pretence to find information, or to get to you in some way.

"Maybe not often, but it happens," Ares said.

"I heard a rumour that Reuben sent one of his younger brothers,

Lucas, to seduce some woman from a rival family." Mannix curled his lip in disgust. "Last I heard, she was pregnant."

I gaped at him while my stomach turned. "That's horrible. Would any of you do anything like that?"

"Not to you," Ice said immediately. "For the record, I've never been asked to do something like that."

"Me either," Mannix said.

"Neither have I, and I wouldn't," Ares said. "Fuck that. I'm not a whore." He pointed a warning finger at Ice, who looked like he was about to joke or contradict him. "Don't say a word or I'll rip your tongue out."

Ice raised a hand in surrender.

"My mother didn't know the Brantley family until after she was with Samuel Bell, right?" I said slowly.

They all looked at me.

"That was what she said," Mannix said. He pressed his lips together. "You think she was sent to seduce him and ended up getting pregnant?"

"I'm prepared to believe just about anything right now." I sighed and sank back deeper against the pillow. "What about that Mack guy? Who is he and where does he fit into all of this?"

"He's hot, isn't he?" Ice's sigh came on the tail of mine.

Mannix cut him a warning look.

"Just looking, not gonna touch," Ice said lightly.

"You better not, because if I have to kill him for touching you, that's gonna create a shit storm." Mannix crossed his arms. "Mack D'Antonio is a friend of Caleb. As much as Caleb has any friends. He's also got more money than Caleb, Reuben, and Bell combined. He's involved in mining or some shit."

"Legal stuff?" I asked.

Ares said, "Some of it's legal, some of it isn't. He does a lot of business here in Dusk Bay. He has a house on the other side of the city, on the promontory. It's about twice the size of this one. He's only there a couple of times of year."

"What a waste." I wrinkled my nose.

"He can afford it," Mannix said.

"Lifestyles of the famous and obscenely rich," I said. It was slightly sickening.

"Obscenely rich is an accurate definition for it," Ice said. "But they still bleed the same."

"Tortured any billionaires lately, have you?" Ares teased.

"Not recently and not nearly often enough." Ice let out an exaggerated sigh. "For what it's worth, sometimes I pretend they're someone other than who they are. That gets me by pretty well."

"If I get my hands on Samuel Bell, he's all yours," Mannix promised. "Just save a little bit for all of us."

"Especially me." I couldn't get the idea of my mother being sent to seduce him out of my head. I considered the possibility it was the other way around, but for what purpose? My mother was no one significant in the scheme of things. Not when it came to the power-play between all these families. As far as I knew anyway.

I'd established by now that the more I learnt, the more I realised I didn't know. She could be a queen in exile, or fuck knows what else.

I shook my head at the thought.

"What do you need to get into Brutham Academy?" I asked.

"Are you thinking of going?" Ice curled a section of my hair around his finger and let it bounce free before curling it again.

"No, I was wondering how and why my mother went there."

Ice's hand stilled. "Most students have to be nominated by their family. Or by one of the more powerful families. If someone works for Caleb Brantley, for example, he could nominate their children to go. Of course, they'd be expected to work for him after they finished their degree."

"Leo nominated me," Ares said softly.

"Me too." Ice went back to playing with my hair. "Only Mannix got in directly."

"My mother must have had ties to the Brantleys long before I was born," I reasoned.

"In some capacity, she must have," Ice agreed.

I didn't want to believe she seduced Bell because she was told to. The idea of her having feelings for him was icky, but it was better than thinking I was an unfortunate accident. A pregnancy that resulted from some kind of power-play.

I couldn't even begin to imagine what that might have involved. A distraction? Some effort to get Samuel Bell on their side? Or maybe the Bell family wanted my mother on their side?

All of this was starting to give me a massive headache.

"I know it matters to you how you came about," Ares said, his tone low and soft, unusually sensitive. "But it doesn't matter to us. We don't care who fucked whom and why. What matters is that you're you and you're ours. All of that shit happened a long time ago. It doesn't change anything."

There was no hint of hesitation or reservation in his voice or on his face. Every single word he said was one hundred percent sincere. If he ever really hated me, he'd put it firmly behind him.

I managed a watery smile. "Thank you. That means a lot. I thought you all might walk away when you knew who my father was." I frowned. "That's not true. I thought you'd kill me. Daughter of the enemy and all that."

"Nothing you could do or be would make us kill you," Mannix said. "You belong to us. End of story. That's how things are going to stay until the end of time. You're stuck with us until we're all old and grey."

He didn't have to add that it was only applicable if we lived that long. We all knew there was a good chance we wouldn't. Charlie's death brought that home better than anything else could have. Then Caleb looking at me like I was some kind of tool to be used however he wanted…

I might end up pushed and pulled between the Bells and the Brantleys and the guys, or I might end up dead. None of that was ideal. Especially the last one. I wasn't ready to be used as a pawn, but I was even less ready to be swept off the board and onto the floor.

"You're stuck with me until you're old and grey too," I told them. "Which will be sooner, because you're older than me and I intend to keep colouring my hair for as long as I can." I grinned.

"And such pretty hair it is too." Ice gripped a bunch of it in his fist and brought it to his mouth to kiss. "I wonder how I'd look with hair that colour."

"Silly," Ares told him. "Just like I would."

"I think he'd look cute," Mannix said. "We could call him Little Red Riding Cock."

"That's Big Red Riding Cock to you." Ice sniffed.

"Yes it—"

We all jumped when my phone rang.

CHAPTER 15
KENNEDY

I leaned over, away from Ice and grabbed my phone off the table beside the bed.

"I don't know the number."

"All in favour of you not answering the phone." Ice raised his hand.

We all looked at Mannix, who was thinking quickly.

"Answer it," he said finally.

"But—"

He cut Ice off. "Answer it. It might be nothing. If it isn't, I want to know about it. Put it on speakerphone."

Reluctantly, I did what he said, then pressed the button to answer the call.

"Hello?" I said tentatively. "Who is this?"

"Kennedy." That was all he said, but I recognised Samuel Bell's voice.

"How did you get this number?" I certainly hadn't given it to him and I didn't know anyone who would.

Bell chuckled. "There's nothing I can't get if I want it. Getting your number was a simple matter."

"Let me guess, if I block this number, you'll try on a different one?" I let Ice pull me back to him and slip an arm around me.

"Yes, but that would be tedious. Don't block this number." There was that, 'I expect to be obeyed,' tone again. That was starting to become normal around here.

"What do you want?" I asked coldly.

"Can't I check up on my daughter?" he asked. "You got home safely?"

"I have a feeling you knew I did," I said. "What do you really want?"

"Did you get my present?"

I frowned. Present? What the hell was he—

Realisation dawned.

"Charlie. That was you." What the ever loving fuck?

"In a manner of speaking," he agreed. "I had my people keep an eye on the gym, to make sure you were okay. They caught him trying to break in, so they dealt with him."

"But the security alarm..."

"Switched off, to avoid drawing attention to the place. If that went off, everyone would have come running and everything would be a lot messier. Wouldn't you agree?"

"Oh yeah," I said sarcastically. "I'm sure it could have been worse than a dead body hanging in my gym. From my silk, which I'm sure you know is my favourite apparatus."

"So I'm told." He sounded like he was reading off a computer screen full of information he or someone had gathered all about me. "You started with gymnastics but your favourite apparatus is a circus trick."

"It's better than being a clown," I said flatly.

He chuckled. "I see you got your sense of humour from me."

"Was that what leaving Charlie dangling like that was? A joke? Because it wasn't fucking funny." His face was going to heavily feature in my nightmares for a while. At least the dreams featuring the guys killing that man outside the masked ball had stopped.

Although, thinking about those masks still made my skin tingle and crawl.

"It wasn't a joke," Bell said smoothly. "It was a warning."

"A warning to me to...what? Stay away from you? A warning that you know where I live and work? Did you do it there because you can't reach me here at home?" It was nice to know somewhere was safe from his reach.

"It wasn't a warning for you," he said slowly and clearly as though he needed me to hear and understand his exact words and meaning. "It was a warning *about* you. That anyone who messes with you will have me to answer to."

His words rattled around in my brain for a minute or two, like those carnival throwing games where the ball rolls around and around the tube before it slowly drops into the hole. Then it rolls down another tube before landing in the wrong place. The number beside the one that would have won the thrower a huge plush hippopotamus.

Yeah, it's happened to me a few times before.

I laughed. "You had your people kill Charlie in my gym as a warning for people to stay away from me?"

"Precisely."

"Who? Who are you warning?" I glanced up at the guys, but they had no more answers than I did judging by the expressions on their faces.

"Your mother, for one," Bell said. "You told her, didn't you? How did she react?"

I knitted my brows. Any harder and I would have made myself a nice, warm scarf.

"She was horrified," I said slowly. "Like any mother would be if their daughter found a dead body at work."

"Not just any mother. One who knows me. I'd wager a million dollars she's already told you I'd have taken you away from her if I'd known about you sooner."

I wouldn't take that bet, because she had.

"What's your point?" I asked.

"My point is, I want her to know I can reach her too. Because of her, we missed out on a lifetime of being together. She's hurt you in ways you can't imagine."

"And yet, the first time we met, you locked me in that room," I said bitterly.

There was a pause, followed by a heavy sigh. "Perhaps not my finest hour."

I snorted. "No shit, Sherlock. For the record, I don't buy this caring father routine you have going on. In fact, I don't think this is about me at all. I think you're pissed off at my mother and want revenge. I was just collateral damage." And I was really, really tempted to hang up. My finger hovered over the phone screen.

"What did she tell you about our past?" he asked.

"What does it matter?" I asked in return.

"What did she tell you?" he insisted.

I closed my eyes and gritted my teeth for a moment, but forced them back open and for my jaw to relax.

"She told me you had a brief fling. That she cared about you but you all graduated and she never saw you again. She said you were supposed to marry…Penelope?"

It was his turn to sound bitter. "I was hoping she'd tell you the truth, because you'd believe it coming from her. Otherwise I would have told you when you were here."

"Spare me if you're going to tell me a bunch of lies," I snapped.

"Not lies. The complete truth. Whether you want to believe it or not is up to you."

I glanced at the guys again. They didn't look even slightly alike, but right now they wore matching sceptical expressions. If that was all we had to go on, we'd look like quadruplets right now.

Ice would find that thought hilarious, but I shoved it out of my mind for now.

"Fine, I'm listening. Tell me what you think your version of the truth is." I was going to need a big pinch of salt, because I doubted a word of it was worth believing.

"You know we met at Brutham Academy?" he started. He continued before I could confirm that I knew that. "She did everything she could to get my attention. At first, I didn't give her much of it. She was gorgeous and all of the boys and a lot of the girls were after her. I thought there was no way she'd be interested in a guy like me. I always had my nose in a book, as they say. The only things I had going for me were my last name and my parents' money. Back then, none of that meant anything to me. I planned to study archaeology and hand the business over to my brother when he was old enough, and finished at the Academy."

He was silent for a beat or two.

"Finally, Helen managed to convince me she really was interested in me. Not my money. Not my name. I fell in love with her. I decided we could have a future together. Get married, have children, live a life away from the violence and crime." He actually sounded sincere.

"We planned to get engaged after we left Brutham. Then I told her about my plans. We argued. Then she admitted her mother was the one who wanted her to go after me. She was a longtime employee of the Brantley family, but she was tired of seeing their wealth and power, while she and her daughter went without. She got Helen into Brutham Academy and set her on the course to change that."

I pictured him sitting at his desk, his eyes closed. Maybe rubbing the bridge of his nose, or his temples. I didn't want to feel sympathy for him. I didn't want to feel anything for him, but he seemed genuine. He also could have been laying a trap I was walking straight into with my soft heartedness.

"So you broke up?" I guessed.

"In a manner of speaking," he said. "I wanted to stay with her regardless of how we started out. My father had other ideas. He decided I should marry Penelope. He offered Helen three million dollars to stay away from me. It was more than Helen would have made being married to an archaeologist, so she took it. I never saw her again. It wasn't until she announced her engagement to Leo that I realised she had a daughter. Our daughter. It seems like she hasn't changed a bit."

I chewed my lip.

How much of it was true?

I suspected a lot was, if not most of it. It sounded exactly how my mother would react. She would have taken three million dollars if it was offered. She was more ambitious than she was sentimental. But to make someone care about her, fall in love with her, then take the money and walk away? What kind of cold hearted bitch would do something like that? If that was the truth, then did I really know her at all? Did I even know myself?

I was starting to think I knew neither.

In spite of that, I said, "How am I supposed to believe what you're saying?"

"Ask your mother. She won't deny any of it. She lied to me since the day we met. I have to wonder if she's done the same to you. She never told you I existed. Never told you this life existed, if I guess correctly? She knew the moment I found out about you, I'd want to see you. Did she insist you move down to Dusk Bay? Did you never think the timing was suspicious, or sudden? It's because she knew what would happen. Everything she does, she does for her own well-being. If you got in her way, she'd climb straight over you, or shove you aside. People call me ruthless, but Helen was always much worse."

"She never locked me in a dark room," I pointed out. She was my mother, she made plenty of mistakes, but she never did anything as horrible as that. At least, none I remembered.

"She sent you to me not knowing I knew who you were," he said. "Knowing you had no clue. Knowing if I caught you, I'd kill you. I'm sorry I locked you in there, but at the time I had no idea what your agenda was. Or if you knew about me. She might have spun some web of lies to make you hate me. She and the people she works with might have sent you to kill me. Once I realise your intentions were a lot more benign, I let you out."

"What about Frank Nixon?" I asked. The man Ice and I tortured to death would have happily killed me.

A heavy silence hung for half a minute.

"I don't know anyone by that name."

"He stalked me and admitted he wanted to strangle me." And worse, but I decided not to mention that. It didn't matter now anyway. "He said you sent him."

That same silence hung again. "I didn't send anyone after you."

CHAPTER 16
KENNEDY

"Do you believe a word of it?" I was still snuggled up beside Ice, with Ares on the other side of me. Before the phone rang, I was sleepy. Now I was wide awake, a million thoughts bouncing around inside my head. "You guys have known about him a lot longer than I have."

I glanced over my shoulder at Ares. His body was pressed against mine, moulded into me like he wanted to crawl inside my skin. I couldn't see his face, but I knew from the sound of his breathing when the conversation irritated him. That was most of the time.

"We've been told about him." Ares sounded accusing, but I wasn't sure who it was aimed at. "I wouldn't say we *know* him."

"He's like the boogie man," Ice said. "Be good or Samuel Bell will get you. Don't say the wrong thing to the wrong people, or he'll get you. You never know who's listening. If word gets back to him, he'll get you. The walls have ears and eyes, and if they see you do anything wrong..."

"He'll get you," I finished for him. "Does that actually happen?"

I knew how easy it was to form a prejudice against something or someone. You only have to look at people's favourite car brand, or their desire to stick to only one type of phone. If you've spent a lifetime being told to hate something, that was usually what you did. Sometimes without questioning the reasoning behind it.

"He did lock you in that room," Mannix pointed out. He sat at the end of the bed, simmering with rage and frustration that threatened to bubble over.

I sat up a little and sighed. "I know."

My ability to hold grudges wasn't going to let go of that one easily. I still wanted to let Ice slice out Bell's kneecaps and use them as serving dishes. Or whatever people did with the kneecaps of torture victims.

"What if everything else he said was true?"

Mannix looked like he wanted to argue, but I went on.

"Consider the possibility for a moment. Charlie broke into the gym and was killed, but nothing was taken. No bombs were left behind. Maybe they *were* there to keep an eye on me."

That was still creepy as fuck, but better than thinking they were there for something nefarious, like killing all of us.

"Frank Nixon never named Bell as the person who sent him," I continued. "He said his boss wanted to send a message that they could get to Leo whenever they wanted to."

"Who else would it be but Bell?" Mannix's voice was tighter than a fly's ass. He, in particular, seemed to be struggling with the idea that Bell might not be as bad as his father always told him he was. His whole life was built on the foundation of the feud between the Bell and Brantley families. That belief was deeply ingrained into every fibre of him. If that was taken away, what was left?

"Does Leo have any other rivals?" I asked. "Maybe Nixon was sent by someone in Bell's employ. Someone who went behind his back?"

"If that's the case, they're not going to live very long," Ice said, sounding sleepy.

Mannix snapped his fingers. "Right. They won't. Bell will find them and make a public example of them. If they exist."

"You don't think they do?" I asked.

He rubbed a hand over the stubble on his chin. "Why go after Leo? Why risk going behind Bell's back to get at him? Leo is powerful, but there are much more powerful players in the game than him. Reuben,

Caleb, their brother Joshua. Daisy Lasalle, Hilton Blake, Ric DiMarco. Hell, Mack D'Antonio is a bigger target than Leo."

I lay back down. "I don't understand any of this," I admitted.

"Bell was probably lying through his teeth," Mannix concluded. "It's what people like him do. They manipulate people to do what they want. Everything he said was just to make you doubt your mother, Leo, and us. That's it. He's trying to plant seeds of doubt and stir up trouble. And it's working."

"I guess so," I agreed. Mannix was right, it *was* working, whether it was some kind of manipulation or not.

"Maybe this isn't about Leo," I said finally. "Maybe it's Bell's attempt to get back at my mother. Like you said, he's trying to get me to doubt her."

That was working too. There was too much truth in what he said. Wasn't that what made someone a good liar? Give the listener just enough truth that it gives credence to the lie. Let the listener do the rest.

"I need to talk to her. I need to know if what he said about my grandmother sending her after Bell, was true." I hardly knew the woman. She'd died when I was three or four. I had her name as my middle name. That was about the extent of it.

"You think she'll admit it if it was?" Ares asked. "No offence, but your mother seems to have her own agenda."

Usually I'd take offence to any words said after, 'no offence,' but in this case he wasn't wrong. I loved her, but my mother often prioritised herself above everything else. I didn't want to think she put herself before me, but the more I got to know her, the more I wondered if everything she did was about her and I was just along for the ride.

"Would she take three million dollars to stay away from someone?" Ice asked.

"I need to ask her that too," I said. "I don't know anything anymore. I don't know if my whole life was a lie."

"If yours was, then so were ours," Mannix growled softly. "But you know what, I don't want to talk about this anymore." He dropped to all fours and stalked up the bed towards me. "I don't want to talk at all."

"Really?" I eyed him. "What do you want to do?" As if I couldn't guess. He was insatiable. So was I. My body throbbed already.

"Everything," he said in a growl that set my body on fire. He lay over me and gripped my sleep shorts. With one jerk, he ripped them apart.

"Hey, those were new," I protested.

He grinned as he tossed both pieces away to either side. "I'll buy you more. Or not. You could sleep naked instead." He backed up his words by grabbing my singlet and tearing that too. "Clothes are over-rated anyway."

"Finally, my dream is coming true," Ice said, a lazy smile on his face. "Mannix and Kennedy walking around all day naked." He glanced over to Ares.

"Dream on," Ares told him. "The world isn't ready for that much awesomeness."

"I think it is," I told him. I turned my attention away from him a moment later when Mannix slipped a hand between my thighs and up into my already wet, hungry pussy.

A shiver passed through me. Between his touch and the way the other two were eyeing me like I was a tasty snack, round one might not last long.

I half expected the guys to touch me, or each other—a girl could hope—but instead they sat back to watch. Okay, I could roll with that. I liked them to look at me, it made me feel pretty. Gorgeous even.

Eyes half-closed, I watched them watching me while Mannix pushed me closer and closer to coming.

All three guys had matching expressions on their faces again, this time appreciating the show, and my body. There was something so overwhelmingly erotic about being the centre of attention like this. Something that drove me hard and fast.

Just before I came, Mannix pulled his hand back.

What the fuck?

I blinked at him and made a face.

He grinned. "Not yet."

"Tease," I growled.

That made him grin even harder. He waited until I came back

down, almost all the way back to earth, before he started tracing minute circles around my clit with his fingertip.

The pressure rose again, more intense this time. I curled my hands around the bedcovers and dug my fingernails into the black cotton fabric.

Like before, when I was about to come, Mannix took his hand off me.

I growled at him, deep in the back of my throat.

Just like before, he was unapologetic. He fixed me with a firm look.

"You'll come when I say you can come. Not before. I meant it when I said your body belongs to me. Everything, including your orgasms. Especially your orgasms."

"Do you want me to beg?" I asked. Because I could beg. It was orgasms we were talking about here.

"That could be fun," Ares said. He looked particularly smug for some reason.

I stuck my tongue out at him.

He stuck his back out at me.

"So mature," Mannix said sarcastically. "Another day I'll make you beg, but today, you'll come when I say you'll come."

"Fuck, it's hot when you're bossy," Ice sighed. "Okay, it's hot when you're not bossy too, but this is totally working for me."

Mannix flashed a smile, then, because apparently he wasn't a complete asshole, he lowered his hand back to my pussy.

I watched his expression through narrowed eyes. If he was going to edge me again, I was going to kick him in the nuts. On the other hand, who was I kidding? I was loving every minute of it.

I loved it even more when he said, "Okay, Princess, come for me."

And come I did, hard and fast. My whole body writhed and bucked, grinding against his hand. The thunder of blood through my ears, the heat of it coursing through my body was worth the wait.

I cried out nice and loud, so the whole house probably heard me. Whatever. I wasn't ashamed of any of this.

"Good girl." Mannix raised his hand to Ice's mouth and let him suck on his fingers.

"Fucking delicious," Ice groaned.

"I know you are." Mannix kissed him quickly, then nodded to me. "Get on all fours."

I did as he ordered. I looked back over my shoulder at him. He gripped my waist in firm, bruising fingers and positioned his cock outside my pussy. In true, merciless Mannix style, he slammed his cock into me as hard as he could.

I cried out in surprise, with a splash of pain, but no hint of complaint. I liked it when they were gentle and I liked it when they were rough. Everything they did to me, every touch was perfect and amazing.

Mannix slid his hands up to cup my breasts. My nipples were rock hard against his palms, eager for him to rub and pinch and squeeze. He did all of those things while pounding into me with firm, even strokes.

I wanted to suggest he couldn't come until I said he could, but I had no words, only groans, moans and pants.

"You feel fucking amazing, Princess," Mannix said breathlessly. "So perfect for my cock. So…"

Whatever else I was, I didn't get to find out, because he came, thrusting frantically and groaning deep and low as bliss claimed him.

He slumped over my back, panting and digging his fingers into my breasts. He stayed like that for a while until he caught his breath, then he slid out of me and flopped onto the mattress.

"My turn," Ice said. He pulled me over until I straddled his hips, then carefully lowered me down onto his thick, heated erection.

His hands on my hips, he helped me to rise and fall, up and down his length. My breasts bounced freely, nipples hard points begging to be touched.

I let him set the speed and rhythm, content to enjoy the way he felt inside me and how my clit brushed against him with each stroke.

He and the other guys were going to be the absolute end of me. And I couldn't get enough of it. Every time they touched me, I wanted more. Every time one of them had their cock inside me it was both enough and not nearly enough all at the same time. I would never, ever get tired of this.

"Beautiful, you feel delicious," Ice said breathlessly. "You make me and my cock both very happy." He looked over at Mannix with half an eye. "You too."

"I know," Mannix said with no hint of humility.

"You're such a dick," Ares told him, but his tone was affectionate rather than purely scathing.

Mannix grinned and went back to watching Ice and I slowly fuck.

Ice wiggled his hand in between us and rubbed my clit as he thrust up into me. "Come for me, Beautiful."

I groaned and angled my body so my clit grazed more firmly over his fingers. I waited for Mannix to tell me no, but he didn't. Evidently he was happy to let Ice be in the driver's seat for a change.

With no one to stop me, and Ice's eyes on me, I came, squeezing his cock so hard he couldn't keep from coming too. His eyes half closed in concentration and he thrust up and up, and up, until he fell still and groaned out his orgasm. His head lifted up off the pillow.

"Hell yeah," he breathed. "So… Fucking… Perfect. So… Ahhh."

He exhaled hard and his head dropped back down.

"I will never get tired of that." He opened his eyes and smiled at me.

"Me either," I agreed.

"My turn," Ares said.

I thought he might go for his paddle and spank me silly but instead slid me off Ice, and rolled me over onto my stomach. He grabbed my wrists and pinned them above my head with one hand. He lowered most of his weight onto me and pried my legs apart with his knees.

With as much mercy as Mannix gave me, he slammed his cock hard into my pussy. If it wasn't for the other guys stretching me for him, it would have hurt like hell.

It still hurt, but instead of crying out in pain, I cried out in pleasure.

He leaned down to whisper in my ear. "You like that?"

I made an incoherent sound, then said, "Harder."

"With pleasure." He pulled all the way out of me, then slammed back in again, twice as hard as the first time. Hard enough to bring tears to my eyes.

"Harder," I said again.

He did, so hard I screamed. It was perfect.

Over and over, he drove himself deep into me. He held nothing back, not one centimetre, not one drop. He was soon breathing hard with the exertion, but never once did he thrust more softly. Never once did he give me anything more than everything, all the way to the hilt. All the way to his balls. They slapped against me with each stroke, a counterpoint to the wet sucking of his cock sliding in and out of my pussy.

"I'm going to fucking come inside you, Firecracker," he said with a grunt. "You're going to take every drop of me like you took every drop of Mannix and Ice. You'll be so full, you'll overflow."

Yes please. His words brought me back to the brink and over. I came harder and faster than I ever had in my entire life. If you asked me what my name was, right then I couldn't have told you. I couldn't have formed a sentence. Not even a word. All I knew was the throbbing of blood through my entire body and the cascade of pleasure. Nothing else existed in that moment.

After a million years in that beautiful space, I started to come down. Just as Ares came, driving in with powerful, determined thrusts.

He didn't say a word, just let out a long, low groan, milking himself in the tight, wet heat of my pussy.

Finally, he slumped, his chest slick with sweat against my back. He still didn't speak, just held me while we caught our breaths in a tangle of arms and legs and satisfaction.

CHAPTER 17
ARES

"I'm not letting you go in there by yourself." I jutted out my chin and stared Kennedy down. She was a badass woman, but I wasn't backing down on this. "I'll tie you to my bed if I have to." She knew I would and we'd both enjoy it too.

She stopped with her hand on the door handle. "You can punish me later." Her eyes lingered on me as she turned away, a smile on the corners of her luscious mouth.

"I will punish you later, but I'm still not letting you go in there alone." I could, and I would, scoop her up, throw her over my shoulder and carry her off somewhere else. Then I'd fuck her so hard she wouldn't be able to walk, much less run away.

Now I thought about it, maybe I should just do that anyway. My cock twitched, ready to leap to attention at a moment's notice.

She sighed. "Fine, but for fuck sake don't make the situation any worse than it already is."

I couldn't see how that was possible. "I'll try to behave. And if I don't, you can punish me." She could do that anyway. Any time.

She glanced back at me and rolled her eyes. She turned the handle and pushed the heavy timber door in on silent hinges.

I'd been in Leo's office a bunch of times, but it always struck me how big it was. The apartment I grew up in was approximately the same size.

Of course, we didn't have a huge, walnut desk, oversized leather chairs, or a view over the ocean.

Leo's house sat on the side of a cliff, leaving nothing but water and sky framed in a massive picture window. If this was my office, I'd get nothing done. I'd either be staring at the waves, or fucking Kennedy in front of the window, both in full view of the world and where no one could see us.

That thought made my balls heavy, so I pushed it away and turned my attention to Leo and Helen. They sat side by side in those oversized leather chairs, their heads together as they talked about fuck knows what. Probably something about how to screw someone over. Wasn't that what rich people spent their time doing?

Leo looked like an older, harder version of Mannix. Same dark hair, same intense eyes, but Leo's hair had a peppering of grey.

Helen's hair was a faded version of Kennedy's, but as far as I was concerned, that was where the resemblance ended. Her nose was sharper, lips not as full. Her breasts were smaller and her skin wasn't dotted with a million, adorable freckles. Her expression was harder too, bitter, like she was convinced the world had fucked her over somehow. She was still a beautiful woman, but paled in comparison to her daughter.

Right now, she and Leo were looking at us with curiosity laced with annoyance. More of the latter than there was of the former. Whatever, I wasn't going to apologise.

"I'm sorry to interrupt," Kennedy said. She didn't sound sorry.

When she first moved here, she would have meant it. She would have snuck back out the door and closed it behind her as silently as she could. No, she wouldn't have come in here in the first place. She would have waited until they came out and then asked to speak to them.

Us guys, we'd encouraged her to go after what she wanted and she was doing exactly that.

Good girl.

Leo put the piece of paper in his hand onto his desk and crossed his legs at the knees.

"It's not a problem, we always have time for you."

Those were the words that came out of his mouth, but his eyes said otherwise. To my surprise, he looked wary. Did he suspect we'd come in here to kill them or something? Should we have?

If Kennedy or Mannix wanted them dead, I had no trouble doing that for them. I was loyal to Leo to a point, but I was loyal to Mannix and Kennedy until the day I died. If they needed a thing done, I'd do it. No question.

"Where are the other guys?" Helen asked. She looked around us expectantly.

"They had some things they had to take care of," Kennedy said. "It's just us at the moment."

Mannix and Ice had to question someone at Ice's workshop. We both wanted to go with them, but Mannix insisted we stay here. Kennedy, to keep her safe, and me to keep an eye on her. I didn't mind being her bodyguard, even if it left me out of other kinds of fun. What was a little torture compared to spending time with a gorgeous woman? The woman I fell hard for, to my surprise. I never expected to feel that for anyone. For a long time, I suspected I wasn't capable of love, just hate, anger and self loathing. The kid who grew up poorer than dirt.

Now, thanks to her, and my brothers, I stood on solid ground for the first time in my life. Brothers in arms, if not by blood. My family. My whole, fucking universe.

Helen looked relieved. She glanced at Leo. I could almost see the thoughts going through her mind. The two of them could deal with the two of us if they needed to.

Kennedy clasped her hands together and stood with one foot ahead of the other. The pose wasn't aggressive but it clearly said she expected to be listened to.

"I got a phone call last night," she said. "From Samuel Bell."

Leo and Helen's response was immediate. They both looked ready to jump out of their chairs. To do what, I don't know, but they were on edge. Jumpy. That made them both dangerous. We'd have to tread carefully.

"How did he get your number?" Helen paled. Her voice was high.

Even if I wasn't trained to hear it, I would have. She was the little mouse now.

"I have a feeling you'd know better than I do," Kennedy said. "If people have enough money they can get whatever they want. How he got it doesn't matter right now. What matters was—"

"What bullshit did he try to feed you?" Helen asked. She was more composed now, ready to shovel bullshit. I trusted her as far as I could throw her. If she wasn't Kennedy's mother…

Kennedy licked her lips. "He said Grandma was working for the Brantley family. That was how you got into Brutham Academy."

Helen hesitated. "That's right. It's not somewhere you can simply apply to and get in. If you want Leo to put in the word for you…"

"I don't," Kennedy said quickly. "Bell also said Grandma wanted you to chase after him."

"She wasn't against it," Helen said carefully. "Sam was different then. He was sweet."

"He said you broke up with him when he said he was leaving the family and wouldn't have money," Kennedy said.

Helen snorted. "Of course he'd say that. He was convinced everyone was after him for his money. He could never accept that I was different. He was…paranoid."

"So you didn't take three million dollars to stay away from him?" I asked. I couldn't help it, the question was burning a hole in my brain.

Helen glanced at Leo. If any of this is news to him, he gave no sign of it. I had a feeling he was in all of this up to his eyeballs too. Shady motherfucker.

"I tried to tell him about you," Helen said eventually. "His father stopped me and made me tell him instead. He said Sam was with someone else and offered three million dollars to look after you. I wasn't going to turn down money to look after my child."

"So you didn't take it in return for staying away from Bell?" Kennedy asked.

Helen shifted uncomfortably in her chair. "That was part of my deal with Sam's father. He'd give me the money to take care of you and I would stay away from Sam. Let him live his life in peace with Penelope. When she died a few years later, his father approached me to remind me of our deal. I said I'd stick to it, and I have. And because of that money, you had a good, privileged life. You've done a lot of things other kids couldn't. Things you wouldn't have been able to do if it wasn't for me making that deal."

She spoke as though she expected gratitude, and lots of it. She didn't get it. Not from Kennedy, and sure as hell not from me.

"Why did you send us to Bell's?" Kennedy said softly. "You knew how dangerous it was. What might happen if we got caught. We all could have died."

Leo rolled his eyes. It wasn't the first time I got the impression he'd be happy if the three of us guys were out of the way.

Helen actually laughed. "I didn't send you, you begged to go. You four insisted you could do it."

"What's really going on here?" Leo asked. "What are you accusing us of?"

Kennedy looked uncertain. "Bell said—"

"A bunch of lies, and you bought straight into them," Leo said. "And you've come in here accusing your mother and I of deceiving you in some way. So your mother didn't tell you who your father was, that doesn't make her suspicious of every little thing that ever went wrong in your life. I welcomed you into my home, into my family, and this is the repayment I get." He included me in the dark look that accompanied his words.

I didn't flinch, but Kennedy swallowed audibly. "I didn't mean to—"

"But you did anyway. What else did Bell say? That we suggested he lock you in that room?" Leo looked even more like Mannix now, face contorted with fury.

"No," Kennedy said quickly. "He said he sent people to look out for me and those people were who dealt with Charlie. He said he was trying to protect me."

Leo let out an ugly, barking laugh. "I knew you were naïve, but not that naïve."

I suspected he meant to crush her spirit a little, but it had the opposite effect.

"I'm not naïve," she insisted. "I'm just done being lied to. I feel like a fucking pawn on a chessboard, moved around back and forth wherever people think I should go."

"Watch your language," Helen snapped.

I was tempted to tell her to fuck off, but bit my tongue for Kennedy's sake. That would only make the situation worse, and Leo may try to kick me out of his office. If he did that, I might end up killing him after all, or at least, punching him in the face.

"What else did Bell say?" Leo asked coldly.

"He said he didn't send anyone after me," Kennedy told him.

"You saw the man with your own eyes," Leo pointed out. "He confessed what he did."

"He never said Bell sent him," Kennedy said.

"He implied it." Leo frowned. "Who else would have?"

"I don't know," Kennedy admitted. "His daughters?" She looked painfully uncertain. She reminded me of a doll whose hands were held by a pair of toddlers. One pulling in one direction, the other pulling in the other, neither having any intention of giving up.

"I wouldn't put it past that pair of snakes," Leo agreed. "Either way, they came from the same place. The Bell family. None of them can be trusted."

"None of them?" Kennedy echoed.

He realised the implication of what he said and his mouth opened and closed a couple of times.

"You know what I mean," he said finally.

"Do I?" she asked. "I have Bell blood running through my veins. Do I have any Brantley blood?" She glanced at her mother. "What about Cassani or DiMarco?"

"Not that I know of," Helen said. "But my mother did work for them for a long time, so anything is possible."

When Kennedy gave her a sideways look, she added, "It's unlikely. My parents had a good, strong relationship."

"Right. So I'm more Bell than anything else," Kennedy concluded.

"No, you're half Knight." Helen placed her hands palm down on the arm of the chair and started to push herself to her feet. "Of course we trust you. Right, Leo?"

The fucker actually hesitated. Only a moment, but it was enough. Leo rose and put a hand on her arm. "Kennedy…"

She shook him off. "Don't. I got the message loud and clear."

She gave them both a scathing look, then turned and marched out of the room, her chin high, back straight.

I knew I was the only one in the room who heard the sound of her heart breaking.

I gave them both a dirty look and hurried out after her.

CHAPTER 18

KENNEDY

"Kennedy, wait!"

I ignored Ares and trotted up the stairs to my room. A few months ago, I would have been blinded by tears. Today, it was anger. I didn't believe for a moment Leo meant anything other than what he said. He was too deliberate, too controlled, to blurt out things he didn't mean.

I stormed into my bedroom and tried to violently shut the door behind me.

Ares grabbed it and stopped it before I got my satisfying slam. It wouldn't have made a sound anyway, I quickly realised. The doors were designed not to be slammed shut.

Fucking tantrum-proof design.

"Kennedy." He closed the door behind me. "What are you doing?"

I stomped into my ridiculously oversized walk-in wardrobe and grabbed the suitcase from the shelf above my skirts.

"If they don't want me here, then I'm leaving." I placed the suitcase on top of the chest of drawers and yanked the zipper open.

I shoved the lid up.

"Fuck." It fell back down on my fingers. I shoved it up again and started throwing in whatever I could put my hands on. Underwear, jeans, T-shirts, a pink sock. Fuck only knew where the matching sock was. Whatever, I didn't care right now.

"Kennedy," he said again. "Would you fucking stop?" He placed his hands on my shoulders, firm enough to stop me from continuing to pack. Not firm enough to turn me around until I was ready to look at him.

That took another couple of minutes.

Finally I turned around and looked up at him.

"Why? You heard them. They don't trust me. Leo can't look past who my biological father is, as if I can help who came inside my mother. Why isn't he blaming her for this? She was the one who kept it from him. From me. She lied to us both. To all of us. Even if she wasn't a gold digger, she dug a hole. Who was the one who got buried in it? I did. Me."

He put his arms around me and let me hide my face in his chest. He was hard, solid and warm. He'd showered an hour ago, after swimming laps in the pool, so he smelled like musk and soap.

"Whatever problem they have, it's their problem," he said, his cheek resting lightly against my hair. "I think Leo is pissed at Helen, but he took it out on you because he doesn't know how to deal with someone he married five minutes ago. He's still thinking with his cock."

I grimaced. Leo's cock was the last thing I wanted to think about. Especially near my mother. Ewww, parent sex.

"Then I'll happily leave them to work it out," I said. "You don't have to come with me."

Okay, I held my breath. I *wanted* him to come with me. I wanted all of them to come with me. If they didn't, if they chose Leo's side…

"Of course I'm fucking coming with you," he said. "You don't get rid of Ares Turner that easily. I wasn't named after the God of war for nothing. It's because I always fight. I don't give in or back down. I'm not gonna start now."

I lifted my head and looked up at him. A watery smile was better than watery eyes. I was *not* going to cry, no way.

"I don't know where we'll go," I admitted. "Or if the others will come with us."

"I'm always in favour of coming with any of you," Ice said. He stepped through the doorway, quickly followed by Mannix. They must have arrived just in time to hear me say that.

Mannix saw my suitcase and his eyes narrowed. "What in the fucking hell is going on?"

I explained in as few words as I could. His and Ice's faces turned redder and redder. Mannix's in particular. By the time I was done, he looked ready to burn the entire house to the ground.

"We're going with you," he said when I was finished. He nodded towards Ice and they both hurried out to pack their own suitcases.

"You should pack yours too," I told Ares.

"I'll help you with yours and then you can help me with mine." He pulled out that stray pink sock and threw it aside before opening my underwear drawer and emptying most of it into the suitcase. "There. All done."

I snorted a laugh and threw in as much of my clothes as I could fit. "I can't just walk around in my underwear."

"I'd prefer you naked," he admitted. "But you might need to leave... wherever we're staying, once in a while."

"If I walked around naked, you three would have to do the same." I closed the suitcase and drew the zipper shut before grabbing the handle and pulling it off the chest of drawers.

"You say that like you think any of us would have a problem with that." He grinned. "I'm not even wearing underwear right now." He grabbed his groin and his grin widened.

I just shook my head at him.

“Wasn’t it you who said the world wasn’t ready for all that awesomeness?”

If we were all naked all the time, how long would it take before they wore out my pussy? Yeah, they wouldn't need to be naked all the time to do that. They were working on it pretty well as it was. I was here for every moment of it.

He grabbed the handle from my hand and rolled my suitcase the rest of the way to the door. We left it there and hurried into his room to throw things into his case. Of course those things included his paddle, some rope, a pair of handcuffs, a different coloured pair of handcuffs, a ribbed vibrator and half a packet of TimTams.

I ate one of the chocolate biscuits while he folded several pairs of jeans and put them inside his black suitcase.

By the time we were done, so were Mannix and Ice.

Mannix's suitcase was black like Ares', but newer. Ice's was bright red and covered in images of various superheroes. Somehow, it was exactly the kind of suitcase I'd expect him to have. It was an interesting contrast to my sky blue suitcase, which was covered in stickers from my favourite bands and authors.

It shouted that I was a nerd, but at least I was a cool nerd.

Ares took the handle of my suitcase again and we made our way back down the stairs.

Staff moved around doing various jobs, but no one gave us more than a second glance. They were all used to us by now, coming and going and doing whatever. They probably assumed we were off on some mission for Leo. Judging by one or two of the glances, they hoped we wouldn't come back. The house had been in turmoil since I arrived. Presumably they were looking forward to a return to the peace and quiet of before.

Whatever it was they were thinking, I wasn't going to dwell on it. For the sake of my sanity, I should try not to dwell on what Leo said either. But yeah, grudges.

We stopped at the door that led directly into the garage. I looked back over my shoulder.

It wasn't until we crossed the threshold that my mother appeared from the direction of Leo's office. She froze at the sight of us and frowned. That deepened when she noticed the suitcases arrayed around our feet.

"What in the world is going on?" She addressed the question to me, as though the guys didn't exist. She might wish they didn't, but that was too fucking bad. We belonged to each other and that wasn't going to change, no matter what my mother thought about it.

"I thought we'd give you and Leo some space," I said lightly. "You are still newlyweds. You should be enjoying the honeymoon period without a bunch of twenty-somethings hanging around, complicating things."

"Even if those twenty-somethings are awesome," Ice said.

She shot him half a glance. She couldn't even spare a full glance before her attention returned to me.

"You don't have to leave," she said. "This is your home. Yours and Mannix's." No one missed the double meaning in those words. It wasn't Ares's or Ice's home. Maybe she'd hoped all of the suitcases were theirs. If that was what she hoped, then she'd be shit out of luck.

"Are you and Leo planning to leave?" I said coolly.

It took a moment for her to realise what I was asking.

When my words sank in, she laughed as though I said something hilarious. "I didn't mean that you could stay because we were going. Let's sit down and have a talk and work things out."

"I'm leaving, Mum," I said simply. "It's time for me to live my life."

"Leo didn't mean anything by what he said." She started to look upset, annoyed. "Don't let one little slip of the tongue come between us all. I'm sure Mannix would prefer to stay here, with his father." She looked at him beseechingly. *Now* she admitted he existed.

"I go wherever Kennedy goes," Mannix said. "We all need a breather from each other."

"It's dangerous out there." Her gaze took us in, one after the other, clearly hoping someone would be on her side. And maybe slightly accusing, like it was the guys who talked me into leaving, not the other way around.

"We'll protect Kennedy," Ares said.

"We'll protect each other," Ice added.

"We should go," Mannix said. He jerked his head toward the car. Once the decision was made, he was impatient to get out of the place.

Mum was wrong, these guys weren't trouble, they were just impetuous. All of them jumped in with two feet, whether they could see where they'd land or not.

Mum put a hand out towards him, but stopped short of touching him. "Wait. Your father—"

"Made his choice," Mannix finished for her. "I hope you two are happy together. We'll be in touch when we get a chance." His expression silently added, 'if we can be bothered.'

"Maybe you should talk to him before we go," I said tentatively. The last thing I wanted to do was come between father and son. Whatever Leo thought about me, was between him and me, not him and Mannix.

Mannix shrugged. "He'll know how to find me if he needs to." He nodded and waved us toward his SUV.

Mum made a noise of frustration and dropped her hand to her side.

"I only did the things I did because I love you." She sounded so defeated, but she answered the question. If she had to choose between me and Leo, she'd choose Leo. Exactly as I expected her to.

I stopped before I climbed into the SUV and walked back to her. I gave her a quick hug and a kiss on the cheek.

"I love you too. I just need some space, that's all. Do me a favour and stay safe. If it's dangerous for me, it might be dangerous for you too."

If Bell was the monster they made him out to be, he might go after her. Although, I remembered the catch in his voice when he spoke of her on the phone. Whatever happened in the meantime, I suspected he really had loved her.

She hugged me back and stood with her shoulder leaning against the door frame. "Call me and let me know you're okay. And if you need anything, you know where to find me too."

I caught a hint of tears before she turned away and shut the door. For a moment, I thought twice about leaving, but then Ice patted the seat beside him and I hopped into the SUV and let the door close behind me with a clunk.

"Are you all right?" Ice asked softly.

I managed a smile. "I will be. Let's get the hell out of here."

"Yes ma'am." Mannix grinned over his shoulder, started the SUV and hit the button to roll the garage door up and out of the way.

"First stop, anywhere but here."

CHAPTER 19
KENNEDY

If I thought it was conflicted before, it was nothing to how I was now.

It was as though someone opened the lid on a thousand piece jigsaw puzzle, and threw the box, and all the pieces up in the air. And then took all the edge pieces to make it harder to put the puzzle back together.

I stared out the window of the apartment Mannix took us to, without seeing anything. We were right on the top floor, with a view over the city and the bay.

I barely noticed. I was too busy trying to sort through thoughts that rushed through my brain like a waterfall. They kept coming, but when I tried to catch them and work through them, they slipped away, pushed by the pressure of another. It left me gasping for breath. And maybe some alcohol.

"I don't know who to believe any more." My breath left mist on the window. It lingered for a few seconds before it dissipated. It perfectly summed up my life lately. Nothing seemed permanent. Nothing but my guys.

"You can believe us." Mannix stepped up behind me and wrapped his arms around me. "None of us would ever lie to you or try to use you."

I leaned back into him, comforted by the warmth of his rock hard body. "I know you wouldn't. You three are amazing. It's everyone else that sucks."

He chuckled, the sound coming from deep in his throat. "Yeah, I figured that out years ago. That's one of the reasons we were so hard on you when we first met you. The guys and I have been a team for a long time. We were all scared that letting you in would change that. Ruin it. What if you only wanted one of us and you split us up? We relied on each other for so long, we didn't want that to stop. You see it all the time. Guy meets girl. Guy stops giving a shit about his guy friends."

"But that wasn't how it went," I said softly.

"No," he agreed. "You fit in with us like…"

"A missing piece of the puzzle?" I asked, the analogy fresh in my brain from my thoughts of only a few minutes ago.

"I was going to say a slice of pizza, but that works too." He chuckled again.

I laughed softly. "I love puzzles, but I prefer pizza."

"Me too," he agreed. "I'm sorry about what my dad said. He can be a stubborn asshole sometimes. I guess that skipped a generation."

I snorted a laugh. "Yeah, you're nothing like him whatsoever." Only a whole lot, but not in the ways that mattered. Mannix's heart was a hundred times bigger than Leo's.

"I'd never treat you like shit." He pressed his cheek against mine, stubble grazing over my skin. "I don't care where you came from, as long as we're not biological brother and sister."

I grimaced, remembering Ice's amusement at that thought.

"I don't think we have to worry on that score. The only chance of that happening would be if Samuel Bell was your father and you look too much like Leo for that to be possible."

"Thank fuck for that," he said.

"What do you believe?" I asked. "About all of this, I mean. The things Bell said versus the things Mum and Leo said."

"Fucked if I know," he admitted. "I think things between your mother and Bell probably fall approximately in the middle of both stories. She went after him for his money and broke his heart. She might've cared about him too. It sounds like they had a bunch of shit working against them, and they let it split them up. I get taking money to take care of you. I mean, you take care of people you love, don't you?"

His tone was suddenly husky as emotion crept in.

"Yeah, you do," I whispered.

"I love you," he said in my ear.

My heart skipped a couple of beats then did a cartwheel or two. "I love you too. For the record, it wouldn't matter how much money Leo offered me. I couldn't stay away from any of you. I wouldn't."

"Hell no you wouldn't," he growled. "We wouldn't let you. We'd hunt you down to the end of the earth if we had to and bring you back."

Ice's words from that night so long ago popped back into my mind.

"I think, sooner or later I will find you. You'll come to me and then we'll deal with you. I'm going to enjoy knowing you'll spend every day wondering if this will be the day when I catch my prey. If this will be the day when you end up in my trap. If this is the day I make you mine. I'm going to enjoy making you squeal, little mouse."

Where once the memory of those words filled me with fear, now they made me shiver with excitement. He'd made me squeal many times since then, always in a good way.

"I know you would," I said finally. "If I ever end up at the end of the earth, it's not because I ran away."

"Of course not," he agreed. "Why would my princess run away from this? " He pressed his semi-erect cock into my hip.

"I can't think of a single reason." I wriggled my hip against him until he groaned. "Who owns this place anyway?"

"Don't change the subject," he growled. He turned me around and cupped my cheeks with his hands. "But because I know you won't give up until you get an answer, I do. I bought the place about a year ago, for those times I needed to get away from my father. Or if I didn't want anyone to know I was in town."

I looked up at him. "You and the guys were here that night? After what happened with Eric during the masked ball? So if anyone found him and tried to trace it to you, Leo could claim you weren't in Dusk Bay."

He tilted his head slightly. "Exactly. We came back here to wash his blood off us. We talked about the little mouse who saw us, as Ice kept saying. He said he smelled a woman, and that you'd find us. If he was anyone else, I would have gone after you that night. I would have hunted you down. But Ice...he was adamant, and you know how he can be."

"He was right, I did find you," I said softly. Not long ago, the thought of them washing that man's blood away would have freaked me out. Now, it was kinda hot.

"Yep." Mannix smiled. "You turned up right under our noses." He glanced down for a moment, then back up again. "I'm sorry we scared you that night. If we had any idea you were there..."

"What would you have done?" I asked.

He smiled softly. "I would have taken you back into the ball and made you spend the rest of the night dancing with me. By the end of the night, you would have been mine."

"I'm yours anyway," I whispered.

I admit, that all sounded a lot more romantic than the way the night actually went. I would have enjoyed dancing with him, and letting him try to win me over. I might even have allowed him to succeed.

How different things might have been from the very start. Easier in some ways, but less interesting in others. Not to mention, if I never found those masks, or never saw them in the first place, I might still be in the dark about who the guys really were.

He brushed his knuckle over my cheek. "Yes, you are. Body, mind and heart, all belong to me. To us. And every bit of us belongs to you."

I smiled softly. I liked the sound of that.

"It's funny how things work out. If you asked me that night where I'd end up, I never would have guessed it would be here. With you three. The mysterious, masked men who cut a man's throat in the forest." Yeah, no one would have predicted any of that. What would I have done if they had?

Oh right, probably hop on the first train out of Dusk Bay and never look back. Thank fuck that wasn't how it turned out.

"When you put it that way, it sounds romantic." He smiled lopsidedly. "Like something out of a novel."

"A dark romance maybe," I said with a slight laugh.

"That's the best kind." He grinned. He brushed his lips over mine.

A thought occurred to me and I had to give it voice in spite of not wanting to know the answer. Not wanting to break the mood of the moment.

"Is Leo going to be pissed off with you for leaving?" I asked. "I don't want to cause any trouble between you and him."

I seemed to be good at that lately, getting between him and his father, between my mother and Leo. Would I be in the middle of Bell and my sisters too? I couldn't imagine a universe where Lila would ever want to acknowledge my existence, much less show me any sisterly affection. Honestly, the feeling was mutual, but still…

"If there's any trouble between me and him, it's because he caused it," Mannix said firmly. "He knows how I feel about you. He must have known any suggestion he made that he couldn't trust you wouldn't go down very well. Not with your mother and sure as fuck not with me." He sucked in an irritated breath. "I'll talk to him when I get a chance."

"Not if it's going to cause any trouble." I looked at him, silently pleading him not to do anything rash. "I'm sure he didn't mean anything by it. Can we let it go? Confronting him could make everything a hundred times worse."

I didn't know what someone like Leo would do to his son as punishment for pissing him off, but I could take a few guesses. Whatever it was, it wouldn't be pleasant.

"Don't worry about me," Mannix said dismissively. "I can stick up for myself." He sounded like he was very certain he was invincible. He wasn't and that was what terrified me. At the end of the day, we were all just regular people.

Okay, maybe not regular, but none of us was immortal and I didn't want to lose a single one of my guys.

"I know you can," I told him. "I don't want anything to happen to you. Is that so bad?"

"Nothing is going to happen to me," he assured me. He curled his fingers in my hair, pulled me to him and slammed his mouth onto mine in a fierce, possessive kiss.

Whether his plan was to shut me up or make me forget the conversation, it worked. The jumble of thoughts disappeared from my brain like steam. It might have manifested as condensation, because I was suddenly very, very wet.

He slipped his hands down my ass and lifted me up until I wound my legs around his waist. He turned us around and pressed my back against the window.

"Princess," he murmured between kisses. "I'll never stop wanting you." One hand held me in place while the other slid up my shirt and across my flat belly.

"Same with you," I said breathlessly. I'd come a long way from the virgin the guys first met. Now I couldn't get enough of any of them. I couldn't imagine a time when a touch, a whisper, a kiss wouldn't make me wet. These three guys drove me wild and I loved it. I loved them.

He tugged down the front of my bra and pinched my nipple.

It was hard enough to hurt, but in a breathless voice, I said, "Yes. Just like that." It felt so incredibly good. Everything he did felt good, but I was in the mood for something extra, something rougher. I wanted to feel him everywhere.

He pinched again, harder this time.

I moaned. If he wasn't careful, I was going to come against his stomach, with layers of clothes between us. I wanted him buried deep inside me, his cock filling my pussy to the brim.

"Fuck." Ice spoke suddenly from behind Mannix.

"You can have your turn later," Mannix muttered. "Kennedy and I are—"

"I'll take my turn later, but that's not the problem right now," Ice said, his voice higher than usual. Frantic enough to make me look up and over at him.

His eyes were on the window.

"What?" Mannix snapped.

"Something out there is on fire," Ice said. "And it looks like exactly where the gym is."

CHAPTER 20

KENNEDY

"Fucking hell."

By the time we arrived at the gym, the building was well and truly ablaze. Black smoke poured out the roof. Flames licked the sky. The heat was so intense, we couldn't have gotten within a block of the place, even if the police weren't keeping people out.

The air was already thick, hot and acrid. My eyes stung and watered from the smoke. The smell was going to cling to my nostrils for days. The sight—that would live with me forever.

"It's toast." I brushed tears off my cheeks.

Two fire trucks were parked outside, their crews hosing the building as best they could. At this point, all they could hope to was to stop the fire from spreading.

Of all the things that happened in the last few weeks, this made me feel the most defeated. I could make up with my mother, and get over all the things that were said and done. I could deal with what I'd said and done. But this… This was different. This was personal.

More than that, it was a loss for all the kids who enjoyed using the gym. They'd all be devastated.

I was devastated.

"Anyone want to take the bet that this wasn't an accident?" Ares asked. His tone held no hint of amusement, only anger that simmered like mine. The barely contained urge to swear loud and long, and maybe punch something.

No one answered him.

Not one of us thought for a minute this was anything but deliberate. Someone had come along and, just like that, set my business on fire.

The worst thing about it? The seemingly ever-growing list of people who might have done it.

No, the worst thing was the way the community relied on the gym. The way the kids did. Everything inside it was replaceable, but that would take time. Time these kids would be missing out. It was unfair to me, but it was even more unfair to them. None of them did anything wrong.

Ice slipped an arm around me and pulled me to him. "I'm sorry. This sucks, big time. We'll figure out who did this and make them pay for it. I don't mean with money."

That earned him a faint smile. "I didn't think you meant money. Can I get first dibs on the pliers?"

How slowly could I tear out a toenail? How much could I make it hurt?

I realised I was digging my fingernails into the palms of my hands and forced myself to relax slightly. Any more pressure and I'd make myself bleed. It wasn't my blood I wanted on my hands right now. I wanted whoever did this to suffer. I wanted them to cry and feel defeated like the cowards they were.

They fucked with me. I could fuck back.

"I've got something a lot more fun than those." He grinned. "I've got this—" He stopped talking when a couple of police officers walked past. He watched them, then mouthed, "I'll tell you later."

I nodded. This definitely wasn't the time or the place for talking about torture devices.

I admit though, he piqued my curiosity. What could be worse than I already saw? Was it worse than using a nail to put out someone's eye? Because that was literally the worst thing I could think of right now.

I had a pretty good imagination, but my knowledge of torture devices was lacking. A shortfall Ice was doing his best to rectify. He was very generous in sharing his favourite hobby, and work, with me. He was lucky he could do something he loved, and got paid for it. He was the poster child for job satisfaction. And it was much safer for him to be doing that than running around being a serial killer, or whatever else he'd have been doing if this life hadn't found him.

"I should let my mother know I wasn't inside," I said. So we didn't part on the best of terms, she'd still like to know I wasn't dead.

Right?

Honestly, I could use a hug from her right about now. After all that went down, she was still my mother. She loved me and I loved her.

In spite of that, I couldn't bring myself to call her. When I pulled my phone from my pocket, I tapped out a brief but concise text message and pressed send. I watched the screen until she read it, then ignored the phone when it rang. I'd talk to her later.

The phone stopped ringing, then started again a moment later. She tried a couple more times, then apparently gave up.

Finally, she sent me a message that read, "Glad you're okay, sweetheart. Call me." That was it. Short and to the point. At least she wasn't worried about me.

I sighed and responded with a thumbs up emoji, in spite of feeling very thumbs down right now. And a whole lot of crying emojis.

On the outside, my eyes were more or less dry, but on the inside I was struggling to hold it together. If it wasn't for the guys, I probably would have lost it. It wasn't every day you literally saw something you loved go up in smoke.

Zero stars out of ten. Would not recommend. I wouldn't even wish it on my worst enemy. Whoever that was right now. Pick one. Bell, Leo, Lila… Hell, I didn't have a clue anymore.

"I guess it wasn't her then," Ice said. "People who do shit like this don't usually try three or four times to contact you."

It hadn't occurred to me my mother was involved in some way, but I was happy to follow his reasoning. If she did this, she wouldn't have responded so quickly. Those might be thin straws I clutched at, but I gripped on tight for dear life.

"I hate to say this," Ares started, "but Ice is right. Whoever did this is probably somewhere close by, watching our reaction." He looked around, then stuck his middle finger in the air. "Just in case."

Ice grinned and did the same.

Mannix rolled his eyes and shook his head at them.

"That only leaves a bunch of other people." I sighed. "Bell. My biological younger sisters. Fuck only knows who else at this point."

"You have more enemies than I do," Ice said admiringly. "Assuming they are enemies, that is. And assuming this is about you."

Mannix nodded his agreement. "The assholes could be trying to get back at us for something we did. The fire could have started in the gym we're rebuilding, not the gymnastics. I hate to brag, but I have an enemy or two." He actually looked proud of the fact, like he flexed mentally.

Mobster men.

Okay, men in general, but these ones in particular. They had absolutely no shame whatsoever. It was one of the things I loved the most about all of them. They lived each day as it came, right on the edge. It was exciting, apart from shit like this.

"More like three or four," Ares said with a grunt. "Just off the top of my head, I can think of that many people who hate your guts. Give me a couple of secs and I'll think up a few more."

"Thanks," Mannix said sarcastically. "Love you too, bro."

Ares rolled his eyes. "I didn't say I'm one of them, I'm just saying you have enemies, that's all. So do I. We share most of the fuckers."

"It's nice of you to argue over who is more disliked than whom to make me feel better," I started, "but I have a feeling when all the ash has settled, they'll find the fire started in the existing space. Undoubtedly with some kind of accelerant. The security cameras will be toast too, but they probably fucked with the feed anyway."

When this was over, I was going to sit down and invent a better security system. One that couldn't be turned off whenever people felt like it. I was getting really tired of people messing with my stuff. Maybe the guys would help me rig one up that would shoot lasers at anyone who tried to fuck with it.

Yeah, there's that holding grudges thing again. Whatever, it was justified.

"You know what the ironic thing is?" Ice asked. "That people don't hate me. They think I'm the goofy sidekick to these two." He nodded towards Mannix and Ares. "But in a way, I'm more dangerous than both of them put together."

He paused again when the police walked past the other way.

"That is ironic," I said once the police were out of earshot. Almost as ironic as the fact people apparently hated me, when I'd spent most of my life studying hard and trying to do the right thing. Look where that got me. Three hot boyfriends and an inferno.

My life was one long moment of fucked up, crazy shit. Topped with a bunch of orgasms. Talk about conflicting.

My phone rang again.

I considered ignoring it, but when I glanced at the screen. I recognised the number.

I looked up at Mannix. He didn't need to ask, my expression told him everything he needed to know.

"Answer it." His tone was decisive, but he was clearly not happy about it.

With the crowds gathered around, and the police moving back and forth, to contain the gathering crowds, I decided it was better not to put the call on speaker phone.

I pressed the screen to accept and held it to my ear.

"Hello," I said warily.

"Kennedy," Bell said, his voice faint over the sound around me. "Are you all right?"

I slipped out from under Ice's arm and walked a few steps away so I could hear better. "I'm fine. Why?"

He was silent for a moment. I almost heard his eyes rolling.

"You think I wouldn't hear about an inferno at my daughter's business?" he asked. “I probably knew before the fire trucks were called.”

"Did you start it?" I asked bluntly. That would explain why he knew before anyone else.

His response was immediate and firm. "No. I had nothing to do with it. If anyone who worked for me did, they might as well have locked themselves inside the gym. Their lives won't be worth shit."

"How am I supposed to believe you?" I wanted to, if only to cross someone off my list. If only because he seemed committed to convincing me he was in my corner. Maybe Leo was right and I was naïve, but I was getting tired of hating people, and being angry and scared.

"What would I have to gain by doing that?" he asked.

"Um, you'd upset me, get back at me for what I tried to do to you, set my business back by months, if not years." If I decided to rebuild, that was. "With the added bonus of attacking the guys' gym they're building next door." There was probably more, but that was all I could think of right now.

"All good points," he said. "But I have no desire to do any of those things. If I came after those boys, I'd do it more directly than this. Arson is so…tacky. In addition, I own several businesses on the street. Putting them at risk wouldn't be very smart, would it?"

"That depends on what you want to achieve," I said. "Some people would consider it collateral damage. Those businesses are insured, aren't they?"

"Of course they are, but I assure you, it wasn't me. Nor was it anyone acting under my orders. Whoever did it, they waited until my people left before they acted. They were watching, presumably hoping to pin this on me. Or at least, to avoid having any witnesses."

The problem was, he made too much sense. He was good at doing that.

"If it wasn't you, then who was it?" I asked. "One of my delightful sisters?"

"It better not be," he growled. "They should be at school right now." His tone suggested if they weren't, they could also lock themselves in my gym for all their lives would be worth after this.

I almost felt sorry for them. Almost.

Even if he wasn't a monster, he was clearly not an easy man to live with. Maybe I was better off not growing up with him in my life. I'd never know the answer to that.

"I'm running out of people to blame," I said. "If you have any ideas, or suggestions, I'm listening. And don't suggest any of the guys did this. They wouldn't do it and, anyway, I was with them."

He actually chuckled. "If they did, I'd want front row tickets to whatever you did to them in retribution. I know some people refer to them as the Devils of Dusk Bay, but I doubt anyone has seen anything compared to a pissed off Bell woman."

"If this is a redhead thing—" I was really tired of people suggesting we had no soul or had horrible tempers or whatever. My hair colour didn't dictate my personality.

"This is an, 'I can see you're a strong willed, intelligent woman,' thing," he replied. "I suspect we're more alike than you think."

"I have to take your word for it, because I hardly know you," I told him.

"That wasn't my fault," he said quietly. "If I had my way—"

"Do you have any idea who did this?" I interrupted. "Enemy of the family I haven't met yet? Any more siblings I don't know about?"

"You have a stepbrother, although his mother and I aren't together anymore. Zachary wouldn't have done this, but he's also away at school. There's only one more person I can think of. An enemy of the family you *have* met."

I listened as he continued to speak. My blood turned colder and colder.

CHAPTER 21

KENNEDY

"Are you sure about this?" I put a hand on Mannix's rock hard bicep.

"Yes," he replied curtly. He half closed his eyes and drew a breath in through his nose. He let it out through pursed lips, opened his eyes fully and looked at me. "Sorry, I shouldn't take it out on you."

"You weren't taking it out on me," I said lightly. "You're right to be...disconcerted. Bell said a lot of conflicting things. Potentially, all a bunch of crap."

"Yeah, well, we'll find out, won't we?" He kissed my cheek and gave the other guys a nod.

I laced my fingers through his. Slow, but determined, we walked out of the apartment and climbed into the SUV.

The drive was short, and we did it in silence, each lost in our thoughts. Except Ice, who seemed to be humming the theme song to the movie *The Omen*.

When I looked over my shoulder at him, he grinned.

Of course he was enjoying this. He was probably hoping to get his chance to shine.

That may just happen.

Mannix parked the SUV beside an empty building a couple of blocks from what was left of the gym. While the fire hadn't reached the businesses on either side, both the gymnastics and the construction of the gym were gutted.

We weren't allowed in yet to survey the damage, but according to the authorities, there was nothing left. Apparently their investigation was ongoing. Judging by the expression on the investigator's face, they'd rule the fire as an accident and walk away with however much they were paid to say that.

None of us were fooled.

I briefly wondered how much it would cost for the truth, but decided it wasn't worth it. Besides, they'd likely been threatened with their lives if they admitted it. That was literally a dead-end not worth pursuing. I hated to let it go, but this was Dusk Bay. That was how things here went. Sometimes it worked in our favour, sometimes not.

Mannix unlocked the door and we stepped inside the cavernous space. He hit the light switch. Several lights in the ceiling illuminated the space.

"It's a blank canvas, as they say." He stepped aside to let us enter and looked around, his chin raised. "It should do for what we need."

It should have smelt dank and dusty, unloved and unused. Instead, the smell of lavender and some kind of cleaning agent hung in the air. The more I thought of it, the more I realised I shouldn't be surprised it was fresh. Mannix would have seen to it. We probably missed the cleaning crew by a matter of minutes.

As if he guessed what I was thinking, he said, "The place was full of dust and spiders. I wasn't bringing my woman into this space. Or my bros," he added at the last moment.

"I don't mind a few spiders," I said. In spite of what people said about Australia, it wasn't the wildlife that tried to kill me, it was other people.

"But I appreciate you being thoughtful enough to have it cleaned before we came here." I didn't want him to think I took anything he did for granted. Everything he did, he did for a reason. To take care of us. Being possessive and controlling was his love language.

He smiled smugly. "So, what do you think? Is it the perfect space, or is it the perfect space?"

I laughed at his question and took a minute or two to look around carefully. In spite of the phrasing, I knew he wanted an honest answer. If this wouldn't do, he'd find me another one. And another one. Until he found somewhere that would work for what I needed.

I had to be careful whenever I mentioned anything, in case he went out and got it for me. I mean, I didn't really *need* a private jet, so I kept thoughts like those to myself. Although, it was Mannix. If I had the thought, he'd figure it out. He was nothing if not astute when it came to reading people. All of the guys were. I guessed it came with the territory.

I tilted my chin and looked up. "The ceiling is high enough." I could already picture the silks hanging. Three, maybe four of them. None with dead bodies tangled in the polyester.

One side of the space could work for gymnastics equipment. The other for tumbling, trampolining and various acrobatic skills. A section at the front would be perfect for practising cheerleading. If I could find someone to teach it. Kids could come here to learn a variety of skills and have a great time doing it. I admit it, the thought was exciting.

"Are you sure there's nowhere for a climbing wall?" Ares asked. "Or an indoor pool?"

"We have both of those in the apartment building," I pointed out. None of the guys had stopped their daily exercise routine since moving there. If anything, they were working out more often. I joined them whenever I could. That would be easier since I finished my last uni class. I passed with a high distinction, so all I had to do now was officially graduate. My cybersecurity business would have to wait for a while. I wanted to rebuild the gym first.

"You can never have too many climbing walls or indoor pools," Ice said.

I rolled my eyes at him. "We're not having either of those here. Wherever you guys set up your gym, you can do what you like." I knew they wouldn't really interfere with this. Just like I knew they would let me interfere with their plans if I wanted to. But I wouldn't. I had my baby and was happy to let them have theirs.

Ice pouted playfully, but then grinned. "I love it when you get all bossy like that. It makes me want to ask you to chain me to the ceiling and use my tools on me."

"Be careful what you wish for," I told him.

That just made him grin even more.

We turned as the door rattled and opened.

Leo stepped inside, followed by my mother.

He looked around, appraising the space.

She hurried over to me to give me a hug. "I was worried about you. After what happened to the gym, I was hoping you'd come home. How absolutely terrible all of that was. Leo has been speaking to the fire inspector, trying to get some answers. He said they've been vague at best."

I bet they have, I thought. Funny how that goes.

I forced a smile. "It was a shock. They may never know what happened. I'm assuming there was an electrical fault no one knew about. It might even have started next door, with the construction. There were tons of power tools over there. It only takes one to ignite and boom. The whole thing is alight."

I didn't have to fake the sadness or frustration as I spoke, even though the words were blatantly ridiculous. Not one single person in the room believed it. Mum clearly wanted to, I saw it on her face.

I let her have it. For now. She'd know the truth soon enough.

"So this is going to be your new gym." Leo looked at me with guarded eyes.

I smiled as though nothing bad ever happened between us. "That was what Mannix was thinking, yes. He said he bought the building ages ago, and never quite knew what to do with it. It's bigger than the old space, so I think it'll be perfect. What do you think?" My tone was all dutiful stepdaughter, like I wanted nothing more than to make amends. Like we asked them here to build bridges.

He regarded me for a moment longer, then looked around again. "I'm no expert on gymnastics, but if you say it's a suitable space, I don't see why you shouldn't move forward with the rebuild."

"I was hoping you'd say that," I said sweetly. "I guess the fire wasn't such a bad thing after all."

"Maybe it was an omen," Ice suggested. "The universe telling you to spread your wings."

The smallest flash of irritation crossed Leo's face, but it was so brief I almost missed it. If I wasn't watching him, I wouldn't have noticed.

"Yes," I agreed. "It's like the universe took away something small with one hand and gave me something big with the other. With the added bonus that no one was hurt when the gym went up in flames."

"That's the important thing," Mum agreed. "The place could have been filled with children. Just imagine what could have happened." She shuddered. "What would have happened if you were in there? I could have lost you." She brushed tears off her cheeks.

The hug I gave her was genuine. I needed it as much as she did. It felt good to touch her, smell the rose scent she always wore. When was the last time we really connected like this? Too long.

"You didn't lose me. No one was hurt. We're all fine. Besides, you can't get rid of me that easily."

She leaned her head against my shoulder and I held her while she cried for a minute or two. When her soft, silent sobs finally subsided, she lifted her face and sniffled.

"I'm so sorry I dragged you into everything. Right from the start, I should have stepped away from all of this. We had that money, we could have started a completely new life somewhere else. Anywhere else."

If someone offered her time machine in that exact moment, so she could go back and change the past, I didn't think she'd hesitate. That was one difference between us. I held a grudge, but I didn't hold on to regrets. You couldn't change what happened in the past, no matter how hard you tried. All you could do was move forward and work with the situation whether it was created by you or someone else. And maybe pull out a few toenails here and there.

I suspected Mannix would disagree. Not the could change the past, but that you shouldn't let anyone create situations for you. Whatever happened, wherever he went, he liked to be in the driver's seat. I couldn't imagine a time he'd step back and let anyone else take control. He was alpha through and through. A force of nature. He'd bring the destruction, then make a path through it for the rest of us.

"I have a funny feeling I would have been sucked into it sooner or later." I offered her a small smile. "The universe would have brought me to these guys," I jerked my head toward Mannix, Ice and Ares, "one way or another."

"Damn right it would," Ares said. "Either way we would have hunted you down."

"Even if we had to kidnap you and keep you tied up until we convinced you," Ice said.

Mum gave him a funny look, but smiled. "I'm sure you would do exactly that too. You all seem smitten with my daughter."

"She's the best thing we have," Mannix said. "Her and each other." He gave his father a look. His face was almost expressionless, but there was something burning in the back of his eyes. For a moment there, I almost would have sworn I saw flames dancing in there. Any minute now, they'd shoot out and engulf us all.

"Young love," Leo said sarcastically. "You think the world would end if you broke up. It won't."

"We're not going to break up," Mannix said. "There's something else we want to show you." He gestured towards the back of the space. "Something I know you'll approve of."

Leo looked sceptical, but followed him into the back corner, where the ceiling lights barely reached.

I hooked my arm around Mum's and walked behind the others.

"Like Kennedy said, I bought this building a while ago. I wasn't sure what to do with the space up here, but there's an extensive space below."

I've never seen a smile as dark as the one that graced Mannix's lips at that moment.

He pulled a key out of his pocket and unlocked a door in that back corner.

I half expected it to creak as he opened it, but it moved on silent hinges, opening onto darkness.

Mannix leaned in and clicked the lights on over a set of stairs that led down.

I wasn't sure who looked more nervous, Leo or my mother.

I squeezed her arm. She'd know what this was about soon enough.

Mannix started down the stairs and the rest of us followed.

CHAPTER 22

KENNEDY

This was my first time down here, but the guys told me what to expect. It was still impressive. At least twice the size of Ice's present workroom, but somehow less dank, in spite of also being underground.

Several brand-new sets of chains were bolted to the ceiling, each approximately two metres apart. Brackets for more were set into the wall. Three chairs were screwed into the floor, also two metres apart. Here and there were a bunch of other devices, the uses of which I could only guess at. They looked nasty.

In the centre of the room was what looked like nothing more horrifying than a kitchen island. It was topped with stainless steel and had drawers all around it. A double sink was set into the surface.

"I wanted a stove, but Mannix said no." Ice gave him a sideways look.

Mannix rolled his eyes. "You have that." He nodded towards the wall. Inset into the concrete was what looked like the kind of oven they used in cremations.

"I bet you the first thing that goes in there is pizza," Ares said.

"Now you mention it, that's exactly what I'm using that for." Ice grinned. "Disposing of evidence and cooking pizza. Ares, you're a fucking genius." He slapped Ares on the back.

Ares waved him away. "No shit. Of course I am."

"This is all very interesting," Mum said uncomfortably. "I've never seen…this side of things before."

"You don't know what you're missing, Mum," Ice said cheerfully. "I can call you Mum, right? I mean, you're my girlfriend's mum so—" He shrugged.

She gave him an awkward smile, like she wasn't quite sure where he fit in a space like this. "I suppose that's all right, Isaac."

"If I'm going to call you Mum, then you should call me Ice." He gave her a big hug. After a moment, she hugged him back.

It was the sweetest thing I saw all day.

"This is impressive," Leo said. "But I don't recall giving the authority to make another torture room."

"You didn't," Mannix said coldly. "I did. I wanted you to know I had everything under control when I took over from you."

"That won't be for a long time," Leo said. He eyed the chains nervously.

"Maybe not," Mannix agreed. "But maybe it will be soon." He walked towards his father, his steps slow but deliberate.

Leo backed up. "What do you think you're doing?"

"Good question," Mannix said. "But I have better ones. When did you find out Kennedy was Samuel Bell's daughter?"

Leo's jaw twitched. "When Kennedy told us." He didn't meet Mannix's eyes or mine.

Ice made a noise like a game show buzzer. "Incorrect. Try again."

Leo shot him a venomous look, but quickly returned his gaze to Mannix. "I'm not sure what you're trying to imply here."

"I'm not implying anything," Mannix said. "I'm saying you knew before Kennedy told any of us. I'm saying you're the one who sent Frank Nixon after her. I'm saying a lot more than that, but I'm giving you a chance to defend yourself."

Mum frowned at Leo. "Leo? Did you know?"

He scoffed. "Of course not."

Mannix nodded to Ice and Ares.

Both guys closed in on either side of Leo. Before he could react, they shoved him a handful of steps back to the chains. He writhed, grunted and tried to pull away, but they grabbed his arms, hauled them up and snapped manacles around his wrists.

"What the fuck do you think you're doing?" he growled.

"This." Ice walked over and pressed a button on the wall. The chains started to rise, pulling Leo's hands up higher above his head.

"If you won't tell us the truth voluntarily, then we're going to have to use more drastic measures," Mannix said. His voice was colder than a blizzard. He *was* the blizzard. Anyone caught in his path was fucked. The time for deceit was over.

I would have hated to be at the receiving end of his icy fury.

Mum looked panicked. "Kennedy, I didn't—"

"I know you didn't," I said quickly. "You would never do that to me." I hadn't thought Leo would either, but here we were.

I could see him scrambling, trying to think of what to say and how to get himself out of this. At the same time, he was getting angrier.

"If you think for a minute you can get away with doing this to me, think again. All four of you will pay for this." He shot daggers at Mannix with his eyes. They looked like toothpicks compared to Mannix's expression.

Mannix was pissed off with his father and wasn't going to be intimidated by him. Not anymore.

"Kennedy, did you have dibs on the pliers?" Ice opened a drawer and pulled out a set. He offered them to me but I shook my head.

"Under the circumstances, I think I'll leave it to the experts."

He nodded graciously and stepped away. He approached Leo, opening and closing the pliers as he went.

"Let's start again," Mannix said with an unusual display of patience. "When did you know Samuel Bell was Kennedy's father?"

Leo eyed the pliers, fear creeping onto his face. "I—" His throat bobbed as he swallowed. "I've always known. I was at Brutham Academy with Helen. I knew when she was involved with Sam. I lost track of her for a while, but when I found her again, she had a kid. It didn't take a genius to work out whose it was."

"But you chose not to tell anyone," Mannix said.

Leo's tongue swept over his lips. "I decided to sit on the information until it became useful."

Mannix nodded. "Why did you send Frank Nixon after Kennedy?"

"Leo would never do that," Mum argued. "Kennedy is like a daughter to him. Right, Leo?" She looked as though she wasn't sure what to believe, or who, but she desperately wanted answers.

"He wasn't supposed to hurt her," Leo said, his voice low as though he didn't want to say the words out loud. "He was supposed to scare her."

"He did that," I said. "He said he was sent to kill me. To show you his boss could get to you anytime he wanted to."

"He was told exactly that," Leo confirmed. "That was all he knew to say. People like him, they don't need to know all of the facts. They're there to do what they're told."

"Just a worthless drone to send to their deaths," Ares said coolly, meaningfully.

Leo looked him straight in the eyes and said, "Exactly."

Ares snarled and might have lunged at Leo if Mannix hadn't raised his hand and indicated for him to stay back.

"That's all any of us are to you," Ares said bitterly. "Pawns in your twisted fucking game."

"You're exactly what you want to be," Leo said. "Exactly what you signed up for. Money, power, obedience. Don't pretend it bothers you now."

"I'm not pretending, asshole," Ares snapped. He stepped away, grumbling under his breath.

"You sent someone after my daughter?" Mum looked disbelieving.

"I needed her and the boys to believe Samuel Bell did it," Leo told her. "I needed them so angry they'd go after him. So angry they'd want revenge. Anything less and they wouldn't have been fully committed."

"You set it up so someone would almost kill my child, for the purpose of sending her and her boyfriends to a place that also might have gotten them killed?" Mum's face turned all tiger mother angry.

I thought she might grab the pliers from Ice and use them on her husband herself. Look, I can’t say I’d try to stop her.

"I knew Bell must have known by then that Kennedy was his," Leo said, unflinching. "He would have been watching out for her, so he could tell her himself or whatever fucked up game he decided to play. I wanted the four of them angry enough that they wouldn't listen to him. Or believe him. If they did, it would weaken them and their mission. Put them at risk."

"Like you give a fuck if we're at risk," Ares snarled. "If we died, you wouldn't shed a tear."

"If *you* died I wouldn't," Leo told him. "Except the money I put into your training would be wasted."

"I'm starting to think you're not very nice," Ice said. "You'd be sad if I died, wouldn't you?"

Leo just looked back at him.

It was probably better he didn't answer, since Ice stood with an implement of torture in his hands.

"We're not supposed to be nice," Mannix said. "It's who we are. But we don't screw each other over."

"No, but we do screw each other," Ice said.

Mannix glanced over and nodded to indicate his agreement with that statement.

He walked back and forth in front of Leo a few times before he stopped and said, "What about the fire?"

Mum gasped. "He wouldn't…"

Leo must have known by then how fucked he was, because he didn't hesitate anymore.

"That was directed at Kennedy. From the moment that *bitch* came into our lives, she's turned everything upside down. For a while, I thought we could ride out the storm, but when she made Mannix move out, I was fucking done."

"I didn't make anyone move out," I said coldly. "You made it clear what you thought of me and I left. The guys made up their minds. If there's any kind of gap or rift between you and Mannix, it was there long before I turned up."

I stepped towards him. "It's there because you don't see him as a son. You see him as a chess piece you can move around however you want. And if he gets knocked out of the game—" I shrugged. "No big deal. Right? You just hand everything over to your other son or whoever the fuck else."

For once, my mother didn't tell me to watch my language. She was too busy gaping at Leo like she was staring at a stranger. She might as well have been. He was far from a nice guy. He was every bit the mobster. Dangerous, ruthless, remorseless.

"Did you ever care about me?" she asked softly.

He turned to her. "Of course I did. I do. I love you. I only did what I did for the good of the family. And because I was—"

Mannix interrupted. "If you say because you were following orders, I will have Ice rip off your eyelids. Yeah, there are orders you need to follow, but you have enough autonomy that you don't need to fuck with me or the people I love in order to follow them. You could have told Kennedy who her father was and we would have thought of something else. There was no need for all the bullshit you did to her. None of it."

He stepped away, then moved back again. Every part of him was tightly controlled, from his movements to his expression. He knew exactly what he was doing.

"You know what? I understand why you did what you did. It's how we operate, isn't it? Do whatever you have to do to get what you want and don't let anyone stand in the way." When Leo started to interrupt him he snapped, "Shut up. It's my turn to speak."

He was silent for a minute or two before he continued, "You had a job to do and this was the best way to do it. To convince us. To avoid putting us in a position of vulnerability. To give us the best chance of succeeding."

"Exactly." Leo started to look hopeful. He might just escape this without being tortured. "I was doing what had to be done."

Mannix nodded. "I can respect that. The fire…you just got angry, right? No one was hurt and it turned out well because upstairs is a much better space. So in a way, you did us a favour." His voice was so tight I was surprised it didn't snap in two.

Leo nodded vigourously.

"But you did something unforgivable," Mannix added. "Something unnecessary. Something I don't tolerate, and neither does Ares or Ice. And you did it in front of Ares."

Leo looked confused.

Mannix slipped a hand into his pocket and pulled out a gun.

"You touched Kennedy."

He raised the gun and shot Leo twice in the left side of his chest.

CHAPTER 23

KENNEDY

"You killed Leo Cassani." Caleb's words were delivered as a statement, not a question, but he clearly wanted an answer.

"I did." Mannix met his gaze without wavering or flinching.

I didn't know how he did it. Personally, I wanted to pee my pants. Everything since Mannix shot Leo went by in a blur. The guys disposed of his remains. Mannix immediately contacted Ric DiMarco and told him what he'd done. We ate and slept and existed for two days until we got the call to come here.

The house Daze shared with Ric and Gunnar, and Hilton when he was in town, was big and imposing. Tastefully decorated, of course, and opulent, but the presence of Caleb and his older brother Reuben made being here nothing less than intimidating as fuck.

All of them reclined in armchairs, looking like judge, jury and executioners, even Daze, who greeted me like an old friend.

So far, Reuben hadn't said a word. He merely sat and watched the proceedings, and expression of mild irritation on his face. He was handsome, for someone twice my age, and he had that air about him. The one that suggested if he told a woman to get on her knees, she'd do it without hesitation. And he knew it.

"Why?" Caleb demanded.

In the same monotone voice, Mannix said, "Because he wasn't acting in the best interests of our family or the organisation."

My gaze wandered across the room and settled on Gunnar, Mannix's older brother.

He looked troubled, and grieving. Conflicted at the same time. Leo was his father, but he clearly wanted to believe Mannix wouldn't have killed him if he had a choice. That was better than him immediately assuming Mannix was in the wrong and baying for his blood. Daze had a hand on his knee, suggesting they'd had this conversation at least once in the last couple of days. Daisy Lasalle seemed like the kind of person who would encourage him to hear his brother out, for both their sakes.

"Explain," Caleb said.

Mannix did, in as few words possible. He described how Leo sent Frank Nixon after me and set fire to the gym. He didn't mention killing Leo because he touched me, or any bitterness for sending us after Bell. We'd discussed all of this and agreed none of that mattered. Caleb would only want to hear how Leo wasn't acting in his and Reuben's interests.

Caleb looked more and more annoyed as Mannix spoke.

"Does Leo's widow want retribution?" Caleb asked.

It was me who answered that question. "No. My mother agrees what Leo did was unforgivable and is grateful his execution was quick." She had a lot more to say than that, and a bunch of tears, but that was the gist of it.

In the end, she chose me over Leo.

"Gunnar Cassani, you've previously said you don't want to take over your father's interests." Caleb turned to Mannix's brother.

Gunnar shrugged one shoulder, but shook his head. "I have enough responsibility as it is. I'm happy to let Mannix have it. Dad's will was more than generous to me."

Caleb glanced over to Reuben, who nodded.

"All right then. Mannix Cassani, you can take your father's place in the organisation. I expect you understand your responsibilities and that we expect you to always behave and act in the best interests of the organisation."

Caleb fixed him with an intense expression that held an underlying threat no one missed. If Mannix put a toe out of line, especially in the next couple of years, they wouldn't hesitate to take him out.

"I always have and I always will," Mannix stated.

Caleb nodded. "Then there's one more order of business. The biological paternity of Kennedy Caroline Knight."

I winced. Did he have to bring my middle name into it?

We'd already rehearsed this. I lifted my chin. "My loyalty is with Mannix and this organisation. However, I'd like permission to maintain contact with Samuel Bell, in the capacity of an intermediary between the two families. We believe I might be able to intercede before any further blood is shed on either side."

Neither Caleb nor Reuben tried to hide their scepticism, but Reuben finally spoke.

"Under the condition all interactions are held with full transparency. If you're seen to act outside our interests, steps will be taken to remove you from the situation."

That was the most diplomatic way I'd ever heard anyone say they were going to kill someone else. I wondered if either Brantley brother ever let their hair down, or did they leave that to their youngest brothers?

"I understand," I said finally. "I don't foresee seeing, or speaking to, him without one of my guys present. If not all of them."

Reuben nodded. "See you don't." He stood and left the room without another word.

Caleb nodded to Ric and Hilton and did the same.

It wasn't until then that the air in the room relaxed, almost visibly.

Daze hopped up from her chair and came over to give me a hug. "I'm so glad that turned out okay. I really hate having to ask the staff to clean blood off the hardwood."

I wasn't sure if she was joking or not, but I hugged her back. "Did you think they'd execute us for what happened to Leo?"

"It's impossible to tell," she admitted. "Some days they'll order someone killed, just because they're in a bad mood. Fortunately, you caught them both on a good day."

I stared at her for a moment. "If that was them in a good mood, I'd hate to see them in a bad mood."

She laughed. "Right? They aren't the friendliest men at the best of times."

Hilton gave her a look, complete with arched eyebrow, as though she said something treasonous, which she probably had.

She responded by being unruffled and blew him a kiss. "He can't say it's not true." They clearly adored each other.

I suspected she got away with a lot. I wanted to be her when I grew up. I had three adoring guys, but none of us were in the position to say whatever we thought, or do exactly whatever we wanted. Not yet.

Although, now we were only a step below her and her guys. I knew Mannix intended to do everything he could to stay there. We had power, influence and all of Leo's assets behind us. We were as close to untouchable as people got. It would be very easy to get intoxicated on all of it.

Daze took my arm and led me aside. "Is your mother really okay? I have a daughter myself and if any of my guys sent someone after her, he'd be lucky to get the quick death Leo got. In fact, I'd happily hand him over to Ice and tell him to make sure he lives for as long as possible. And as horribly as Ice can make his last days. No one messes with my kid."

I believed every word she said. It didn't matter how much she adored Hilton, Ric and Gunnar, they'd pay dearly if they did what Leo had.

"I'm not sure if I'd say she's okay," I said slowly. "She genuinely cared about Leo. She's still in shock over everything." For someone who had been embedded in this life since she was my age, seeing Leo shot in front of her was still incredibly difficult and confronting.

As for me, it replaced masks and dark rooms in my dreams. Dreams that weren't as bad as the nightmares. My subconscious must have known it was the only way that day was going to end. Known and accepted it.

Part of me wanted to feel bad, but as the guys took Leo out of the chains and hefted him into the hot oven in the wall, all I felt was relief.

He got what was coming to him and Bell pointing the finger at him turned out to be right.

Until Leo admitted what he did, I wasn't sure chaining him in Ice's new workroom was the right thing to do. If Bell was wrong and Leo was innocent, we might well be the dead ones now. Leo wouldn't have forgiven us for our assumption or restraining him the way we had.

We'd rolled the dice and thank fuck the gamble paid off. We could have paid dearly. Leo's attitude to me tipped me off that maybe he did the things Bell suggested he did. None of the guys took much convincing. That was how they lived. Whatever they did, they were all in.

"We're taking good care of her," I added. "All of the guys adore her. She lost her husband, but she gained three sons." Ice, in particular, adored her. He followed her around the apartment, making sure she had fresh coffee and warm slippers. He even went out and bought her several new pairs of bed socks.

I told him it wouldn't be winter for another few months, but he shrugged it off and grinned in true Ice fashion.

"It's never too early to get ready for winter. And look, this pair has ducks all over them. I couldn't resist. Don't worry, I bought things for you too. Lacy things. I would have brought some for Mum too, but according to Ares, that would be weird." He shrugged.

He would never be anyone but his own, unique self, and we all loved him for it.

"That's awesome." Daze smiled. "Nova loves having three fathers. If one says no, she goes running to another one of them. Although, they don't tell her no very often. She has them all wrapped firmly around her little finger." She held up her pinky.

I laughed. I bet if the guys and I ever had children, the same thing would happen. They'd have an abundance of love and attention. What more could anyone want for a kid?

Children were a long way off for me, if we ever had them at all. Right now, I had enough to deal with without bringing a little human into the world.

"I should go before Reuben and Caleb upset the staff." Daze made a face and hurried away after I nodded.

I wondered if upsetting the staff meant leaving them in tears, or on their knees. Maybe both.

"We did it." Mannix stepped up behind me and slipped his arms around me. Ice and Ares did the same, until we were all enveloped in a group hug.

"Yes, we did," I agreed. "We get to live another day or two."

Mannix chuckled. "I'm the head of my family, just like it was always supposed to be. And I have my girlfriend, my boyfriend and my bro."

"Boyfriend," Ice echoed. "I like the sound of that."

"I like the sound of bro," Ares said softly.

He'd been quieter for the last couple of days. He'd seen Leo as a kind of father figure. Realising Leo didn't see him as any kind of son clearly stung. He didn't break down and cry like my mother had, but I caught him several times looking out the window, his lips pressed together so tight they were almost white. I could almost forgive the things Leo did to me, but not this. Ares was a self-proclaimed badass motherfucker. Leo turning on him was not all right. It wasn't the way you treated someone who looked up to you.

"And I have three boyfriends," I said.

"I really, really like the sound of that," Ares said.

I looked him in the eye and said, "You'll always have us."

He smiled. "Fuck yeah I will. I'm not letting any of you go."

"I love all of you," I said.

"We love you too." Ice pressed his forehead to mine.

"Yes we do," Mannix agreed. "And the four of us have some celebrating to do."

CHAPTER 24

KENNEDY

"We thought there was something you should deal with first." Ares held a black cotton drawstring bag in his hand.

I sat on the edge of the couch and eyed him doubtfully.

"Who is 'we'?"

"All of us." He flicked a finger in the direction of Mannix and Ice. "But it was my idea."

"If this goes badly, it was definitely your idea," Mannix agreed.

Ares flipped him off.

"We were all in on it." Ice gave both of them a look, then turned his gaze to me. "If it goes badly, it's the fault of all of us."

"Please tell me there's not a disembodied head in there." I grimaced. The bag was big enough.

The guys shared a glance.

"Not a head, no," Ares said slowly.

"Hunter and Parker Brantley's cocks?" I guessed. Honestly, I didn't want those either.

"Maybe you should just show her," Ice suggested.

"Yes, maybe you should just show me," I agreed.

Ares teased the bag open. He put his hand inside and pulled something out.

My heart stopped for a second or two.

"I told you this was a bad idea," Mannix said.

"No," I said quickly. "It's okay." I reached for the mask. It wasn't the one Mannix wore the night they killed Eric Parcell, but I recognised it anyway.

I looked up at Ares. "This was yours?" It was dark purple, with swirls on the forehead and the cheeks. Understated, like its wearer.

"Yeah." Ares shrugged. "I figured if you saw them up close and personal, they wouldn't be so freaky."

"Facing my fears and stuff like that." I turned the mask around in my hands. In this context, it was nothing but plastic, with elastic to hold it in place. Nothing scary at all, except some residual unease about that night. That was what this was about. Putting that unease to rest, once and for all.

"Exactly," Ares said. "You're not scared of much, but these masks made you run away once. I didn't want you to find them again and take off."

I glanced up at him and smiled. "I wouldn't, but I appreciate you doing this for me. Would you put it on?" I handed it back to him.

"Whatever my Firecracker wants." He placed the bag on the coffee table and pulled the mask down over his face. It sat just above his mouth, leaving his grin exposed. "See, totally harmless."

"Yes, you are," Mannix teased.

Ares rolled his eyes at him. He snagged the bag back up and dove back in again. He pulled out another mask.

This one was gold and black, and looked like some kind of cat.

"Ice's." Ares handed it to him.

Ice pulled it on and gave me a rakish smile. "Well hello there, little mouse."

It wasn't until then I realised the irony of his mask. Cat and mouse. Where once I would have been freaked out, now I laughed softly.

"Should I pour you a saucer of milk?"

He grinned. "I'd prefer cream." He slid over to Mannix and ran a hand over the front of his jeans.

"Soon, pussy," Mannix told him. He held out his hand. Ares pulled out his mask and handed it to him. He turned to me and pulled it over his face.

This one was definitely the creepiest one of all. Not just because I saw it that night, or on my mother's wedding day, but because it covered his mouth with a very Mannix-like sneer. It reminded me of when we first met. He'd looked at me like he hated me on sight. The feeling was more or less mutual at the time.

Now, I didn't hate him and I wasn't afraid of the mask. Or any of them.

"Better, Princess?" Mannix asked.

"Much better," I agreed. When he reached to take it off, I put out a hand to stop him.

"Can you leave it on?" I looked at the other two. "You too. Just for a little while."

Mannix put a hand on the back of my head and drew me closer to whisper in my ear. "Are you saying you want us to fuck you while we're wearing these?"

I drew my lower lip in between my teeth and thought while I let it slide loose. "Would that be weird? Because I think it would be kinda hot." They killed a man in these masks. They made the guys look sinister, dangerous. Sexy.

"Whatever my Princess wants, my Princess gets," Mannix said. He reached down to tug my t-shirt up and over my head. My bra quickly followed.

I grabbed the hem of his shirt and yanked. He slid his arms out and placed his hands over his face to hold the mask in place while I pulled it off the rest of the way.

"You know what we should have done." Ice sat beside me on the couch and started to trace circles around my nipples with his fingertip. "We should all have masks that cover all of our faces. Then we could swap them and not know who was who. Of course, then my mouth would be covered." He leaned in to lick one of my stiff peaks.

"We could always put a blindfold on Kennedy," Ares suggested.

"Definitely," Mannix agreed. "But not today. If she wants to see us like this, then that's how it will be." He grabbed my knees and yanked me forward until I flopped down onto my back.

Ares grabbed my feet and held them up to make it easier for Mannix to pull off my shorts and panties. Smiling under the purple mask, he bent my knees and spread my legs wide, opening me out for them all to see.

"Shame your mouth is covered," he said to Mannix. He all but shoved him aside and dove his face down between my legs.

Mannix grunted and undid his jeans before he grabbed the back of Ice's head and guided him to his already erect cock.

Ice eagerly opened his mouth and let Mannix slide his cock between his lips.

Fuck, that was hot every time.

I grabbed one of Ice's thighs and pulled him over closer. I turned my head and put my own mouth on his cock. He responded with I sounded like a pleased grunt and twisted a little further so I could take him in deeper.

The same time, Ares teased my clit with his tongue, sometimes using only slight pressure, sometimes using a lot. Apparently he was inspired by Mannix edging me the other night. Pussy tease.

Instead of arguing or getting frustrated, I focused on sucking and licking, and tracing lines and circles around Ice's magic cross while Ares pushed me closer to the edge, then pulled me back again a handful of times.

Finally, he licked with more persistence. He slipped his fingers inside me and hooked them around to work me inside and out.

"Come for us," Mannix said. He was the only one who didn't have his mouth full. Maybe having it covered wasn't so bad after all, he could boss us around.

I hung on to Ice's cock with one hand while I took my mouth off him and came. I arched my back, lifting up off the couch. My face tilted back, I shouted toward the ceiling.

Ice grunted in response. His cock throbbed in my fingers before he came, spilling himself down my cheek and chest. Strings of pearly cum decorated my skin and hair.

"Fuck, yeah," Mannix said breathlessly. "You look even more beautiful like that."

I smiled back at him.

Ares knelt in front of me and gripped my hips to pull me onto his thick, rock hard cock.

I groaned unashamedly. "You feel so good."

"So do you." He gave me a minute or two to get used to him, then started to thrust rapidly, but evenly.

I watched him. I watched all three of them. One fucking me, one having his mouth fucked, one with the only part of him visible, his eyes, closed.

Yeah, those masks definitely weren't scary anymore.

"Touch yourself," Ares said.

Without hesitation, I placed my hands down between us and found my clit. With two, slow fingers I started to circle and rub myself.

Mannix pulled out of Ice's mouth, and turned him around until he was bent over the couch beside me. He grabbed a tube of lube up off the coffee table and squirted out a finger full. He rubbed his fingers over Ice's rear hole and tossed the tube aside, before positioning himself behind the other guy. He gripped Ice's hips and drove himself slowly inside.

"Fuck, that feels amazing," Ice said. "So full."

"So tight," Mannix grunted.

Holy shit, that was also hot.

Ares leaned forward to nip and bite my nipples, hard enough to hurt and leave marks. Just how I liked it.

I couldn't keep myself from coming again, stimulated by my touch and the thrusting of his cock. I locked my eyes on Mannix's as the stars exploded around me. I think I shouted, but I didn't know. All I knew was the incredible sensation and the way he came from watching me. His hips rolled, pushing him deeper, harder, quicker into Ice's ass.

Ice ground himself back against Mannix, drawing out his orgasm even longer.

"Fuck, yeah," Mannix managed to say. It sounded as though his teeth were clenched behind his mask.

Ares followed right behind, pounding into me, his whole body leaned over me as he came.

It wasn't until we all slumped down that Mannix slipped his mask back off his face and tossed it onto the coffee table.

Ice followed suit a moment later. "I don't know what I prefer to do with a mask on, kill or fuck. It might be a tie."

"Both at the same time?" Ares said as he pulled off his own mask.

Ice sighed exaggeratedly. "Now that would be living the dream. We should do that sometime."

"Whatever you want, babe," Mannix said as he pulled his cock out of Ice's ass.

"Yes." Ice grinned. "You guys are the best. The best family an Iceman ever had."

"The best family I ever had too," Ares agreed. He sat up a little, content to leave his cock inside me for a while longer.

"Yeah, you guys are all much better than the alternative," Mannix said dryly.

Ice patted his cheek. "You did the right thing, killing Leo. He couldn't get away with doing the things he did. Especially touching Kennedy." That seemed to be the worst part of it in their books.

Personally, I thought everything he did added up, but it was too late to argue anyway.

All I could do was smile and say, "I'm a lucky girl to have you guys. I don't know what I'd do without any of you."

"You never have to find out," Ares said softly. "You'd have to kill us all to get rid of us."

"In that case, I guess we're stuck with each other forever." That sounded perfect to me.

EPILOGUE

KENNEDY

"I'm glad you got through it all okay." Samuel Bell sipped his espresso. It didn't surprise me that he drank it black and unsweetened. He seemed to like living on the edge. That must be a mobster thing.

"I take it my assumptions about Leo were correct?"

I sipped my own coffee and looked across the table to him. "All of it," I agreed.

"It doesn't mean we're friends," Mannix told him. He sat between me and Bell on one side. Ares and Ice sat on the other.

"But it doesn't mean we can't be friends in the future," I said, giving Mannix a meaningful look.

He shrugged. "Maybe. We'll see."

"Old habits are difficult to break," Bell said. "Especially when you spend your whole life learning them." He was clearly talking about himself as well.

"I guess it takes someone who hasn't been indoctrinated to see both sides," I said.

"As long as they don't let themselves be led in the wrong direction." Bell raised an eyebrow at Mannix.

"Or the right direction," Mannix said. He matched Bell's expression.

Bell rolled his eyes, but a smile tugged at the corners of his mouth.

"Whatever you say. Do me one favour though. If you ever come after me again, please stay the hell off my desk."

He sipped while my face burned. Of course he had cameras in his office.

Awkward.

"I've explained to Chloe and Lila that you've surrendered all claim to the leadership of the Bell family," Bell said, potentially steering the conversation in a less embarrassing direction. "That doesn't mean you're excluded from my will."

"She doesn't need your money," Mannix snapped.

"Probably not, but she's still my daughter," Bell said, unruffled. "She'll get her share. Not that I intend to die anytime soon." He put down his cup on the smooth, timber surface of the coffee shop's table. We'd agreed any get-togethers we had should take place in public, so no one could accuse us of conspiring against the Brantleys.

"However, I've given my other daughters the task of earning their place as the head of the family. Chloe is older, but Lila is more ruthless."

"How are they going to earn that place?" I asked carefully.

"They'll earn it at Brutham Academy," he said. "First year is the way the Academy differentiates between those who are worthy and those who aren't."

I frowned. "Wait, isn't that how a bunch of students die?"

"It is," Bell agreed.

I gaped at him, but Mannix actually looked impressed.

"Whichever twin survives gets to lead the family," he said. "They may both survive, but this year should clearly indicate which of them is strong enough to step into my shoes." Bell looked as though he didn't find anything even slightly wrong with any of this.

"What if one of them comes to me for help?" I asked.

"There are no rules," Bell said bluntly. "If they come to you and you choose to help them, that's your call. If you choose not to help them, that's also up to you."

Well, shit. That wasn't even the most fucked up thing I'd heard since I'd come to Dusk Bay, but it was pretty fucked up. I was almost starting to like my father, but I was very grateful I hadn't grown up in his world. I was even more grateful I'd already surrendered any claim to the leadership of the Bells. I had a feeling if I hadn't, this battle, or tournament, or whatever you want to call it, would include me too.

Hard pass.

"Wow," Ice said softly. "Let the games begin."

Thank you for reading! The games begin in Heartless, Brutal Academy book 1.

ABOUT THE AUTHOR

Maggie Alabaster writes reverse harem romance.

She lives in NSW, Australia with one spouse, two daughters, one dog, and countless birds.

Jo Bradley writes contemporary romance.

Sign up for Maggie's newsletter! Sign Up!

Join Maggie's reader group! Join here!

Follow Maggie on Bookbub! Click here to follow me!

Check out Maggie's website- www.maggiealabaster.com

Sign up for Jo's newsletter

ALSO BY MAGGIE ALABASTER

Ruck Boys

Filthy Ruck

Hard Ruck

Twisted Ruck

Sparrow and the Mafia Kings

Possessive

Ruined

Corrupted

Pucking Dark Hearts

Pucking Hearts Collide

Pucking Forbidden Hearts

Pucking Hardened Hearts

Dusk Bay Demons

Puck Drop

Breakaway

Power Play

Brutal Academy

Book 1 Heartless

Book 2 Cruel

Book 3 Vengeful

Court of Blood and Binding

Book 1 Song of Scent and Magic

Book 2 Crown of Mist and Heat

Book 3 Sword of Balm and Shadow

Book 4 Whisper of Frost and Flame

Dark Masque

Book 1 Bait

Book 2 Prey

Book 3 Trap

Saving Abbie

Book 1 Pitch

Book 2 Pound

Book 3 Session

Book 4 Muse

Book 5 Rhythm

Book 6 Encore

Novella Venomous

Saving Abbie books 1-4

Saving Abbie books 4-6 + Venomous

Ruthless Claws

Book 1 Ivory

Book 2 Crimson

Book 3 Elodie

Harmony's Magic

Book 1 Summoned by Fire

Book 2 Summoned by Fate

Book 3 Summoned by Desire

Shifter's Vault

Book 1 Discarded

Book 2 Deceived

Book 3 Disgraced

My Alien Mates

Book 1 Star Warriors

Book 2 Star Defenders

Book 3 Star Protectors

Academy of Modern Magic

Book 1 Digital Magic

Book 2 Virtual Magic

Book 3 Logical Magic

Complete Collection

Summer's Harem

Book 1: Shimmer

Book 2: Glimmer

Book 3: Flicker

Complete collection

Short reads

Taken by the Snowmen

Jingle All the Way

Also by Maggie Alabaster and Erin Yoshikawa

Caught by the Tide

Book 1–Pursued by Shadows

Book 2 Pursued by Darkness

Book 3 Pursued by Monsters

ALSO BY JO BRADLEY

Dusk Bay Sharks

Prequel Novella Sidelined

Spike

Punt

Intercept

Snap

www.ingramcontent.com/pod-product-compliance
Lightning Source LLC
Chambersburg PA
CBHW020326030826
48979CB00020B/234
9781763506398